the
soho p
book o

80s

short fiction

edited by
dale peck

the
soho press
book of

80s

short fiction

SOHO

Compilation and introduction copyright © 2016 Dale Peck

See page 579 for permissions information.

Published by Soho Press, Inc.
853 Broadway New York, NY 10003

Library of Congress Cataloging-in-Publication Data is available upon request.

ISBN 978-1-61695-546-5
eISBN 978-1-61695-547-2

Interior design by Janine Agro, Soho Press, Inc.

Printed in the United States of America

10 9 8 7 6 5 4 3 2 1

the
soho press
book of

short fiction

table of contents

Between Courage
and Despair:
A literary antidote
to the 1980s

Introduction

We cringe when we think about them. Shoulder pads and acid wash. K cars and the Portland Building. *Rambo*, hair metal, and the travesty of the Moscow and Los Angeles Olympics. And, oh yeah, the Cold War and the Gipper, who personified the time over which he governed more completely than any president since Eisenhower, if not FDR.

Let's start there: Ronald Reagan, a '50s throwback as unrepentantly unoriginal as Elvis's cover of Big Mama Thornton's "Hound Dog" (hell, he even ripped off Elvis's haircut), a John Wayne manqué who conceived of international politics as if it were a script for one of the Duke's wartime propaganda films (never mind that Wayne was playing a bastardized version of his own cowboy hero), a modern-day Nero lusting after an office for which he was manifestly unqualified, and succeeding to it only because of the cryptocratic machinations of a shadow government of oligarchs and con artists. In other words, the personification of the military-industrial coup d'état Eisenhower had warned us about twenty years earlier, Warholian in execution, Orwellian in effect.

We'd had bad presidents before. Stupid presidents even. Pierce, Johnson, Harding spring to mind. Reagan was something new. His tenure completed the theatricalization of American politics, concentrating unprecedented power in a telegenic figurehead whose policies, like his speeches, were crafted by handlers who not only put the words in his mouth but the ideas in his head: *The American Presidency*, a mockumentary by Lee Atwater, produced by Michael Deaver, starring Ronald *Bedtime for Bonzo* Reagan. To call Reagan an actor-turned-politician is to give his acting career credence it doesn't merit. Even so, he brought a method sincerity to politics he could never muster for his films, and this seemed all it took to create the myth of the Great Communicator, *paterfamilias* meets *pater patriae*, smiling genially as he sold the American public one bottle of snake oil after another. His less flattering sobriquet, the Teflon president, was more apt, yet neither it nor the pyramid scheme of scandals it referenced did any real damage to his reputation. Not Debategate, not Iran-Contra, not the open door between the administration and lobbyists or the surrender of the EPA and HUD to the very corporations from which they were supposed to protect citizens or the spree of financial and media deregulation that led to the $160 billion S&L crisis and the transfer of authority from elected officials to the broadcasters who now set the political agenda, nor even the refusal to mention the word "AIDS" during the entirety of his first term. Not even the *ex post facto* revelation of Alzheimer's tarnished his legacy. His was leadership through lifestyle, after all, not cerebration. He didn't have ideas, he had ideals, and of all the ways his presidency betrayed the American experiment, not least the uncountable trillions spent on video game technologies (SDI, the Peacekeeper missile, the Stealth bomber) and the era of preemptive wars they require, the most damaging may ultimately prove to be the anti-intellectual populism he ushered in as the dominant mode of civil discourse. To all those who say the US could never elect a Donald Trump, I say: we already did. His name was Ronald Wilson Reagan.

It may be that history—whatever "history" is anymore—remembers the '80s as the last analog moment when human beings were what we had always been, before we're fully digitized into whatever hive creature information technology is in the process of creating. Hence our amused nostalgia over the music and the fashion and their air-brushed, hair-sprayed accoutrements. Yet it seems clear, too, that the normalization of postmodernity was well underway by the time Nancy Reagan talked one of the First Family's backers into dropping $200K on a new set of White House china. Millennials tend to associate postmodernism with a sophisticated if neurotic (and sometimes tedious) interplay between the object that is the case and all its previous and possible iterations, but for much of the second half of the twentieth century the postmodern condition was a source of crippling anxiety for artist and working stiff alike. The past seemed to have exhausted the possibilities of identity, the future destined for Armageddon, while the present, well . . . the present was jacked, economically and politically, intellectually and aesthetically.

If the angst reached its zenith in the 1970s (Watergate, the fall of Saigon, gas lines, the hostage crisis), its nadir came in the '80s. Enervated by the tremors of punk and disillusioned by the failures of the Congressional class of '74 and the impotence of the Carter presidency, America sighed a collective "What the fuck" and decided to ring out the end of empire/end of days with the indulgence of third-century Romans. Ronnie's simulacrum of a presidency was only the most obvious manifestation of our retreat, but if you looked around you could see the signs everywhere. Tell someone you liked the '80s (even someone who lived through them, someone who should know better) and they'll immediately assume you're talking about *Thriller* or *Top Gun* or *Bonfire of the Vanities. Like a Virgin, Raiders of the Lost Ark, The Color Purple, Pyromania, The Terminator,* one of those robust novels of the not-so-distant past by Doctorow or McMurtry or Morrison or Stone or Kennedy or Updike or Roth or . . . Or Paula Abdul's choreography, or Julian Schnabel's paintings, or Donald Trump's personal style, or Gianni Versace, or Denise and Robert Venturi, or nouvelle cuisine, or the Harmonic Convergence, or a poster of a pair of battered pointe shoes . . . It's a motley collection, admittedly, linked by nothing more than temporal proximity and an unironic commitment to various forms of regressive cultural assumptions. Its failings were as evident then as they are now (as, for that matter, are its strengths), but as with the rampant sexism and racism of America's great cultural bloom in the '30s, '40s, and '50s, they're also irrelevant, at least in regard to their status as cultural totems rather than aesthetic objects. Twenty-five, thirty years on, a nostalgia inherent in the work itself has reified into sepia shellac, rendered all the more jaundiced by the smug paternalism with which people who consider themselves technologically or psychologically sophisticated regard the artifacts of more primitive—"innocent"—eras.

Still, if the aesthetic ideology of a decade can be reduced to a slogan, that slogan would have to be Gordon Gekko's infamous "Greed is good." The line itself is forgetable. What makes it emblematic is the fact that audiences were supposed to find it, like, *evil*, when the truth is it represented their values more accurately than Charlie Sheen's puling coming to consciousness ever could. Like the best Hollywood directors, Oliver Stone understands that cinema trades in visual symbols rather than narrative, but like the worst (which is to say, like most of them) he's never managed to replace story with other ways of making meaning, with the result that *Wall Street* ends up selling the excesses it purports to denounce far more persuasively than the straight-and-narrow path it pretends to endorse. Which, who knows, was maybe the intention. Stone isn't a complete idiot, after all. On some level, he had to know his audience didn't want a dingy semidetached house in Queens any more than he wanted to make an honest but less commercially appealing movie. They wanted the blockbuster lifestyle: the Upper East Side penthouse, the Armani suit, the promise beneath Darryl Hannah's Marilyn Monroe minidress. Tiger blood *avant le lettre*. But more than they wanted any given material marker, they wanted not to have to do anything to earn it. They wanted the "money for nothing" the Dire Straits song waved under their noses, in a four-and-a-half-minute narrative that contains more dramatic irony than *Wall Street*'s leaden two-plus hours. Not that irony counted for anything: like every future stockbroker's understanding of Gekko's greed line, like George Will's blinkered endorsement of "Born in the USA" and a nascent generation of stalkers and victims slow dancing to "Every Breath You Take," it didn't matter that you weren't in on the joke. That the joke was at your expense. It mattered only that you got what you wanted and that *no one made you feel guilty about it.*

The greedy American was nothing new. Nor was the innocent American. These Americans were as greedy as their forebears but they couldn't claim previous generations' näiveté about the sources of American prosperity. But rather than repudiate their materialism, they took denial to a new level: they wanted not to be accountable for it. For their boorishness, for their avarice, for their emphatic failure to empathize. They wanted to be wrong and to be rewarded for it. This is practically the definition of decadence, but it's a decadence Huysmans or Proust would hardly recognize, let alone the emperor from some last-gasp interval of Chinese or Ottoman profligacy. Unfettered capitalism had reduced debauchery to brands rather than objects, transformed nihilism to celebrity rather than self-indulgence or mortification. Everything—cars, art, faces—was reduced to burnished surfaces that couldn't help but reflect what they were meant to conceal: the replacement of an inner life by mass production and the dollar value placed on same. People effaced themselves not by scourging the flesh or denying their connection to nature but by pretending to be the masks they wore. If the effect tended toward neurasthenia, its origins lay in a more banal complacency. Call it greed, call it fear, call it the apotheosis of kitsch: the '80s oozed intellectual and aesthetic flatulence, but even that was circumscribed and dull, less *Gargantua and Pantagruel* than that kid in *9 ½ Weeks* who could fart the theme to *Jaws*—but only the first note.

But for all that, the '80s get a bad rap. When the dominant ethos is so patently meretricious, so devoid of originality, morality, or any other claim to a thinking person's attention (let alone admiration), it becomes irrelevant, if not simply invisible to those who haven't decided to trade on their privilege or otherwise cash in. Think Weimar between the wars, Adorno, Brecht, Gropius et al., flourishing even as fascism seized the German psyche; or the samizdat of Brodsky and Bulgakov and Solzhenitsyn mapping the constraints of a Russian reality that stood in stark contrast to the hegemonic claims of Soviet orthodoxy.

What I mean is, the 1980s I just described wasn't my 1980s. My 1980s didn't simply reject Ronald Reagan, it ignored him: ignored everything that made him possible and everything he made possible. My 1980s was peopled by outsiders: by nerds, eggheads, Goths, drug addicts, and dropouts; by bitches and lezzies, faggots and trannies, and people who had only just started (at least in music and movies and books) to call themselves niggers. ("I, Debbie, nigger faggot cunt crippled by my sawed-off dick": Laurie Weeks's declaration of allegiance to the disenfranchised and reviled is rooted in Lennon/Ono's "Woman Is the Nigger of the World" and Patti Smith's "Rock N Roll Nigger," but occupies a swiftly changing cultural landscape somewhere between Bret Easton Ellis's "I hate hanging out with niggers anyway" and Essex Hemphill's "Are you funny, nigga?") My 1980s turned on this kind of appropriation and reappropriation. It was fired by the zeal of the hippies and flower children and Civil Rights marchers, but without the earlier generations' sense that momentum was on their side. The outlook was pessimistic, fractured, contradictory. We railed and rallied against a corrupt, homogenous mainstream in a language as expedient as political jargon always is (c.f., "mainstream," a buzzword whose only consistent meaning was that it discredited anything to which it was applied), but we never really thought things would change, or about what we would do if they did. The only thing we knew for sure was that the show was being put on by assholes and imbeciles and we had no desire to join them, which is why protest was only occasionally labeled as such, and more often manifested as refusal.

But in the shadows and the margins, in dingy bars and night clubs, in indie bookstores and record shops and seedy apartments in the East Village and Harlem and the Haight and Compton, an alternative culture began to sprout. Indeed, the '80s was the period when "alternative" became an aesthetic descriptor, "indie" too. Both terms were as nebulous as the "mainstream" to which they stood in opposition, but no less persuasive for that. If the mainstream was characterized by sameness—whiteness, maleness, the concession to a mercenary standard of universality—then the alternative was marked by difference, not just to the mainstream but, crucially, to itself. Mainstream was a gravitational singularity, obliterating distinction (even if only notionally) by shrinking everything to the market's yardstick, whereas indie was dispersed across the orbital bodies just outside the event horizon (and occasionally getting sucked in). There were similarities in the outliers' songs and stories and movies, certainly, but nothing you'd call a program, let alone a school. This isn't to say that the work was ignorant of history, of ideas. In fact it was often steeped in "theory" (yet another buzzword), but support for one or another formal mode was tempered by the knowledge that the aesthetic shifts and rifts in literature, art, music, etc., had always privileged the making of meaning over identity, which is the polite way of saying that the various "experimental" modes to which previous generations of avant-gardists and enfants terribles had declared allegiance were no more innocent of racism, misogyny, or homophobia than the culturally normative realism to which they had organized in opposition. For the first time a substantial number of artists—and their audience—were willing to say that moral concerns trumped formal ones. The new work drew from a welter of sources and styles—realist and postmodern, figurative and conceptual, punk and rap and New Wave—and paired them with an equally diverse array of points of view. I originally wrote "married" rather than "paired," but the liaisons were as suspicious of monogamy as they were of every other aspect of heteronormative patriarchy. Artists weren't endorsing one method, one identity, over another, but simply trying to make them tell. In particular, the distinction between fiction and nonfiction collapsed. A piece of writing might run in a magazine as an essay and later show up in a book of short stories, or a short story might later find its place as a chapter in a memoir. Or the genre tags were simply left off, and it was up to the reader to decide if a piece was "real" or "made up." The labels didn't matter. What mattered was revealing the world and its beleaguered citizens rather than torturing them with edifying or otherwise aspirational myths that no one could (or should) hope to live up to.

Not that the disjunctions were always amicable. As with the rivalry between East Coast and West Coast hip-hop (okay, not *exactly* like the East Coast/West Coast split—there weren't any guns), the literary world made much of the antagonisms between writers, between crews, even though the distinctions had more to do with marketing labels than the way a given writer conceived of his or her work. The New Narrativists supposedly hated the minimalists for being too mannered, the dirty realists (who might or might not have been the minimalists) hated the post-punks for their sloppiness, and everybody hated the Brat Pack because they were making all the money. Yet the New Narrativists were no more unified than the groups to which they were purportedly in opposition, even less so the dirty realists and the minimalists and the Brat Pack, whose most common shared trait was probably a revulsion for the belittling or otherwise misleading tags by which they were sold.

Still, some similarities were visible, which time has only served to highlight. The return of/reinvention of parataxis (in lieu of what Robert Glück called the "La Brea Tar Pits of lyricism") the shift in narrative focus from institutions (marriage, corporations, the military) to individuals, above all the insistence on constricting consciousness to its physical container: to the body, whose movements and sensations didn't exactly circumscribe the self, but nevertheless made it possible, and meaningless in any other context. This is a literature of the flesh: of its shifting loci of pleasure and pain, as Foucault, uncoupling sexuality from Freudian pathologies, labeled them; of its frailties; of its futile but inevitable gestures toward transcendence. Lynne Tillman: "This is a Herculean task never before recorded. An adventure with my body. In forever." Raymond Carver: "The body is still unidentified, unclaimed, apparently unmissed." Jim Lewis: "The human body is the best picture of the human soul." The language echoes metaphysics but the context is always (comically, banally, painfully) concrete: a woman attempting to remove a diaphragm; a news account of a body found in a river; a man who's shot himself in the foot. Depending on how you interpret it—and this is the work's genius, the closest it comes to universality—its obsession with the body is either a capitulation to the Cartesian construct of the head in the tank or an absolute rejection of it. Which is to say: the new writers suffered from the same postmodern anxieties about the epistemological relationship between the self and the world as had the post-war generation, but they didn't allow that to derail an engagement with the information delivered by the senses, only to temper any conclusions at which they might (seem to) arrive. John Keene: "Thus his musings, when written down, gradually melded, gathered shape, solidified like a well-mixed mâché, and thus, upon rereading them he realized what he had accomplished was the construction of an actual voice. The final dances of youth, dim incandescence. Willow weep for me. And so, patient reader, these remarks should be duly noted as a series of mere life-notes aspiring to the condition of annotations."

Notes maybe, but notes to, for, *from* life—real life, life-as-it-is-lived, and not the beginning-middle-end stuff that fiction had always insisted on, as if life were a sculpture on its plinth rather than a gas drifting through, merging with, the void. This was a literature that engaged with time more honestly than any that had come before. Most writing concerns itself with the relationship of the present to the past and the future. This was a literature of moments. Of successive moments, because the forward flow of time is inexorable, but not necessarily linked moments: if one action followed another, the first action wasn't always depicted as causal—even if, say, the second action was death from AIDS and the first was unprotected sex with an HIV-positive person. Hence what Dennis Cooper referred to as a "widespread disbelief in a future and a refusal to learn from the past," which observation served as a kind of psycho-social barometer for most of my early career. Yet this anomie was balanced by what Robert Glück described as a need to "convey urgent social meanings while opening or subverting the possibilities of meaning itself." The most urgent of these "meanings" undoubtedly concerned the AIDS crisis, which was to the Blank Generation what World War I was to the Lost Generation. AIDS disproportionately affected people who fell into one or another disenfranchised minority, which was widely perceived as the reason behind the Reagan administration's criminally sluggish response to the epidemic. But it was more than that. AIDS was a medical crisis, and a political one, but it was also existential, because if anything united the diverse members of the counterculture, it was sex. From the litany of lovers in Lynne Tillman's "Weird Fucks" or Susan Minot's "Lust" to the gritty pornography of Gary Indiana's "Sodomy," the neonatal voyeurism of Suzanne Gardinier's "How Soft, How Sweet," or the inculcation of shame in Jamaica Kincaid's "Girl," copulation was almost always a liminal experience, the lens through which the artifice of identity could be seen most clearly. "He used sex as a means of communicating," Sam D'Allesandro writes in "Giovanni's Apartment": "I need sex as a way to get into heaven." Or Sarah Schulman in *After Delores*: "She saw something special in me. She trusted me. And I was transformed suddenly from a soup-stained waitress to an old professor." Perhaps the only feeling more pervasive than alienation from the revanchist ethos of Reagan's '80s was the refusal to succumb to it, to validate it or accept its judgments. Writers found strength in the very traits that had been used to vilify them and, fertilized by desire and fear and determination, a new literature flourished in the tiny spaces between courage and despair.

The '90s ruined everything, of course. The boom went on so long it produced a generation that believes it can have whatever it wants. Liberal or conservative, aesthete or infidel: identity and ideology don't have to inconvenience anyone anymore. You can vote against gay marriage and pay your gay hairdresser $500 to cut your hair like Ellen Page's. You can espouse environmentalism but still drive an SUV and jet off to India or the Caribbean for vacation. You don't have to choose between Björk and Beyoncé, between the Hamptons or the Hudson Valley: you can have it all. Even now, when the go-go '90s are a distant memory, the prevailing ethos seems to be "Get what you can" (or maybe "Get it while you can") and this is just as true in literature as it is in the rest of life. The fractured antirealisms of the 1980s were supplanted by a recidivist postmodernism even as an ever-assimilationist realism tied its fortunes to politically expedient notions of identity, a lose/lose development that reduced the aggressive insecurities of '80s alt-lit to easy ironies or even easier pieties. What I mean is, the stories in this anthology aren't just a corrective to the excesses of the Reagan-Bush era. They're an admonition to ours as well.

It should be said, though, that the goal of this anthology isn't to define a canon or a school, only to dismantle one—or two, or three, or a dozen. The parameters of what remains are as idiosyncratic as its writers; as its readers. It starts, by one measure, with Baldwin and Becket and Burroughs, and ends with Bolaño, Didion, Ferrante, Knausgard, Sebald. By another measure it starts with the first line of Brad Gooch's "Spring": "It's not dark yet, but it's getting there," and ends with the last line of David Wojnarowicz's "Spiral": "I am disappearing but not fast enough." It starts with Dorothy Allison's "I tell the stories and it comes out funny," and ends with Amy Hempel's "She wants my life." It starts with Gil Cuadros's "Thoughts of the world seem woven of thread, thinly disguised, a veil," and ends with

Rebecca Brown's "Above the crowded street, the hospital, you fly." "Her body feels like someone else's," writes Suzanne Gardinier: "As she lies there with her head on my father's chest she admits for several seconds that it feels like a prison, in which she must serve out the term of her life."

"In that extended instant after sex," Christopher Bram observes, "before you remember you are not alone, I felt pleased with myself and the life I lived."

"Out in the snowy East of Long Island," Kevin Killian answers, "I bent over Frank O'Hara's grave and traced his words with my tongue, the words carved into his stone there: 'Grace to be born and to live as variously as possible.'"

"But then the war came," Gary Indiana writes, "which ended a good deal one might have looked forward to."

"Looking back on it," Mary Gaitskill sums everything up, "I don't know why that time was such a contented one, but it was."

A note on chronology: Decades only rarely oblige the calendar by confining themselves to their numerical delineation (perhaps reflected in our perverse insistence that they start in the tenth year of their predecessor, and end in their ninth). The stories in this anthology were all either written or published between 1980 and 1992, which is to say, the Reagan-Bush years, which seem to me to form a cohesive period in American culture, markedly different from the 1970s (which didn't really start until the fall of Saigon and Nixon's resignation) and the Clinton '90s, when the genuine prosperity of the boom years succeeded in commodifying aesthetics in a way that Reaganomics never could. I apologize if my title misled anyone, but what can I say? *The Soho Press Book of Short Fiction from 1980–1992* is no one's idea of sexy.

Weird Fucks
A Novella in 13 Chapters

Lynne Tillman

CHAPTER 1: There's a Snake in the Grass

I'm on my way, one of four NYC college girls, heading for Bar Harbor, Maine, to spend the summer as a chambermaid, waitress, or piano player. Bar Harbor is on Mt. Desert Island, linked with the mainland by one bridge only and, we are warned, if there is a fire, we might all be caught on the island. Only two lanes out, they caution in dour Maine tones, and the only way out.

Bar Harbor is full of Higginses. There are three branches of the family, no one branch talking to the other two. We took rooms in Mrs. Higgins' Guest House. Willy Higgins, a nephew to whom she didn't speak, fell in love with me. He was the town beatnik, an artist with a beard and bare feet. He would beat at the door at night and wake all four of us. I'd leave the bedroom Hope and I shared to be embraced by this impassioned island painter who would moan, "I even love your dirty feet."

I was in love with Johnny. Johnny was blond and weak, his mother an alcoholic since his father died some years back. Johnny drove a custom-built racing car which had a clear plastic roof. He was a society boy.

The days for me were filled with bed-making and toilet-cleaning. I watched the motel owner make passes at women twice my age who couldn't read. We had doughnuts together at six A.M. I would fall asleep on the beds I tried to make.

At night Hope would play cocktail piano in bars and I'd wait for Johnny. Mrs. Higgins watched our comings and goings and spoke in an accent I'd now identify as cockney. She might have been on the front porch the night Johnny picked me up in his mother's station wagon. We drove to the country club in the middle of the night and parked in the rough behind a tree. We made love on the front seat of the car. I actually thought of F. Scott Fitzgerald. He asked me to put my arms around him again. He whispered in my ear that, although he knew many people, he didn't have many friends. He asked if I minded making love again. This would be my third time.

The rich boys who were sixteen and devoted to us NYC girls robbed a clothes store in Northeast Harbor. They brought the spoils to our apartment. Michael, a philosophy student and the boyfriend of one of us, insisted the stuff be returned within twenty-four hours or else he'd call the cops. The next night Bill returned the tartan kilts and Shetland sweaters that hadn't been missed. But he dropped his wallet in the store while bringing it all back and somehow or other the cops were at our door the night after. They spotted me as the ringleader. We went to Bangor for our trial and got fined $25 each as accessories. They called it a misdemeanor. The newspaper headline read Campus Cuties Pull Kilt Caper. I didn't really want to be a lawyer anyway, I thought.

Johnny never called back again. I dreamed that Mrs. Higgins and I were in her backyard. I pointed to a spot in the uncut lawn and said with alarm: There's a snake in the grass.

A guy who hawked at carnivals wanted me to join the circus and run away with him. I was coming down from speed and learning to drink beer. Some nights we'd go up Cadillac Mountain and watch the sunrise. Bar Harbor is the easternmost point in America, the place where the sun rises first. I pined away the summer for Johnny and just before heading back to NYC heard that his mother had engaged him to a proper society girl.

CHAPTER 2: An East Village Romance

I was a slum goddess and in college. He looked something like Richard Burton; I resembled Liz. It was, in feeling, as crummy and tortured as that.

George had a late-night restaurant on St. Marks Place. I'd go in there with Hope, my roommate; we'd drink coffee, eat a hamburger. Fatal fascination with G behind the counter—his sex hidden but not his neck, his eyes, his shoulders. He called me "Little One." "Little One," he'd say, "why are you here?

What do you want?" I'd sit at the counter with hot coffee mug in hand, unable to speak, heart located in cunt, inarticulate.

José was George's best friend and George had a Greek wife who was not around. The guys and I hung out together. $1 movies at the Charles. Two-way conversations between artists (they were both sculptors) while I hung, sexually, in the air. José had a red beard, George had no beard, just grayish skin in the winter. "Little One," he'd say, "what do you want?" He'd trace a line on my palm as if it were a map of my intentions.

Still, with so much gray winter passion, no fucking. Night after night, nights at the counter, count the nights. I met his wife who dried her long black Greek hair in the oven. They are separated. It is a recent separation and I am passionately uncaring. I am in love. I take trips with other people to places I can't remember. I spend hours talking with an older woman called Sinuway who gives me a mirror to remind me I am beautiful. She disappears.

José reminisced about the fifties when beatniks roamed the streets. In those days George made sidewalk drawings. One time José recounted, "George was very drunk—very drunk, heh George—and drawing a young girl's portrait. For hours and hours because he'd fallen asleep behind the easel, his face blocked by the paper. Remember, George?" Stories like these passed the time. Weeks passed.

George, José and I were in George's room and José put a ring on my finger then left the room. George and I were alone. He undressed me and put his hand on the place between my breasts. He undressed me in the doorway and fucked me. It went fast after so many weeks, like a branch breaking off a tree. The time had come. It was a snap.

"I want to write a poem," he said, his cock still hard. "Oh, I don't mind," I said, dressing as fast as I could. I wanted to be indifferent, not to burden him with my lack of sophistication. He had an ugly look on his face. Perhaps he was thinking about his recently separated wife drying her hair in the oven while he fucked a young woman.

Back at St. Marks Place I headed home, thinking this might be a reason for suicide. All that time, the perfunctory fuck, that poem he would write. It was all over. I phoned Susan who still lived at home; her life wasn't plagued with late-night restaurants. "What would you do," I asked. "Forget it," she said, "it's not important."

Later that night Hope and I went out again and I met Bill. He traced a line from my palm up my wrist all the way to my elbow.

CHAPTER 3: A Very Quiet Guy

Bill and I left Hope and went to the Polish Bar not four doors from George's late-night restaurant. Beer ten cents a glass. We drank and drank; I told Hope I'd be home soon and wasn't.

Somehow we were upstairs in somebody's loft. Bill had red hair and brown eyes. He was very tall and wore a flannel shirt. We made love all night long, this kind of sleepless night reassuring. His rangy body and not much talking. He'd keep tracing that line from my palm to my elbow, the inner arm. He disarmed me. It was easy to do.

Early morning at the B&H dairy restaurant, our red faces like Bill's hair. Breakfast with the old Jews in that steamy bean and barley jungle. Romance in the East Village smelled like oatmeal and looked like flannel shirts. Our smell in the smell of the

B&H. George and José walk in and it was a million years ago, those weeks of gray passion and one snappy fuck. Sitting with Bill, so easily read, I smile at them. George looks guilty and embarrassed. I feel wanton and he is history.

Bill and I started to go together. He told me about his wife from whom he was separated. She was on the other coast. That seemed like a real separation. Bill was quiet and often sat in a corner. I thought he was just thinking. I introduced Michael, the first hippie I knew, to Nancy, my best friend. We spent New Year's together on 42nd Street, Nancy kissed a cop, the guys pissed on the street and Michael pissed in the subway.

Bill and I started a fur eyeglass-case-making operation which I was sure would catch on. We convinced Charley, owner of the fur store on St. Marks Place, that those scraps of fur would make great eyeglass cases. A fur sewing machine was rented and placed in the basement of the fur store. Bill and I passed nights sitting side by side, silently, in old fur coats, stitching up cases which never did get sold. Bill grew more and more quiet.

My father had his first heart attack. The subways were on strike and I took long walks to Mt. Sinai in my fur coat to visit my father in the intensive care unit. The first night he was in the hospital I couldn't go home. I slept on the couch at Nancy's mother's apartment. In the morning Nancy stood by the couch, anxious because the sheet covered me completely, like a shroud, and she wondered how I could breathe.

One night Bill fucked me with energy. Spring was coming and so was his wife, he told me later. I stormed out of the fur store, yelling that I would never see him again, and fumed to the corner where I stood, having nowhere to go. That fuck was premeditated—wife here tomorrow, do it tonight. I turned back and returned to Bill and Michael who said, "We knew you'd be back. You're too smart for that."

We went to Nancy's and suddenly I was sick, throwing up in her mother's toilet bowl. Bill held my head, my hair. He took me to my apartment and made me oatmeal. Left me propped up in bed with a pile of blankets and coats over me. Three days later, I awoke, my flu over.

His wife had a beautiful voice and was as tall as he was. And while I could get him out of my system, he couldn't get out of the system. He didn't want to resist the draft; he desperately wanted to pass the tests, especially the mental test. When he received his notice telling him he was 1-A, he tried to kill himself. Slit his wrists. Last time I remember seeing him he was sitting in an antique store, rocking, near the window. We waved to each other.

CHAPTER 4 : No/Yes

I threw caution to the wind and never used any contraception. Nancy finally convinced me I might get pregnant this way and made me an appointment at Planned Parenthood. It was a Saturday appointment and that night I had a date with John, a painter from the Midwest, a minimalist. So the doctor put the diaphragm in me and I kept it in, in anticipation of that meeting. Besides, I had lied to the woman doctor when I said I knew how to do it—I was afraid to put it in or take it out. Let it stay there I thought, easier this way.

We met at the Bleecker Street Cinema and watched a double feature. Godard. Walked back to his place below Canal Street. We made love on his bed and he said, "I'm sorry. This must be one of my hair trigger days." "What does that mean?" I asked. He looked at me skeptically. It was difficult, very difficult, for men to understand and appreciate how someone could fling herself around sexually and not know the terms, the ground, on which she lay. He said, "It means to come too quickly." "Oh," I said, "that's all right." I kept comforting men. He fell asleep fast.

I awoke at three A.M. with just one thought. I had to get the diaphragm out. If it were possible and not already melted into my womb or so far up as to be near my heart or wherever diaphragms go when you're ignorant of where they can go.

I pulled a rough wool blanket around me and headed for the toilet in the hall. John awoke slightly and asked where I was headed. "For a piss," I said.

The heavy door opened into a dark hall. The toilet door opened, just a toilet and no light. I stood in the dark and threw my leg up on the toilet seat as shown in various catalogues not unknown to the wearer.

Begin searching for that piece of rubber. Think about Margaret Sanger and other reassuring ideas. Can't reach the rim. Reach the rim; finger slips off. Reach it, get it and pull. Can't get it out. It snaps back into place as if alive. Go into a cold sweat. Squat and try. Finger all the way up. Pull. Then try kneeling. I'm on my knees with my finger up me, the blanket scratching my skin. It seems to be in forever. This is a Herculean task never before recorded. An adventure with my body. In forever.

I pulled the blanket up around me and stood, deciding to leave it in for now and have it removed surgically if necessary. In a colder sweat I left the dark toilet to return to the reason for all this bother. I couldn't pull the loft door open. It seemed to be locked or blocked. I began banging heavily against the metal door. Hot sweat now. When John finally opened the door he found me lying flat out on the blanket, a fallen angel, naked at his feet. I'd fainted. He revived me and we were both stunned. "The door," he said, "was open." That's what they all say. He gave me a glass of water and we went back to bed.

The next morning, even though he said our signs were right, my fainting had indicated other signs. Signs and more signs. I walked toward Canal Street and a sign on the wall read Noyes Electrical Company. I read No/Yes Electrical Company. No/Yes, I thought, that's a crazy name for a business.

CHAPTER 5: An American Abroad

Rome was hot and strange in the summer. Nancy and I had been in Europe three weeks. We were tourists on the Spanish Steps. She met a Spaniard called Juan and I met his friend called Ricardo. Ricardo and I didn't get along very well and he thought I was an "egoist" as I tried out my college Spanish. All my sentences began with Yo and I was either tired, hungry or hot. Nancy and Juan began a five-year relationship that had her living in Yugoslavia for four of those years. Ricardo returned to Madrid.

Mao appeared one day at the steps. He was tall, thin and brown, a French Vietnamese. Suddenly he was my boyfriend and we were going to go to Greece together. Ours was a silent love affair and I'm not sure how we reached a decision like we were going to go to Greece together. My French was slightly worse than my Spanish, always akin to the pen of my brother is on . . . I believe we used interpreters, particularly when we fought. I discovered that I was sullen in both French and

Spanish, but the languages, on my primitive tongue, seemed to lend themselves to moodiness.

Together, Mao and I did all the right things like eating in a poorhouse run by Franciscans and trying to get into one of the numerous movies being made in Rome. About fifty of us were taken on a forced march to a suburb outside Rome where Anita Ekberg or some other blonde star looked down on us from her balcony to single several of us out as looking like hippies. The rest of us were sent back to Rome, not right for the part.

Juan and Nancy wanted to sleep outside in the gardens of the Villa Borghese. Though I had a hotel room, Mao and I decided to join them. They disappeared behind a tree, some several yards above us on a small hill. Mao and I spread our blanket on the ground, took off our pants, made love and fell asleep. He was very beautiful and the lovemaking was nothing much at all.

It was a hot night and very still in the garden. I awoke, feeling light shining down on me. There are lights shining on us, the headlights of a cop car. Two policemen are standing at the foot of our blanket. They shine flashlights. Mao stands up pulling on his trousers. I can't find mine, they're hidden somewhere and I try to pull the blanket around me as my hand feels the ground, looking for them. But those Italian cops are fast, fast to spot a piece of ass. "Nuda, nuda," one yells, pointing at my ass as if I were already behind bars or in a zoo. My ass I figure is probably reflecting the light of the moon. I wonder if this image could ever be seen as romantic. The other echoes his cry: "Nuda, nuda." Now we're in for it, I think, semi-nude fornicating hippies found in elegant Borghese gardens. An international incident.

I become hysterical, nuda nuda, still searching for my

clothes. I find them, put them on and stand up behind Mao, who is attempting to hide me from the cops. This gesture is futile and indeed ridiculous, as if Adam and Eve could hide from the authorities. They're not at all interested in Mao. I decide to play dumb. I point at my head and my chest, emphatically declaring, Stupido americana, stupido americana. I'm not at all sure of the agreement, but I figure they'll get the point. And the point is that if I admit I'm an idiot, particularly an American idiot, Americans are hated in Europe, if I admit all this, they may go easy on me. Mao stands by the blanket. They lead me to the cop car. I'm being taken away.

They push me into the back seat of the car. One cop gets into the driver's seat and the other tries to slam the back door after me. I shove my leg out so that he can't close the car door, unless he wants to cripple me. I leap out of the car and go running into the night. I keep running and the cops don't follow, they just get back into their car and drive away.

Nancy had watched from safety, behind a tree. Said it was the funniest thing she's ever seen. Like a Keystone comedy. Mao and I continued to communicate badly with one another until I said something which hurt him deeply—something I never understood, perhaps it translated poorly—and he left Rome, or so a friend of his interpreted.

Nancy went off with Juan and someone who called himself a friend of Juan's, seeing me alone, offered me his sister's house as hospitality. I fell asleep in the front seat of his Mercedes as we drove away from Rome toward what I supposed were the sub-urbs. I awoke in the car which was parked next to a field. After he raped me, he said, "Now we go to my sister's house." It had seemed pointless to fight him off and then go running around the Italian countryside in the dark when I had had a taste of what the police were like. He thought, because I hadn't resisted, that I liked it.

Two days later I got out of Rome, following the sun to Greece, hitching with a sixteen-year-old English boy who carried my rucksack on top of his. On the Continent, only, can one trust Englishmen to be old-fashioned.

CHAPTER 6: Coming of Age in Xania

I was sitting on a sidewalk in Athens, sitting on the curb in front of a shoe store. Jack saw me and called out, "Are you an American?" and I answered, "Yes," and told him I was looking for a hotel. "Share mine," he said, "a dollar a night."

Jack was from Chicago, a spoiled and wealthy Irishman who wanted to write. He had just gotten to Athens from Tangier. He had reddish hair, pale skin and eyes Carla would have called "sadist blue." He was recovering from an unhappy love affair which, having ended badly and to his disadvantage, made him vindictive and self-righteous. I didn't want to travel alone and he looked like a life-saver. We went to Crete and he hated me or at least it seemed that way. "Look, Jack," I told him, "you can stay in the house I'm renting but our being together is insane since you criticize me constantly." He didn't argue this point and we agreed to be housemates only. But Xania is a small city and a small Greek city at that and a young woman doesn't leave a man simply. Or at all. Friends of Henry Miller littered the island and all would later descend on me for my unfairness to Jack, who was drinking so much now.

I had fallen in love with Charles who arrived with Betsy and her child. She was separated from her husband. He had remained in their native land, South Africa. Charles told me that he and Betsy were friends. They seemed like adults to me, the big-time, and when Charles looked at me longingly, I returned the look. At first we were secretive. Betsy, who was older and probably wiser, seemed to take this in her stride and Charles moved out, into his own room near my rented house. Jack still slept in my bed and every night I would leave my house and go to Charles' bed. He wanted to be a writer too. Jack and I would have pleasant talks together on the terrace. We'd smoke some grass and he'd talk about his broken heart. Things seemed ok and in fact they were extremely bizarre.

The first week in Xania I was cast, in my naïveté, as the young thing who arrives in town and enters a world she doesn't understand. This was my screen role in Charles Henri Ford's film *Johnny Minotaur*. I had been given Ford's address by a Greek called Stephanos. He approached me on the Spanish Steps, urging me to go to Crete and look up Charles Henri. He said Charles would want to put me in his movie. Luckily for Charles Henri who left Xania shortly after filming Jack and me in a classic beach scene—I wore a skirt and held a black doll in one hand, a pinwheel in another—he never saw his second heroine descend into her role.

Xania is made for secretive strolls, its lanes curve from house to house. I took these turns recklessly, leaving my house every night, strolling a curved lane to Charles' bare room where we would lie together on his skinny cot. Morning would come and I'd stroll back to my house. Breakfast at the Cavouria restaurant and a swim before lunch. I took to going fishing and the fishermen would smile as I walked down the pier to the tower and cast my line into the sea. I never caught anything.

Betsy continued to be civil to me. We went dancing at a taverna where the Greek sailors did their famous carrot dance. Charles didn't come and I sulked. Betsy was understanding and her graciousness made me uncomfortable. We watched a sailor place a carrot at his crotch and another sailor hack away at it with a sharp knife. I went to sleep outside the taverna in Betsy's car and woke to find Greek sailors peering through the car windows. I was driven home.

The strolls continued. Charles was good-looking, moody, given to short-lived enthusiasms and other things I can't remember. Jack and I socialized with Greek waiters. Waiters have always been partial to me—my mother has always said I had a good appetite. One such waiter took us for really good food in a place where men who looked like officers cracked plates over their heads, even though this was then against the law. The waiter took us to his home and fed us some plum booze that's thick as a hot night. Jack and I went home and I went for my usual stroll. Several weeks later it was common knowledge that the waiter's common-law wife wanted to kill me. Alfred Perles, his wife, and Betty Ryan—the friends of Miller—all accused me of destroying Jack. It was the right time to leave.

The woman who took care of my rented, decrepit house and lived just across the lane offered to wash my hair and bathe me. I hadn't had a hot bath in two months. She heated the water in a huge black cauldron over a fire in front of her house. She sat me in a plastic tub. She even scrubbed my back. I felt she had some sympathy for me, and had watched, from her position in the chorus, other, similar young women.

There was no love lost. Charles slept at my house on my last night in Crete, Jack having sailed away, alone, almost nobly, a week before. I refused to make love with Charles, complaining of the heat and the bugs, and as a final indignity kept my underpants on and slept over the covers, while he slept beneath them. Charles and Michael, who had played Count Dracula in Ford's movie, drove me to the airport. On a similar ride one year later Betsy's husband who had come, I imagine, to win her back, would be killed in a car crash. I made it back to Athens.

CHAPTER 7: A Pass for the Night

Jos and I had been living together eight months, first in London and then in Amsterdam, where he and I ran a cinema and a film cooperative. He was in Utrecht visiting his girlfriend and I was in our room, wearing my Victorian nightgown and suffering. It was as if I were still taking speed—couldn't sleep, the night was ragged and endless. It wasn't easy to find sleeping pills or tranquilizers in Amsterdam. The Dutch were more into natural drugs, like hash. Later heroin.

Piet was a painter who lived just around the corner; he had been in a Godard film, was traveled, had a French wife who often left him; he was tough. He might have some pills.

I threw my fur coat over my nightgown. It was winter. In Amsterdam one can visit unannounced. I put on a pair of old-fashioned shoes and headed out in the middle of the night. It was snowing, all white out, like my nightgown.

An American named Marty was with Piet. Both had similar reputations. It was odd to see them together. I had met Marty a week before on the night I'd received notice from Jos that he wanted to move out, that he wanted us to live separately. He loved me, he said. I knew from the loveletters left on our bed that Jos was fucking someone else. This is the stuff that tries our souls. Oh, we hadn't been happy. I felt I was being finished off, planed down. After his phone call, I went, unhinged, to Cathrine's, where Marty happened to be. I cried as if I knew him or as if he weren't there. Cathrine handed me a joint. Misery became an awful joke. "Marty," I laughed, "do you know a man for me?" His response, and I can't remember it exactly, indicated he was a man. I couldn't understand why a man would want a woman in pain. I wasn't sophisticated about sadomasochism.

That was a week ago and here I am in Piet's studio with Marty, and I'm an inmate with a pass for the night. I kept on my heavy fur coat to hide my nightgown, which made my presence even more eccentric. We listened to Dylan's latest album. Piet didn't have any pills, just hash. Marty said, "I like your shoes." It was an erotic comment, slightly perverse from his lips. He said he wanted to photograph me. I wish he had. I would have liked a picture like that, in the same way that I've always wanted to steal one of those US Post Office pictures of the Ten Most Wanted.

He stayed until 5 A.M. We fucked. I was a ghost. He left to return to his Dutch wife, to awaken in their bed. I didn't care at all. "Stay beautiful," he called out as he closed the door behind him. I stayed awake for several more nights.

By the time Jos returned I had accepted my destiny, the universe and his leaving our room. I wanted him to go. He didn't. And then I accepted that too. Marty, seeing Jos and me together, never flirted with me again, though we remained friendly. I wasn't sure if it was disinterest or respect for another man's territory. I didn't really care either way. I was the one who finally moved out of the room on the Anjelierstraat (Angel Street). But that was not the end.

Chapter 8: Lies in Dreams

Breaking up is hard to do. After more than a year with Jos, I went alone to Paris and London. Jos followed; my parents and one of my sisters were in Paris but I didn't introduce them to him. He wasn't supposed to be there. I went to London and Jos and I lived together again, briefly, in that city until we had to find another room. Searching for a room in London proved too much for our poor spirits. Jos returned to Holland.

I met John at a film festival in London, thought he was an interesting man. He told me he was a poet and a publisher and might publish my work. Since I had no work to publish, I didn't pursue him. He pursued me. One morning Jos left for Holland and that night John was at my door. We went to see Warhol's *Bike Boy*. John's uncanny instinct for the kill would reappear, but not for another two weeks. He would come calling and I'd never be at home. He'd leave word that he'd been. I became interested and sent a postcard telling him I was going to New York and Amsterdam but would see him when I got back to London. I was blasé. That night John appeared and found me. This moment having built to a fevered pitch, it was love at the front door. Then we had some tea.

I had not remembered any of our previous conversations,

held at the film festival. He told me that we had had a long discussion about why I could not watch Otto Muehl's film *Sodoma* in which an animal is killed, and at the same time I was not one of those who wanted to stop Muehl from making a live action in the theater itself.

That second but first evening we joined my friends Susan and David for dinner and, later, a lecture at the Etherius Society. Got stoned during dinner and dropped a Van Morrison album from quite a height onto the record player after being told "one can do things better when stoned." This reminded me of that line in Djuna Barnes' story about her sister, "She sugared her tea from too great a distance."

The Etherius Society's leader was Charles King, a medium who believed himself to be in direct contact with the Venutians. The Society held its meetings at the end of the Fulham Road and in the basement of what appeared to be an ordinary English house. London always gives the appearance of the very ordinary. The lecturer was dressed in a business suit. John and I were in no ordinary state. The audience was mixed—old, young, artists, housewives and businesspeople. The lecturer spoke for two hours or what seemed a lifetime. John and I laughed without sound. Our faces were impacted with mirth and, though the lecturer glowered at us as he spoke about the Venutians and the Martians, we really couldn't help ourselves. It was when the tape of Charles King's conversation with the head Venutian played that some awful guttural sound came from me. "Come in, come in, Venus," King called. And the head Venutian answered, "Nim Nim two two, Nim Nim two two, I can hear you, old chap." The lecturer was furious now and John who was used to how ordinary

English craziness is was able to control himself. The lecturer continued to stare straight at us and said, "We are now going to say the Venutian prayer. The lights will dim. And I would like to say one thing. You can snigger at the Martians but you cannot laugh at the Venutians."

And so we fell in love and that night slept side by side in a large bed while another man slept in another bed in the same room. We did not fuck. I felt we had anyway, that his body had moved into mine. And then he did move in. I met all the English concrete poets and learned to drink tea from morning to night. We invented Fluff, a kind of joke about how we were existing, which turned out to be our relationship. When we made love he refused to go down on me but wanted me to suck his cock. And when he looked at me I turned to lava.

I went to Amsterdam to tell Jos it was over. In true romantic fashion I did this from a sickbed; I'd sent him a telegram the day before saying that I was too ill to come to him. Jos came to me and sat on the edge of my bed for an hour as I spoke about why we couldn't go on. He was silent. (In the excess of my passion for John, I met another Englishman at one of Amsterdam's canals and we made love too. I threw away his telephone number and regretted this later.)

I returned to London and crazed days and nights with John. We shared a room on Lancaster Road near the Portobello Road. Our life was made of tarts, tea, cream and constant visits. One young man we visited, a poet, died the next year. His girlfriend later made love with John. I later made love with a close friend of John's. We all were trying to continue connections that had once been.

John wore a thick wool robe and I wore a Japanese kimono that was always open to him. My thoughts were Spenserian; I was the true love and even if I were to go he would know the false from the true. I went to New York and stayed two months, sleepwalking around the city, seeing friends, going places, possessed. Nancy hardly knew me. I earned money to return, and when I did, went to Susan and David's. They told me John had been acting very strangely. So I phoned him and he hardly said hello. The next day he phoned me and asked me to come see him. He told me he was encased in glass. We spoke for more than an hour. He refused my presents and presence. He had gotten very thin and cut his hair short; he looked like a monk. I left his room and spent two months, waiting, in a Victorian nightgown. Anyone who has ever worn a Victorian nightgown knows its meaning, it is the gown of an inmate. I took Valium and waited, would see John on the Portobello Road on rare walks out.

Over an Indian dinner a friend of his told me John was living with another woman. It was just after I'd bitten into a piece of food wrapped in silver paper. It was the beginning of the end of true romance, a fall that lasted two years.

I dreamt that I was with my father in my home town. We are driving around the 20th Century Fox Estate. My father asks if I can settle down again and I say I don't know. Suddenly I am running wildly, wildly, down a wide path with trees lining each side. A man on horseback approaches and I leap out of the way only to hit a smaller horse, a pony. The pony drops to the ground. The man dismounts. My father reappears. The horseman looks very sad. "He's not dead," I cry. "I merely hit him." "No," the horseman says, "he's not dead, but he is blind. We'll have to shoot him." I scream.

I told John's friend the dream—he is the one I, woodenly, make love with in the future—and the friend said that there are lies in dreams too. I avoided speaking to people for a while.

CHAPTER 9: Suspicions Confirmed

By now everyone knows that Valium is one way to get over a love affair. After taking those pills long enough, life becomes intensely fair: everything is the same. In this condition I visited friends and acquaintances with equanimity. Even people I didn't like. At one home I met Tim, a fringe Hollywood exile, actor and public relations person for something or other. He was also a photographer. I met him and went home without expectation of particular interest, this being one of Valium's cachets.

One week later the phone rang in the middle of the night. He said he'd been trying to reach me for a week, had even wired an office in New York at which he thought I worked. His enthusiasm only intrigued me.

He arrived with flowers and bought me steak. We got stoned and Tim called his friend Harold, a black Englishman who seemed to represent to Tim all that was cool and noble in the world. Harold invited us to his girlfriend's house outside London, and drove us in his car. I sat in back which was all right with me as I had become morose and paranoid. We were all very stoned, and I assumed we wouldn't arrive at the home of the ambassador from, I was told, a small African nation. Harold was dating the ambassador's daughter.

Sitting alone in the back seat of the car, I kept thinking that Harold was driving sideways, that the road was giving way at every turn, that the car might fly into the air. I distrusted Tim inordinately, and Harold was looking at Tim, and not at the road. Their laughter encouraged my worst fears.

We arrived at the ambassador's house and were introduced to his children. Harold's girlfriend was the eldest daughter. She led us to the basement which had been converted into a game or conference room. It was filled with six oversized leather lounge chairs. Like every ambassador's daughter I've ever met, she had been educated in a French convent. The four of us sat in chairs much too big for us. I grew more and more alarmed. I hadn't the slightest desire to fuck Tim but there seemed no way out. There was an inevitability about the night. I was being driven places I didn't want to go. The mode was ineluctable.

Harold drove us back to the city and dropped us at my place. Tim and I smoked some African grass. I stared at him, and he became recognizable. "You look," I said, "like my father's charcoal gray Perry Como sweater." He looked at me quizzically but still advanced. I couldn't understand why, I thought my remark was devastating.

Tim's stupidity was dangerous. When finally we were fucking, he was given to calling out, "That's some cunt. That's some cunt." In my condition his love-talk became absurd exaggeration. He made too much of a good thing (I thought). His enthusiasm grew as I retreated inside, and as if to draw me out, to reach me, he whispered bloodlessly, "I'd like to kill you with my cock." That was it. I knew it—in bed with a dangerous maniac who wants to kill me with his cock. All my suspicions were confirmed. This whole evening I was hanging on the edge of the fence, rigid with suspicion that was now given credence.

I drew back from his embrace and looked at his eyes which had narrowed. "That's horrible." I said, "I can't continue." It was impossible to prove to him that I was not crazy. The blind leading the blind and other such homilies come to mind. Besides I was in no position to argue.

It turned out that the wife I didn't know about was coming back from her vacation and I wouldn't have to see Tim ever again. When he left the next morning he gave me his sweater to keep.

CHAPTER 10: Just an Accident

I was staying away from men and lived and worked in Amsterdam where I found it easy to do so. A Dutchman let me use his back room and I camped there for the good part of a year. The Dutchman was depressed and cynical. I knew he wanted me to leave and, when Carla suggested I join her and George Maciunas for a trip around the Greek islands (George wanted to buy one), I had to get there. Jos found me some money, a six hundred guilder scam, and I went by train to Greece. Three days and two nights on the Athens Express in a compartment with a Greek man from Thessaloniki who fed me feta cheese, bread and olives. I read Jane Austen while on the train and feared that I might have to marry the Greek man, as several Greek women would pass our compartment and give us knowing smiles. I'm not one not to smile back and was relieved when he got off at Thessaloniki and I was not with him.

Carla and I settled again in Xania and she left before I did. I got very brown and into a little trouble, saying goodbye only because my money had run out. I returned to Amsterdam.

Jack Moore once said, "We are all going to be in Munich for

the 1972 Olympics." I nodded, "Oh, yes?" and found myself there in the summer of 1972, along with twenty or more actors in Jack's theater company, The Human Family.

The hill of garbage, the rubble from World War II outside Munich since the postwar cleanup, is the site of the Olympiad. An artificial lake separates the games from the Spielstrasse, play street, where artists from Western Europe, Japan and America are to perform. The lake is polluted. The Olympics committee spent millions of marks to make Kultur at the games.

The Human Family was a participation theater group, using films, music, video and slides. I helped organize the production and directed some of the films. In Munich I also became a performer in the theater group, something I would ordinarily never do, having a horror of appearing in public, acting on a stage, but this was an extraordinary situation, more surreal than Meret Oppenheim's *Fur Teacup and Saucer*. I wrote postcards to friends, extolling this quality, and mentioned the thighs of the athletes.

The Spielstrasse abounds with German romantics who never die. Every tourist has some piece of equipment around the neck, arm or back. Busloads of varying nationalities embark, disembark, to watch theater pieces, clowns, conceptual artists, and then cross back over the polluted lake to see the games.

The German romantic I met was called Karl. He was political, did yoga seriously and ate macrobiotic food. We spent several evenings in The Human Family's common room. Karl whispered and blew in my ear for three hours.

Our theater company performed every night. The piece began on the top of the hill. We ran downhill, each with a flashlight in both hands, waving our arms in the shape of the infinity symbol. I spent a good part of each day anxiously awaiting the run downhill. Even with our flashlights on, I was certain we couldn't be made out and I was afraid of rolling down the hill. But my fear about rolling downhill was small compared with what I felt about jumping onto the stage and going into slow motion. We were wearing overalls, too. Twenty of us in gray uniforms. After moving very slowly, we were directed to stare out at the audience which should have gathered at the foot of the stage. From this bunch each of us was to choose a person to encounter and bring him or her up on stage. It was, for me, the worst kind of popularity contest. At the end of the piece we handed out donuts—the piece was also known as the Donut piece—and everyone danced around gaily to Shawn Phillips music written especially for the production. Our group earned the reputation for being very high, happy people, and often other Spielstrasse workers joined us for the dance.

Charley was one such worker. It took me some time to consider Charley seriously. Thinking in the midst of the Olympics, and while a member of a theater group that makes donuts its symbol, thinking was hardly possible. Charley just entered my life. He smiled a lot and so did I.

Then the Israelis were murdered, and everything stopped. I didn't know what was going on. No one did.

Charley came to see me. I was alone. The rest of the company had gone to the country. We spread all the pillows on the floor and lay down. The door opened and three members of the West Indian steel band—they lived rhythmically across the lane—walked in. We were both naked and the men stood over Charley and me. They seemed to have no intention of leaving. What with our group's easygoing reputation on the Spielstrasse, this might have been expected. We asked them to go, and they did. A few minutes later one came back and asked if he could be next. That's the way it began.

The Spielstrasse was closed because of the murders, "the political situation," as it was called, but the games were allowed to continue. All the theater groups and artists met to protest the trivial way in which Kultur was treated. The meetings ended in futility. The Japanese director Shuji Terayama and his group, which performed in costumes of black, red or white, succeeded in getting back on to the Spielstrasse. They started a fire and burned down their set, they burned everything. The flames could be seen for miles.

Everyone was going home. Charley asked if he could come with me to Amsterdam. I was surprised. Even more surprised when I discovered he already had a child, whose mother was a smart and crazy amphetamine-head. They lived in Paris.

We returned to Amsterdam and lived and worked together for more than a year. I hadn't lived like this for a while, and it was healthy to be fucking regularly. But Charley and I never did have much to say to each other. One day he came to me and said we shouldn't live together anymore; I lost him to a commune and his best friend, whom I couldn't stand to be around. It was hell for a couple of months and, when the hell was over, I rarely if ever thought of him again. This alone struck me as demeaning. A physicist once told me that one view of our universe is that its stability is an accident, that thousands upon thousands of relationships are unstable and that chance alone holds ours together.

CHAPTER 11 : Lean Times

Watching an English television play reminds me of life with Roger, an English actor I lived with for two months. Charley and I had split up, work at the film cooperative was impossible—no one cooperated. The book I'd finished editing a year before still wasn't published and into this hole came an English acting company. The play they brought to Amsterdam was adapted from a novel a friend had written and the author being a friend, the cast became friends too. Of course no one makes friends that easily.

It was Edward whom the author told me to look up, but I looked instead at Roger who was playing pinball after the play. It was, oddly enough, Valentine's Day. Two years before I'd written a short story on this day about the day and this year I found myself falling in love again. It is safer to stay indoors.

Three nights later Roger and I walked around Amsterdam, drinking in several bars, walking around and around, the way one can in Amsterdam, the city having been built in a semicircle. "Not tonight," I told Roger. We ended up at four A.M. in an Indonesian fast-food joint on the Leidesplein and ate peanut-covered meat. Shaslik.

Economics affects our life specifically: I had no money and no place to live since leaving the film cooperative. I had been living off the fat of the land and now, further into the seventies, there wasn't so much excess. Everything was getting tighter. After all those flowers and assassinations, optimism had died. Business went on as usual. Lean times. Roger had a small house in London and a rented cottage in Norfolk.

Our third night in Amsterdam we smoked and ate some hash. We took a walk and as we walked I felt we weren't getting anywhere. There may be no progress, but still I felt we weren't moving at all. Roger was staying in a small hotel, the one set aside for English actors when they came to Amsterdam. They came often—Dutch theater is lamentable. He said as we got closer to the hotel, "How are we going to get to my room?" The usual question of getting past the room clerk. With all the wisdom I could muster I replied, "We'll just walk up the stairs." Roger was amazed at this profundity, so simple, so direct, and indeed the way to his room was just past the room clerk and up one flight of stairs. The route to Roger himself was not so direct.

The next morning he left the hotel to stay at Mimi's house. I couldn't tell from the way Roger described Mimi and her situation if he was in love with her or she with him. In any case he described her primarily as a friend and an older woman, as if that would invalidate her. Later she and I became friends, and Roger's deviousness was reflected in phrases like "an older woman." It was hard for me to fuck Roger with Mimi below us in her solitary bed. The next night Roger agonized about whether or not we could make it with each other.

That Roger would leave town soon made our week intense, sweet. There's nothing like the promise of absence to make presence felt. When he left my bed to cross the Channel, Charley came to see me and asked me to live with him again. We could squat a house, he said. I figured his coming to me had to do with smell but he was two weeks late and I wanted to get the hell out.

Spring in London. I filmed Roger in Hyde Park and in the garden. I baked apple pies, wrote poems about making apple pies—rhyming pie with die—and took to watercolors again. What an interesting couple we made. We went to his cottage in Norfolk. Listened to Stevie Wonder on the radio and I wrote letters about cricket, actors, country life; my letters were shaped with Jane Austen in mind. She was my model for the genteel English country life. The English have got cottage life down, like having tea at four. We visited the neighboring Lord and had a discussion about tied cottages. The pound may have dropped as we spoke.

We returned to London. I took a job in the neighborhood, making twenty pounds a week for a five-day regime. And we shared the cost of living together. I continued to cook. Susan visited from Amsterdam and noted that she thought I was playing house. I was very serious when I played, though. Roger thought my friends were weird and I thought his superficial.

My book was up in the air and my plan was to return to Holland, read the proofs and come back to Roger and our routine life. Roger's heart, about which I heard a great deal, made it hard for him to be honest. He never wanted to hurt anyone. And while he liked me, he was still in love with the one before me. The day I left for Holland she moved right back in. Roger didn't let me know this, his heart was so big, for months and months.

I went to Eastern Europe with my sister, happy to be away, unhappy about Roger, again returning to Amsterdam. Roger called, after those months had passed, to give some apologies. Still later we held a conversation that clarified matters further. He thought because I had posed in the nude for a drawing course and had worked on a sex paper, he thought I would introduce him to the mysteries.

CHAPTER 12: Going to Parties

Living in New York City and going to parties. The last ritual, attending parties. Kathy introduces me to Scott who is kneeling and I kneel too. My knees begin to hurt and I stand over him. I'm sure he's queer with his Lou Reed hair, overalls and big glasses. I watch him dance. Not bad. I lose everyone I know and Scott and I begin to dance. He's very tall and I can't see his face which is hidden anyway by his glasses. The masked man. A bad song comes on and we lean against the wall. "Let's go to my place," he says, "and we'll come back in a little while. It's real close." That's friendly, I think, and say ok and off we walk in an area unfamiliar to me. His loft is farther than a few blocks and it's raining. Maybe he's not homosexual.

The loft is six flights up and I begin by bounding the stairs two at a time. "Take it easy," he says, "there's a lot more." I enter the loft panting. My eyes are attuned to small Dutch quarters and the amount of space he has makes us both look small, insignificant.

Scott turns on The Wailers and we continue dancing. It's that movie when the dance becomes The Dance. He says, "You were making eyes at me." I tell him I wear glasses. We're lying on the bed. By now I realize he's heterosexual and this is the fashion. "Are you Kathy's boyfriend?" I ask, suddenly. "Not anymore," he says, "we're both hot to trot." I'm not sure what anything means and insist, drunkenly, that we go back to the party. He thinks I'm upfront. "Since we're not going to fuck," he says, "wanna see my sculpture?" And next find myself seated inside a vibrating box.

Everything seems funny. I feel both innocent and wild. "Hey, little girl, you don't have to hide nothing no more. You haven't done nothing that hasn't been done before." Kathy walks up to me, "you've been with Scott?" "Yes," I say, "what about it?" She clears the decks and not only clears them but also indicates she has aimed me at him. "He's a good fuck," she says, and walks off. Is he or am I being passed on? There's something bloodless in the modern age.

Scott watches the discussion and says, "I coulda hit you for talking to Kathy." "Look, it's funny, Scott, don't you see?" We're dancing again, nearer to the wine and a Puerto Rican woman who really dances and I dance with her and smoke some grass and get given hash and Scott walks up and says (again), "Let's go."

We do the same walk, in the same night, up all those stairs, but there's a difference. "Harder this time," he says. Of course, I think. His roommate is at the far end of loft. I know he's here but can hardly see him. More California wine and the television on by our heads. My head is turned toward it but I am not watching. Pulling off our clothes, on the bed, he thinks I'm watching the movie. I am and I'm not. It's just on, a forties movie, and it fits right in, somehow, with everything else. The guy at the far end of the loft is snoring. Scott and I are fucking. "Did you come?" he asks. "Not this time," I answer. "Next time," he says. "I trust you," I say. But I can't sleep. The wine, grass and sex. Parched throat. Water. Need water. "Get me some too," he says. It's dark and I take the long walk down the naked loft. That naked walk to get a glass of water. For a piss, or for water, so familiar in unfamiliar territory. Don Juan should see me now, gait of the warrior in a New York City loft. I find everything and return carrying two full glasses of water. I hand one to Scott. Cold water hits him in the face and he thinks I did it purposely. "You bitch," he says, just like in a forties movie. Then I know. He wants that. He keeps calling me Bitch. There's something refreshing about this reversal: a masochistic man. "No," I say, "I wouldn't do that, pour cold water on you in bed."

He's fast asleep. I can't sleep. Why can they always sleep? Are men better sleepers? The windows bang heavy during the night. The rain bangs against the windows. I look at Scott, closely now. No hair, no glasses. He looks like a little baby and has a small mouth. By the light of the storm, he looks like an alien. A young alien. I have to stop this and sleep. I know more about his cock than his face. Big cock, small mouth. The sun is coming in through the windows and I'm watching it. The light is dark as the rain continues.

In the morning Scott tells me he's into being macho. "How do you mean?" I ask. "Well," he says, "it's sort of feminism for men." I tell Scott I have an appointment, which seems like a lie but isn't. With whom he asks. Sally, I say. Sally Blank? he is incredulous. Yes I say. "She's a good fuck," he reports. "This is just like high school," I say. "Oh," he goes on, "and you don't know all of it. Anyway, Kathy is using this material for her novel. She uses the gossip." At least that isn't new. He calls me bitch again as I dress and then he undresses me and my belt buckle makes a clumsy sound in the big, empty room. "Why didn't you start this before I got dressed?" I ask. "You moved too fast," he says. His big hand touches, hardly touches my cunt, and we fuck again, not drunk or stoned. Lots of light now. "You feel so good," he says, "and I have to piss." He gets out, gets up and goes to piss. Stay for pancakes? Can't I stay.

He walks me to the door wearing a terry cloth robe that just barely covers his tight ass. Lifts me high, kisses me and unlocks the door. It's pouring outside.

Some months later, we've remained friends. Scott asks how he can meet a woman. "I'm confused," he says. "That's it," I say. "What?" he asks. "That. Just let her see you've vulnerable. It works every time. Women are suckers for sensitive men." The advice works. I'm invited to his loft dancing-wedding party a year later. The bride and groom wear dark colors and both have closely cropped hair.

CHAPTER 13: The Fourth of July

I should have known better. Upper middle class guys from Westchester are trouble and can't fuck. But look at that I say to myself, he's in therapy, talks about his mother with affection, wants to know something about me. The modern man aware of female independence. I'm not attracted to him though he's handsome in a way I find reprehensible—slick, well-dressed, clean but sweats a lot. Still he's so normal. The bait taken, Josh beat at my conditioned barriers and I let him in.

It's my first Fourth of July in the USA in seven years. And it's the Bicentennial at that. I'm not sure what people are celebrating but Americans like parties. We watch fireworks from a roof on Canal Street. The approach to the roof is the most dangerous aspect on this pacific evening. For while Amy had predicted bombs and dutifully warned Sidonie, a French friend, to stay off the streets, five million people walk around Lower Manhattan, watch the tall ships, and eat. I eat Polish sausage and drink German beer.

The party begins tentatively as most do. But it is the Fourth of July and people want to have a good time. The dancing starts slowly and builds up, people secreting into the group one by one, then two by two. Martha knocks herself out on this hot night doing an energetic lindy then disappears. A man with a moist face approaches me from behind and asks me to dance. There's something about being asked to dance that takes me back to sixth grade parties. Being asked to dance in this way and by a stranger is so American and perfectly right for the Fourth of July. He's sweating which keeps me at arm's length until he asks serious questions which soften me to him. I dance with him for a while but dismiss myself graciously, saying I'm going to the bathroom. I want to find Sidonie and see if she'd be interested in this earnest man, in Josh.

Red, white and blue chalk marks are drawn on my forehead. It's not the mark of Cain but still one can't help making an association like that. Judy has lines over her mouth, more like a clown. Things seem to be heating up with old lovers walking in and out, the party filling democratically with people one wants and one does not want to see. I introduce Sidonie to Josh but she's not interested and neither is he. It's not that easy. We dance again and he leaves, giving me a kiss on the cheek and the ritualized "I'll phone you."

Patsy and I do a vicious dance, a tango of sorts; the time is right for dancing in the streets and movements such as these. I tell Scott that this week he is not one of my favorite people and he takes this seriously, so we don't speak for months.

Firecrackers keep popping off and everything feels slightly evil. For the urban dweller whose adventures are limited to sexual ones, the Fourth of July has nothing to do with America's independence. One's own independence is severely circumscribed anyway. We play out the hunt we can.

Josh phones two nights later when I had all but forgotten him. His voice is reassuring and certain. We meet the next night at a Chinese restaurant, joined by Martha and her friend Don. Martha and Don are blond and fairskinned, Josh and I are dark-haired and tan.

Alone in a bar we talk familiarly about recent problems and the women he used to live with. This is the usual fare. I am still not attracted to him but consider this my failing. I tend toward men who aren't as nice. He says, "But we haven't talked about your writing."

And he walks me home and since I have not changed my feelings toward him, I don't want him to go out of his way for me. He insists that he is doing what he wants to do. This kind of statement comes right out of therapy and I recognize it—he's taking responsibility for his actions. Still, he strikes me as sensible. We walk to my street near Wall Street, talking all the way, and he invites me to a party the next night. By now he knows I'm leaving for San Francisco in a few days. This has created for him an urgency to see me more. I don't distrust this. I ask if I can bring Sidonie to the party and he says, "Yes, of course."

The party is on the Bowery. We pass alcoholics fighting over shoes. Across the street from his friend's party, there is a fire in a flophouse. It's like leaving a war zone when we enter the party. The men and women are spotless and fashionable and they are artists. Lots of good food and drink. The discrepancy can be watched, like a movie, out the window. A few drinks and I begin to appreciate Josh because he is so very attentive. This is a form of flattery that is most convincing, particularly at a party. When I was fourteen I discovered that boys would fall in love with me if I listened to everything they said. A strong sense of integrity prohibited me from continuing this form of seduction. And, in addition to integrity, there was the problem of having to continue to listen to them.

We dance and I still don't want to make love with him. I get drunker in order to overcome my disinclination, even disgust at the prospect. I am sure I don't want him because he's so nice, is like the boys I grew up with, and so openly likes me. I feel trapped. And it's kind of comfortable.

We return to his loft and I see his paintings, which are done

on the back of the canvas. This interests me because it is in
sharp contrast to his regular guy demeanor. "You're less open
than you appear," I say to him, surprising him with this insight.
I immediately forget it, as if it were only academic, and sit on
the couch beside him. Noticing my reluctance he thinks I'm
nervous about making love with him for the first time. This
amuses me inwardly but I cannot share my amusement with
him. He begins to talk about "the situation" and I know I'll
either do it or I won't so I say, "Let's go to bed." A lot of per-
formers get on the stage like that, just jumping on. Besides, I
think to myself, this is an act I know with and without feeling.
I am trying to get over a reluctance, the reason for which I do
not know. The mechanics of sex make it easier for a woman to
betray herself, which leads perhaps to her having different feelings about sex from a man whose sex organ is always a sign. We
make love and once it's over I feel relieved, like having gone to
the dentist and just having one cavity.

When we awaken in the morning, I feel like talking, not
rushing from his bed. By this time I'm involved—in something. Uninspired sex can win a masochist. It certainly makes
sex not at all central to the relationship; it's so easy to forget.
And so I felt that I really liked him and was not just attracted
to him. Here is Puritanism, liking someone because the sex
is bad.

I'm excited about leaving New York and having met a nice
guy I can introduce to my friends. So I introduce Josh to lots of
my friends, feeling certain and calm. He says I can phone him
collect whenever I want. He phones me every week I'm away
and I send romantic cards. I'm away for five weeks and don't
make love with anyone else, partly out of this strange loyalty I
develop like a rash when rubbed by certain kinds of men, partly

because San Francisco didn't abound with men I could make love with. This combination appeared to be fate. Fatal.

When I get back to New York City, it is still hot. I phone him, leaving a message on his machine. He calls later and we meet that night. Everything seems to be going as it should. But he can't get it up. Says he is anxious about a show coming along faster than he expected. There's nothing to do about impotence except be understanding. But it was awful and not at all like the dream I had of my return to New York—he had made a painting that, when shot with a water pistol, moved in mysterious ways often called orgasmic.

We both bury the lack of lovemaking as if it's just one of those things. Josh asks me to go to the Hamptons with him for the weekend but when I phone the next day to find out when we're leaving, he begs off, and says he wants to be alone. That he'll call me when he returns. Says there's nothing wrong between us.

Sunday night passes, and Monday, it could've been a long summer weekend. Josh never calls and I am the one, finally, to call him. He speaks to me as if I were a foreigner, a greenhorn who has the wrong expectations about America.

One year later he comes up to me in a bar and, smiling, asks, "How are you and what are you up to now?" I look at him blankly and answer "The same." "You're distant," he says to me, surprised, even hurt by my disdain. He hadn't been a one-night stand, a temporary shelter like a glassed-in bus stop on a busy, rainy city street. Anonymous and more or less alienating, or sexy, depending upon one's mood. He had attenuated the one-night stand into something more difficult to get over. For a while I was meaner in the clinches, not so easy to fool. There are some things I just won't forgive.

Girl

Jamaica Kincaid

Wash the white clothes on Monday and put them on the stone
heap; wash the color clothes on Tuesday and put them on the
clothesline to dry; don't walk barehead in the hot sun; cook
pumpkin fritters in very hot sweet oil; soak your little cloths
right after you take them off; when buying cotton to make yourself a nice blouse, be sure that it doesn't have gum on it, because
that way it won't hold up well after a wash; soak salt fish overnight before you cook it; is it true that you sing benna in Sunday
school?; always eat your food in such a way that it won't turn

someone else's stomach; on Sundays try to walk like a lady and not like the slut you are so bent on becoming; don't sing benna in Sunday school; you mustn't speak to wharf-rat boys, not even to give directions; don't eat fruits on the street—flies will follow you; *but I don't sing benna on Sunday at all and never in Sunday school*; this is how to sew on a button; this is how to make a buttonhole for the button you have just sewed on; this is how to hem a dress when you see the hem coming down and so to prevent yourself from looking like the slut I know you are so bent on becoming; this is how you iron your father's khaki shirt so that it doesn't have a crease; this is how you iron your father's khaki pants so that they don't have a crease; this is how you grow okra—far from the house; because okra tree harbors red ants; when you are growing dasheen, make sure it gets plenty of water or else it makes your throat itch when you are eating it; this is how you sweep a corner; this is how you sweep a whole house; this is how you sweep a yard; this is how you smile to someone you don't like too much; this is how you smile to someone you don't like at all; this is how you smile to someone you like completely; this is how you set a table for tea; this is how you set a table for dinner; this is how you set a table for lunch; this is how you set a table for breakfast; this is how to behave in the presence of men who don't know you very well, and this way they won't recognize immediately the slut I have warned you against becoming; be sure to wash every day, even if it is with your own spit; don't squat down to play marbles—you are not a boy, you know; don't pick people's flowers—you might catch something; don't throw stones at blackbirds, because it might not be a blackbird at all; this is how you make a bread pudding; this is how you make doukona; this is how to make pepper pot; this is how to make a good medicine for a cold; this is how to make a good medicine to throw away a child before it even becomes a child; this is how to catch a fish; this is how to throw back a fish you don't like; and that way something bad won't fall on you; this is how to bully a man; this is how a man bullies you; this is how to love a man, and if this doesn't work there are other ways, and if they don't work don't feel too bad about giving up; this is how to spit up in the air if you feel like it, and this is how to move quick so that it doesn't fall on you; this is how to make ends meet; always squeeze bread to make sure it's fresh; *but what if the baker won't let me feel the bread?*; you mean to say that after all you are really going to be the kind of woman who the baker won't let near the bread?

So Much Water So Close to Home

Raymond Carver

My husband eats with good appetite but he seems tired, edgy. He chews slowly, arms on the table, and stares at something across the room. He looks at me and looks away again. He wipes his mouth on the napkin. He shrugs and goes on eating. Something has come between us though he would like me to believe otherwise.

"What are you staring at me for?" he asks. "What is it?" he says and puts his fork down.

"Was I staring?" I say and shake my head stupidly, stupidly.

The telephone rings. "Don't answer it," he says.

"It might be your mother," I say. "Dean—it might be something about Dean."

"Watch and see," he says.

I pick up the receiver and listen for a minute. He stops eating. I bite my lip and hang up.

"What did I tell you?" he says. He starts to eat again, then throws the napkin onto his plate. "Goddamn it, why can't people mind their own business? Tell me what I did wrong and I'll listen! It's not fair. She was dead, wasn't she? There were other men there besides me. We talked it over and we all decided. We'd only just got there. We'd walked for hours. We couldn't just turn around, we were five miles from the car. It was opening day. What the hell, I don't see anything wrong. No, I don't. And don't look at me that way, do you hear? I won't have you passing judgment on me. Not you."

"You know," I say and shake my head.

"What do I know, Claire? Tell me. Tell me what I know. I don't know anything except one thing: you hadn't better get worked up over this." He gives me what he thinks is a *meaningful* look. "She was dead, dead, dead, do you hear?" he says after a minute. "It's a damn shame, I agree. She was a young girl and it's a shame, and I'm sorry, as sorry as anyone else, but she was dead, Claire, dead. Now let's leave it alone. Please, Claire. Let's leave it alone now."

"That's the point," I say. "She was dead. But don't you see? She needed help."

"I give up," he says and raises his hands. He pushes his chair away from the table, takes his cigarettes and goes out to the patio with a can of beer. He walks back and forth for a minute and then sits in a lawn chair and picks up the paper once more.

His name is there on the first page along with the names of his friends, the other men who made the "grisly find."

I close my eyes for a minute and hold onto the drainboard. I must not dwell on this any longer. I must get over it, put it out of sight, out of mind, etc., and "go on." I open my eyes. Despite everything, knowing all that may be in store, I rake my arm across the drainboard and send the dishes and glasses smashing and scattering across the floor.

He doesn't move. I know he has heard, he raises his head as if listening, but he doesn't move otherwise, doesn't turn around to look. I hate him for that, for not moving. He waits a minute, then draws on his cigarette and leans back in the chair. I pity him for listening, detached, and then settling back and drawing on his cigarette. The wind takes the smoke out of his mouth in a thin stream. Why do I notice that? He can never know how much I pity him for that, for sitting still and listening, and letting the smoke stream out of his mouth . . .

He planned his fishing trip into the mountains last Sunday, a week before the Memorial Day weekend. He and Gordon Johnson, Mel Dorn, Vern Williams. They play poker, bowl, and fish together. They fish together every spring and early summer, the first two or three months of the season, before family vacations, little league baseball, and visiting relatives can intrude. They are decent men, family men, responsible at their jobs. They have sons and daughters who go to school with our son, Dean. On Friday afternoon these four men left for a three-day fishing trip to the Naches River. They parked the car in the mountains and hiked several miles to where they wanted to fish. They carried their bedrolls, food and cooking utensils, their playing cards, their whiskey. The first evening at the river, even before they could set up camp, Mel Dorn found the girl floating face down in the river, nude, lodged near the shore in some brandies. He called the other men and they all came to look at her. They talked about what to do. One of the men—Stuart didn't say which—perhaps it was Vern Williams, he is a heavy-set, easy man who laughs often—one of them thought they should start back to the car at once. The others stirred the sand with their shoes and said they felt inclined to stay. They pleaded fatigue, the late hour, the fact that the girl "wasn't going anywhere." In the end they all decided to stay. They went ahead and set up the camp and built a fire and drank their whiskey. They drank a lot of whiskey and when the moon came up they talked about the girl. Someone thought they should do something to prevent the body from floating away. Somehow they thought that this might create a problem for them if it floated away during the night. They took flashlights and stumbled down to the river. The wind was up, a cold wind, and waves from the river lapped the sandy bank. One of the men, I don't know who, it might have been Stuart, he could have done it, waded into the water and took the girl by the fingers and pulled her, still face down, closer to shore, into shallow water, and then took a piece of nylon cord and tied it around her wrist and then secured the cord to tree roots, all the while the flashlights of the other men played over the girl's body. Afterward, they went back to camp and drank more whiskey. Then they went to sleep. The next morning, Saturday, they cooked breakfast, drank lots of coffee, more whiskey, and then split up to fish, two men upriver, two men down.

That night, after they had cooked their fish and potatoes and had more coffee and whiskey, they took their dishes down to the river and rinsed them off a few yards from where the body lay in the water. They drank again and then they took out their cards and played and drank until they couldn't see the cards any longer. Vern Williams went to sleep, but the others told coarse stories and spoke of vulgar or dishonest escapades out of their past, and no one mentioned the girl until Gordon Johnson, who'd forgotten for a minute, commented on the firmness of the trout they'd caught, and the terrible coldness of the river water. They stopped talking then but continued to drink until one of them tripped and fell cursing against the lantern, and then they climbed into their sleeping bags.

The next morning they got up late, drank more whiskey, fished a little as they kept drinking whiskey. Then, at one o'clock in the afternoon, Sunday, a day earlier than they'd planned, they decided to leave. They took down their tents, rolled their sleeping bags, gathered their pans, pots, fish, and fishing gear, and hiked out. They didn't look at the girl again before they left. When they reached the car they drove the highway in silence until they came to a telephone. Stuart made the call to the sheriff's office while the others stood around in the hot sun and listened. He gave the man on the other end of the line all of their names—they had nothing to hide, they weren't ashamed of anything—and agreed to wait at the service station until someone could come for more detailed directions and individual statements.

He came home at eleven o'clock that night. I was asleep but woke when I heard him in the kitchen. I found him leaning against the refrigerator drinking a can of beer. He put his heavy arms around me and rubbed his hands up and down my back, the same hands he'd left with two days before, I thought.

In bed he put his hands on me again and then waited, as if thinking of something else. I turned slightly and then moved my legs. Afterward, I know he stayed awake for a long time, for he was awake when I fell asleep; and later, when I stirred for a minute, opening my eyes at a slight noise, a rustle of sheets, it was almost daylight outside, birds were singing, and he was on his back smoking and looking at the curtained window. Half-asleep I said his name, but he didn't answer. I fell asleep again.

He was up this morning before I could get out of bed—to see if there was anything about it in the paper, I suppose. The telephone began to ring shortly after eight o'clock.

"Go to hell," I heard him shout into the receiver. The telephone rang again a minute later, and I hurried into the kitchen. "I have nothing else to add to what I've already said to the sheriff. That's right!" He slammed down the receiver.

"What is going on?" I said, alarmed.

"Sit down," he said slowly. His fingers scraped, scraped against his stubble of whiskers. "I have to tell you something. Something happened while we were fishing." We sat across from each other at the table, and then he told me.

I drank coffee and stared at him as he spoke. Then I read the account in the newspaper that he shoved across the table: ". . . unidentified girl eighteen to twenty-four years of age . . . body three to five days in the water . . . rape a possible motive . . . preliminary results show death by strangulation . . . cuts and bruises on her breasts and pelvic area . . . autopsy . . . rape, pending further investigation."

"You've got to understand," he said. "Don't look at me like that. Be careful now, I mean it. Take it easy, Claire."

"Why didn't you tell me last night?" I asked.

"I just . . . didn't. What do you mean?" he said.

"You know what I mean," I said. I looked at his hands, the broad fingers, knuckles covered with hair, moving, lighting a cigarette now, fingers that had moved over me, into me last night.

He shrugged. "What difference does it make, last night, this morning? It was late. You were sleepy, I thought I'd wait until this morning to tell you." He looked out to the patio: a robin flew from the lawn to the picnic table and preened its feathers.

"It isn't true," I said. "You didn't leave her there like that?"

He turned quickly and said, "What'd I do? Listen to me carefully now, once and for all. Nothing happened. I have nothing to be sorry for or feel guilty about. Do you hear me?"

I got up from the table and went to Dean's room. He was awake and in his pajamas, putting together a puzzle. I helped him find his clothes and then went back to the kitchen and put his breakfast on the table. The telephone rang two or three more times and each time Stuart was abrupt while he talked and angry when he hung up. He called Mel Dorn and Gordon Johnson and spoke with them, slowly, seriously, and then he opened a beer and smoked a cigarette while Dean ate, asked him about school, his friends, etc., exactly as if nothing had happened.

Dean wanted to know what he'd done while he was gone, and Stuart took some fish out of the freezer to show him.

"I'm taking him to your mother's for the day," I said.

"Sure," Stuart said and looked at Dean who was holding one of the frozen trout. "If you want to and he wants to, that is. You don't have to, you know. There's nothing wrong."

"I'd like to anyway," I said.

"Can I go swimming there?" Dean asked and wiped his fingers on his pants.

"I believe so," I said. "It's a warm day so take your suit, and I'm sure your grandmother will say it's okay."

Stuart lighted a cigarette and looked at us.

Dean and I drove across town to Stuart's mother's. She lives in an apartment building with a pool and a sauna bath. Her name is Catherine Kane. Her name, Kane, is the same as mine, which seems impossible. Years ago, Stuart has told me, she used to be called Candy by her friends. She is a tall, cold woman with white-blonde hair. She gives me the feeling that she is always judging, judging. I explain briefly in a low voice what has happened (she hasn't yet read the newspaper) and promise to pick Dean up that evening. "He brought his swimming suit," I say. "Stuart and I have to talk about some things," I add vaguely. She looks at me steadily from over her glasses. Then she nods and turns to Dean, saying "How are you, my little man?" She stoops and puts her arms around him. She looks at me again as I open the door to leave. She has a way of looking at me without saying anything.

When I return home Stuart is eating something at the table and drinking beer . . .

After a time I sweep up the broken dishes and glassware and go outside. Stuart is lying on his back on the grass now, the newspaper and can of beer within reach, staring at the sky. It's breezy but warm out and birds call.

"Stuart, could we go for a drive?" I say. "Anywhere."

He rolls over and looks at me and nods. "We'll pick up some beer," he says. "I hope you're feeling better about this. Try to understand, that's all I ask." He gets to his feet and touches me on the hip as he goes past. "Give me a minute and I'll be ready."

We drive through town without speaking. Before we reach the country he stops at a roadside market for beer. I notice a great stack of papers just inside the door. On the top step a fat woman in a print dress holds out a licorice stick to a little girl.

In a few minutes we cross Everson Creek and turn into a picnic area a few feet from the water. The creek flows under the bridge and into a large pond a few hundred yards away. There are a dozen or so men and boys scattered around the banks of the pond under the willows, fishing.

So much water so close to home, why did he have to go miles away to fish?

"Why did you have to go there of all places?" I say.

"The Naches? We always go there. Every year, at least once." We sit on a bench in the sun and he opens two cans of beer and gives one to me. "How the hell was I to know anything like that would happen?" He shakes his head and shrugs, as if it had all happened years ago, or to someone else. "Enjoy the afternoon, Claire. Look at this weather."

"They said they were innocent."

"Who? What are you talking about?"

"The Maddox brothers. They killed a girl named Arlene Hubly near the town where I grew up, and then cut off her head and threw her into the Cle Elum River. She and I went to the same high school. It happened when I was a girl."

"What a hell of a thing to be thinking about," he says. "Come on, get off it. You' re going to get me riled in a minute. How about it now? Claire?"

I look at the creek. I float toward the pond, eyes open, face down, staring at the rocks and moss on the creek bottom until I am carried into the lake where I am pushed by the breeze. Nothing will be any different. We will go on and on and on and on. We will go on even now, as if nothing had happened. I look at him across the picnic table with such intensity that his face drains.

"I don't know what's wrong with you," he says, "I don't—"

I slap him before I realize. I raise my hand, wait a fraction of a second, and then slap his cheek hard. This is crazy, I think as I slap him. We need to lock our fingers together. We need to help one another. This is crazy.

He catches my wrist before I can strike again and raises his own hand. I crouch, waiting, and see something come into his eyes and then dart away. He drops his hand. I drift even faster around and around in the pond.

"Come on, get in the car," he says. "I'm taking you home."

"No, no," I say, pulling back from him.

"Come on," he says. "Goddamn it."

"You're not being fair to me," he says later in the car. Fields and trees and farmhouses fly by outside the window. "You're not being fair. To either one of us. Or to Dean, I might add. Think about Dean for a minute. Think about me. Think about someone else besides your goddamn self for a change."

There is nothing I can say to him now. He tries to concentrate on the road, but he keeps looking into the rearview mirror. Out of the corner of his eye, he looks across the seat to where I sit with my knees drawn up under my chin. The sun blazes against my arm and the side of my face. He opens another beer while he drives, drinks from it, then shoves the can between his legs and lets out breath. He knows. I could laugh in his face. I could weep.

Stuart believes he is letting me sleep this morning. But I was awake long before the alarm sounded, thinking, lying on the far side of the bed, away from his hairy legs and his thick, sleeping fingers. He gets Dean off for school, and then he shaves, dresses, and leaves for work. Twice he looks into the bedroom and clears his throat, but I keep my eyes closed.

In the kitchen I find a note from him signed "Love." I sit in the breakfast nook in the sunlight and drink coffee and make a coffee ring on the note. The telephone has stopped ringing, that's something. No more calls since last night. I look at the paper and turn it this way and that on the table. Then I pull it close and read what it says. The body is still unidentified, unclaimed, apparently unmissed. But for the last twenty-four hours men have been examining it, putting things into it, cutting, weighing, measuring, putting back again, sewing up, looking for the exact cause and moment of death. Looking for evidence of rape. I'm sure they hope for rape. Rape would make it easier to understand. The paper says the body will be taken to Keith & Keith Funeral Home pending arrangements. People are asked to come forward with information, etc.

Two things are certain: 1) people no longer care what happens to other people; and 2) nothing makes any real difference any longer. Look at what has happened. Yet nothing will change for Stuart and me. Really change, I mean. We will grow older, both of us, you can see it in our faces already, in the bathroom mirror, for instance, mornings when we use the bathroom at the same time. And certain things around us will change, become easier or harder, one thing or the other, but nothing will ever really be any different. I believe that. We have made our decisions, our lives have been set in motion, and they will go on and on until they stop. But if that is true, then what? I mean, what if you believe that, but you keep it covered up, until one day something happens that should change something, but then you see nothing is going to change after all. What then? Meanwhile, the people around you continue to talk and act as if you were the same person as yesterday, or last night, or five minutes before, but you are really undergoing a crisis, your heart feels damaged . . .

The past is unclear. It's as if there is a film over those early years. I can't even be sure that the things I remember happening really happened to me. There was a girl who had a mother and father—the father ran a small café where the mother acted as waitress and cashier—who moved as if in a dream through grade school and high school and then, in a year or two, into secretarial school. Later, much later—what happened to the time in between?—she is in another town working as a receptionist for an electronics parts firm and becomes acquainted with one of the engineers who asks her for a date. Eventually, seeing that's his aim, she lets him seduce her. She had an intuition at the time, an insight about the seduction that later, try as she might, she couldn't recall. After a short while they decide to get married, but already the past, her past, is slipping away. The future is something she can't imagine. She smiles, as if she has a secret, when she thinks about the future. Once, during a particularly bad argument, over what she can't now remember, five years or so after they were married, he tells her that someday this affair (his words: "this affair") will end in violence. She remembers this. She files this away somewhere and begins repeating it aloud from time to time. Sometimes she spends the whole morning on her knees in the sandbox behind the garage playing with Dean and one or two of his friends. But every afternoon at four o'clock her head begins to hurt. She holds her forehead and feels dizzy with the pain. Stuart asks her to see a doctor and she does, secretly pleased at the doctor's solicitous attention. She goes away for a while to a place the doctor recommends. Stuart's mother comes out from Ohio in a hurry to care for the child. But she, Claire, spoils everything and returns home in a few weeks. His mother moves out of the house and takes an apartment across town and perches there, as if waiting. One night in bed when they are both near sleep, Claire tells him that she heard some women patients at the clinic discussing fellatio. She thinks this is something he might like to hear. Stuart is pleased at hearing this. He strokes her arm. Things are going to be okay, he says. From now on everything is going to be different and better for them. He has received a promotion and a substantial raise. They've even bought another car, a station wagon, her car. They're going to live in the here and now. He says he feels able to relax for the first time in years. In the dark, he goes on stroking her arm . . . He continues to bowl and play cards regularly. He goes fishing with three friends of his.

That evening three things happen: Dean says that the children at school told him that his father found a dead body in the river. He wants to know about it.

Stuart explains quickly, leaving out most of the story, saying only that, yes, he and three other men did find a body while they were fishing.

"What kind of body?" Dean asks. "Was it a girl?"

"Yes, it was a girl. A woman. Then we called the sheriff." Stuart looks at me.

"What'd he say?" Dean asks.

"He said he'd take care of it."

"What did it look like? Was it scary?"

"That's enough talk," I say. "Rinse your plate, Dean, and then you're excused."

"But what'd it look like?" he persists. "I want to know."

"You heard me," I say. "Did you hear me, Dean? Dean!" I want to shake him. I want to shake him until he cries.

"Do what your mother says," Stuart tells him quietly. "It was just a body, and that's all there is to it."

I am clearing the table when Stuart comes up behind and touches my arm. His fingers burn. I start, almost losing a plate.

"What's the matter with you?" he says, dropping his hand. "Claire, what is it?"

"You scared me," I say.

"That's what I mean. I should be able to touch you without you jumping out of your skin." He stands in front of me with a little grin, trying to catch my eyes, and then he puts his arm around my waist. With his other hand he takes my free hand and puts it on the front of his pants.

"Please, Stuart." I pull away and he steps back and snaps his fingers.

"Hell with it then," he says. "Be that way if you want. But just remember."

"Remember what?" I say quickly. I look at him and hold my breath.

He shrugs. "Nothing, nothing," he says.

The second thing that happens is that while we are watching television that evening, he in his leather recliner chair, I on the sofa with a blanket and magazine, the house quiet except for the television, a voice cuts into the program to say that the murdered girl has been identified. Full details will follow on the eleven o'clock news.

We look at each other. In a few minutes he gets up and says he is going to fix a nightcap. Do I want one?

"No," I say.

"I don't mind drinking alone," he says. "I thought I'd ask."

I can see he is obscurely hurt, and I look away, ashamed and yet angry at the same time.

He stays in the kitchen a long while, but comes back with his drink just when the news begins.

First the announcer repeats the story of the four local fishermen finding the body. Then the station shows a high school graduation photograph of the girl, a dark-haired girl with a round face and full, smiling lips. There's a film of the girl's parents entering the funeral home to make the identification. Bewildered, sad, they shuffle slowly up the sidewalk to the front steps to where a man in a dark suit stands waiting, holding the door. Then, it seems as if only seconds have passed, as if they have merely gone inside the door and turned around and come out again, the same couple is shown leaving the building, the woman in tears, covering her face with a handkerchief, the man stopping long enough to say to a reporter, "It's her, it's Susan. I can't say anything right now. I hope they get the person or persons who did it before it happens again. This violence . . ." He motions feebly at the television camera. Then the man and woman get into an old car and drive away into the late afternoon traffic.

The announcer goes on to say that the girl, Susan Miller, had gotten off work as a cashier in a movie theater in Summit, a town 120 miles north of our town. A green, late-model car pulled up in front of the theater and the girl, who according to witnesses looked as if she'd been waiting, went over to the car and got in, leading the authorities to suspect that the driver of the car was a friend, or at least an acquaintance. The authorities would like to talk to the driver of the green car.

Stuart clears his throat, then leans back in the chair and sips his drink.

The third thing that happens is that after the news Stuart stretches, yawns, and looks at me. I get up and begin making a bed for myself on the sofa.

"What are you doing?" he says, puzzled.

"I'm not sleepy," I say, avoiding his eyes. "I think I'll stay up a while longer and then read something until I fall asleep."

He stares as I spread a sheet over the sofa. When I start to go for a pillow, he stands at the bedroom door, blocking the way.

"I'm going to ask you once more," he says. "What the hell do you think you're going to accomplish by this?"

"I need to be by myself tonight," I say. "I need to have time to think."

He lets out breath. "I'm thinking you're making a big mistake by doing this. I'm thinking you'd better think again about what you're doing. Claire?"

I can't answer. I don't know what I want to say. I turn and begin to tuck in the edges of the blanket. He stares at me a minute longer and then I see him raise his shoulders. "Suit yourself then. I could give a fuck less what you do," he says. He turns and walks down the hall scratching his neck.

This morning I read in the paper that services for Susan Miller are to be held in Chapel of the Pines, Summit, at two o'clock the next afternoon. Also, that police have taken statements from three people who saw her get into the green Chevrolet. But they still have no license number for the car. They are getting warmer, though, and the investigation is continuing. I sit for a long while holding the paper, thinking, then I call to make an appointment at the hairdresser's.

I sit under the dryer with a magazine on my lap and let Millie do my nails.

"I'm going to a funeral tomorrow," I say after we have talked a bit about a girl who no longer works there.

Millie looks up at me and then back at my fingers. "I'm sorry to hear that, Mrs. Kane. I'm real sorry."

"It's a young girl's funeral," I say.

"That's the worst kind. My sister died when I was a girl, and I'm still not over it to this day. Who died?" she says after a minute.

"A girl. We weren't all that close, you know, but still."

"Too bad. I'm real sorry. But we'll get you fixed up for it, don't worry. How's that look?"

"That looks . . . fine. Millie, did you ever wish you were somebody else, or else just nobody, nothing, nothing at all?"

She looks at me. "I can't say I ever felt that, no. No, if I was somebody else I'd be afraid I might not like who I was." She holds my fingers and seems to think about something for a minute. "I don't know, I just don't know . . . Let me have your other hand now, Mrs. Kane."

At eleven o'clock that night I make another bed on the sofa and this time Stuart only looks at me, rolls his tongue behind his lips, and goes down the hall to the bedroom. In the night I wake and listen to the wind slamming the gate against the fence. I don't want to be awake, and I lie for a long while with my eyes closed. Finally I get up and go down the hall with my pillow. The light is burning in our bedroom and Stuart is on his back with his mouth open, breathing heavily. I go into Dean's room and get into bed with him. In his sleep he moves over to give me space. I lie there for a minute and then hold him, my face against his hair.

"What is it, mama?" he says.

"Nothing, honey. Go back to sleep. It's nothing, it's all right."

I get up when I hear Stuart's alarm, put on coffee and prepare breakfast while he shaves.

He appears in the kitchen doorway, towel over his bare shoulder, appraising.

"Here's coffee," I say. "Eggs will be ready in a minute."

He nods.

I wake Dean and the three of us have breakfast. Once or twice Stuart looks at me as if he wants to say something, but each time I ask Dean if he wants more milk, more toast, etc.

"I'll call you today," Stuart says as he opens the door.

"I don't think I'll be home today," I say quickly. "I have a lot of things to do today. In fact, I may be late for dinner."

"All right. Sure." He moves his briefcase from one hand to the other. "Maybe we'll go out for dinner tonight? How would you like that?" He keeps looking at me. He's forgotten about the girl already. "Are you all right?"

I move to straighten his tie, then drop my hand. He wants to kiss me goodbye. I move back a step. "Have a nice day then," he says finally. He turns and goes down the walk to his car.

I dress carefully. I try on a hat that I haven't worn in several years and look at myself in the mirror. Then I remove the hat, apply a light makeup, and write a note for Dean.

> *Honey, Mommy has things to do this afternoon, but will be home later. You are to stay in the house or in the back/yard until one of us comes home.*
>
> *Love*

I look at the word "Love" and then I underline it. As I am writing the note I realize I don't know whether *back yard* is one word or two. I have never considered it before. I think about it and then I draw a line and make two words of it.

I stop for gas and ask directions to Summit. Barry, a forty-year-old mechanic with a moustache, comes out from the restroom and leans against the front fender while the other man, Lewis, puts the hose into the tank and begins to slowly wash the windshield.

"Summit," Barry says, looking at me and smoothing a finger down each side of his moustache. "There's no best way to get to Summit, Mrs. Kane. It's about a two-, two-and-a-half-hour drive each way. Across the mountains. It's quite a drive for a woman. Summit? What's in Summit, Mrs. Kane?"

"I have business," I say, vaguely uneasy. Lewis has gone to wait on another customer.

"Ah. Well, if I wasn't tied up there"—he gestures with his thumb toward the bay—"I'd offer to drive you to Summit and back again. Road's not all that good. I mean it's good enough, there's just a lot of curves and so on."

"I'll be all right. But thank you." He leans against the fender. I can feel his eyes as I open my purse.

Barry takes the credit card. "Don't drive it at night," he says. "It's not all that good a road, like I said. And while I'd be willing to bet you wouldn't have car trouble with this, I know this car, you can never be sure about blowouts and things like that. Just to be on the safe side I'd better check these tires." He taps one of the front tires with his shoe. "We'll run it onto the hoist. Won't take long."

"No, no, it's all right. Really, I can't take any more time. The tires look fine to me."

"Only takes a minute," he says. "Be on the safe side."

"I said no. No! They look fine to me. I have to go now. Barry . . ."

"Mrs. Kane?"

"I have to go now."

I sign something. He gives me the receipt, the card, some stamps. I put everything into my purse. "You take it easy," he says. "Be seeing you."

As I wait to pull into the traffic, I look back and see him watching. I close my eyes, then open them. He waves.

I turn at the first light, then turn again and drive until I come to the highway and read the sign: SUMMIT 117 Miles. It is ten-thirty and warm.

The highway skirts the edge of town, then passes through farm country, through fields of oats and sugar beets and apple orchards, with here and there a small herd of cattle grazing in open pastures. Then everything changes, the farms become fewer and fewer, more like shacks now than houses, and stands of timber replace the orchards. All at once I'm in the mountains and on the right, far below, I catch glimpses of the Naches River.

In a little while I see a green pickup truck behind me, and it stays behind me for miles. I keep slowing at the wrong times, hoping it will pass, and then increasing my speed, again at the wrong times. I grip the wheel until my fingers hurt. Then on a clear stretch he does pass, but he drives along beside for a minute, a crew-cut man in a blue workshirt in his early thirties, and we look at each other. Then he waves, toots the horn twice, and pulls ahead of me.

I slow down and find a place, a dirt road off of the shoulder. I pull over and turn off the ignition. I can hear the river somewhere down below the trees. Ahead of me the dirt road goes into the trees. Then I hear the pickup returning.

I start the engine just as the truck pulls up behind me. I lock the doors and roll up the windows. Perspiration breaks on my face and arms as I put the car in gear, but there is no place to drive.

"You all right?" the man says as he comes up to the car. "Hello. Hello in there." He raps the glass. "You okay?" He leans his arms on the door and brings his face close to the window.

I stare at him and can't find any words.

"After I passed I slowed up some," he says. "But when I didn't see you in the mirror I pulled off and waited a couple of minutes. When you still didn't show I thought I'd better drive back and check. Is everything all right? How come you're locked up in there?"

I shake my head.

"Come on, roll down your window. Hey, are you sure you're okay? You know it's not good for a woman to be batting around the country by herself." He shakes his head and looks at the highway, then back at me. "Now come on, roll down the window, how about it? We can't talk this way."

"Please, I have to go."

"Open the door, all right?" he says, as if he isn't listening. "At least roll the window down. You're going to smother in there." He looks at my breasts and legs. The skirt has pulled up over my knees. His eyes linger on my legs, but I sit still, afraid to move.

"I want to smother," I say. "I am smothering, can't you see?"

"What in the hell?" he says and moves back from the door. He turns and walks back to his truck. Then, in the side mirror, I watch him returning, and I close my eyes.

"You don't want me to follow you toward Summit or anything? I don't mind. I got some extra time this morning," he says.

I shake my head.

He hesitates and then shrugs. "Okay, lady, have it your way then," he says. "Okay."

I wait until he has reached the highway, and then I back out. He shifts gears and pulls away slowly, looking back at me in his rearview mirror. I stop the car on the shoulder and put my head on the wheel.

The casket is closed and covered with floral sprays. The organ begins soon after I take a seat near the back of the chapel. People begin to file in and find chairs, some middle-aged and older people, but most of them in their early twenties or even younger. They are people who look uncomfortable in their suits and ties, sport coats and slacks, their dark dresses and leather gloves. One boy in flared pants and a yellow shortsleeved shirt takes the chair next to mine and begins to bite his lips. A door opens at one side of the chapel and I look up and for a minute the parking lot reminds me of a meadow. But then the sun flashes on car windows. The family enters in a group and moves into a curtained area off to the side. Chairs creak as they settle themselves. In a few minutes a slim, blond man in a dark suit stands and asks us to bow our heads. He speaks a brief prayer for us, the living, and when he finishes he asks us to pray in silence for the soul of Susan Miller, departed. I close my eyes and remember her picture in the newspaper and on television. I see her leaving the theater and getting into the green Chevrolet. Then I imagine her journey down the river, the nude body hitting rocks, caught at by branches, the body floating and turning, her hair streaming in the water. Then the hands and hair catching in the overhanging branches, holding, until four men come along to stare at her. I can see a man who is drunk (Stuart?) take her by the wrist. Does anyone here know about that? What if these people knew that? I look around at the other faces. There is a connection to be made of these things, these events, these faces, if I can find it. My head aches with the effort to find it.

He talks about Susan Miller's gifts: cheerfulness and beauty, grace and enthusiasm. From behind the closed curtain someone clears his throat, someone else sobs. The organ music begins. The service is over.

Along with the others I file slowly past the casket. Then I move out onto the front steps and into the bright, hot afternoon light. A middle-aged woman who limps as she goes down the stairs ahead of me reaches the sidewalk and looks around, her eyes falling on me. "Well, they got him," she says. "If that's any consolation. They arrested him this morning. I heard it on the radio before I came. A guy right here in town. A longhair, you might have guessed." We move a few steps down the hot side-walk. People are starting cars. I put out my hand and hold on to a parking meter. Sunlight glances off polished hoods and fend-ers. My head swims. "He's admitted having relations with her that night, but he says he didn't kill her." She snorts. "They'll put him on probation and then turn him loose."

"He might not have acted alone," I say. "They'll have to be sure. He might be covering up for someone, a brother, or some friends."

"I have known that child since she was a little girl," the woman goes on, and her lips tremble. "She used to come over and I'd bake cookies for her and let her eat them in front of the TV." She looks off and begins shaking her head as the tears roll down her cheeks.

Stuart sits at the table with a drink in front of him. His eyes are red and for a minute I think he has been crying. He looks at me and doesn't say anything. For a wild instant I feel something has happened to Dean, and my heart turns.

"Where is he?" I say. "Where is Dean?"

"Outside," he says.

"Stuart, I'm so afraid, so afraid," I say, leaning against the door.

"What are you afraid of, Claire? Tell me, honey, and maybe

I can help. I'd like to help, just try me. That's what husbands are for."

"I can't explain," I say. "I'm just afraid. I feel like, I feel like, I feel like . . ."

He drains his glass and stands up, not taking his eyes from me. "I think I know what you need, honey. Let me play doctor, okay? Just take it easy now." He reaches an arm around my waist and with his other hand begins to unbutton my jacket, then my blouse. "First things first," he says, trying to joke.

"Not now, please," I say.

"Not now, please," he says, teasing. "Please nothing." Then he steps behind me and locks an arm around my waist. One of his hands slips under my brassiere.

"Stop, stop, stop," I say. I stamp on his toes.

And then I am lifted up and then falling. I sit on the floor looking up at him and my neck hurts and my skirt is over my knees. He leans down and says, "You go to hell then, do you hear, bitch? I hope your cunt drops off before I touch it again." He sobs once and I realize he can't help it, he can't help himself either. I feel a rush of pity for him as he heads for the living room.

He didn't sleep at home last night.

This morning, flowers, red and yellow chrysanthemums. I am drinking coffee when the doorbell rings.

"Mrs. Kane?" the young man says, holding his box of flowers.

I nod and pull the robe tighter at my throat.

"The man who called, he said you'd know." The boy looks at my robe, open at the throat, and touches his cap. He stands with his legs apart, feet firmly planted on the top step. "Have a nice day," he says.

A little later the telephone rings and Stuart says, "Honey, how are you? I'll be home early, I love you. Did you hear me?

I love you, I'm sorry, I'll make it up to you. Goodbye, I have to run now."

I put the flowers into a vase in the center of the dining room table and then move my things into the extra bedroom.

Last night, around midnight, Stuart breaks the lock on my door. He does it just to show me that he can, I suppose, for he doesn't do anything when the door springs open except stand there in his underwear looking surprised and foolish while the anger slips from his face. He shuts the door slowly, and a few minutes later I hear him in the kitchen prying open a tray of ice cubes.

I'm in bed when he calls today to tell me that he's asked his mother to come stay with us for a few days. I wait a minute, thinking about this, and then hang up while he is still talking. But in a little while I dial his number at work. When he finally comes on the line I say, "It doesn't matter, Stuart. Really, I tell you it doesn't matter one way or the other."

"I love you," he says.

He says something else and I listen and nod slowly. I feel sleepy. Then I wake up and say, "For God's sake, Stuart, she was only a child."

Aphrodisiac

Christopher Bram

The revolving drum of the multilith printer spun with a rhythmic chatter. Sheet after sheet of clean white paper shot beneath the drum, then jumped into a cradle, each page stamped with Carpenter's face and politics.

It was unnerving. Imagine being in love, and suddenly the object of your affections begins to divide, multiply in a sort of amoebic frenzy, until the world holds a hundred duplicates of the unique person who'd earned your total devotion. What then?

The original Carpenter stood beside the machine, adjusting the feed of paper, correcting the ink flow, talking to me over the gentle noise of the machine. His smooth, boyish face was tilted forward and a sheaf of blond hair was caught behind one lens of his old-fashioned steel-rimmed glasses. Carpenter was twenty-eight, three years older than I, but the only thing about him that looked adult were his hands. They were oversized and tough, ridged along the edges. I have always had great respect for his hands.

"No. I've been meaning to come by and see you people," Carp was saying. "Or at least let you know what was up. But I've been occupied with this." He gestured at the stack of handbills rising in the cradle.

It was lunch hour, and Carp was using his free time to run off material for his city-council campaign. Every few years Carp ran for city council, affiliating himself with one or another of the left-wing groups that seemed to come and go in Richmond with the life expectancy of a fruit fly. He had vanished from view a month before; and although I knew about the campaign, I couldn't quite believe that it was the only reason he was staying away. He had to know what was going on, and if he did, he would want no part of it. Carpenter had always been a terrible moralist. I had driven all the way across town during my lunch hour to learn how much Carp knew, and I stood there now in the empty print shop, watching Carp, feeling out of place in my three-piece suit.

"That's the only reason you haven't been around?" I asked. "There's nothing wrong?"

He looked at me, surprised. "Not at all. What could be wrong?"

"Nothing," I mumbled. I invented a reason. "Cathy thought you might be bored with us."

"*Bored?* Lord, no. I'm sorry I haven't been able to see y'all. But this nonsense—"

"Good. Cathy'll be glad to hear that. She was afraid you'd gotten tired of hobnobbing with the bourgeoisie."

He prodded the last sheets of paper through the machine and cut off the power. "On the contrary."

So he didn't know after all. The news pleased me and I could enjoy watching the rubbery way he moved when he stooped to stack his bills and posters. "You like some help with that?" I asked.

"Nope. Friendship doesn't require it."

"For crying out loud, Carp. Carrying your propaganda's not going to subvert me. Besides, that's what you're *supposed* to do," I said, picking up a bundle and trying to hold it so that the ink didn't rub off on my vest. "Subvert, pervert, and seduce. You're not a very good socialist, you know."

"I'm a *r-r-rotten* socialist," he said with a grin and led the way out back to his car.

It took several trips to fill the trunk and I was able to brush clumsily against him each time we passed; for the moment, that was all the contact I needed. Carpenter and I shook hands, promised to visit each other as soon as the election was over, shook hands again and parted. My afternoon at the insurance office was spent reviewing claims, but the work soothed me; I knew I had another life hidden beneath my button-down respectability.

During the next few weeks we saw Carp only in the form of his campaign leaflets and posters. The bills I had seen being run off by the hundreds were suddenly all over town. There were other candidates, and a flood of other people's posters, but it was only Carp's that I noticed. The photograph was old, something saved from a previous campaign; he was dressed in a Robert Hall jacket and the kind of narrow necktie worn by working-class grandfathers. He looked exactly like a kid dressed up for church back home in Nansemond County. Printed beneath the picture were the words *Socialist People's Party*. The incongruity of picture and caption made me think of the bland high school photos you see in the newspaper under such headlines as HONOR STUDENT SLAYS OWN FAMILY.

The picture was suddenly everywhere; the whole world seemed to have been papered over with Carpenter's face. Wherever I went, surfaces mocked me with his beaming-boy image, the boy in the Sunday school suit, the Socialist People's candidate. He was on telephone poles, on alley walls, on the soaped-over windows of shops that had gone out of business. He even peered winsomely from a wastebasket in the downstairs lobby of the insurance office. Cathy thought it might be funny to peel a poster off and tack it up in the apartment; she called me a stuffy prig when I wouldn't let her.

Cathy and I weren't very happy in Richmond. We had never been very good at meeting strangers, but when we lived in Maryland we had Cathy's family and a few of her friends from college. The only person we knew in Richmond was Andrew Carpenter. Carp and I had come from the same county in southside Virginia. When I met him, he was already halfway through college; I was still in high school. I trailed after him like a puppy, thinking I was only attracted to him because he was what I, foolishly, wanted to be: an intellectual. It was only now, after the insurance company had transferred me to Richmond, that I understood the real reason for the attraction; I understood only because I had tripped over backwards and fallen into it again. Here I was, happily married, and not only had I fallen in love with somebody else, I had fallen in love with a guy.

It bothered me, but not in the way I might have expected. There was no guilt, perhaps only because I was too busy wondering what I could do with this new feeling. I liked the feeling very much and did not want to throw it away. The obvious thing would have been to go to bed with Carp, but I wasn't sure what you could *do* in bed with him. Even if I were capable of it, I thought there should be something beyond that, perhaps something like marriage. I wondered about adoption.

Several weeks without Carpenter passed. Cathy was as bored with Richmond as I was, so bored she finally overcame her snobbery and insisted we buy a television. We hunted for things to keep each other entertained. A week before the election we drove out to the University of Richmond to see *Children of Paradise*. I'd found out that a film society was going to show it and reported the news to Cathy as though it were a gift just for her. But I wanted to see it as much as she did. Our isolation in Richmond had made us very dependent on each other; all our pleasures and desires seemed to blur together. The blurring was nice, in a way, but I found myself missing the sharp edges things had had when we were first discovering each other. Now, we were too easy with each other, even at night when we went to bed.

Cathy was all shivery and excited after the movie. It was a clear, cold October night and we delayed our return home by walking around the campus. I tried to put my arm around her, but she kept breaking away to wave her hands and repeat a favorite line or remember some lush scene. I was very happy, too. Under a streetlight I stopped her and asked to hear the line Arletty uses to invite the actor into her room.

"Hmmmm? Which one?"

"You know. Right after he asks if her door is locked."

She displayed her big teeth in an enormous grin. I often tease her for having a mouth like a cupboard full of china. "Oh, I *love* it!" She clapped her hands and grabbed me by the collar to pull me down to her level. She gave her head a shake, pretending to get into character. Eyeing me from beneath her hood of disheveled hair, she mimicked Arletty's seductive purr: "*What do I have that thieves can steal?*" Then she burst out laughing and shoved me away.

I watched her parade down the walk, her head thrown back so far she couldn't see. She nearly fell over a fire hydrant. I continued my amused strut behind her and didn't catch up again until she had stopped in front of a kiosk plastered with one of Carpenter's posters. She leaned against it and hooked one arm over the picture, pretending it was real. "Be nice to see Andy again. In flesh and blood, I mean."

I clutched her hand and pulled her away. "See him soon enough," I said.

We resumed our walk, leaning against each other's shoulder for support. "You're not bored by Carp?" I asked. It was a silly question, but I wanted an excuse to talk about him. From the start, she had made it clear she enjoyed his company. The first time we had had him over to dinner, Cathy was charmed by the way he had repeatedly interrupted his defense of socialism to identify each piece of classical music played on the stereo with the Warner Brothers cartoon he had first heard it in.

She clicked her tongue. "You keep insisting I should be bored by Andy. Believe me, Scott, I'm not. I actually *like* the goof. And not just because he's your friend, either."

"But why? You've got nothing in common."

"Maybe that's it. Maybe I find him . . . *exotic*." She growled the word. "I don't know. Why does anyone like anybody else? Well for one thing, he's not an insurance person."

"Then you find *me* boring?"

"Oh, get out of here." She butted my shoulder with her head. "Your *friends*, dope. Your friends and Daddy's. Insurance people always seem the same. Cynical about everybody and everything except themselves."

"They're not really friends."

"Okay then, acquaintances. Oh, you know what I mean. But don't worry, Scottie. You're different. You're a mutant."

I gave Cathy a squeeze around the waist and softly whispered in her ear, "And you're my little mutant, too." Our shoulders began to ache; we had to straighten up.

The walkway climbed a small hill and gradually swung to the left. There were fewer lights here and as we walked we saw a full moon slowly shift into the gap between the tall, black dormitories. Close to the horizon the moon looked enormous, as wonderfully theatrical and fake as the canvas disc used for the Pierrot mimes in the movie. I began whistling one of the tunes that had accompanied the mimes.

"Funny thing," said Cathy, wearily, "but I've gotten so used to seeing Andy's face all over town, I can't even look at the moon without seeing that goof in it."

I laughed with her over her silliness. My eyes, too, were twisting the lunar geography into a copy of Carpenter's face, but I proudly believed my reasons were more dangerous and exciting than Cathy's.

Love. Sloppy, romantic love. Love so clichéd you saw the loved one in the moon. It takes no talent to fall in love, but I was proud to be in love with Carp. I may have been disturbed that I didn't know what to do with it, but I wasn't bothered by the unnaturalness of the love. I was already familiar with natural love, the domestic kind I shared with Cathy. Love with her was love that justified, protected, soothed; it was as commonplace and necessary as a loaf of bread. No matter what tensions might develop between us, my dumb faith in the success of domestic love created the feeling that there was a safety net strung beneath us and that we were absolutely free from danger. It was my love for Carpenter—a sort of ecstatic nervousness—that now supplied me with the missing danger.

Election day. Cathy and I had not been residents of Richmond long enough to be able to vote, but after dinner I suggested we visit Carpenter and sit out the returns with him.

Cathy studied me for a moment, then screwed up her mouth and shook her head. "I don't think we should. He's probably off with some friends. Don't you think?"

"If I know Carp, I'll make a bet he's alone reading. He could probably use some company."

"You really think so?" She was skeptical. Cathy has always been leery of spending evenings with strangers. I promised and teased her into giving in.

Carpenter lived on the edge of the Fan district in a small upstairs apartment behind a shoe repair shop. I had seen the place only once before: walls painted a clinical shade of white, a few straight-back chairs and an unvarnished desk, a wooden floor with no carpet. Tacked above the desk was a solitary picture: an overripe figure of Death towed a frightened monk by his cowl toward places unknown. It was a morbid picture, but oddly it seemed a humanizing touch in the stark setting of the room. An exposed flight of stairs descended from his doorway to the alley.

"So this is where Andy lives?" said Cathy as she followed me up the rattling stairs. The flaking frame shook under our combined weight.

"I've pointed it out to you," I said, rapping on the door.

"Have you?" Holding her embroidered purse against her throat, she looked over the rail at the pile of cans and flattened boxes below. "I don't think so. Are there any rats down there?"

"Big black socialist rats," I said, irritated by her sudden delicacy. She seemed to be in one of her prim and stuffy moods tonight.

The knob turned with a sharp snap and the door opened. A stocky woman with rust-red hair faced us. "Yeah?" she said, arrogantly cocking her head as though she expected us to sell her something. Pop music played in the room behind her.

A female. I was stunned to find a female in Carpenter's doorway. It was a possibility I had never considered.

"Something we can do for you?" the woman asked impatiently, her eyes as black and tiny as the heads of carpet tacks.

"We've come to see Andrew Carpenter," I stammered.

She bellowed into the apartment, "Hey! Turkey! You got visitors!"

"Don't be rude. Ask them in," Carp quietly commanded.

The woman shrugged her big shoulders, motioned us inside, and closed the door.

I advanced nervously, my head bent forward. All over the floor were empty beer cans and jar lids filled with cigarette butts. Next to Carpenter's stocking feet was half a bottle of red wine.

He sat rigid in a chair in the center of the room. I was afraid we had stumbled in on something that shouldn't be stumbled in on, but when my eyes finally reached Carpenter's face, I found his smooth cheeks pocked with two enormous dimples and a grim that lifted his eyeglasses halfway up his forehead. "Why, *hello* there," he said warmly. "What brings you people down here tonight?"

"Cordial visit," I said, working up a smile. Cathy stared at the red-haired woman. "We thought you might like company on your big election night. If we're disturbing any—"

"Marsha's my co-worker." Carpenter waved his cup at Marsha, who was studying Cathy. "We had Marsha's gang of undergrads over earlier, but they wanted to get drunk and we'd run out of beer. Political campaigns are supposed to be kept well oiled with alcohol. I keep forgetting that fact." Carp himself did not seem at all well oiled; he spoke with his usual sober cheerfulness. "Marsh. These are the friends I was telling you about. That's Cathy there. And her husband is Scott."

"Pleased to meet you," Marsha said with a smirk. She looked somewhere in her late twenties and wore jeans and a floppy, untucked shirt. Whenever she moved, her breasts bounced inside the shirt like a pair of cats squirming in a bag. She spoke with a deep, bearish voice. "You're the insurance salesman."

"Oh, nothing that adventurous," I said with a nervous laugh. "I don't do any actual selling. I just march figures up and down sheets of paper and make sure they all arrive at the same place. Like the exercises they gave you over and over again in third grade, only now I get paid for it."

"If you don't like your work, get out of it," she said and turned to Carpenter. "You need more chairs. I'll get the one in the bedroom."

"You sit here," said Carpenter, setting his own chair beside Cathy. She smoothed her coat behind her and cautiously lowered her bottom to the chair. She looked down at the radio that sat on the floor, tuned to an AM station. "Marsha's," Carp explained.

No, I didn't like Marsha. And it worried me that she was familiar with Carpenter's bedroom.

"Well, what do you think your chances are with the election?" I asked, trying to forget about Marsha.

"He doesn't want to get elected," Marsha snarled, bringing in the chair. She pushed the chair at me and added, "He's chicken. If he thought he might win, he'd never run."

Carpenter only smiled at the attack and drank his wine. More cups were brought out; Carpenter sat cross-legged on the floor and poured the rest of the bottle. "Marsha's an interesting person," he said, watching the liquid rise to the same level in each cup. "The token southpaw in the V.C.U. sociology department. According to her, I'm much too conservative, Tory radical. Oh well. I've been called worse." Marsha snorted in agreement. "But it's thanks to her that my name's splashed all over town. She's got the kind of dedication rarely found outside a meeting of Young Republicans."

"Screw you," said Marsha.

More insults followed, and the exchange turned into an argument on politics. Marsha insisted on the need for strong, decisive action. Carpenter advocated a quieter approach. They spoke as though Cathy and I weren't even there. I was able just to sit and watch for clues to their relationship. It was Marsha's strident tone that worried me most; she seemed positively marital, as if she already had him. In Carp's voice, I found nothing. He spoke just as he always did, spinning his ideas with his slow, rural drawl. The southside Virginia accent didn't match the ideology under discussion. It made me think of Gary Cooper cast as Trotsky. Cathy was looking lost and bored and I felt guilty for having misled her. Every now and then I tried to give her a special glance and a nod to let her know she had my sympathy. Her cup of wine sat on her knee untouched. She answered my concern with a brittle smile.

"I know you've heard me say it a hundred times," Carp said. "But if you're going to be a southpaw in this country, you've got to keep your goals limited."

"Must be pitiful to be a defeatist at such an early age," said Marsha.

"Perhaps. But when you have big plans, it's easier to become disillusioned. You get disappointed, maybe overreact, and end up on the other side."

"I hear you," said Marsha. She greeted the possibility with a lip fart, then shifted her nail eyes towards me. "Is that what happened to you?"

"Me? What?" The need to answer took me by surprise. "No, I was never . . . I've been friends with Carp but I . . . at no time. No. I've not been a socialist. Never." I looked around the room for help.

"No," said Carp, smiling kindly. "Scottie's always been a capitalist lackey."

"I see," said Marsha, leaning back. "Very good. I was afraid you were a sellout. But you're the real thing, huh?"

I assured her I was, and attempted a few jokes about the sins I'd committed in the name of the oppressor class. None of the jokes took, and Marsha began to hammer at me about the halfheartedness of my beliefs. Why this? What did I really think about the world I lived in? Carpenter had never violated me in this way, never poked and forced me to twist my feelings into ideas I knew nothing about. I waited for him to come to my aid again, but he simply sat there, amused by what was going on. He had a misplaced faith in my ability to defend myself. Cathy was too lost or bored to help me. I was left to myself, and trotted out the only argument I have ever used on the subject of revolution. "Suppose . . . suppose you're a fish living in a dirty bowl. You got the choice of either putting up with the filth and mess of the dirty water or you can jump out, flop around on the carpet. Maybe get eaten by the cat. So I've decided to stay in the bowl and accept all the imperfections as part of life." I have always been a little proud of that argument without completely believing it. I folded my arms together, assuming that would be the final word and that we could move on to more interesting questions. Such as was Marsha sleeping with Carpenter?

Marsha slammed her heel against the floor. "You can *change* the bowl you live in, you smug little jerk."

Cathy suddenly woke up "What're you two getting so nasty for?" she muttered to her shoes. "You're only talking about *ideas*. Nothing to get nasty about."

"That's only what *they* want us to believe," said Marsha, leaning closer to Cathy and speaking to her as if to an equal. "That these things are *only* ideas. They want us to believe that there's real life over here, and ideas over there, and no connection between the two." Marsha glared at me. "And they want us to think that real life is only a dirty fishbowl you can never change but only talk about. Like the weather."

"In Marsha's mind, *they* are men," Carpenter explained, shaking his head and not making it clear whether or not he agreed with her.

Marsha began to twist a strand of her hair around one finger.

"That's a vulgarization of what I believe," she muttered, then picked up the wine bottle and examined it. "Empty," she said. "Pitiful the party has to end so soon. We ought to get some more wine."

I jumped out of my chair and rubbed my hands together. "No, it's getting late, I'm afraid. Cathy and I should be moving on."

Cathy looked up at me over her shoulder. "We don't have to go, do we, Scott? It won't hurt us to stay a little longer."

"You want to stay?" She surprised me. I looked her up and down, wondering about her motives. It seemed masochistic for her to want to stay any longer. "Well. Whatever you say," I said reluctantly. I was afraid of making a scene by insisting we leave. "Uh, since I'm up," I said to Carpenter, "why don't I go get the wine?"

Marsha rose, clomped over to the desk and picked up an Army jacket. "I'll go too."

"That's not necessary."

"Hey, Marsh. Why don't you stay here?" said Carp.

"Nope." She turned to me. "I can show you the best place," she insisted, and before I could object again, Marsha and I were outside, headed for the car. With her sneakers planted on my dashboard, Marsha gave directions.

As soon as we were moving down the street she turned to me and said, "Tell me. I'm curious. How come you're foisting your wife on poor old Carp?"

I couldn't understand what she was talking about and spent a good twenty seconds trying to understand before I finally said, "Come again?"

"She's in love with him, isn't she? I always thought your kind kept their wives locked up whenever something like that happens. Never imagined a husband would offer personal delivery. I guess I should find it admirable." She tittered through her nose. "Unless it's just bourgeois kinkiness."

This was hilarious. I couldn't believe it. I nearly choked trying to hold back my laughter. She was so damn right in her general picture of what was going on. And so damn wrong in the particulars. "You know, you're nuts," I said. "What gives you a crazy idea like that?"

"Come off it. You don't have to pretend with me. Sweet little things like that can never hide their feelings. Soon as she walked in, the place smelled like love and kisses."

"My wife is no 'sweet little thing,'" I said, dutifully going to Cathy's defense.

"But she *is*. Sweet, frail, *Cosmopolitan* girl. Not her fault, though."

I didn't like to hear Cathy mocked like this. "I can't . . . I can't *imagine* how you'd see what you see. You wouldn't talk like that unless you were in love with Carpenter yourself."

"Me?" There was a laugh like pebbles dropping onto a snare drum. "If I ever fall in love—and I won't—it'll never be for the likes of good old Carp."

"Then why are you being such a bitch about it?"

"I merely report the obvious."

We pulled up in front of a delicatessen. Marsha ran inside with long, leaping strides. *Cathy in love with Carpenter. Husband delivering wife. Sweet little thing.* Very droll. I kept turning it around and around in my head until Marsha returned with the wine.

Marsha kept her mouth shut for several minutes. I was hoping for complete silence, when she suddenly shifted sideways in her seat and confessed, "I'm needling you. Scott. Can't you see that? I have no objections to what you're doing. It goes along with everything I believe. Sexual democracy." She came closer to me. "But I'm curious why you're doing it. It's not the norm for people of your ilk. Something like this runs against the grain, doesn't it? Or are you and your wife so bored you'll jump at anything?"

"My *ilk*? You think you have me pegged, don't you?"

"I know you a lot better than you think. You're one of those types who thinks to himself, 'I'm complicated. I'm so wonderfully complicated.'" She mimicked my thoughts with a squeaky whimper. "And you take great pride in it. Cozy sensitivity. But, you know? You're not really so complicated. A few contradictions, a few hypocrisies. Things you could reconcile if you put your mind to it. Only you don't want to bother. It would put an end to the cozy notion you're a deep person."

Marsha settled back into her seat. I was relieved to have some distance between us again. I took refuge in silence.

"Of course, you realize your wife doesn't have a black man's chance with Carp."

I refused to rise to the bait.

"Perfect nickname. Carp. He's a cold fish, all right." She waited for a reply, then snidely added, "Your wife might as well be flirting with a fag."

"Carp's gay?" I asked, trying to hide my sudden interest.

She shifted her big shoulders. "I don't know. You know him better than I do. Is he?"

One of the many idiotic things about the whole idiotic mess was the fact that I did not know Carpenter's sexual affiliation. Through all the years of our friendship, all the letters and visits, there had never been mention of a girlfriend and never any mention of the alternatives. Whenever the subject of love or lust came up, Carpenter only smiled and wiggled his head until the subject went away.

"Don't know," I said to Marsha.

"Might as well be for all the luck she's going to have. Couldn't get him to do *anything* with me," she said, and sighed, "much less fall in love. Not that I'd want that. The love part, I mean."

"You asked Carpenter to go to bed?"

"Why not?" she said, wistfully indifferent.

"And what did he say?"

"I think he laughed. Carpenter can be a jerk."

When we arrived at the apartment, Marsha made a big show of stomping noisily up the stairs, as if to warn them of our return. There was a clownish grin on her face.

We entered and found Cathy and Carpenter exactly as we had left them, seated six feet apart. Cathy's look of discomfort was gone; she appeared relaxed and easy, and not even Marsha's return disturbed her. The radio had been changed to an FM station: a baroque fanfare of trumpets added to the happiness.

"Mountain chablis," Marsha announced proudly, stripping the bag from the bottle. She broke the seal and the wine was passed around while we returned to our positions in the circle. I tried to be sociable by asking for news of the election.

"Andy's writing a book," Cathy declared. She was quite excited that Carpenter had confided this to her; the outcome of the election seemed to interest her as little as it did the candidate.

"He's always writing some book," I said. "What's this one about?"

"It's, uh, fictional institutions."

Carpenter politely corrected her. "Institutional fictions. Assumptions about reality that make up the basis of different social institutions." He gave himself an embarrassed sigh.

Marsha smiled at me, apparently reading my thoughts and highly amused by them. But she could not have been reading them correctly. I gave no consideration at all to her goofy ideas about Cathy's affections. Marsha was a joker, I decided. I felt a fondness for her now that I knew she had failed and that I wouldn't have to compete against her. And I felt a great fondness for Cathy because she seemed happy now and I no longer had to feel responsible for her discomfort. I was set free to sit back and enjoy the fact that I was in love with Carpenter.

Marsha left shortly after midnight, and things became very peaceful. There were times when there was nothing to say, but there was no embarrassment over the stretches of silence.

As Cathy and I got ready to leave, Carpenter said he was pleased the nonsense was over and that he'd be free to see us more often. There was a prolonged exchange of smiles and handshakes, then Carp watched from his open door as Cathy and I made our way down his stairs.

The interior of the car was cold as a refrigerator; the heater did not begin to ease the cold until we were halfway to the suburbs. Cathy stretched over the console and huddled close to my side.

My head ticked with possibilities. In the narrow space of a couple of hours, I had found my path blocked and then had found the obstacle totally imaginary. Carpenter was available after all; my love had come through the ordeal stronger than before and I knew I would have to act on it. I would take my chances; I would actually do something with this incredible feeling I carried. There would be love, out in the open, danger-ous love, love so strong it would be indistinguishable from fear. The only question was how to move Carpenter to join me in it.

"You've certainly been spacy tonight," said Cathy, her face buried in my coat.

"Yeah? Just toward the end. I got to thinking about things. You were pretty spacy yourself. At the beginning."

"Was I?" she asked sleepily. "Yeah, I guess so. We're not the world's greatest guests. Wonder if we could get tutored somewhere on social charm. Take night classes in party behavior, maybe."

"Don't know."

"Oh, doesn't matter. I think we could've acted any old way and Andy wouldn't have minded. Scott? Did you think that girl and Andy were lovers? I mean when we first walked in, did you think that?"

"Hard to imagine her being anyone's lover. Too dogmatic. Too much the—you know." I wanted to say "bitch" but the word angers Cathy. "Why? Did you think that?"

"At first. But I talked to Andy while you were out and I got the impression they were barely friends. She really was too dog-matic. I feel sorry for people like that. They must be very lonely before they can go and get like that."

I had heard Cathy express similar sympathy for her father, for my older brother, and before she had met him, for Andrew Carpenter. When I stopped at the next traffic light, I was able to bend over, kiss the top of her head, slip my hand beneath her long hair, touch the down on her neck.

There was eerie energy in our lovemaking that night. Sex again became the invention of two teenagers petting under the bushes, only with adult privacy now, and no restraints. Each intimate move was smoothly answered and there was a slippery, licensed roving of hands and mouths. I did not fake any of it. I could not pretend it was Carpenter who shared me. No, it was definitely Cathy whose knees and shoulders, breasts and hair were the targets of all my energy and it was irrelevant that the energy had been created by my feelings for Carpenter.

In that extended instant after sex, before you remember you are not alone, I felt pleased with myself and the life I lived. Gradually, I reawakened to Cathy, and found her looking at me with one open eye.

"You—" she began lovingly, and never finished. Suddenly, she rose up on her knees and stretched her body like a cat. She sank down again and rested her chin on my chest.

We lay like that for a very long time. I could look past the loops of her hair and see our legs, stacked together like hand dipped candles.

"Know what?" she finally said. There was a bit of flirtation in her voice, and the warm breath with the words tickled my chest.

"What?"

"Kind of funny but—"

"Yes?" I closed my eyes and brushed my hand up and down the solid muscles on either side of her back. I was waiting to be teased or complimented.

"I think I have a slight crush on your Andrew Carpenter."

She spoke too soon to disguise it. And all along I had thought her excitement had been in response to mine, that it had been something I created in her. "Do you mean . . . you're in love with him?"

"*Noooo*. Nothing stupid like that. Do you think I'd tell you if it was something like that?" She hugged me around the waist and giggled, then looked up at me with her lower lip sucked behind her front teeth, grinning while she watched and waited for me to share her amusement.

My hand drew tiny circles on the cooled mounds of her bottom.

"No," she said. She had to shift her eyes away from my face. "No. It's just a silly crush. All in my head. Nobody could *really* fall in love with Andy." There was a tremor in the pupils of her eyes as they looked straight into mine again. "You dope!" she suddenly laughed. "You have nothing to fear," and she reached up to sweep some hair back from my forehead.

From
Pet Food

Jessica Hagedorn

The sign dangled from the fire escape in front of the shabby
building:

STUDIO APT. FOR RENT

I entered the lobby of the dimly lit building, one of those
Victorian San Francisco dwellings that must've been grand in
the early 1900s. Times had certainly changed—the neighborhood had quietly deteriorated and the building had decayed

right along with it. It still had marvelous dark wood panelings and art nouveau, daffodil-shaped lamps along the walls, but the carpets were stained and faded, and you could smell the grease emanating from the apartments. Another faded sign in the lobby read:

STANLEY GENDZEL — MANAGER — APT. 1

COLLECTOR OF ANTIQUES — PARROT MAN EXTRAORDINAIRE

I hesitated before knocking on his door. Bells tinkled faintly, and someone came toward me down the dark, dank hallway. I put my suitcase down and whirled around to face the young man who stood there, staring at me. Could this be Stanley Gendzel? I wondered.

Barefoot, the young man held a large orange cat in his arms. The cat gazed at me with the same dispassionate curiosity.

The young man and the cat bore a striking similarity—the young man with copper-colored skin, slender and beautiful, with his ominous lion's mane hair, the color of brown fading into reddish gold, much like the extraordinary cat's thick fur. After a few moments, the young man put the cat down, and we both watched it scurry away into the darkness.

"I'm looking for the manager," I said.

The young man smiled. "Manager?"

Oh no, I thought, this couldn't be Stanley Gendzel!

"I'm looking for a place to live," I said, as firmly as I could. Looking for an apartment of my own was one of the momentous decisions of my life, and I was determined to act as adult and businesslike as possible.

"Oh," the young man said, still being playful with me. "A *place*. You need a place."

"I certainly do," I retorted.

"Then you need to see Stanley," he said.

There was a moment of silence, and we looked each other over like two animals sniffing each other out.

Suddenly he said, "Let me show you my guitar."

I shook my head. "No."

"Let me show you my cello."

"No." Where was Stanley Gendzel?

"Let me show you my saxophone."

"No!"

"Let me show you my soprano saxophone."

"Hmmmm . . ." I was getting curious.

"Let me show you my bass saxophone."

"Oooh . . ."

He was relentless. "Let me show you my bass clarinet."

"Oh dear," I sighed, slowly wearing down.

My favorite instrument. I looked him dead in the eye. "Upright or electric?"

He grinned. "Both."

It had been a long day. I decided I must be falling in love, and to hell with Stanley Gendzel. "Well," I said, "maybe . . ."

His grin widened, and suddenly—like magic—the dank and forbidding hallway seemed less gloomy. "My berimbau? Caxixi? Sansa?"

He was so enthusiastic and strangely radiant I had to give in.

"OKAY!" I responded, smiling back at him and taking his hand.

I followed him up the first flight of stairs, and he pulled out the gleaming gold key and unlocked the door to an apartment. The living room was littered with every kind of musical instrument imaginable, and an orchestra of children was playing. Their faces were painted like ornate African and Balinese masks. Bells hung from the ceiling. We began to dance in slow motion, lost in some kind of trancelike, sensuous waltz.

My first and only lover so far had been Junior Burgess, who could sing as compellingly as Smokey Robinson, seducing me sweetly with his voice while telling me stories of all my favorite Motown groups. But this young man who held me in his arms was different. He made me so nervous I blurted out "I love you" in the middle of our dance.

His face was devoid of expression, like the cat who sat purring in the room, so sure of its regal beauty. "I know," he said, not unkindly.

"My name is George Sand," I told him shyly.

"I know," the young man said.

"Your name is Rover," I said.

"Exactly," he replied, twirling me around the room. I don't know how much time we spent in that room, the children's orchestra continuously serenading us with their dissonant circus music, the purring orange cat never once taking his amber eyes off our dancing bodies. And I didn't care.

I floated out of Rover's apartment in a daze, starting back down the stairs in my second attempt to locate the mysterious Stanley Gendzel, manager of this illustrious building. I dragged my battered suitcase behind me, unsure of what had just happened. All I remembered was that late afternoon softly changed into darkness, and the children's orchestra stopped playing, and Rover and I stopped dancing, unwinding slowly like two figures twirling on top of a music box. The big orange cat rubbed against our legs, and Rover picked him up and carried him in his arms, stroking his fur gently. He kissed me on my lips, then once—very tenderly—on each of my eyelids. "I will see you again," was all he said.

A darkly beautiful Sephardic Jewish woman came bounding up the stairs as I was on my way back down to Stanley Gendzel's apartment. She seemed to be in her early twenties, dressed in interesting layers of clothing my friend Boogie would've called "flea market glamor." Crocheted doilies had been sewn together into a lacey shirt worn over red satin pajamas. The pajamas were stuffed into embroidered Nepalese boots. She was carrying a blender in one hand and a large black portfolio in the other.

"Hey," she called out, in a friendly way. "You new in the building? Silver Daddy's new piece of cheese, perhaps?"

"Uh, no."

She peered at me from under the thick fringe of her black eyelashes. "My name is Momma Magenta," she finally said.

"Hi. I'm George."

She never flinched. "You're very much his type, you know. Are you Indian or something? Mexican? Italian, somewhat?"

"No, not any of those," I said wryly.

"What about Japanese? That's Silver Daddy's new trip. THE JAPANESE . . . he's busy editing an anthology of esoteric Japanese poets. 'O Momma Magenta,' he's always telling me, 'you've got all the right ingredients. Long black hair, black eyes, big tits, a small waist, and a big ass . . . but you aren't JAPANESE!' I'm always showing him my portfolio, you know," she chattered confidentially. "After all, Silver Daddy's one of America's oldest living legends, with plenty of connections in the art world. But all he ever wants to do around me is talk about pussy."

"Oh. You're an artist?"

Momma Magenta was obviously pleased that I had asked this question. "Yeah, that's right. I do rock n' roll posters. Wanna see my portfolio?"

"No thanks. I don't have time. I'm looking for a place to rent."

"Well, you've come to the right place, sweetie. Silver Daddy owns this building, see. He's what you might call a bona fide *artiste* and slum landlord all rolled into one. He lives on the top floor, in his fashionable ghetto penthouse. You're in luck Silver Daddy just ordered Stanley Gendzel to kick one of the tenants out. He was a poet from New York named Paolo. Trouble was, he was a smack freak, and broke all the time. HEY—wanna buy a used blender?"

I started down the stairs. "No thanks, really. I think I should go see about renting this apartment," I said, waving goodbye to her.

"Good luck with Stanley,'" she waved back. "Don't let *him* chew your ears off. And don't be surprised when Silver Daddy invites you up for one of his famous dinner parties."

Something that resembled a shriveled-up spider with bushy eyebrows for antennae opened the door. "Whadda ya want?" he croaked, looking me up and down.

"I'm interested in renting the apartment," I said. "Are you Mr. Gendzel?"

"Yup. I'm Stanley Gendzel. Come in, come in." He stepped aside to let me through the door. I pretended not to notice that all he had on were faded, yellow boxer shorts. A large green parrot was perched on his shoulder.

He ushered me into his grimy kitchen and pulled out a chair for me. For a long while no one said a word. I watched Stanley scratch the bird's head, cooing softly to the creature. Then he pulled out a box of birdseed and nonchalantly placed some seeds on the tip of his tongue. The parrot pecked the food off the old man's outstretched tongue while the old man stared at me suspiciously.

"Are you a college student?" he asked suddenly, when the parrot finished his dinner.

"No, I'm a poet," I blurted out, wondering if I'd said the wrong thing.

Stanley was visibly upset. "A poet! Not another one!"

It had been such a long, grueling day that between my mother and Auntie Greta's hysterics and Momma Magenta's aggressiveness, I decided I just couldn't accept Stanley's disapproval. I had to convince this strange man that I had to have the apartment this very evening. Besides, it was getting late and I was hungry.

"Yes," I said, as calmly and politely as possible. "I'm a very responsible person, in spite of what you might think. How much is the rent?"

"Well," Stanley said, scratching the parrot's head once again, "it's one of the worst studios in the building. That heroin addict never cleaned up after himself. Always sipping grape soda and munching Twinkies! It's a wonder he's still alive. Left behind reams and reams of paper—some with writing on it, some without. I didn't have the heart to destroy his work, even though Silver Daddy didn't think too highly of it. He ordered me to go in there and disinfect everything and burn all the boy's manuscripts. Imagine! I just couldn't do it," Stanley repeated, shaking his head slowly.

"I'm glad you didn't. I'm sure Paolo would appreciate it," I said.

"Humph!" Stanley snorted. "Paolo didn't appreciate anything—that's why he was so self-destructive. Anyway, I haven't cleaned the place at all, so you can have it for eighty dollars a month, no cleaning deposit necessary. The toilet works, and if you wanna paint it, Silver Daddy will insist on raising the rent, so I wouldn't advise it. Just leave well enough alone."

I got up to go. "Thanks very much, Mr. Gendzel."

"What'd you say your name was again?" he asked.

"I didn't. My name is George Sand."

"Interesting name for a young girl. You look very interesting, by the way. You wouldn't happen to be Japanese, would you?"

"No, I'm from the Philippines, actually. My mother brought me here when I was very young," I replied.

He seemed totally disinterested. "Oh. *The Philippines*. All I remember is that big fuss about MacArthur. Well, it doesn't really matter. I'm sure Silver Daddy will invite you to dinner as soon as you move in. It's part of the rituals around here, his own way of getting to know each tenant. The only one he never invited was Paolo . . ."

"Perhaps I'll show him some of my poems."

Stanley Gendzel arched one of his extravagant eyebrows. "He'd be utterly delighted, I'm *sure*. That's the right attitude to take with that old lecher! He's working on some Japanese translations right now, y'know. Had some Japanese nobility up there helping him out. Flew her all the way from Toyko. Called her Camembert for short. She called him Daddybear."

The only thing I had when I moved in was a sorry-ass little suitcase crammed with notebooks and journals, a pair of jeans or two, and a memory of my mother Consuelo's face when I went out the door of her house. When I finally telephoned to say I was all right, Auntie Greta picked up the phone and answered in a solemn voice, "Good evening . . . the Sand Residence."

"Hello? Auntie Greta?" My own voice seemed unusually high to me.

"My dear George—are you all right?"

"Yes. I got a place—my own apartment. Is Mom there?"

"Your mother can't come to the phone, dear. She's not feeling well," Auntie Greta said.

"You mean she won't talk to me."

He cleared his throat. "Let's just say your mother is under sedation—high blood pressure, you know. She couldn't handle your leaving us too well."

"Well, tell her I'm all right. I'm living on Webster Street," I said.

"Webster Street??? Webster Street and what???"

"Oh, you know—near the freeway," I replied. I knew what was coming.

"Dios mio! You're living in *that* part of town?" Even Auntie Greta couldn't bring himself to say it: the ghetto. Bodies bleeding on the front steps of my building, virile young things with guns as erect as their dicks, leaping in and out of Chinese grocery stores. My mother's darkest fears.

I sighed. "Don't worry, Auntie Greta. There's a famous person living in this building. His name is Silver Daddy. He's my landlord."

"I've never heard of him," Auntie Greta said.

"Of course not," I retorted, exasperated. "You don't read the papers, except for the movie listings. Mom doesn't read the papers, either. Well, if you did, you might know about his column in the Sunday arts section. He writes on all the new stuff going on in the art world."

Auntie Greta was obviously offended. "Well, I don't know

about that, young lady. I do read the paper from time to time! I know you've always thought yourself above us."

"Oh Jesus, there you go sounding like my mother," I said.

"You know what they say—association makes for assimilation. Listen, George, do you have enough locks on your doors and windows?"

"Yes."

"I'll break the news to your mother gently. And please, dear, keep in touch. Are you getting a phone?"

"No. But there's a pay phone in the lobby," I said.

"A *pay* phone! In the *lobby*! OH MY GOD!" Auntie Greta groaned.

I figured it was better if I hung up first.

Welcome to de Ghetto

From my new apartment window, I watched Silver Daddy stroll down the street. He wore a leather cowboy vest that accentuated the paunchy belly that jutted out as he walked. There was something grand about the way he swaggered, in spite or because of his weight. Like a futuristic Santa Claus so sure of himself he sees nothing, he stopped under my window and called up to me, his icy blue eyes twinkling and his silver moustache gleaming. Ho-ho-ho.

"Are you the new tenant?"

"Yes. My name is George Sand."

"I know," Silver Daddy said. "Stanley told me. This is all very interesting. You must come to dinner this evening and meet my family." I seemed to have no choice in the matter. We arranged a suitable time, and he strolled away, turning around halfway up the block to tell me that my new neighborhood would be a good education for me.

"Bleeding bodies happen almost every day in America," Silver Daddy said ominously. "You simply must face up to it, George."

Persimmons

Tinkerbelle, Silver Daddy's secretary-companion, led me into the dining room of Silver Daddy's spacious ghetto penthouse. A wooden refectory table was set for four people with earth-toned Japanese bowls and ivory chopsticks. A slender vase filled with white chrysanthemums stood at the center of the table. Chinese masks and cubist paintings by Silver Daddy hung on the walls. Navajo baskets and Nigerian carvings were strewn haphazardly but deliberately around the room.

Tinkerbelle watched me with curious detachment as I wandered around, politely studying Silver Daddy's rather bland attempts at painting. Tinkerbelle was in her early thirties, a small-boned woman with shoulder-length brown hair and horn-rimmed glasses. She was wearing her standard uniform: nondescript plaid skirt, white Ladybug shirt, and a conservative cardigan sweater. Everything about her was mousey, but she emitted a certain nervous energy as she scurried around the room, chain-smoking Gauloise cigarettes. Bored with the paintings and artifacts, I decided to be friendly and start a conversation.

"Are you the one helping Silver Daddy out with the translations?" I asked her.

Tinkerbelle seemed rather offended. "Have you been

talking to the tenants? If so, you've been grossly misinformed. I am Silver Daddy's secretary—his right hand, so to speak. I sometimes also do the cooking for him," she added, primly.

"Oh," I said, immediately intimidated by her Dame Edith Evans manner.

"Silver Daddy is a gourmet chef, among other things," Tinkerbelle continued, with a great deal of pride. "He taught me how to cook international dishes. I hope you like sushi."

"It's actually one of my favorites," I said.

"Good. We're having a complete Japanese menu tonight: miso soup, sushi, sashimi, and daikon. Silver Daddy's on one of his kicks."

Suddenly, Silver Daddy's precocious fourteen-year-old daughter grand-jetéed into the room. An aspiring ballerina with feline green eyes and long dark hair pulled back into a ponytail, she wore a pink tutu, pink tights, and pink satin toeshoes. She held out her hand and spoke with a puzzling accent that constantly shifted from French to Bela Lugosi pseudo-Hungarian.

"Good evening," she said, "you must be George. My name is Porno. I'm Silver Daddy's teenage daughter."

I shook her hand. "Pleased to meet you," I said, somewhat startled.

"AND HERE HE IS, LADIES . . . AMERICA'S OLDEST LIVING LEGEND: MY ESTEEMED FATHER, SILVER DADDY!!!" Porno announced brightly, like an emcee in some decadent Berlin cabaret.

Tinkerbelle bowed as if on cue, and I followed suit. Silver Daddy sauntered into the room, wearing a long black kimono, with a red sash tied around his Sumo wrestler waist.

I handed him a gift-wrapped package, trimmed with origami birds. "I brought you some persimmons."

He sized me up slowly with his icy blue eyes. "DELIGHT-FUL! Remind me to tell you one of my persimmon anecdotes someday. You know what they taste like, don't you?"

"No," I said, shaking my head.

"**Japanese pussy**, of course!" He chuckled at his own joke. Porno and Tinkerbelle clapped their hands and laughed along with him. "Shall we sit down and have dinner?" Silver Daddy gestured towards the table. "You must tell us all about yourself, George."

We all sat down except Tinkerbelle. She flitted about like a dragonfly, serving the food, bringing dishes in and out of the room, smoking her endless cigarettes.

"You're named after *the* George Sand, aren't you?" Silver Daddy asked me.

"Actually, my parents thought they were being funny. I don't think they had any idea who she really was," I replied.

Silver Daddy frowned. "How *painful*. Have you ever read any of her novels?"

"No. "

"Oh, you *must*!" Porno chimed in. "I read all her work by the time I was twelve."

Unimpressed by his daughter's enthusiasm, Silver Daddy pointedly ignored her. "At least read her biography," he advised me. "There are some good ones available these days. You may find it illuminating. She was a most interesting personality—particularly when she ran around with that musician Chopin!" He paused. "I hope you brought your work."

I hesitated before answering. "I did. I wasn't sure if l should, but—"

"Don't be silly," Silver Daddy interrupted. "*I expected you to.* How do you like the miso soup? Tinkerbelle made it herself, from scratch."

"It's organic," Porno said, with the same enthusiasm. "Soybean's the best thing for you. I was raised on it. Wasn't I, Daddy?"

"Yes," Silver Daddy sighed. He turned to me. "Her mother was a health food fanatic. Died at an early age."

"No, she didn't!" Porno declared, visibly annoyed. "You're always saying that! Mama is alive and well in Arizona. Your *first* wife died at an early age. In childbirth, I believe," Porno added, with a hint of irony.

"Having a baby is like shitting a giant watermelon," Tinkerbelle suddenly intoned, sitting down at the table. She nibbled at her sushi.

"I wouldn't know," I murmured, blushing.

"Well, that's all right," Porno said, "'cause Tinkerbelle knows. Tinkerbelle likes to think she's an authority on all subjects—don't you, Tinker, dear?"

"It's your father's influence," Tinkerbelle replied coolly. "Have some more sashimi, Porno."

In a mournful, basso profundo voice, Silver Daddy began chanting:

> *There was a young man*
> *from St. John's*
> *who went out to bugger*
> *the swans,*
> *when up stepped the porter*
> *who said, "Take my daughter—*
> *them swans is reserved*
> *for the dons."*

Once more, Tinkerbelle and Porno applauded and giggled. "Daddy, you're getting more academic in your old age," Porno said.

"It's difficult having a movie star for a daughter," Silver Daddy said, stiffly.

I looked at the smiling Porno. "I didn't know you were in the movies."

"We don't talk about it much around here," Porno said. "Daddy forbids it."

"I only forbid it because I'm not sure of my feelings," Silver Daddy said. "You're only fourteen years old. What would your mother have said if she knew? She's probably turned over in her grave by now."

Porno began pouting, her full, luscious lower lip trembling with emotion. "There you go again," she accused her father. "Mama's not dead. Your first wife is dead. Mama lives in Arizona. And she doesn't care about me, one way or the other."

Gazing at me with her green cat-eyes, she said, "Daddy likes to think he's ahead of his time, but he can't cope with the fact that I make pornographic movies."

"Is that how you got your name?" I asked, losing my appetite.

"Yes. It's my stage name. **I hate my real name.** Can you imagine some one as hip as Silver Daddy calling his daughter RUTH?"

"May I have some more sushi, please?" I asked Tinkerbelle, trying to conceal my embarrassment. All I'd wanted was a good meal and a positive start in my career.

"Have as much as you want," Silver Daddy said grandly. "I love young girls with hearty appetites."

"You certainly do," Porno said.

"RUTH!" Silver Daddy barked, his icy blue eyes crackling. "You're getting out of hand. I wish you'd shut up."

I started to get up from the table. "Maybe I should leave . . ."

Tinkerbelle was horrified. "You can't do that. You haven't finished your dinner."

"Certainly not," Silver Daddy agreed. **"I won't allow it!** Don't let family intrigues spoil the evening for us, George." He took a deep breath. "NOW—it's time for my persimmons."

I sat back down. Tinkerbelle handed Silver Daddy the bowl of persimmons.

Silver Daddy attacked the persimmons, slurping noisily and lasciviously. Once in a while he would look at me meaningfully. Porno watched her father eat the fruit with a dreamy look in her eyes.

"Daddy, do you know the title of my next film?"

He never stopped eating. "WHAT?" he grunted.

"*Persimmons!* I thought of you right away" She paused, but when her father didn't react she began directing her comments to me. "I'm going to star in the loveliest film," she began, in her childlike, faraway voice. "I shall lie spread-eagled on top of a concert grand piano, and my mouth shall remain open throughout the entire movie. See my mouth? I've been told I have the most sensuous mouth since Ingrid Bergman in *Notorious*—don't I, Daddy?"

Silver Daddy reached for another persimmon.

"Two Arabian stallions prance around the room, their luxurious manes occasionally brushing against my extremely sensitive nipples," Porno said, a slight smile at the corners of her mouth. "The opening scene will be shot in slow motion, of course, with lots of diffused light and all that sort of thing. Then, Van Cliburn enters the room, totally unaware that I'm lying naked on his grand piano, and proceeds to play an extremely tacky rendition of 'Moonlight Sonata.'"

"Hmmm. One of my favorites," I murmured.

"Would you like some tea, or coffee?" Tinkerbelle asked me.

"Coffee."

Tinkerbelle scurried out of the room, puffing on her Gauloise cigarette.

". . . As I writhe sinuously atop the concert grand," Porno went on, by now oblivious to everyone, "a leering Aubrey Beardsley-type dwarf waddles into the room, carrying a dome-covered silver platter. He removes the dome to reveal a quivering, asthmatic anteater. The anteater, of course, has no idea what's going on. He crinkles his snout in the direction of my gaping, nubile honeypot."

I was so mesmerized by this scenario that I was unaware of Tinkerbelle at my elbow, pouring coffee in my cup. Porno seemed like she was going deeper into a trancelike state.

"I lift up one leg in agonizing slow-motion, as the anteater's tongue slithers slowly out. The whole thing is going to be choreographed like an excruciating, torrid ballet—by me, of course . . ."

"I didn't realize you were so talented," I said.

She ignored me. "The sticky tip of the anteater's tongue explores my swollen clitoris, and I arch my supine back as a leering dwarf giggles. Van Cliburn sweats as the music crescendos, his flair in electric shock reminiscent of Elsa Lanchester in *Bride of Frankenstein*. The anteater, disappointed at having found no ants, turns away from my juicy honeypot and is suddenly grabbed by a leering dwarf, who by this time has an enormous hard-on."

She paused, and for a moment her cat-eyes focused on me. "You know, little men have the biggest dicks, sometimes."

She said this with a combination of innocence and matter-of-factness that reminded me of my friend Boogie.

"The leering dwarf pulls down his knickers and buggers the struggling anteater, who can't escape the dwarf's powerful embrace," Porno said, panting excitedly. "Van Cliburn, oblivious to everything around him, is still crescendoing as five West Indians calypso into the room."

I gulped my coffee.

"Ahhh," Silver Daddy said, sucking on another persimmon, "neo-colonialism! The fucker and fuckee."

Neo-Colonialism

"The first West Indian has a dick that's long and thin, like a buffalo's," Porno said, breathlessly. "He enters me in the usual missionary position. I moan. He comes fast, like a junkie. The second West Indian has a dick that's pointy, like a Masai spear. He turns me over—quickly, quickly—and enters me from behind, humping me like a horse. No, no," she gasped, "not like a horse! Like an angry wolf!"

"An angry wolf in *heat*," Silver Daddy added, solemnly.

Porno nodded in agreement, her green eyes glittering. "He pulls out and comes all over Van Clibum's elegant, brand-new tuxedo. Van Cliburn doesn't care, he continues his 'Moonlight Sonata' crescendo. The third West Indian has a dick that's not too long, but rather thick and awesome. I can't wait. He wraps my legs around his broad shoulders and proceeds to fuck me DEEP, with long, masterful strokes. By this time, the leering Beardsleyesque dwarf has rolled underneath the grand piano, grunting like a sow as he buggers the terrified anteater. Meanwhile, the fourth West Indian places his hook-shaped dick into my luscious, foaming, strawberry mouth."

"More coffee?" Tinkerbelle poured me a second cup.

"Thank you," I said. "It's very good."

"It's Blue Mountain coffee," Tinkerbelle informed me. "Silver Daddy orders it especially from Jamaica."

Porno had shut her eyes, looking more ethereal than ever. "The fifth West Indian is a beautiful, degenerate fawn—the only other star in the film. He sucks my prominent, aching nipples as he beats off his dick, which happens to be the longest, thickest, most cobralike dick anybody would ever want to see. By this time, I am shrieking and gasping for breath—in between dicks and tongues in my mouth, my honeypot, and God-knows-where-else!"

She opened her eyes. "The fifth West Indian finally comes—like Niagara Falls—a never ending stream on my breasts, my eyes, and my warm creamy belly. He wipes his dick in my long straight hair, murmuring endearments in Spanish, Portuguese, French, and patois. Van Cliburn finally collapses, like a ragdoll on his piano stool. The leering dwarf reaches a violent orgasm, strangling the puzzled and terrified anteater."

Silver Daddy smiled at no one in particular. "Salvador Dali enters the room, unlocking a cage filled with yellow butterflies—"

"Yes!" Porno exclaimed, radiant. "The butterflies hover over my sleeping body in the still, now-empty room. The film ends."

No one said anything much after that. Tinkerbelle had settled into a smoke-filled reverie of her own, and Silver Daddy retreated into his bedroom with my manuscripts. After my fourth cup of coffee, I excused myself and went downstairs to my apartment. They didn't bother to say goodnight.

My apartment was really a one-room studio, with a dingy closet of a kitchen and a gloomy bathroom where the roaches liked to hide. The best thing about it was the bathtub, a massive boat with lion's paws that had definitely seen better days. I loved filling it with warm water and just sitting in it for hours, thinking. Unhappy with the mattress on the floor I was using to sleep on, I had even considered turning my wonderful bathtub into a bed.

I had left the apartment pretty much in the same state I had found it—the floor littered with papers of every shape and size, including newspapers. Almost all the papers belonged to the poet Paolo, although lately I had gotten in the habit of discarding my poems and stories in the same way—using the sheets of paper as rugs, haphazard decorations on the floor that floated in the air when the wind blew through the apartment.

I had taken to tacking some of my poems, finished and unfinished, on the walls next to or on top of the poems Paolo had glued on like wallpaper. In an eerie way, it made me feel safe and comfortable.

I called Boogie and invited him to see my new home. He seemed highly amused by my surroundings as soon as he walked through the door. I was impressed by his appearance—Boogie had always been very pretty, and his multicultural looks confused a lot of people. He could pass for Latino, Asian, even Native American. His eclectic way of dressing never betrayed the toughness behind the elegance, and I loved the way his beauty drove men and women crazy. Nothing seemed to disturb him, an attribute that could sometimes make me angry. But when I was feeling good about myself, I could think of no one else in the world whose opinion mattered more.

Tender Vittles

"Rover, Rover . . . ," I called out softly. "This cat that is sometimes an animal and sometimes a man—where are you, Rover?"

Rover appeared suddenly, lounging like an alley cat on the fence next to my apartment building. I hadn't seen him since our first encounter, and I missed him terribly. He leaped down nimbly off the fence, landing directly in front of me and grinning.

"Oh, Rover, where've you been? I've got so much to tell you."

"Really? Hey, George, I got somethin' for you. Somethin' very important to me." He grabbed me and pulled me toward him, startling me at first. Then we started dancing around wildly on the sidewalk. I was puzzled by his behavior, but then I got caught up by the sheer exuberance of the moment.

"I know why I love you," Rover said, kissing me passionately.

"Why?"

"I'll never tell."

"I love you back," I said. "I need to see you more. So much has been happening since I last saw you. I'm working on this musical project."

"Tell me about it," Rover said, playfully.

We went upstairs to my apartment and made love for hours. I fell asleep. When I awoke the room was dark, and Rover had disappeared, leaving his white guitar behind him. A sheet of music paper lay on the pillow next to me:

Loving You Was Better Than Never At All
by Rover The Cat (BMI, ASCAP, MEOW)

A new song. I was overwhelmed by a sudden, terrible loneliness. I never had the chance to tell him about my musical
project, and I was afraid I would never see him again. I got up
from the disheveled bed, looked for my notebook, and began
to write.

Sex Story

Robert Glück

Brian undid the buttons of my levis one by one, pulled down my pants and Egyptian red cotton briefs; white skin and then my cock springs back from the elastic—"Hello, Old Timer." A disappointing moment when possibilities are resolved and attention localized, however good it's going to be. So it's going to be a blow job—that's nice. So it's going to be sex—nice, but less than the world. That blow job defined the situation, then a predictable untangling of arms and legs and stripping off shoes and clothes, my jeans, his corduroys, lighting sand candles, putting on records, closing straw blinds, turning back sheets, turning off lights. Brian has a way of being naked a few minutes at a distance—he politely averts his eyes so I can study him unself-consciously.

"From his small tough ears, his thick neck came down to his shoulders in a long wide column of muscles and cords that attached like artwork to the widened 'V' of his clavicle, point-ing the way to his broad, almost football padded shoulders and then down to those muscular arms, covered with blond hair. The tits were firm, and never jiggled, though the nipples were almost the size of a woman's, and seemed always to be in a state of excitement. A light patch of blond hair was growing like a wedge between them, and a long racing stripe of blond hair led the eye down over the contour of his rippling stomach muscles, past the hard navel, and streamlined down to a patch of only slightly darker pubic hair. There, in all its magnificence hung the 'Doug.' Its wide column of flesh arched out slightly from his body, curving out and downwards in its solidness to the point-ing tip of its foreskin where the flesh parted slightly exposing the tip of a rosebud cockhead. The width of the big cock only partially hid a ripe big sack behind it, where two spheric globes of his balls swelled out on either side of it. The cock hung down freely, without the slightest sign of sexual arousal, and still it spanned downward a full third of the boy's young strong legs.

'Turn around slowly," Cliff said to Rags, unbuttoning his own shirt and pulling it back off his torso . . ."

That was from *Fresh from the Farm* by Billy Farout, pp. 20–21. I want to write about sex: good sex without boasting, descriptive without looking like plumbing, happy, avoiding the La Brea Tar Pits of lyricism. Brian is also golden, with a body for clothes, square shoulders, then nothing but the essentials decked out with some light and pleasant musculature. He carries his shoulders a little hunched—the world might hit him on the head—which goes with a determined niceness that can become a little grim, like taking the bus to the LA airport to meet me. But if he has his blind spots, Bruce, Kathy, Denise and I said in various combinations over cups of coffee—well, who doesn't? It's that this one doesn't correspond to ours. Five years ago Brian painted a picture of a house and had many delusions about it. Finally he went to live in the relative safety of its rooms. I can understand that. Brian looks like anyone. Rags looks like no one; he's an alluring nightmare that reduces the world to rubble. Really, I could never grasp Brian's looks, a quality I admire. When I understand his face, solve it into planes and volumes, factor in blond hair and green eyes, then he turns his head a little, the essential eludes me and I must start all over. Sometimes he's intact as a fashion model emitting sunlight. Sometimes he's a fetus, big unfortunate eyes and a mouth pulled down, no language there, fingers and toes waiting to be counted.

I knelt and returned his blow job, his body tensed toward me and his cock grew in my mouth according to his heartbeat, each pulse a qualification that sent me backward to accept more. I was not completely in favor of his cock—it seemed indecisive—but he didn't care about it either. When I praised him—"the charm of its shape"—he shrugged and the compliment didn't register. It was his ass, full and generous, that we concentrated on.

He more or less pushed me onto the bed and tumbled after me, raising our exchange a level by blowing me while looking into my eyes. He's giving me pleasure and looking at me, keeping me focused. I'm acknowledging that. There's no way to dismiss this by saying I'm lost in a trance, by pretending I

ROBERT GLÜCK

am not myself. Still, I make up an escape clause—I say: I put myself entirely in your hands and what I know you desire is to put yourself in mine, so I demand what I know you want me to want. I stood and commanded him to blow me, to do this and that: crawl behind and rim me while I masturbate myself. Brian replied, "As James Bond used to say, 'There's no mistaking that invitation.'" A tongue in your ass is more intimate than a cock anywhere; I receive the sensation inside my groin, in my knees and nipples and wrists. Now this was like a porno movie, or the sex ads in the gay newspapers:

Top (Father, Cowboy, Coach, Cop) wants Bottom
(Your prisoner and toy)—and conversely.
29-34? Small waist, W/M, Fr a/p, Delicious tongue
worship your endw. Lean back & watch yr hot rod
get super done, Sir. Don't any of you with long
poles want to be shucked down and get some
down-home Fr?
EXHIBITIONISM, j/o, facesitting,
Close Encounters in Venice.

What made it sexy? Probably the posture that isolated sex, isolated fantasy. He blew me and I took one step backward. He murmured, loving to crawl forward. The gesture, economical and elegant as a hawk's wing, pointed toward a vista that was not geographical.

I lifted him and we kissed passionately, our first real kissing filled with deep tongues and assy fragrance, running my tongue over his lips, each tooth defined by a tongue, our saliva tasted the same, he played with our cocks and I carried him to the—no, first he knelt and licked me, licked my feet and legs, tongued between my toes. "I don't like pain but I don't mind a good spanking." I obliged, spanking him on one cheek, then the other, while he blew me and masturbated himself. Then I had to piss and Brian made coffee. What if friendship and love are extras tagged onto sexuality to give it a margin of safety, of usefulness, and the relations between subject and object, usually dismissed as a set of perversions, were the heart of sex? Brian slipped into the bathroom while I was thinking and pissing. To my surprise he knelt and drank from my cock, looking at me. I wonder what I'm getting into, I said to myself, getting into it.

Still in the bathroom: "I sit on your lap and you talk to me like a father." What if desire and power take the form of "Law" as we experience it, whether as the "father" or the "cop." "Have you been a good boy?" "I have a special treat for you." "Are you going to do a good job?" Whispered while tonguing his ear and raining kisses on his neck and cheek—all the language of blackmail and instrumentality, its context shifted to pleasure. Brian dutifully replied to his father's cock, not daring to raise his eyes. These few phrases established father and son, where desire is accumulated and forbidden, yet we remained animals exploring pleasure, teasing prostates with inserted forefingers up to the first and second knuckle, learning by heart each other's cock better than our own, needing to touch all his skin with my tongue: the tonguing of nipples until erect and then little bites accepted resistingly, tongue around the ears, inside the head, his curls of blond hair a county line for a tongue going out of town, down the backbone, pause, into the crack, pause, testing the asshole—clean as a whistle, tidy boy—tapping with the slightest pressure, knocking again and again to produce a moan, the straining backward, the gasp of a penetration. Caressing him there satisfied me as though I were touching all of Brian at once.

That got old and the kettle whistled. We settled back in bed with the coffee. There was no way around it, he loved me. It was plain to see in his melting eyes. More, in the steadiness of that melting gaze: he made me more naked than without clothes. I hadn't been loved that way for years; my relief was so fierce you could call it passion. Brian loved me quickly and thoroughly, without a credit check on my personality. I felt abashed.

Responding to my thought he told me the story of his falling in love (which I fill in):

Brian and two women friends traveled from LA to San Francisco to spend Halloween with me. Brian wanted us to portray Earth, Wind, Fire and Water, and accordingly made costumes and masks which he brought along. They were brown, baby blue, scarlet and royal blue, with matching sequins and feathers. I forget which was mine but I rebelled when I saw the scanty muslin toga. "I'll make my own costume," I said, and so we went as Earth, Fire, Water, and a bumblebee. I drank—scared and belligerent. A blur of emotions. In a bar: "I'm a BUMBLEBEE, asshole." We returned home; the scenario indicated passionate happy lovemaking for hours and hours. I dreaded it. Instead I drank a half pint of brandy on top of the evening's beverages. That was October. I hadn't divested myself of the summer's construction project in LA, an escalating nightmare of fraud and anxiety. Ed and I formally separated in June; I desired him in the same way that I still require a cigarette, a physical call. I hardly drink, I never drank. Depressed, I ate Viennese pastry. Ed said he knew when I was upset because I left doilies around the kitchen.

I drank myself into a crying jag. I peeled off my sweaty cigarette-smelling bumblebee outfit and cried on Brian's hot skin. Sometimes I paused, then a stronger wave would submerge me and carry me up. Crescendo. The pain registered as isolation. My body really hurt, my skin hurt, so I decided I'd better eat bread to absorb the alcohol. Besides, crying had made me claustrophobic. It was five in the morning. I got up feeling like Monday's wash, put on one of my abject T-shirts and sat down in the kitchen, wearily sniveling and cramming saltines down my throat. "And that," said Brian, "is when I fell in love with you."

We were on our sides more or less tangled up. His free hand meditated on the slimness of my waist, the power of my shoulders and chest. I basked in his general radiance. I loved his waist and the gold of his skin, I wanted to fold myself into it. Then he slid down and kissed my cock the way you kiss lips. He said, "I love your cock." He said it with more fervor than customarily applied to a sweet nothing, and so lapidary that I assured myself I would remember it during that amount of "forever" which is to be my portion. I've been reading Jane Austen. He said it to my cock's face, and I thought Oedipally, "A face a mother could love." "How's your mother?" And, "How's her emerald collection?" I liked to hear him recite her stones. I think Brian felt he betrayed her a little, that my eagerness and the question itself was not in the best taste; "Gimme a break," he would say. And here I am justifying his fears. But really I viewed her collection as a victory, a personal domain wrested from so much that was not hers. I liked its lack of utility and sexual shimmer. I liked the war that each piece represented, complete with siege, ground strategy and storming the fort. Her collection was an Aladdin's hoard, not an investment. She had: (1) A diamond and emerald bracelet, groups of four each alternating around. (2) A diamond ring that Brian says doubles as a Veg-a-matic. (3) A diamond and gold brooch set on an inch-wide gold bracelet (Brian's favorite).

(4&5) Two pairs of diamond and emerald clips. (6) An emerald brooch, geometric design within a rectangle. (7) Many pearls. (8) A large emerald ring. Plus opals and a few token stones.

Brian's mother angles back a little of her own power in the going currency of charm and attractiveness. She's not the Enemy.

I met the enemy at a gay resort on the Russian River. It felt strange to be there, surrounded by money and its attendant —available and well-groomed flesh. Until that day I spent my vacation at a small neighborhood beach where nakedness was not so much a declaration. Each morning I took Old River Road to about five yards from the Hacienda Bridge, veered right and coasted down a steep grade that carried me back to an older level of houses and crossroads beneath the bridge. Like a dream: *there is a world underneath this one and it's here now.* I parked at the end of Hummingbird Lane, stepped over a barbwire fence and its PRIVATE sign, took a darkly congested path—maple trees and blackberry bushes—which became sunnier—manzanita and buck brush—opening out to the hot sun and an arid span of rock and sand bleached white right up to the river's channeled coolness. Naked people lay as far from each other as possible. The air was white and deadlocked from reflected heat, it made the sunbathers look like quick sketches. When I wet my lips I almost tasted the remote breeze that stirred the tops of the laurel and Douglas fir growing up the opposite hillside. I couldn't hear the river; a loud buzzing sound came from the spellbound air, the inactivity, the heat, my own breath—I either submitted to it or felt anxious.

That stretch of river held a special attraction for me. A few white alders grew on a little island. Next to the island there was a small rapids with an alder overhanging it, and someone had tied a rope around a branch. A swimmer could grab hold of the rope and be carried up by the water—lithe and quick—legs, belly, everything washed and washed. Buoyed up like that, if I submerged my head a giant roaring surrounded me. It was so pleasurable I could endure it only a few minutes. I was bored, alone, diffused—there was no ground to be me pursuing my aims, no margin for the anxiety of perspective, resolution into categories. Gradually I spent more time dangling from that rope; finally I tied myself to it although I feared drowning. What a pleasurable agony each moment is as it dilapidates into the next. The water rushed, brought my body to a point, it felt good.

My friend Sterling came up from San Francisco and stayed at a gay resort, which is how I found myself lying nakedly with him beside a swimming pool along with fifty other men. I was comforted by the smell of chlorine and hot cement. We looked like a David Hockney that had gotten out of hand; the sun was spinning ribbons in the water and also cooking eight thousand pounds of shellacked gay flesh. Sterling introduced me to suntan oil. His friend Tom, the enemy I mentioned before, had joined us. We repositioned ourselves to the full sun. I was on my stomach, drowsy, and Sterling absentmindedly put his hand on my left asscheek, he put his hand on my ass, he put his hand on my ass and he kept it there, he kept it there—I didn't move a muscle and basked in his hand more than in the sun, pleasure spread to the back of my legs, my lower back and my nipples— not a muscle, he'd think I was uncomfortable, his hand was hotter than the sun on my other cheek—somebody said, "Bob's got an ass like a peach." Sterling, who's black, said, "Not that much color." I suggested wintermelons. "What?" said Sterling. *"Wintermelons . . . "* "What did Bob say?" asked Tom. "He said *wintermelons,*" Sterling answered.

Tom gazed abstractly down at his unformulated body, master of all he surveyed. The afternoon passed and much conversation got said and forgotten, but information about his wealth gathered like nuggets or objets d'art set mentally side by side on a mantle. Instead of ormolu clocks and Chinese epergnes, I counted three houses—mansions—in San Antonio, a farm in upstate New York, two houses in Florida, a ranch in the Panhandle, three houses in San Francisco, and condos in New York City and Palm Springs. These were his proud investments; he'd made this million on his own, not resting on the laurels of his inherited millions from Gulf Oil. Answering me, he said, "My watch cost $8,000. Look, it's a twenty dollar gold piece with a diamond nob, set in a gold case."

Tom furnished much food for thought. It shocked me that he was so undefined. At thirty he still had his baby fat, aimless good will. He wore the most conventional plastic leather outfits. Never in his life had he voluntarily read anything more detaining than a magazine. Was *this* the Pomeranian Earl of Rochester, his overbright eyes leering subnormally under his peruke? I expected manners, Jane Austen, nice debates as to who takes precedence at dinner, fine points. How else do you know you're different from the servants?—and the people who run your farms and rent your apartments? When I returned from the toilet he joked, "Did everything come out all right?" And later he asked it *again*.

How could all that wealth be condensed in this fatuous presence? The answer: it wasn't. The wealth stayed where it was, intangible. Maybe Tom's character grew vague by way of response. Tom doesn't live on top of his servants; his property remains as abstract as the money it equals. Even the fifty Persian carpets he treasures wait in constant breathless readiness to be traded or sold. So manners might be beside the point, the tweed and horses of his seniors a tip of the hat to feudal wealth. But how can I attack Tom's life and still defend his sexuality? When Sterling, Tom and I walked back to my car we passed a bunch of "youths" whiling away the day lounging on their pickups, and despite Tom's bank account they started yelling: "Death to Faggots," "Get Outta Town," "Kill Queers," etc.

Tom became vivid for me in one passage that afternoon. Is it surprising that the medium of his transformation should be pleasure? We were cooling off in the shallow end, watching the suntan oil slick make marbled paper patterns on the pool's surface. We acknowledged a passing physique, a body that summed up what's happening these days. Tom attempted a joke about fist-fucking that included a reference to a subway entrance. I said that I could understand the erotic charge of bondage and discipline, of water sports and so on, but I could never grasp fist-fucking's sensuality. Was it homage to the fist and arm, that masculine power engaged, taken on because inside you? Tom responded with patience and expertise, accustomed to making things clear to laymen. He said that most fist-fucking is beside the point because it stops at what he called the trap. I think that's a plumbing term. He said that the colon makes a right-hand turn and then loops up all the way to the diaphragm. He drew the arch on my torso with his forefinger. If you negotiate that turn and forge ahead, your hand is a membrane away from the heart—in fact, you can actually hold your lover's beating heart. More than that, after a while your two hearts establish a rapport, beat together, and what physical intimacy could exist beyond this?

I let out a long breath. I was a little stunned. Until then, being naked, I felt naked. Facing this vista of further nakedness, I felt dressed and encumbered as a Victorian parlor.

I joined Sterling; I lay face down on an orange plastic cot and dozed. Troubling images: We're on top of a pyramid. The Aztec priest holds a stone knife in one hand and in the other he lifts the still-beating heart above its former home, the naked warrior, whose lower back balances on a phallic sacrificial stone. He's held by half-naked priests at the hands and feet, his body still spasming and arching. That from the eighth grade. There were no undressed white people in my textbook. Did the compilers feel that Indians did not possess enough being to be capable of nakedness? If I were that picture everyone's cock would be hard as the stone knife.

And this from Anne Rice's *Interview with a Vampire:* "Never had I felt this, never had I experienced it, this yielding of a conscious mortal. But before I could push him away for his own sake, I saw the bluish bruise on his tender neck. He was offering it to me. He was pressing the length of his body against me now, and I felt the hard strength of his sex beneath his clothes pressing against my leg. A wretched gasp escaped my lips, but his bent close, his lips on what must have been so cold, so lifeless to him; and I sank my teeth into his skin, my body rigid, that hard sex driving against me, and I lifted him in passion off the floor. Wave after wave of his beating heart passed into me as, weightless, I rocked with him, devouring him, his ecstasy, his conscious pleasure."

The vampire's erotic charge consists of just this meeting of heartbeats, yet our hero consumes the life he is experiencing. Rice weaves homosexuality into vampire society. Does she think it will make the dead deader or more alive? "The pleasures of the *damned*," "the *pleasures* of the damned"; in "Carmilla," once

Le Fanu underscores his vampire's grief, you are free to enjoy by proxy her lesbian embrace: "She used to place her pretty arms about my neck, draw me to her, and laying her cheek to mine, murmur with her lips near my ear, 'Dearest, your little heart is wounded; think me not cruel because I obey the irresistible law of my strength and weakness; if your dear heart is wounded, my wild heart bleeds with yours. In the rapture of my enormous humiliation . . .'"

So death accompanies this heart stuff. And some would say, do say, that Tom's journey through the anus is a trip to the underworld. Yet this is all very far from the harmony of Tom's description, far from the particular realm of pleasure that expresses the urge to be radically naked. Tom isn't dead, neither are his partners. As Tom and his friend get dressed, culture, ideology and conflict enter simultaneously, saying we are supposed to be alone, discontinuous. We experience this as safety. We experience as transgression the penetration of our boundaries, fusion with another, and they warn us that this transgression is fearful as death. Naturally the vampire always wears a criminal half-smile. This guilt, even if slightly embraced, even if an inch stepped toward, becomes a sexual apparatus increasing the pleasure it decreased, a second ego becoming its own opposite.

I woke up on the plastic cot in the sunlight and shade, looking at a grid of sun the cot stenciled on the cement, thinking over and over *Orfeo ed Euridice, Orfeo ed Euridice*. I forgot who I was; the music and sunlight seemed more real. It was not the composer's name, or—I think—the trip through hell. Not even the "Dance of the Furies" to which I did my situps every morning. It was the following band I recalled, "The Dance of the Blessed Spirits," so limpid and noble that I would lie back exhausted and just float.

Sterling was by my side; the rest of the pool area was mostly deserted. He told me a story about his mother which reminded me of Brian's mother and her emeralds. While Brian's mother operated in that middle-class locus of power, the parents' bedroom, Sterling's mother went outside of the house, changing the terms. Sterling grew up in San Antonio where his father, a gambler also named Sterling, had married in his forties a woman twenty years younger. Along with other business ventures, Sterling Sr. ran a "buffet flat." He usually had a mistress but age brought respectability, and now he confines himself to real estate and Adele. Sterling recalls only one fight from his childhood. He can't remember why, but Sterling Sr. slapped his mother. They were in the kitchen; Adele stood in front of a stove filled with a complicated Sunday dinner. She yelled, "You want a fight, motherfucker? I'll give you a fight!"—and she systematically threw at her husband: muffins, potatoes, roast, salad, peas, collard greens, gravy and peach pie. Sterling Sr. stood uncertainly for a moment, weighing the merits of an advance. Finally he broke for the front door. Adele followed. She continued throwing the household at him, including, Sterling said with a pang, a cranberry glass lamp with lusters. Sterling Sr. jumped in his car and started to pull away but Adele got a rifle and blew out his tires. He skidded to a service station, changed tires, and spent a few days in Dallas. This noisy exchange triggered in Sterling's mom a meditation; its theme was power. At that time Adele worked for a travel agency. Her employers, an alcoholic white couple with liberal views, absconded to Mexico with the advance receipts for a tour of the Holy Land, leaving the agency more or less to Adele. She moved it to the black section of San Antonio and became financially independent. On one of her guided tours of Los Angeles she acquired a lover;

they met there for years. All this strengthened Adele's marriage. The two went past the inspirational bitterness of events to the events themselves, and now they are enjoying their sunset years, closer than ever.

"What's a buffet flat?"

It's a railroad flat, a long maroon hallway with many rooms: one room had two men doing it, another had two women doing it, and really each room had anyone with anyone, doing it. It's a sexual buffet. You paid an entrance fee to watch or act. I like the town meeting aspect of this. Also there were stars whom the audience egged on; 1910—big hats and skirts—or the twenties, a little tunic of dark spangles. Against that antique clothing nakedness becomes more naked.

What if I am a black woman who propositions one of these talented big fish. What a smile I'm capable of, I flash him one of these. I'm wearing a black beaded tunic I mentally refer to as my star-spangled night and the streets aren't paved. Want some tequila? Just a splash. What if we're naked together, clothes tossed over a chair and he only fucks me in the missionary position. What if I ask after a while if that's all.

What if he says, "Baby, I'm just warming up, just giving you a taste." I am the bottom man and this river is the top man, lithe and muscular with two handfuls of flesh. I am a bottom, the person who really controls is the bottom and sex is the top and I arrange for it to take my streaming body and clear me of names and express me and bring me to a point. This is pleasure and I'm no fool.

Brian said, "Jackie Kennedy made the pillbox hat famous. She made Halston famous, she made sleeveless dresses famous, she made Valentino famous. She made Gucci famous."

"Thrilling words," I said, "I can only add that the discovery of the individual was made in early 15th-century Florence. Nothing can alter that fact. Don't you think that's interesting? I do." Brian laughed at me and said, "You're like e=mc², always brimful of meaning." Then he asked conversationally, "Don't you think your cock is more interesting? I do." I thought it was a likely topic and finished my coffee. "Or am I putting words in your mouth?" he continued, taking my cock in his mouth and laying his head on my lap, still looking up at my face. I replied, "I reckon I'll just kick back and get me some old-fashioned, down-home French." Brian looked like a fetus. Then he sat up and said, "We boys in the back room voted you Mr. Congeniality." "What makes me a great catch?" I asked, falling into his arms so he'd have to catch me. "Looking for compliments?" "I just want to see if our lists tally." Then, seriously, "You know, I have a very beautiful couch." By way of response Brian tickled me, which escalated into wrestling. I lost because I wanted to see what he would do with an immobilized me; he held me down and started licking my torso while I mock resisted even though I was hard. "Want a frozen Reese's Peanut Butter Cup?" he asked my extravagantly arching neck. I pictured them stacked neatly in his freezer. Coffee, Kools and peanut butter cups were Brian's staff of life. I followed him into the kitchen, past his new room arrangement that I had just admired upside down through the bedroom door.

Brian lived in a bungalow in Venice, CA—a bedroom, living room and kitchen. He furnished the living room with a mattress, a box spring, a large palm, a poster-size print of a sepia photograph of women in long skirts carrying rifles in the Mexican Revolution, and another poster of a Hiroshige woodblock print (*36 Views of . . .*). The room was spotless and these five elements constantly found new spatial relationships. I followed him: a small deco kitchen with a total of four dishes, three cups, two one-quart stainless steel saucepans, mismatched flatware for two and a half, and a knife. I liked the cups, Mexican enamel with a decal of an innocent nosegay.

We stood in the dark kitchen kissing; that got old. He wanted to sit on my lap. I was so aroused I was wide open. We mutual masturbated like that and kissed—I was gasping. I caught our reflection in the window and it was funny to see us so localized inside these giant sensations of pleasure, my hips and muscles permanently cocked.

That got old so I carried him to the kitchen table where he squatted like a frog and I fucked him. My own body knows what his experienced: each time my cock touched a certain point hot and icy shivers radiated outward. I burn and freeze. If you have a man's body that is what you would feel. A cock's pleasure is like a fist, concentrated; anal pleasure is diffused, an open palm, and the pleasure of an anal orgasm is founded on relaxation. It's hard to understand how a man can write well if he doesn't like to be fucked. There's no evidence to support this theory; still, you can't be so straight that you don't submit to pleasure. Ezra Pound claimed his poetry was a penis aimed at the passive vulva of London. Perhaps that's why his writing is so worried, brow-furrowed. We dallied with coming for a while but decided no. Brian loved to be carried and pleasure made me powerful, sent blood to my muscles and aligned them. I lifted him from the table and fucked him in the air.

It was great sex—not because of the acrobatics, not even because he loved me and showed it and showed it, but because we were both there, very much of us, two people instead of two porno-movie fragments. Brian knelt in front of me, sucking the cock that fucked him. That's one—among many—of the things I wouldn't do. Don't do too often. It's not so bad, but all I think is now I'm doing this and what disease will I get. I quickly brush the cock with my hand like kids sharing a bottle of coke, certain that no germs are killed, just so something besides my lips touches it first. I admired Brian's range and mobility; his sexuality makes little concession to the world. I contrasted him favorably with myself. Brian is more sexually alive than anyone I know. A shower of sparks spills off his skin like inside a foundry. I'm a little more cautious, a little less generous. Let's say I had to avert my eyes.

I had to piss, Brian smiled, I laughed—a light went on about all the coffee he kept feeding me. Ed, whose dream life still seems definitive, described pissing into epic Busby Berkley waterfall fantasies, erotic masterpieces of technical know-how. I presented to Brian the difficulty of pissing when hard, but in the spirit of the great director he assured me that when there's a will there's a way. All the same, these particular golden showers were intermittent. Kneeling, he put his head between my legs—I pissed on his back, then slowly in his mouth. Because the temperature was all the same I couldn't tell what was cock, mouth or urine, like pissing in a lake, just feeling warmth and a pressure outward. I envied Brian the clarity of his position.

Not sex, but my concern for you makes this story vulgar. You see I named it before you could. Brian and I were both so powerful, admiring each other's power. Surely power and sexuality seek each other out, even if ultimately they are held in a suspension. But our force was opposite to the kind that oppresses and controls, so it engendered permissiveness and generosity. Like the strategies of the two mothers who wanted to reclaim their lives: on the one hand, power lies in understanding the given terms and using them as leverage; on the other hand, power changes the terms. In literature, the former is *technique*—I want to create beautiful things (precious stones); the latter, *strategy*— I want a dynamic relation with my audience (my husband).

I scooped Brian up, kissed him and carried him back to bed. He asked me if I'd like to hear about his confinement in a mental institution. He asked so politely that I understood he wanted to tell me about it: "You have to understand I repeated the story about 498 times during the first two days—doctors are even more curious than you—but I'll try to make it fresh." (It's true he talked as though he were composing a letter.) He began, "Well, Bobbo, it's like this:

"I'd been whittling my life down so that smoking a cigarette became an actual activity. I just broke up with a boy named Aaron who lived about three blocks away. I used to visit him in his new apartment and model for a painting called *The Junkie*. It showed me sitting in a pile of garbage with a needle in my arm."

"You sat there with a needle in your arm?"

"After I went nuts, Aaron told me he never found anyone who could hold the pose as long. I was taking a visual perception course taught by a woman named Edith Hammer. She was a great teacher; she'd show different works from different times and compare their visual components. After my second class I had an acute guilt attack, rushed to an art supply store and bought a large square canvas, paints and brushes. I rushed home to the apartment I had shared with Aaron but now occupied alone, and started painting.

"At first the idea seemed lyrical and intelligent: to make a cross section of reality in the form of a house."

"Sounds like an idea to me. Meaning and Safety."

"The windows were shaped like coffins and corresponded

to gravestones above. The windows opened on a blank horizon. Above was a cemetery scene illustrating a story from my mother's childhood; it showed my grandmother and my aunt sitting under a tree, my mother as a child running to them, and my uncle as a baby watching the whole thing from behind the tree. It was done in mottled brilliant colors and I was very excited about it.

"I would wake up every morning and see something else and keep working, drawn deeper into it. I saw duality in everything; the painting helped me break down reality into its basic components and I thought if I saw past the duality I'd get to the nitty-gritty. Meanwhile it was getting a little scary. I titled the painting *The Conception and Evolution of Brainchild's Unity Theorem*, and when I printed that on a piece of paper and thumbtacked it to the lower corner, the gesture completed the delusion. I thought I had brought the symbol to reality—that some presence came from my painting through the white of the clouds which were unpainted, thus being a void. Then I had the terrifying conviction that I somehow evolved myself through the painting to be God.

"The more I tried to reason it out, the deeper I got. I tried burning the frame I had made in my bathtub, thinking if I partially destroyed the painting I could save myself. I was afraid if I burned the whole painting I might die or the world might end. I started schlepping the painting. I took it to school—'nice'—and then to Miss Hammer—'spiritual.' I wanted to throw up.

"Finally after a visit to my friend Mary Dell (with the painting)—no one seemed to be able to deal with what was going on with me. I called Mary Dell back that night and she drove me to the hospital where I lied and said I had insurance and committed myself. The admitting shrink thought I was tripping."

Brian had finished. I felt trapped by his story: his years felt like a graph with sadness as both scales. It struck me that the same qualities—generosity, emotional presence—that paved the way for all this distress also made him good at love. Should I charge in and set up squatter's rights in his experience? He wasn't dejected, didn't call for support or even sympathy. Just because of that, he seemed to test my aptitude for sympathy and support. I feared Brian might want to be saved, and how could I do that? Then I realized he just wanted me to pay attention. With tremendous exertion I asked him some interested questions. How long was he in? Nine months. Jesus! Did they try to cure him of being gay? (I squeezed his cock.) Yes, although they didn't succeed. (He squeezed my cock.) But in the end the violence of Brian's story was so much a condensation of dream to me that I was falling asleep; sleep was a cliff that I fell off, drifting slowly as a parsley flake in a jar of oil. Did he have to wear a uniform? Yes. They sedated him most of the time.

Our bodies had turned around. We looked up at the ceiling, absentmindedly playing with our own or each other's cocks, which enhanced my detached response to Brian's story. As a postscript he added: "Aaron embraced the Bahá'í faith and swore himself to celibacy. He now lives in a trailer in Champagne, Minnesota, and calls me occasionally to ease the Way. The painting ended up in my shrink's office closet. I moved to Los Angeles and found a job as the manager of the toddler's department at Saks." (I see him looking like the sun in his linen suit. He's saying—with his hand over his heart—to a bullying child, "Hey, gimme a break.")

In the silence that followed we applied ourselves to each other's body more creatively; we dribbled on some Vaseline Intensive Care lotion while Brian speculated that probably gay men have younger cocks because of the oils and lubricants. Truman Capote wrote that we also have youthful necks and chins, I added, because of all the sucking. I recalled an Isherwood quotation: "Of course it would never have occurred to any of them to worry about the psychological significance of their tastes." I copied this passage on my journal page after three recipes for potato salad.

I don't think "disturbed" people are more healthy than "normal" ones, but sometimes there is a fine line, or no line at all, between "disturbed" and oppressed. Driven crazy is more like it. Are oppressed people more sexual? Other forms of discourse—languages of production and ownership—have been denied us or disowned. By default we are left with sex and the emotions—devalued as Cinderella at the hearth. And then we become—maybe—Cinderella at the ball. Then we are blamed for embracing sex and we will be a bone in the throat of people who don't. It's the same with the popular cultures of gays, people of color, the working class. They are feared because they draw energy away from "productive goals." And they are colonized, neutralized and imported into our stagnant mainstream culture. Sex is a sign of life. If sex is relegated to gays as a sign of our devalued state—becoming the shimmer of jewels— it's strange to me that the Left hasn't broached the topic of pleasure. You could say the Left leaves it to Freud, but where is pleasure in all his systems and epi-systems? In all that dominant where is the tonic, the home key?

Brian asked, "What would you like?" A thought sailed by, "It would be nice if you . . ." Here inspiration failed—I was dejected, couldn't grasp the rest. It was growing light. I felt a little scared to be doing this for so many hours, a little "disturbed." I thought of the Marquis de Sade, perpetually feverish, energy spiraling out because it's mental, disconnected from physical rhythms, busy, busy, busy. I wanted my borders back; I wanted to curl into myself intact as a nautilus shell and let my sleeping mind group and regroup to absorb and master this experience. I said, "Masturbate me as slowly as you can." We lay on our backs, side by side and head to foot. This is really a solitary activity for two in that your attention equals your sensation, and the hand on the other's cock requires as little care as the hand that grasps a branch in the Russian River. We masturbated each other slowly, achingly gathering up skin into folds which were meditative and inward turning as the mantle of a 14th century Madonna; then in a reversal experienced as a huge change from night to day, or the turning in some great argument, we brought our hands down. It made us gasp. The pace was excruciating. We were permanently aroused, erectile tissue flooded and damned up, and so we enjoyed a kind of leisure and Mozartian wit. I knew from the first with Brian that we would continue. Love and friendship aside, you can tell on a first meeting that it will take more exchanges to accomplish the various sexual permutations—know by the way he touches you rather than by positions and tastes.

I could just see the top of Brian's sunny head over the horizon of his chest. Silence, gasps—out of the blue he said, "You would have looked like dynamite in that toga."

What if I'm fucking on the grass in ancient Rome like we always do on Wednesday night. Is it Thursday? What's one day? Nothing—you turn around and it's dark, the tick and tock of day and night. What if I'm the woman? I'm languidly stretched out on the grass fanning myself with a spray of flowering myrtle. When he enters me I'm spread open as a moth, I'm all colors. What if I'm the guy when I feel someone on me and wham!—I've got a cock up my ass—I never saw the guy before and I *still* haven't seen him but I ride his cock—why not?—I'm riding it across a continent of skin. I feel like a sandwich, the pleasure's in the middle because no one has had or knows this much—I can't see, I'm bellowing and I start to come, it begins in my ass as a pinpoint of light a thousand miles away. I move closer to it with a religious sense of well-being and when I come I shout a little prayer—I shout *Je-Sus!*

What if I'm fucking this boy and his orgasm is so absolute it leaves me gasping.

What if I'm watching the three of them calling on their gods and gasping their extravagance—their arms and legs, their skin filled with rosy orifices, they look like an anemone. First I'm the woman, then I'm the man, then I'm Catullus, then I'm an observer remembering a poem, the distance becoming erotic.

He's going to make us into a poem, I've heard better lines. What if he takes us to his villa and merely to pluck at my nipples he feeds me olives pickled in caraway, dormice dipped in honey and rolled in poppy seed, sausages, orioles seasoned with pepper, capons and sow bellies, blood pudding, Egyptian and Syrian dates, veal, little cakes, grapes, pickled beets, Spanish wine and hot honey, chickpeas and lupins, endless filberts, an apple, roast bear meat, soft cheese steeped in fresh wine, tripe hash, liver in pastry boats, oysters and hot buttered snails, pastry thrushes with raisin and nut stuffing, quinces with thorns stuck in them to resemble sea urchins, because I'm handsome.

Some people like sex, most men don't. What if I'm blowing him, I look up as he brings down a knife—I either die or don't die. I'm alone at night in bed, someone's moving silently up the stairs—this was to be a sexual rendezvous but instead he intends to wrap a wire around my neck. I don't die but my erection's gone. I must begin again: what if he puts his hand under my tunic, his finger up my ass and I squirm down on it, why not? My girl's laughing—dildos shaped like birds and fish. He's moaning *Nostra Lesbia, Lesbia ilia, ilia Lesbia*—what is this, Latin? This guy's obviously educated.

Orioles must be aphrodisiac or maybe it's the situation because all we want to do is fuck, we can't keep our clothes on, we go to it, showing off for him. I love how our eyes go blank and then we think with our bodies. She licks it like a cat with her rough tongue, or like licking ketchup off your forefinger—one two, that's all. Then men come and lift me and hold my legs and body while he fucks me and I'm blowing somebody, it's fantastic, all I ever want to do is this.

Brian and I were working ourselves around to coming; we enjoyed the sense of absolute well-being and safety that precedes orgasm. By now we were on our knees kissing urgently and masturbating ourselves. Our cocks felt a little ragged and wanted the master's touch. Masturbation can *feel* better, although I favor a penetration for emotional meaning. Still, that was hardly necessary since we filled up the house to overflowing, and besides, we weren't planning to have a baby.

Orgasms come in all shapes and sizes, sometimes mechanical as a jack-in-the-box—an obsessive little tune, tension, pop goes the weasel—other times they brim with meaning. And other times, like now, they are the complimentary close that signals the end of a lengthy exchange. I recall a memorable climax, a terrific taste of existence in the summer of '73. I was with Ed; we weren't doing anything special but the orgasm started clearly with the fluttering of my prostate, usually a distant gland, sending icy waves to my extremities. Then a hot rush carried my torso up into an arc and just before I came a ball bearing of energy ping-ponged up and down my spine.

Brian and I curled into each other. Our semen smelled faintly of chlorine. Sunlight glittered off or was accepted by the domestic surfaces. On our way to falling asleep we exchanged dreams:

Bob: I dreamt that an alligator lives in my kitchen wall; it cries brokenheartedly on the weekends. A cannibal rabbit with sharp teeth lives there too. A pathetic shabby man who looks like Genet keeps beckoning to me, appearing at a distance everywhere, even on the Greyhound bus I take to escape him, standing up the aisle and beckoning. These characters fill me with dread. I know they can't hurt me in themselves—they are intensely defeated, already claimed by death to such an extent that I writhe backward rather than associate with them.

Brian: I dreamt this while I was nuts. A group of nuns in black and white floated on the surface of a foreign planet. They were only heads, like that creature in the space movie. In their hands they carried candles that vibrated colors and gold. Everything on the nuns' side was grey and dead, but where the candles were, the light created moving patterns of color and electricity.

Bob: One day Denise, following a recipe of mine, made baked apples in wine. But something went awry and they turned out hard and sour. That night I dreamt there was a new kind of elephant called an Applederm, and its babies were called Apples.

Brian: I was at a party with my father. Our hosts—a family—were noticeably absent, which made me angrier and angrier. I followed my father into the dining room to placate myself with some food and as I looked up I realized it was my parents' apartment. There was laughter from the other room and someone said, "All our hearts are the same here."

Bob: I dreamt this around puberty. I was making love with

my little sister on her bed but the springs squeaked and I was anxious because my family in the next room might hear us. So we became bumblebees and hovered above the bed, buzzing and buzzing, and when we touched stingers I came. (I never told anyone my bumblebee dream, had forgotten it for years. I felt that now Brian could know me in one piece—what wasn't in the dream he could extrapolate.)

Brian: I stood in a room that was all black and white and because the dream was in color it was beautifully vivid. Black and white tiled floor, white walls, black and white solid drapes. As I looked around the room I saw a black bed from classical Greece, white sheets and in the bed a boy, sun-tanned with platinum blond hair. The contrast between him and the black and white setting filled me with joy; I moved closer passing through veils of black and white (remember duality?) and as I kissed him I awoke with the overwhelming erection that only dreams can provide.

Brian and I sometimes exchange letters. In the latest, Brian told me he is moving in with a lover. I felt a pang that I had no right to turn into any claim—the pain augmented by the fact that Sterling moved out of my life without leaving a forwarding address. I had been curious about the story Brian painted from his mother's childhood.

He answered:

"The image was based on one of my mother's frequent outings with my grandmother, my great aunt Kate and her uncle Ollie. Kate's husband, Hugo, died young and on weekends my grandmother and Kate would pack a picnic and make a day of visiting Hugo. I'm not sure why this is so peculiar to me. Maybe because that's my mother's impression of it. More likely it's that Be-Be (our name for my grandmother) and Katie were so unaware of the irony of taking children to play in a cemetery. I made my mother the embracer and my uncle the observer. Later, Katie was institutionalized along with both her daughters, who somehow were not in on these trips. I met Katie when I was six and she would definitely win my most terrifying-person-I-ever-met award. She had straight black hair cut severely across with straight long bangs. She sat hostilely on my grandmother's sofa, barely acknowledging our family's presence. She also scared the shit out of my father. She eventually died in a hospital singing Irish lullabies to herself.

"My grandmother held her own in the strange department. In her sixties she had to have one of her eyes—including the lid—removed. Instead of wearing a patch, Be-Be opted for glasses with a large plastic artificial eye attached to one of the lenses. It had a bizarre effect, particularly when she napped. What can I say about riding the subway with her—that people stared? that I got angry? It made me dislike people and love her. She would call and invite me to lunch. 'We'll go out!' she'd say expansively, as if The Acorn on Oak were the world. I gave her a feather boa one Christmas and we were thick as thieves after that. She loved to dance, drink. She would come out of the bathroom with hair she had just bleached platinum, make a '20s pout in the mirror, say, 'Your mother and I are both blonds,' and giggle. She was great.

"When Be-Be died, she presented a unique problem

to the undertaker. My mother insisted that the coffin be open in the Irish tradition. The undertakers were perplexed—should they put Be-Be's glasses on her and create the disconcerting effect of a corpse with one eye open? In the end that's exactly what they did, and dressed in her favorite red beaded gown, Be-Be said goodbye.

"Moody in her earlier years, Be-Be became senile later. I'd go to her apartment and cook dinner. I loved her very much. In the hospital she suddenly became lucid and rose to the occasion of her death. She said, 'You always learn something. Now I'm learning about tenses. How long is this going to take?' Then she removed her rings, one by one, and placed them on the nightstand for my mother."

In the Cemetery Where Al Jolson Is Buried

Amy Hempel

"Tell me things I won't mind forgetting," she said. "Make it useless stuff or skip it."

I began. I told her insects fly through rain, missing every drop, never getting wet. I told her no one in America owned a tape recorder before Bing Crosby did. I told her the shape of the moon is like a banana—you see it looking full, you're seeing it end-on.

The camera made me self-conscious and I stopped. It was trained on us from a ceiling mount—the kind of camera banks use to photograph robbers. It played us to the nurses down the hall in Intensive Care.

"Go on, girl," she said. "You get used to it."

I had my audience. I went on. Did she know that Tammy Wynette had changed her tune? Really. That now she sings "Stand by Your *Friends*"? That Paul Anka did it too, I said. Does "You're Having *Our* Baby." That he got sick of all that feminist bitching.

"What else?" she said. "Have you got something else?"

Oh, yes.

For her I would always have something else.

"Did you know that when they taught the first chimp to talk, it lied? That when they asked her who did it on the desk, she signed back the name of the janitor. And that when they pressed her, she said she was sorry, that it was really the project director. But she was a mother, so I guess she had her reasons."

"Oh, that's good," she said. "A parable."

"There's more about the chimp," I said. "But it will break your heart."

"No, thanks," she says, and scratches at her mask.

We look like good-guy outlaws. Good or bad, I am not used to the mask yet. I keep touching the warm spot where my breath, thank God, comes out. She is used to hers. She only ties the strings on top. The other ones—a pro by now—she lets hang loose.

We call this place the Marcus Welby Hospital. It's the white one with the palm trees under the opening credits of all those shows. A Hollywood hospital, though in fact it is several miles west. Off camera, there is a beach across the street.

She introduces me to a nurse as the Best Friend. The impersonal article is more intimate. It tells me that *they* are intimate, the nurse and my friend.

"I was telling her we used to drink Canada Dry ginger ale and pretend we were in Canada."

"That's how dumb we were," I say.

"You could be sisters," the nurse says.

So how come, I'll bet they are wondering, it took me so long to get to such a glamorous place? But do they ask?

They do not ask.

Two months, and how long is the drive?

The best I can explain it is this—I have a friend who worked one summer in a mortuary. He used to tell me stories. The one that really got to me was not the grisliest, but it's the one that did. A man wrecked his car on 101 going south. He did not lose consciousness. But his arm was taken down to the wet bone—and when he looked at it—it scared him to death.

I mean, he died.

So I hadn't dared to look any closer. But now I'm doing it—and hoping that I will live through it.

She shakes out a summer-weight blanket, showing a leg you did not want to see. Except for that, you look at her and understand the law that requires *two* people to be with the body at all times.

"I thought of something," she says. "I thought of it last night. I think there is a real and present need here. You know," she says, "like for someone to do it for you when you can't do it yourself. You call them up whenever you want—like when push comes to shove."

She grabs the bedside phone and loops the cord around her neck.

"Hey," she says, "the end o' the line."

She keeps on, giddy with something. But I don't know with what.

"I can't remember," she says. "What does Kübler-Ross say comes after Denial?"

It seems to me Anger must be next. Then Bargaining, Depression, and so on and so forth. But I keep my guesses to myself.

"The only thing is," she says, "is where's Resurrection? God knows, I want to do it by the book. But she left out Resurrection."

She laughs, and I cling to the sound the way someone dangling above a ravine holds fast to the thrown rope.

"Tell me," she says, "about that chimp with the talking hands. What do they do when the thing ends and the chimp says, 'I don't want to go back to the zoo'?"

When I don't say anything, she says, "Okay—then tell me another animal story. I like animal stories. But not a sick one—I don't want to know about all the seeing-eye dogs going blind."

No, I would not tell her a sick one.

"How about the hearing-ear dogs?" I say. "They're not going deaf, but they are getting very judgmental. For instance, there's this golden retriever in New Jersey, he wakes up the deaf mother and drags her into the daughter's room because the kid has got a flashlight and is reading under the covers."

"Oh, you're killing me," she says. "Yes, you're definitely killing me."

"They say the smart dog obeys, but the smarter dog knows when to disobey."

"Yes," she says, "the smarter anything knows when to disobey. Now, for example."

She is flirting with the Good Doctor, who has just appeared. Unlike the Bad Doctor, who checks the IV drip before saying good morning, the Good Doctor says things like "God didn't give epileptics a fair shake." The Good Doctor awards himself points for the cripples he could have hit in the parking lot. Because the Good Doctor is a little in love with her, he says maybe a year. He pulls a chair up to her bed and suggests I might like to spend an hour on the beach.

"Bring me something back," she says. "Anything from the beach. Or the gift shop. Taste is no object."

He draws the curtain around her bed.

"Wait!" she cries.

I look in at her.

"Anything," she says, "except a magazine subscription."

The doctor turns away.

I watch her mouth laugh.

What seems dangerous often is not—black snakes, for example, or clear-air turbulence. While things that just lie there, like this beach, are loaded with jeopardy. A yellow dust rising from the ground, the heat that ripens melons overnight—this is earthquake weather. You can sit here braiding the fringe on your towel and the sand will all of a sudden suck down like an hourglass. The air roars. In the cheap apartments on-shore, bathtubs fill themselves and gardens roll up and over like green waves. If nothing happens, the dust will drift and the heat deepen till fear turns to desire. Nerves like that are only bought off by catastrophe.

"It never happens when you're thinking about it," she once observed. "Earthquake, earthquake, earthquake," she said.

"Earthquake, earthquake, earthquake," I said.

Like the aviaphobe who keeps the plane aloft with prayer, we kept it up until an aftershock cracked the ceiling.

That was after the big one in '72. We were in college; our dormitory was five miles from the epicenter. When the ride was over and my jabbering pulse began to slow, she served five parts champagne to one part orange juice, and joked about living in Ocean View, Kansas. I offered to drive her to Hawaii on the new world psychics predicted would surface the next time, or the next.

I could not say that now—next.

Whose next? she could ask.

Was I the only one who noticed that the experts had stopped saying *if* and now spoke of *when*? Of course not; the fearful ran to thousands. We watched the traffic of Japanese beetles for deviation. Deviation might mean more natural violence.

I wanted her to be afraid with me. But she said, "I don't know. I'm just not."

She was afraid of nothing, not even of flying.

I have this dream before a flight where we buckle in and the plane moves down the runway. It takes off at thirty-five miles an hour, and then we're airborne, skimming the tree tops. Still, we arrive in New York on time.

It is so pleasant.

One night I flew to Moscow this way.

She flew with me once. That time she flew with me she ate macadamia nuts while the wings bounced. She knows the wing tips can bend thirty feet up and thirty feet down without coming off. She believes it. She trusts the laws of aerodynamics.

My mind stampedes. I can almost accept that a battleship floats when everybody knows steel sinks.

I see fear in her now, and am not going to try to talk her out of it. She is right to be afraid.

After a quake, the six o'clock news airs a film clip of first-graders yelling at the broken playground per their teacher's instructions.

"*Bad* earth!" they shout, because anger is stronger than fear.

But the beach is standing still today. Everyone on it is tranquilized, numb, or asleep. Teenaged girls rub coconut oil on each other's hard-to-reach places. They smell like macaroons. They pry open compacts like clamshells; mirrors catch the sun and throw a spray of white rays across glazed shoulders. The girls arrange their wet hair with silk flowers the way they learned in *Seventeen*. They pose.

A formation of low-riders pulls over to watch with a six-pack. They get vocal when the girls check their tan lines. When the beer is gone, so are they—flexing their cars on up the boulevard.

Above this aggressive health are the twin wrought-iron terraces, painted flamingo pink, of the Palm Royale. Someone dies there every time the sheets are changed. There's an ambulance in the driveway, so the remaining residents line the balconies, rocking and not talking, one-upped.

The ocean they stare at is dangerous, and not just the undertow. You can almost see the slapping tails of sand sharks keeping cruising bodies alive.

If she looked, she could see this, some of it, from her window. She would be the first to say how little it takes to make a thing all wrong.

There was a second bed in the room when I got back to it!

For two beats I didn't get it. Then it hit me like an open coffin.

She wants every minute, I thought. She wants my life.

"You missed Gussie," she said.

Gussie is her parents' three-hundred-pound narcoleptic maid. Her attacks often come at the ironing board. The pillow-cases in that family are all bordered with scorch.

"It's a hard trip for her," I said. "How is she?"

"Well, she didn't fall asleep, if that's what you mean. Gussie's great—you know what she said? She said, 'Darlin', stop this worriation. Just keep prayin', down on your knees'—me, who can't even get out of bed."

She shrugged. "What am I missing?"

"It's earthquake weather," I told her.

"The best thing to do about earthquakes," she said, "is not to live in California."

"That's useful," I said. "You sound like Reverend Ike—'The best thing to do for the poor is not to be one of them.'"

We're crazy about Reverend Ike.

I noticed her face was bloated.

"You know," she said, "I feel like hell. I'm about to stop having fun."

"The ancients have a saying," I said. "'There are times when the wolves are silent; there are times when the moon howls.'"

"What's that, Navaho?"

"Palm Royale lobby graffiti," I said. "I bought a paper there. I'll read you something."

"Even though I care about nothing?"

I turned to the page with the trivia column. I said, "Did you know the more shrimp flamingo birds eat, the pinker their

feathers get?" I said, "Did you know that Eskimos need refrigerators? Do you know *why* Eskimos need refrigerators? Did you
know that Eskimos need refrigerators because how else would
they keep their food from freezing?"

I turned to page three, to a UPI filler datelined Mexico
City. I read her MAN ROBS BANK WITH CHICKEN, about a man
who bought a barbecued chicken at a stand down the block
from a bank. Passing the bank, he got the idea. He walked in
and approached a teller. He pointed the brown paper bag at
her and she handed over the day's receipts. It was the smell of
barbecue sauce that eventually led to his capture.

The story had made her hungry, she said—so I took the elevator down six floors to the cafeteria, and brought back all
the ice cream she wanted. We lay side by side, adjustable beds
cranked up for optimal TV-viewing, littering the sheets with
Good Humor wrappers, picking toasted almonds out of the
gauze. We were Lucy and Ethel, Mary and Rhoda in extremis.
The blinds were closed to keep light off the screen.

We watched a movie starring men we used to think we wanted
to sleep with. Hers was a tough cop out to stop mine, a vicious
rapist who went after cocktail waitresses.

"This is a good movie," she said when snipers felled them
both.

I missed her already.

A Filipino nurse tiptoed in and gave her an injection. The
nurse removed the pile of popsicle sticks from the nightstand—
enough to splint a small animal.

The injection made us both sleepy. We slept.

I dreamed she was a decorator, come to furnish my house.

She worked in secret, singing to herself. When she finished, she guided me proudly to the door. "How do you like it?" she asked, easing me inside.

Every beam and sill and shelf and knob was draped in gay bunting, with streamers of pastel crepe looped around bright mirrors.

"I have to go home," I said when she woke up.

She thought I meant home to her house in the Canyon, and I had to say No, *home* home. I twisted my hands in the time-honored fashion of people in pain. I was supposed to offer something. The Best Friend. I could not even offer to come back.

I felt weak and small and failed.

Also exhilarated.

I had a convertible in the parking lot. Once out of that room, I would drive it too fast down the Coast highway through the crab-smelling air. A stop in Malibu for sangria. The music in the place would be sexy and loud. They'd serve papaya and shrimp and watermelon ice. After dinner I would shimmer with lust, buzz with heat, vibrate with life, and stay up all night.

Without a word, she yanked off her mask and threw it on the floor. She kicked at the blankets and moved to the door. She must have hated having to pause for breath and balance before slamming out of Isolation, and out of the second room, the one where you scrub and tie on the white masks.

A voice shouted her name in alarm, and people ran down the corridor. The Good Doctor was paged over the intercom. I opened the door and the nurses at the station stared hard, as if this flight had been my idea.

"Where is she?" I asked, and they nodded to the supply closet.

I looked in. Two nurses were kneeling beside her on the floor, talking to her in low voices. One held a mask over her nose and mouth, the other rubbed her back in slow circles. The nurses glanced up to see if I was the doctor—and when I wasn't, they went back to what they were doing.

"There, there, honey," they cooed.

On the morning she was moved to the cemetery, the one where Al Jolson is buried, I enrolled in a "Fear of Flying" class. "What is your worst fear?" the instructor asked, and I answered, "That I will finish this course and still be afraid."

I sleep with a glass of water on the nightstand so I can see by its level if the coastal earth is trembling or if the shaking is still me.

What do I remember?

I remember only the useless things I hear—that Bob Dylan's mother invented Wite-Out, that twenty-three people must be in a room before there is a fifty-fifty chance two will have the same birthday. Who cares whether or not it's true? In my head there are bath towels swaddling this stuff. Nothing else seeps through.

I review those things that will figure in the retelling: a kiss through surgical gauze, the pale hand correcting the position of the wig. I noted these gestures as they happened, not in any retrospect—though I don't know why looking back should show us more than looking *at*.

It is just possible I will say I stayed the night.

And who is there that can say that I did not?

I think of the chimp, the one with the talking hands.

In the course of the experiment, that chimp had a baby. Imagine how her trainers must have thrilled when the mother, without prompting, began to sign to her newborn.

Baby, drink milk.

Baby, play ball.

And when the baby died, the mother stood over the body, her wrinkled hands moving with animal grace, forming again and again the words: Baby, come hug, Baby, come hug, fluent now in the language of grief.

Spring

Brad Gooch

It's not dark yet, but it's getting there. Brad and Bobby are sitting on the concrete-block edge of a foundation for a new house on Winola Avenue. So far only the basement has been dug out of what used to be an empty lot. The lot next door is still empty: grown-over grass and a big old chestnut tree with thick trunk, knotted branches, and floppy leaves, almost tropical except for their Northern dark green pigment, near black in this twilight. The sky is blue and its moon, a heavy hanging half, past full, is manila. The two lots together had been used for a whiffle ball field. Now the boys in the neighborhood have to play longways which makes them feel cramped.

Brad's family's house is right across the street. It is a double-block, and he looks over every so often, wondering if anyone is watching him. Brad is a little pudgy with a bland face, dark skin, and a crew cut but without the front wave that sticks up on most crew cuts. He told the barber to trim it down. The front wave is an aggressive swish that he feels is reserved for others. He is twelve or thirteen. Dressed in a striped T-shirt (striped crossways), dark corduroys with patches sewn on the knees, low white tennis shoes, and colored socks. Ankle-high PF-Flyers or Keds are another fashion which he feels excluded from. He is dangling his legs, tapping the wall erratically with the backs of his heels, humming.

Bobby's family is a little farther up the street. Their house is a double-block also, but divided into a top and bottom half rather than a left and a right half like Brad's. Bobby's family lives in the bottom half. His father works in a brewery; his mother makes Italian spaghetti as a housewife and a caterer. She is pretty fat, wears lots of makeup, is friendly, and once gave Brad the frames from her old imitation-pearl eyeglasses which Brad had admired and tried on when he came over for dinner.

Bobby is sitting sideways, facing Brad. He has his knees hunched up in front of him. Has long straight brown hair, a thin animal face, and a bony body. Has on a sleeveless T-shirt and, over that, a cotton shirt with repeating Revolutionary War drum designs, black pants that show the scuffs from the concrete, brown tie shoes and socks. He keeps stretching his neck and twitching around his jaw.

Spring is just beginning in the neighborhood. The air smells sweet. A breeze rustles Bobby's shirt. Brad stares into patches of thick fruit trees in the yard next door. Some birds are flying around, making their last noises before it gets too dark. Both boys are dirty, especially their hands and faces.

Bobby: What do you want to do?

Brad: I don't know. What do you want to do?

Bobby makes a face. They have this exchange a few times a day, sometimes for five or ten minutes at a stretch.

Bobby: I said last time. It's up to you.

Brad: What time is it?

The street is still active. Cars go by every few minutes, some with headlights, some without. They either pass quickly or (fathers coming home from work) slow down to turn into one driveway or another. Brad checks to see if one of the cars belongs to his father who works as an accountant. His mother stays pretty much at home. He just finished supper with her a half-hour ago. It was iced tea, potato salad, a brown cooked meat, creamed corn, swirled ice cream for dessert.

Brad: I want to tell dreams.

Bobby: No. Not now.

Brad: Well, tell me what you said in confession on Saturday.

Bobby: I can't.

Brad: Why not?

Bobby: It's against my religion.

Brad: Who else was there? Was Terry there?

Bobby: Maybe.

Just then a convertible goes by. The guy driving is alone in the front seat. In the back, Duane, a tall blond early drug-user, is sitting with two teenage girls on either side, giggling and kissing him. The car horn blares steadily, a low almost mournful sound, from down at the Pierce Street corner.

Brad: He went to the pool last summer.

Bobby: Did you see him?

Brad: No, but he spit on me once.

Bobby: (dubious) Where?

Brad: I was going to Vacation Bible School. In the summer. He was up on a second-floor porch and he spit on me all the way across the street.

Bobby: Did it hit?

Brad: Right on my hand.

Bobby: What did you do?

Brad: Wiped it off with my handkerchief. Then I threw the handkerchief away and told my mother I lost it.

Bobby: I wouldn't let anyone spit on me.

Brad: Well, it just got me a little. Just on this side of this finger.

Bobby takes out a tube of Brylcreem from his back pocket, all rolled up like a toothpaste tube. He squeezes a dab on his palm and rubs it into his long brown hair, slicking it back. Light from the moon shows up the wet parts.

Bobby: (tossing the tube to Brad) Here.

Brad knows just what to do. Puts a dab right on his head, rubs the grease around his scalp freely. Tosses the tube back.

Bobby: We could go for a walk.

Brad: Where?

Bobby: Schoolyard.

Brad: No.

Bobby: We could go in Patsy's yard. They're not home.

Brad: (standing up) You want to cut through here?

Bobby and Brad go over to a low green fence by the yard next door. They jump over. Chained dog barking from the porch. They run past and jump the other fence to Patsy's yard.

Now they're in a more secret part of the neighborhood.

There are yards facing them from the houses behind and yards on either side. The big brown two-story house where Patsy lives with her parents and sister is dark.

Brad: It stinks here.

Bobby: Does not.

Patsy is a good friend of Bobby's, less so of Brad's, although the three of them hang out together, mostly swinging. Patsy has acne, a well-developed body for her age, and is already starting to go out with football players who have driver's licenses. Brad's mother makes derogatory comments about Patsy's family, something about her father having been in jail. Bobby's mother and Patsy's mother are good friends; they go to Mass together on Sunday mornings. Brad's family is Protestant and they never go to church, but he goes sometimes with his friends who go to a Methodist church.

Brad and Bobby head directly for the swings. Brad lays down on the sliding board backwards, his head down toward the bottom, every so often starting to let go, as if he is sliding down, then catching himself on the handles. Bobby swings on a swing, legs way out in front of him.

Brad: So did you ever see Patsy with her clothes off?

Bobby: Once.

Brad: You're cousins or something anyway, aren't you?

Bobby: No. She was just over playing.

Brad: Playing what?

Bobby: Chinese checkers.

Brad: And what happened?

Bobby: Well, we were looking at the stacks of my mother's *Playboys*.

Brad: Your mother's?

Bobby: Or my father's.

Brad: Yeah?

Bobby: So she said she'd show me and she took off her clothes.

Brad: What did she look like?

Bobby: Great.

Brad: How would you know?

Bobby: What do you mean, how would I know, I saw her.

Brad: Maybe if she put a bag over her face.

Bobby: Yeah, her face is pretty gross. But her body is beautiful. She has really big pointy breasts. And she has some hair you-know-where.

Brad: She just took them off? And stood there?

Bobby: She just stood there. And turned around. Then my parents were coming. The car drove up. And she went in and got dressed fast.

Brad: Remember that time your mother caught us?

Bobby: I don't think she saw anything.

Brad: Yes she did. I'm sure.

Bobby starts swinging so fast and so high now that he can't continue the conversation. Brad climbs back down the ladder from the sliding board. Goes for a walk in the backyard. He smells some bushes. Squats over a line of yellow flowers.

Brad: (shouting) Do all flowers open in the day and shut at night?

No answer.

Brad goes over to a green hose and turns on the spigot. He sits on the back steps and sprays water in different directions. A woman walks out of the house next door and comes over to the fence. She is all dressed up in a red tissue-papery dress that tutus out, going down only to her knees. She is carrying a box-shaped purse made out of glass.

Mrs. Evans: Do you have permission to do that?

Brad: Sort of.

Her husband comes out dressed in a light blue suit with a white carnation in the lapel. He stands tall and silent next to her. Bobby slows down his swinging and watches the confrontation, sitting balanced on the edge of his swing.

Mrs. Evans: How sort of?

Brad: We're all in a club. Of which Patsy is the treasurer. Bob over there is president. And I'm secretary. We share all property in common. If I was away, Pat could come sleep in my bed. That's how it works. Plus I'm doing her, them, a favor by watering their lawn.

Mrs. Evans: Well, this isn't Patsy's house. It belongs to her parents. And since they don't belong to your club, I think you'd better get moving.

Brad gets up and turns off the hose. Then he walks back to the swings and cricks his neck, motioning to Bobby to come with him. They head for the back wood fence and start to boost themselves over.

Mrs. Evans: Not that way.

Mr. Evans: (simultaneously) Oh no you don't.

Brad and Bobby slump back to the ground. They walk past the Evanses, down the driveway, and are back on the sidewalk of Winola Avenue. Bobby turns around and says goodnight. They say goodnight back, almost musically, as they get into their Ford Galaxie. Brad just keeps walking, unwilling to forgive or forget.

They are walking down Winola toward Pierce Street, which is a big street filled with traffic, gas stations, tractor and truck repair factories. This is the street where you get the bus to go into Wilkes-Barre.

Brad: Let's do this. I'll say the name of the family whose

house we're walking by. And you say one thing about them. Then you say the name and I'll do it. Until we get to Pierce Street. I'll start. Flaskis.

Bobby: Tony Flaski plays basketball. One day he turned a hose on you and now you can't play with him.

Brad: Okay, you say the next name.

Bobby: Gleason.

Brad: Mrs. Gleason's husband died a few years ago. She paid us one day to paint her front porch. Smiths.

Bobby: The Smiths go to the same church you do. I always forget what they look like. They don't have any kids. McCarthy.

Brad: Her husband died too. And now her and Jamie McCarthy live in that garage converted into a house. He was in the car with the Kilgallen kid who was killed on the way back from Harvey's Lake on Fourth of July weekend. And he dropped out of school. Crease.

Bobby: Larry Crease made you kiss his sneakers one day on my front porch. My father saw it through the window.

Brad: I never did that I just pretended to do it. You can't tell the difference. Lease.

Bobby: Rob was one of the guys in the circle when we had that contest I told you about in the lilac bushes. Remember?

Brad: Next.

Bobby: Miknoffs.

Brad: Miknoffs are Jewish too. Marcia and I used to play Fish. She has a crush on me.

Bobby: And what's this creep's name?

They have come to the white corner house with a dentist's shingle hanging on a post by the driveway. On the back porch a thin-faced woman is sitting on a lounge chair made of flexible tan rubber strips leafing through a colorful women's magazine by the light of a mosquito-killing candle. She watches the boys go by, her eyes peering cautiously above the gloss.

Brad: (sotto voce) I don't want to talk about him. He's just a greaser hood. That's why he locked us in the cellar. We fixed him, though.

Bobby: You mean your father did, calling. Do you think she recognized us?

Brad: Let's stop. We're here.

It is now pitch black. Around nine o'clock. They are on Pierce Street with cars whizzing by. Lots of electric lights from headlights, billboards, stores, eating joints. The two of them look very small in the glare. They aren't talking much because there is too much noise.

Brad: (shouting) Let's get fruit.

Bobby: (regular speaking voice) What kind?

Brad: (shouting) Any kind. Wait and see.

They keep walking until they get to an outside fruit stand, the Orange Grove Market. They look around at the fruit, disappointed.

Bobby: Maybe a vanilla Popsicle.

Brad: Let's go to the Pierce Street Market.

Bobby looks a little shocked because that market is much farther away. Under the train trestle. Near the park and the river. But Brad has already started off so Bobby goes too. It takes about two minutes to pass under the trestle. Scared of being in the dark with cars passing much closer to their bodies, no division between sidewalk and street. Out into the artificial light again. Soon to get to the second market, which is actually a supermarket with cars parked in marked diagonal spaces. They go in the doors which zoom open as soon as Bobby stamps on the corrugated pad.

They head up the side aisle which is where all the fruit is, light beaming down, frigid air rising all around. Brad sticks his head in over the fruit, feeling the cold, smelling the insulated smell.

Brad: Which ones are you gonna buy?

Brad starts looking at the oranges. He wants an orange, but doesn't want to have to buy a whole plastic bag with a dozen. He just wants a fruit to hold in his hand and eat. Bobby heads straight for a coconut and picks it up, triumphant.

Bobby: Coconut.

Brad: What do you do with that?

Bobby: I know what to do with it. I lived in Florida for a while, remember?

Bobby's mention of living in Florida always scares Brad. He feels as if there are secrets to Bobby and to the whole world that he doesn't know. That anyone looking at him and Bobby could tell the difference in experience between someone who has lived in Florida and someone who has not.

Brad: How do you eat it?

Bobby: You get a hammer and you open it. Then you eat the white meat and you drink all the milk. It's sweet.

Brad: (zeroing in on one point) And just where are you going to get this hammer?

Bobby: I'll use your head.

Brad: (smugly) My head is more like a coconut than a hammer *for* a coconut.

Bobby: Come on, Brad. Make up your mind. Which fruit do you want?

Brad looks at the bag of oranges. Then at the bag of apples. Feels dissatisfied. Then he sees a pineapple and his problem is solved. Picks up the pineapple.

Brad: (holding it up to the light, exposing its different facets) Do they have these in Florida? I know they do.

Bobby: Millions of them. And in Mexico. Where we stayed at the South of the Border Motel. There they have tacos, which is a kind of sandwich but the bread is more cardboardy and inside is the best . . .

Brad: How do you travel so much? Your father just works in a brewery.

Bobby: There's a lot of money in beer. How much does your father make?

Brad heads off down the aisle, past all the cereals which interest him greatly, then past soups and mayonnaises which interest him less. When he gets to the front, Bobby, less wide-eyed, is already in line. Brad gets behind him. The girl weighs Bobby's coconut. He gets out change to pay. Brad tries to count how much Bobby has in his dirty palm. Then Brad gingerly hands her the pineapple, his hands stinging from the prickles. Brad recognizes the checkout girl as a cheerleader from high school. He averts his eyes. Sees Bobby off to the side with a big smile, trying to get Brad to show he recognizes her. Brad pays, feeling a slight stab as he has just spent one week's allowance.

Brad: (walking out, turning around to Bobby) I'm glad we bought these.

Bobby: Where do we eat them?

They are back on Pierce Street again. When they hit the first avenue after the trestle, Bobby motions with his head to turn down. Brad follows. It is dark. On one side of the street is the football stadium with another large field next to it for softball. The bleachers all around, empty, make a kind of curved dark hole where all noise stops. One of the tall spotlight scaffolds covers over strips of moon, like a fencer's mask. On the side where they're walking is the dark trestle. Trains only go by once every few hours. The first house is still about a hundred yards ahead.

Brad: Let's eat the fruit where we found all the fossils the other day.

Bobby: On top?

Brad: Yup.

Bobby: Are you gonna watch TV tonight?

Brad: I wanna see the presidential debates.

Bobby: I wanna see *Gomer Pyle*. Tonight's the night the sergeant gets the mumps.

Brad: Big deal. When the world's at stake. Let's go.

Brad and Bobby scramble up the trestle, which is about three stories high made, it seems, from a big slag of coal with train streaks running over the top. They keep losing balance and falling in the cutting coal. Their clothes are getting messy and ripped. Once Brad really punctures his palm by falling on top of the pineapple bristles. When he gets to the top, Bobby is sitting there, the moon making his face look like ivory.

Bobby: You have to grab onto the trees to get up.

Brad looks down and notices the trees growing unevenly along the side of the trestle. He had not watched how Bobby had made it.

They both sit down. Brad sits facing in the direction the big city. He can see the dark of the park, a silky string of river, the courthouse lit up with its bald dome to look like the Taj Mahal, and the top of the King's College building with spotlighted statue of Jesus Christ spreading his arms way out. Bobby sits on the other side facing their town. He just sees a lot of roofs and TV antennas. Since they're in a valley, eventually their eyes come up against the same curve of mountains with red

airplane-warning beacons spaced on the ridges every so often.
Brad comes back and joins Bobby.

Brad: I like it up here.

Bobby: You can't see the fossils at night.

Brad: How you gonna eat yours?

Bobby: Like this.

Bobby slams his coconut down on the train tracks. Milk spills
all over and the coconut breaks into a dozen big chunks. Bobby
bares his teeth and begins eating out the inside of one. He hands
a chunk to Brad who chews too. Then Brad takes his pineapple
and throws it against the tracks also. His pineapple just mooshes
into a lump, juice flowing out all over his hands and the rail. He
picks at a few pieces but is not really so interested. Bobby picks
up a chunk and sucks on it.

Bobby: Okay, since you asked before, what's your dream?

Brad: I haven't had any. I just watch that lady next door
through the opening in her fan. She sits there and reads books
all night and watches Johnny Carson. *Her* husband died too.

Bobby: What is it around here? All the husbands are croaking off.

Brad: What about you? Did you have a dream?

Bobby: Last night. A big one.

Brad: How big? What happened?

Bobby: Well, I dreamed I was on this operating table. Like
in a hospital. Or Frankenstein. This was in somebody's house.
I didn't have any clothes on. And I was strapped down to
this flat cold table with straps. And over this part (rubbing
his crotch) there was like a metal jockstrap that came down.
Timmy Wilson was in the dream. He's the one who picks on
me at catechism.

Brad: I know him. What's with him?

Bobby: I don't know. But he came over to my house once with his tape recorder.

Brad: What happened?

Bobby: Come on. Let me tell the dream. So this metal thing clamps down, and Timmy has this dial where he can send volts into my whole body through this. Sometimes he turns it off and on real fast, sometimes so high I scream, sometimes low and I just feel vibratings.

Brad: Did it feel good?

Bobby: Well. Yes and no. I mean, it was torture. But . . . And Timmy didn't have any clothes on. Except this white doctor's coat that was open. You could see his whole front. And his face kept changing. Sometimes he was mean. Sometimes not.

Brad: Well, he is sort of mean. In real life.

Bobby: And then he started getting really bad. Turning it up and up and it hurt. Then I woke up and I had to go to the bathroom.

Brad: (not wanting to stop) What did he say in the dream?

Bobby: Nothing. He just smiled. Or laughed. Oh and someone with a mask over her face came in with rubber gloves and they were cold and felt my body to check for temperature every so often. To make sure I didn't get killed.

Quiet for a long time. Then,

Brad: Did anyone ever eat a sundae off you?

Bobby: What are you talking about?

Brad: But we don't have any whipped cream.

Bobby: Eat a sundae how?

Brad: Like I could put pineapples and whipped cream on your pecker and eat it all off. Then you'll forget that dream.

Bobby: Yeah you'd like to wouldn't you?

Brad: Uh-huh.

Brad starts picking up the pineapple chunks and punching

makeshift holes in the centers with his thumb. Bobby looks around, unzips his zipper and lets his cock show out.

Brad: You have to open it more. Or your pants will get all sticky.

Bobby undoes his thin belt, lowers his pants a little. Has a thick cock and big balls with bristly hair all around. He sits gingerly back on the coal rocks, keeping his arms straight while leaning back to give himself some leverage. Brad slips the sloppy pineapple rings over. Bobby feels back with his arm, finds a coconut section with a puddle of milk still inside. He pours the milk over.

Bobby: Here. This makes it a real sundae.

Brad goes down, slurping theatrically as he eats the pineapple rings and licks off the sweet milk. The smell from Bobby's pubic hair is an intenser version of the sweet breezes of the night, but a bitter taste also cuts through the fruity pineapple and sweet creamy coconut milk. Bobby doesn't make a sound. Seems to be holding his breath.

From faraway the low tone of the train horn begins. It is still miles off. But the tone can already be felt in all the houses in the Valley, especially those near the trestle, a low, almost mournful sound, like a whale's call. Some people hear it through television soundtrack and just feel funny for a minute. Some people, especially young teen-age boys and girls, hear it from their rooms when they are lying on the bed, lights either on or off, and feel a strong pull, a real loneliness that has to be solved. Young kids hear it and are relatively unaffected. Animals perk up their ears for cars, but not for this. Brad and Bobby know they have time. Bobby feels it is up to him to listen so that when the train gets close enough he can warn Brad and they can scratch their way back down the trestle. Brad feels the train sound means more to him than to anyone else.

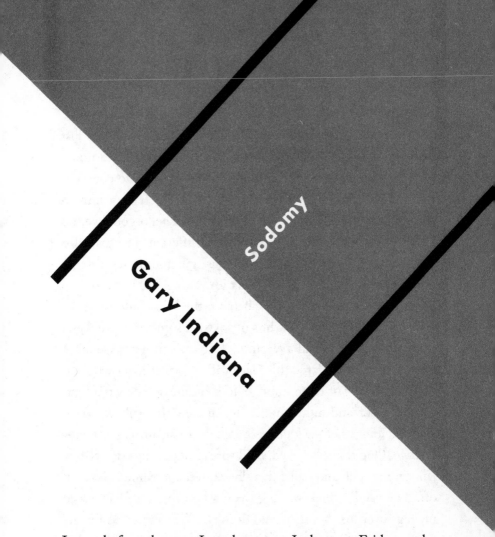

Sodomy

Gary Indiana

It was before the war. I used to meet Jack every Friday at the Oyster Bar in Grand Central. I was employed as a memory typist at a survey firm. Jack worked in publishing. He was my age, twenty-eight. He had the soft brown eyes of a southern boy, full lips and a strong chin. Jack worked out, he had an inspiring physique. His hair was the color of a motorcycle jacket. It looked very glamorous on him.

"Hiya, sweetheart," was Jack's normal greeting. I arrived early, he arrived late. An inflexible pattern.

"Jack," I'd say. "My prince."

He smiled a lot. Even his teeth were sexy. He liked my little romantic things. There was nothing binding in them.

"You look like a million dollars," Jack would say, not just being flattering. Between Friday night and Saturday afternoon, Jack found me totally enthralling. We never had two consecutive nights together and I knew we never would. If I saw him on the street with somebody else it was always hello goodbye, no kiss, no handshake even. Fridays were different. Jack paid for everything, the oysters, dinner, endless gin and tonics, often a bottle of champagne at the end of the evening. We went to strip joints and discos and fist fuck bars on the West Side to dance and score poppers or a few hits of coke. At some hour we'd end up at his place. He had a clean, dark apartment near Avenue A on East 13th. He shared this place with a former lover who was perpetually out of town, on nebulous business. Jack would put on some jazz and light candles, making an atmosphere. We'd smoke a joint, then Jack undressed me with an air of great confidence. One thing he liked, he'd spread honey and strawberry jam on his cock and balls, then kneel over me while I licked it off. The candles flickered big shadows on the wall. Jack eased my legs over his shoulders and drooled saliva across his fingertips, smearing it around my asshole and the head of his prick. He plunged in bluntly then froze with just the tip inside until my muscles relaxed around it, squeezing in deeper a half inch or so at a time. The shaft of Jack's penis was about ten inches long and almost two inches thick. Once he had it in all the way it felt like an iron pipe, but Jack knew how to make it nice, I'd tighten around it if he slid more than an inch of it out. I could twist over onto my stomach without losing any of it. Sometimes Jack carried me across the room, his arms wrapped around my thighs, fucking the whole time like an air hammer. In the mornings we fucked standing up in the shower, and usually once more on the carpeted floor in the living room, dog style, though this second fuck made both of us stoned and hazy for the rest of the day. I really had to struggle to get anything accomplished on Saturday afternoons the whole year and a half I was seeing Jack. But we were hungry for each other. To tell you the truth, Jack was about the only thing that made sense to me at the time.

As things go, it wasn't much. Jack couldn't make love cold sober on Friday, though he did fine on a Saturday morning hangover. The one time we skipped cocktails and the drugs, Jack barely could get it up and flung his wad in about two minutes. I wondered about that, after he apologized and fell asleep: did he invent his lust out of mere alcohol? Was it just convenient, after a hard week at the office, to fuck me instead of looking out for someone else? It's true we had sentiments about each other. But when we really scratched the surface of our real opinions and ideas, it was obvious Jack and I came from two distant planets. I wanted us to have more in common than we did, so I agreed a lot with Jack's dumb ideas; I'm sure he went along with mine, too.

In those last confused years before the war, it was possible for something like Jack's sexual organs to play a key role in my life, along fairly homely lines of supposedly vanquished stereotypes. He never let me fuck him, for example, pleading hemorrhoids. He went down on me from time to time, but mainly he played the man. It was fine for a while but it got boring. He could make me come with his dick, which isn't so common as people suppose; but I never came inside him, and I had the idea that this meant something important. Perhaps it didn't, looking back on 1978.

But there was this, too: I didn't love Jack, and Jack didn't love me. We liked each other's bodies, it went that far. The guy I did love didn't want anything to do with me, not physically anyway. Dean. Dean was an actor in off-Broadway, then. What attracted me to Dean was the certainty of rejection, added to a funny gambler's hope of somehow beating the house, seducing him through sheer will, making the unlikely blossom into heady passions like a million stale Hollywood endings. As a former resident of Nevada, I know perfectly well, and knew then, that no one ever beats the house. However, this never stopped anybody from dropping their mortgage payment on the table at Caesar's Palace and it didn't stop me from being in love with Dean.

Dean's appearance was nothing to write home about, so I figured I loved him for who he really was. He was tall and gangly and his face was full of odd scooped out angles and flatnesses. It had a certain grace, though. People sometimes said he was so ugly he was almost beautiful. Even if they never left out "almost," he was beautiful to me. He was a person for whom I'd gladly have given up my will, if you see what I mean. Anyway, Dean was my comet passing once, and strictly poison. Unattainable people usually turn out weak and ridiculous once your feelings for them go; that happened to me once with a junkie landscape gardener, and another time with an opera queen who had astigmatism. But a certain few prove strong and dangerous: that was Dean, all in all. My wanting him stirred up a deep-buried stratum of nastiness in Dean, an excessive viciousness that sprang from some copious childhood reserve. Some people run away from unsolicited attention, it's the usual thing to do. Others channel these surprising energies and put them to work, the way voodoo doctors set zombies out in the fields to plant cane.

I didn't see Dean so very often at first, because this type of relationship doesn't exactly improve your mental health, even if it does give you something to think about most of the time. We went to dinner occasionally, flirting desultorily and keeping the muck underneath at arm's length. Later, though, there were several periods of intense, daily contact. Dean wasn't a big talker but he had an eloquent physical vocabulary. Silence can tell you a lot of things. Large tracts of emotional sewage passed between us in a wordless miasma. I wanted him desperately. Dean enjoyed this with indecent detachment. Something hideous generally occurred when we saw each other with any regularity. The more I saw him the less I liked him, but that didn't affect my desire for him even slightly. In fact, as I peeled the onion of his personality to its dark center and found more and more to despise, the stronger my need to possess him became. Dean revealed himself as a creature of masks, a manipulator of ambiguities spun in silences as deadening and calculated as surgical anesthesia. After knowing him awhile I started tagging his masks and numbering them in my head. Whenever his blankness became too terrorizing for me to manage I'd do something spiteful to drive him off. Then I'd spend weeks rolling everything around in my head, finding obscure and noble motives for the rotten things he'd done, and in the end I'd miss him. There was something about Dean's physical aura that gave me a weird high. I always broke down and called him. And he always threw himself back into my life with numbing, amnesiac enthusiasm.

We were in a Mexican restaurant once upon a time, and I, with great tequila courage, said: "Dean, I can't see you anymore." I felt strong, too, because Jack had screwed me the previous evening. "I'm in love with you, I want you, you know, physically, and if that isn't what you want it's masochism for me to be around you."

Marimba music poured from two minispeakers near our table. Dean had heard all this before. It bored him. His long face took on a flinching, pained look that I'd recently decided to call Mask Number Three.

"I'm not ready for a physical relationship," Dean said. "I mean, we can be friends, and someday—"

"No, we can't. I can't just will my feelings away and act like they don't exist."

"I'm not saying you have to, I'm just asking you to give me some time."

"Time to do what, Dean? Excite yourself with my frustration?"

"Thanks."

My thought was: if I were a decent human being, I'd accept this situation as it is and love him that much more. But I'm not a decent human being. Decent human beings live in India and perform blessed works among the dying.

"It's making me crazy to see you, Dean. I want you every second. When you aren't there I think about you. Constantly. It's idiotic. You don't love me, I don't even understand what you find tolerable about being with me."

"I do love you, I've told you before, I'm too fucked up right now to get involved with anybody in a, a sexual relationship."

The sense in which we were already involved in a, a sexual relationship was one that didn't elude Dean, exactly. Looking at it now, I think he always had half his mind on what things looked like to other people, and how far he could go without becoming involved in his own actions. In the material sense of sticking parts of his body into holes in other people's. The mind, whatever its penetrative capacity, is, after all, photographically invisible.

"Then we should go away from each other," I told him, not very firmly. "It can only make me bitter against you to want you when you don't want me."

"If you love me the way you claim you do, you wouldn't insist on that physical thing, there are other ways to love people."

I considered these other ways while Mask Number Two, an expression of incipient and sensitively withheld lust, began working itself through the skin of Mask Number Three. Dean was never as convincing onstage as he was across a restaurant table. But we'd done this number so many times that I simply watched the morphology shifting, as if witnessing some geological process beyond my influence. I'd known him for seven months, and registered every nuance of his voice, his eyes, his fingernails. Nothing he did would ever surprise me again. When I tried to break it off, he turned seductive and coy, opened his legs a certain way in a chair, brought his body closer to mine in a room, lit my cigarettes, kissed my neck when my head was turned to the clock on the wall or the exit sign in a cinema; when I responded, he withdrew with a fluttering of petty details, an abrupt assertion of surface. Mask Number One was a glossy, impervious fish face that all desire bounced off like a superball, and its appearance was inevitable. When Dean needed an emotion he pulled the appropriate face out and held it up until the crisis passed.

"Relax," he said at last. Marimbas jingled in stereo as we laughed off another horrid moment. When I think about Dean today, there are always waiters on the periphery of my mental picture, flashing cocktail trays and setting down silverware. And unpleasant music playing, through high distortion speakers.

I never told Dean about Jack, but he must have known a Jack

existed somewhere: when I felt contented, and acted emotion-
ally detached, Dean switched on the full voltage of his charm,
became proprietary, gave notice to my person. He knew, he
must have known, must have studied the problem carefully: if
he'd fucked me in the first place he'd have lost all power over
me. That wasn't what I wanted from him. It was the tangi-
ble aspect of what I wanted him to be for me—my lover, the
person whose flesh was his bed. I wanted him beyond any
simple craving, as a metaphysical principle: not to fuck him,
but to disappear inside him.

This business of being in love, it's nothing but a little dance
around a straw puppet unless the other person plays. Everyone
knows this. What confused me in those days before the war was
that Dean did play, right up to the edge of carnal finality. And
there he flew away, to the next branch, like some mating parrot
in the Amazon. Without letting go of a thing, he kept himself
the most important thing in my life.

This all had its effect on my Friday nights with Jack. My taste
for disconnected sex was turning to nausea. His cock began to
hurt, though it never had.

"I can't, Jack. It's too much."

He pulled out instantly. "It's okay, baby. Let's get some sleep."

"In the morning, Jack."

"Sssh. Shut your eyes. Have a pretty dream."

I didn't even know I was crying. Jack wiped my face with the
heel of his palm.

"You got hurt, baby," he whispered. "How did that happen?"

"I don't know," I sniffled. Jack crinkled the cellophane on a
new pack of Camels. "Because . . . oh, Christ, Jack, because I'm
such an asshole."

A match lit up his face. He frowned, leaned over, and kissed my forehead the way you kiss a small child, holding his cigarette with thoughtful poise.

"We're all assholes," Jack said, with gravity. There was a cheap alarm clock near the bed, its face glowing dimly with a pinkish, defective-looking light. It was new. That apartment had hardly any natural light, waking in it was like waking underwater. We had never known exactly what time it was, on any particular Saturday, for a year and a half: hours had gone past like minutes, minutes like hours. The afternoon sun had always been a stinging surprise.

"I've never been good to you," Jack said, "except in bed."

"That's not true," I said. I kissed the warm flesh of his back. "You've been great. I'm just sorry I'm so fucked up."

I grabbed his arm and pulled him down to me, wriggling free of the sheet, wrapping my legs around his waist. I felt the head of his penis glide through the opening under my spine and pushed myself over his stiffening organ, folding him into me with a kind of mad insistence, arching over him as he lowered his back to the mattress, his lower back crushing my feet. I forced him through me and felt my insides tearing apart, ramming myself down on the thick, stinging prick until I could feel his pubic hair sweating against my balls. I freed my legs and shifted my knees, sinking my weight down against his lower abdomen and then slowly rising until the rim of his dick lay just at the edge of my sphincter muscles, holding him there and then delicately sliding the curled lip of flesh in and out of the slackened opening; I could feel the blood flowing in the veins of Jack's cock, and slid greedily down the hard tube of flesh, rose up again, and now Jack's hips began pounding him into me and out again, I braced myself with my fists buried into the mattress around his hair. I felt my bowels loosening and everything inside being pummeled into shit and blood and pure pain, and finally felt his sperm squirting through me like a random laser, rivers of it splashing across the walls of my intestines, the cock burning like coals as it shrank and very gradually slipped out of my ass and slapped against the sheet.

The bed felt wet and when Jack turned the light on we saw it was soaking with blood, both of us smeared with it, though it seemed to have stopped flowing out of me.

"Jesus," Jack said, pulling the sheet from the bed. He guided me into the bathroom, where he washed me gingerly with a face cloth and wiped the blood off his cock. "Wow, I'm really sorry."

"It isn't your fault," I said. "Anyway, I'm still alive, Jack."

We put a new sheet on the bed. Jack went into the kitchen and came back with a glass of orange juice.

"Have some juice," he told me.

"Oh, Jack."

We studied each other in the dim greenish light of the room. My brains felt scrambled, I could barely focus my eyes. Jack sucked on a Camel, looking bewildered and suddenly much older than himself. Neither of us wanted to say, but it was one of those strange moments when reality foams up around your ears unbidden, so to speak. I put down the juice glass and slid off the bed. Jack picked his underpants from the floor and pulled them on.

"Listen," I told him when I had my clothes on, "you've been great to me, Jack, don't ever think different."

He put his chin on my shoulder and said, "Someday we'll figure out that we really needed each other."

"Uh-huh."

When I thought about it later I realized it was the most upsetting thing anyone ever said to me. It was the last time I went to bed with Jack; a few days later I began taking a lot of speed and went through another strange time with Dean, the last one as it turned out. For some reason Dean was also taking a lot of speed, and since I had the better supply he began turning up at my apartment every morning to replenish himself. By this time I just thought of him as a jerk, and had difficulty finding my former interest in his awkward body and oblique manner. He had always been punitive towards me, but now he seemed coarse and brutal, too. The last day I saw him, Dean said something so baldly insulting that it gave away his contempt for me more directly than he'd intended, and I walked out of the room. Dean followed me into the kitchen. I poured some black coffee into a mug, paying no attention to him.

"Philip, do me a favor."

"What, Dean."

"Don't put on that wounded bird look. It just pisses me off."

"I'm not putting on any look. This happens to be the way my face is. I think I can look however I want in my own apartment, anyway."

"Well, I don't like it."

"I know you don't like it. You don't like it, you don't like it. Maybe you should go find something you do like and stop subjecting yourself to me."

A provocative, familiar silence. Long enough for me to catch myself and apologize. Long enough to read the New York telephone directory aloud.

"If that's how you want it."

"Dean?"

"What."

"This is all just words, you know."

"Meaning what."

"Meaning that we never really discuss what's going on between us, and you like to think if we don't discuss it that it doesn't exist, which is nice and safe for you, but I'm . . ."

"Listen to yourself, will you?"

"Listen to you, listen to the tone of voice you're using right now."

"You're crazy, Philip."

"I know that. So what. Who isn't."

"Yeah, but you're *really* crazy. Do you really want to destroy everything between us over nothing?"

"According to you there isn't anything between us. According to you I'm a nut case like that broad in *Play Misty for Me*, going bonkers because some guy won't fuck her. So why keep coming around, Dean? To cop amphetamine? Clint Eastwood wouldn't do shit like that."

"I care about you, shithead."

I realized we were on the verge of something really irrevocable and said it anyway: "So prove it, Dean. Get out of my life."

And he did. Slunk out, more or less, but with an atmosphere of great pride later on, as if it made any difference. So it ended with Jack and it ended with Dean, and I suppose something new might have started with other people, but then the war came, which ended a good deal one might have looked forward to. A few years later I ran into Dean in a back lot and we fucked on a mattress in a pile of rubbish, but I didn't realize until later that that was him, and I don't think he recognized me either.

The History of the World

Jim Lewis

This man Bill woke up in the big room upstairs in an old house on the edge of some fields where he lived. He blinked in the sunlight, and he rolled over, putting the pillow under his chest

* * *

The dream of a king affected the lives of thousands.   The mouth of the river is a strategic point.   If something was not like anything else it was ignored until it was forgotten.   It rains for days on end; crops are washed away.   As human beings evolve they retain the juvenile characteristics of their ancestors; large eyes, a less prominent jaw, and so on.   A lamb could and resting his chin on his crossed arms, and he listened to the local news on the radio on the table beside the bed. After a few minutes he rose and put on a pair of pants and a shirt and went down to the kitchen, where he put some water on the stove to boil. While he waited for it he wandered through the rooms downstairs; through the kitchen door and into the front hall, from the front hall to the living room, and from the living room to the room with the TV in it, where he sat on the couch and rocked sleepily back and forth, rubbing his thighs with his hands. When he heard the water in the pot boiling over and hissing on the stove's flame he went back through the living room and the front hall, into the kitchen, and he fixed himself some coffee. He spilled some hot water on the formica-top counter as he poured it into his cup.

As he sat at the kitchen table sipping his coffee he ran his hands through his hair. It was windy outside, and he watched through the back window as the wind bent the grass in the fields. What he was thinking about was what the wind was doing. Bill, he said to himself out loud.

He went back upstairs and he went into the bathroom, and he looked earnestly at his earnest reflection in the mirror, and he watched his hand move as he moved it up to rub the side of his neck. He brushed his teeth, and then he turned on the shower, and as he waited for it to heat up he went into the bedroom and sat on the edge of the bed and smoked a cigarette.

---

substitute for a person in a ritual sacrifice without diminishing the people's satisfaction.

We don't trust accounts of events given by people who were drunk at the time, or the insane, or by those who may have some reason for wanting the event to be seen in a particular way. Two-thirds of the earth's surface is covered by water. The domestication of animals helped end man's self-identification with nature.

Individual events of apparently slight importance create severe unrest among

It was a chilly morning, and as he dried himself off after his shower he shivered and goose-pimples rose on his skin. He put his pants and shirt back on, and he put on a pair of socks and a pair of leather shoes. He took a jacket from the back of a chair and he went back downstairs. There was a gun and a few loose bullets in a chest of drawers in the living room, and he carefully loaded the gun and put it in his pocket, and then he walked through the front hall and through the kitchen and out the back door.

He stood in his backyard looking at the things on the ground there; a bicycle with a flat tire lying on its side, a few planks of wood in a pile, some empty bottles, a bucket. He took the gun out of his pocket and felt its weight in his hand.

He shot at the bicycle without really aiming, just to hear the sound—it went *bang*, but the wind took most of it. The bicycle didn't move. He stooped down and picked up a bottle and threw it in the air and shot at it, but he missed, and the bottle broke when it hit the ground.

So he walked around to the front of the house and he stood in the driveway, looking at the road. There was a sign about thirty yards away that said "35 MPH" on it and he looked at it for a few seconds, and then he shot at it, and he missed. So he aimed more carefully, resting the top half of his body against the car. He put a hole in the metal in the loop of the "P," smiling at the sound it made. He put another hole right next to it. Then he

---

the populace.   Traditional folk melodies have no authors.

Some people come back and stay for good; some people come back and stay for a while before leaving again; some people never come back.   The distance between points A and B is indicated by the time it takes to walk from one to the other. They have many weapons but they lack spare parts, so many of them are unusable.

In all civilizations at all times it is common for people to expect the end of the world

walked back around to the back of the house and, after hesitating for a second at the line where the clearing behind the house met the beginning of the fields, he headed out across the grass towards a line of trees in the far distance. He walked slowly. Every fifty yards or so he stopped and turned to look at the house, and each time it seemed to shrink into the space between the ground and the sky. After a while he stopped.

He looked up at the sky, and he looked over to where it lightened before being cut off by the ground, and then he looked back across the fields to his bedroom window on the second floor of the house. He turned in a slow circle, and then he sat down. The grass came up to his shoulders and the wind blew through it, but the ground underneath was hard and still, and he sat there for a couple of minutes. Eventually he twisted around, cramped his left leg underneath him and extended his right leg in front of him, one arm resting on his knee, the other holding the gun off at an odd angle. And he stared at the rounded toe of his right shoe, and wriggled his toes underneath, and then he pointed the gun at them, inhaled, and fired.

There was a bang and the gun moved, and his foot went numb and he was lying on his back, and the ground was spinning underneath the sky for miles around him, and he felt a sweet, warm convulsion in his stomach and his throat, and he turned over, pressed himself up with his hands and vomited on the ground.

---

in their lifetimes.   A still-life of a wave of flowers hangs on the wall where there used to be a mirror.   Existence is not a predicate.
Constraints on gastronomic habits have their origins in hygienic considerations.   The word "delirious" comes from a Latin word meaning "ridge" or "furrow."   The party out of power calls for the implementation of austerity measure.   You owe everybody.   It is possible to control

He remained propped up like that for a while, his upper body perched on his arms, his hips on the ground and his legs wrapped around each other behind him, and when his arms grew tired he spat and pushed himself up until he was on his knees. It was quiet. He could feel his foot throbbing, and by pivoting his shoulders around he could see the ripped toe of his shoe, and he watched it leak blood onto the ground, and watched as the hard ground failed to absorb it. He looked over the grass to the house, on the edge of the fields.

His head was spinning and he got to his feet, but the first step he took shifted his weight to the wounded foot and his leg collapsed and he fell and swore. He had the odd feeling that he was lost, and a brief, urgent desire to find out where he was, and then he remembered. He got up again and started to hop, making it about twenty yards before he had to stop. He could hear himself panting. An airplane hummed overhead. He wondered how bad the bleeding was, and he started towards the house again, stopping from time to time to try to curb his dizzyness. He was sweating a lot. Once, when he had fallen again, he paused to unlace his shoe and he delicately pried it off, wincing and saying Ah! as the pain cut its way through the numbness and the throbbing. He threw the shoe off into the grass as far as he could. The house sat on the edge of the fields, and he made his way towards it.

It took him a long time to reach the clearing behind the

---

the temperature of each room individually.   The English language has no future tense.   In times of economic prosperity the role of women changes. Messengers bring news of troop movements along the border. Familiarity breeds contempt. Alcoholism is a disease.   As the measurement of time grew more accurate the 9-to-5 work day was introduced and standardized, resulting in an increased psychological division between work and leisure.

house, and when he had he stopped to look again at the things on the ground there; they seemed transformed. He was trembling, and his good leg was tired from carrying his weight, and he was afraid it would give way before he could reach the back door. He had been dragging his shot foot on the ground, and it was dirty. The wind blew across his face and chest. He was confused, and squinted at the house for a minute, and nearly lost his balance and tipped over. With a final effort he threw himself towards the back door of the house, opened it, and propelled himself through the doorframe with his hands, paused and looked around, and dropped into a chair by the kitchen table.

His coffee cup was still on the table. Nothing had moved. His sock was dark with clotted blood and soil, and he could see dark red streaks on the floor in a path from the door to his chair. He had tears in his eyes. He had a hard time thinking.

After a minute he pushed himself up from the chair and hopped over to the sink and turned on the water. Propping himself up on his good leg and grabbing onto a paper towel roll in a holder above the sink, he reached down with his right hand and pulled his other leg up and put it in the sink, leaning over backwards a bit to maintain his balance. Gingerly he pulled his sock off, rolling it down his ankle and then stretching it as much as he could. He felt it pull a bit as it separated from the wound, and it hurt.

He couldn't tell exactly what the gun had done; the individual

---

Every major city has a housing shortage.   Immigrants from another country are placed in internment camps for the duration of a war with that country.   The telephone rings a dozen times before someone answers.   Sunlight streams through the windows.   *E. Coli* makes many medical discoveries possible.   Self-immolation is a tradition. During an argument someone loses their temper and some objects are broken. Afterwards toes seemed to be twisted and crushed, there were a few small charred patches, and there was a lot of blood. It looked like a bit of pinkish bone was sticking out. He felt better because he could see it, and he touched one bit of protruding flesh lightly with the tip of his finger, and that made him feel better as well. Blood ran down the side of the sink, and the water from the tap diluted it and washed it in a circle down the drain. He maneuvered the foot with his hand, guiding it into the running water.

The pain was excruciating and he screamed, flinching backwards and losing his balance. He clutched at the paper towel roll but it came easily out of its holder and he fell backwards, his shoulders crashing into the table behind him and his lower back landing on a chair. The chair splintered beneath him and the table jerked backwards a foot or two. He heard the sound of his coffee cup rolling towards the edge of the table and he twisted and lunged at it to grab it before it fell. The table came down under his weight and he watched helplessly as the cup hit the floor and broke into dozens of pieces, and some of them disappeared beneath the refrigerator. After that it was quiet, and he could hear the water running in the sink, and he noticed for the first time that he had left the back door open. Bill, he said to himself out loud, Shit, and he laughed, half buried beneath the broken furniture.

He still held the paper towel roll in one hand; a broken chair leg was sticking into the small of his back, and he pulled it out

---

some time is spent wondering whether the damage is irreparable.   The development of a night-time economy is a result of the invention of the electric light, and an increase in the work force, and changes in moral beliefs.   If X equals Y and Y equals Z then X equals Z.   Garbage in, garbage out. The human body is the best picture of the human soul.   By bouncing lasers off of reflectors on the moon scientists can detect minute shifts in the earth's crust.

with the other hand. He sat up as best he could, and he started wrapping paper towels around his foot, the first few layers soaked up blood and were stained red. Eventually they formed big white clumps around his foot. He pulled himself to his feet and fought back the urge to vomit again. The pain had ceased and the throbbing had begun again, and he hopped back to the sink and took a bottle of aspirin from the shelf above it, emptying five of them into his hand and washing them down with water that he slurped from the faucet. He made his way into the front hall, and then hopped through the living room and into the room with the TV in it, and he fell on the couch, where he sat for a moment, breathing heavily and staring at the telephone. The wind made a slight, soft whistling noise as it blew through a crack in the window-frame.

The birth of the idea of a guilty conscience was as important as the birth of the idea of private property.   The plane has been delayed because of bad weather.   Incarceration is more sophisticated than exile. One hears sound effects instead of sounds.

The Angel

Patrick McGrath

You know the Bowery, I presume? It was on the Bowery that I first caught a glimpse of Harry Talboys. I was a writer in those days, and I lived in a five-story walk-up by the men's shelter. I didn't realize at the time that Harry Talboys lived in the same building, though of course I was familiar with the powerful smell of incense that contaminated the lower floors. It was high summer when I met him, high summer in Manhattan, when liquid heat settles on the body of the city like an incubus, and one's whole activity devolves to a languid commerce of flesh and fluids, the ingestion and excretion of the one by the other, and all sane organisms quite simply estivate. I was certainly estivating; I rose late in the day, and after certain minimal ritualistic gestures of the writerly kind made my way to the liquor store. It was on one of these errands, on a garbage-strewn and urine-pungent sidewalk, beneath a blazing sun, and slimed in my own sweat, that I first encountered Harry Talboys.

He was making stately progress down the Bowery with a cane. Let me describe him: a tall, thin figure in a seersucker suit the grubbiness of which, the fraying cuffs, the cigarette burns and faded reddish wine stain on the crotch could not altogether disguise the quality of the fabric and the elegance of the cut. Very erect, very tall, very slow, on his head a Panama hat; and his face a veritable atlas of human experience, the nose a great hooked bone of a thing projecting like the prow of a ship, and the mouth—well, the mouth had foundered somewhat, but the old man animated it with lipstick! He must have been at least eighty. His shirt collar was not clean, and he wore a silk tie of some pastel shade—pale lilac or mauve, I seem to remember; and in his buttonhole a fresh white lily. (I never saw Harry Talboys without a fresh flower in his buttonhole.) And as I say, he was making his way down the Bowery, and the men from the men's shelter drinking at the corner of Third Street greeted him warmly. "Hey, Harry!" they called; "Yo, Harry!" and he moved through them with all the graceful condescension of royalty, briefly lifting his Panama to reveal a liver-spotted skull devoid of all but a last few wisps of snow-white hair. Watching this performance I was much taken with the dignity of the old fellow, and with his lipstick. Was there, I asked myself, a story here?

Our friendship began well: he asked me into his apartment for a drink. Such a hot day, he said, hanging up his Panama in the hallway and leaning his stick in the corner; productive activity, he said, was quite out of the question. His accent, to my surprise, was old Boston. (I'm from the North End myself.) The odor of incense was strong, and so was the perfume he wore. He was very liberally scented and smelled, in fact, like an old lady, but there was, I detected it even then, something unpleasant about it, a nuance, a suggestion of overripeness in the bouquet.

Are you familiar with the apartments of the Lower East Side? Designed essentially as holding tanks for wage laborers, they do not err on the side of expansiveness. We entered Harry's living room. Crowded bookshelves, a pair of deep seedy armchairs that faced windows with a clear prospect north to the Chrysler Building, and between the windows, on a rounded, slender-stemmed table of varnished black wood, a vase full of lilies. Directly above the lilies, and between the windows, hung a large crucifix, the body of the Saviour pinned to a cross of white ivory with nailheads of mother-of-pearl. Hanging from the ceiling in the far corner of the room, on a length of copper chain, was the censer whence the fumes emanated. No air conditioner, no fan. There was, however, ice in the kitchen, and Harry made us each a large gin-and-tonic. Then he lowered himself stiffly toward an armchair, the final stage of this operation being a sort of abandoned plunge followed by a long sigh. "Cigarettes," he murmured, rummaging through the pockets of his jacket.

"You have no cats," I said.

"Dreadful creatures," he said. "Can't abide them. Your very good health, Bernard Finnegan!"

We drank. He asked me about my writing. I began to explain,

but he quickly lost interest. His gaze shifted to the window, to the glittering blade that the Chrysler Building becomes in the shimmering blue heat of certain summer days. His books impressed me. A good many classical authors—Petronius was represented, Apuleius and Lactantius, and certain of the early Christian writers, Bede and Augustine among others. When I rose to leave, he asked me for my telephone number. Would I, he wondered, have a drink with him again? Yes, I said, with pleasure.

"Gin?"

The censer was, as before, smoldering gently on its chain. It reminded me of my childhood, of chapels and churches in which I had fidgeted through innumerable interminable Masses. Harry's perfume, slightly rotten though it was, one grew accustomed to; not the incense. The stink of it was apparent as soon as one entered the building. I asked him why he burned it.

"Does it disturb you?" he said. He was slicing a lemon on the kitchen counter, very slowly. I was in the other room. The Chrysler Building was glowing in the dusk, and there were red streaks to the west, over the Hudson.

"It makes me feel like a schoolboy."

He looked at me carefully then, those watery blue eyes of his fixing me like a pair of headlights. "Are you a Catholic?" he said.

"Lapsed."

"I too."

He sighed. He became preoccupied. He appeared to be pondering our common connection to the Roman faith. "When I was a young man," he said, when we were settled in our armchairs, "I called myself a Catholic but I lived like a pagan. Oh, I could drink in those days, Bernard! I could drink till dawn.

Today, as you see, after one gin I become"—here he smiled with gentle irony—"desperately befuddled. But then! I was happy with my gods, like the ancients. Do you know what we thought the body was, Bernard, back in the Twenties? A temple in which there was nothing unclean. A shrine, to be adorned for the ritual of love! We lived for the moment, Bernard—the purpose of life was to express yourself, and if you were unhappy that was because you were maladjusted, and if you were maladjusted it was because you were repressed. We were excitable, you see, and if there was one thing we would not tolerate"—he turned toward me in his armchair—"it was boredom! Dullness! Anathema!" He gazed off into the night. There was a silence.

"Go on," I said.

"It didn't last. I remember coming back to New York in 1929 . . . My friends all seemed to be dead, or married, or alcoholic . . ." Another pause. "I don't suppose you know the *Rhapsody in Blue*?" He hummed the opening bars, and there was suddenly a tone, in the thickening and aromatic dusk, of intense melancholy, rendered all the more poignant by the slow, faltering cadence of the old man's melody. He said little more that evening, and when I rose to leave he was distant and abstracted. He did apologize, though, for being "such a wretched host."

The summer progressed. In a gin-blurred heat haze we slipped into August. I spent two or three hours a day at my table and told myself I was working. In fact I made several verbal sketches of Harry Talboys; to what use I would put them I had no clear idea at the time.

The thunderstorms began—brief showers of intense rain, with lightning and thunder, which did nothing to disturb the pall of stale heat that clung to the stinking city. They ended as

suddenly as they began, and left the streets still steaming and
fetid. It occurred to me that I should more actively prompt
Harry to reminisce. I wondered if, between us, we might not
produce a memoir of the Twenties? We would call it *An Old
Man Remembers the Jazz Age*, or something of the sort; lavishly
illustrated with photographs from the period, it would stand
as an expressive personal document of modern America in the
innocent exuberance of its golden youth. The more I thought
about it, the surer I felt that such a book was needed. I mentioned the idea to Harry when next I saw him. "I knew an angel
once," he murmured. "That was in the Twenties."

It was, they said, the hottest summer in thirty years, and there
was a distinct possibility that the garbage men would go on
strike. A rather grisly murder occurred in an abandoned building over on Avenue C; the body was mutilated and drained
of all its blood. The *New York Post* suggested that a vampire
was on the loose. My own habits became increasingly nocturnal, and my productivity declined still further. I did manage to
spend one afternoon in the public library looking at material
from the Twenties, and made up a list of questions to put to
Harry, questions which I hoped would release a rich flow of
anecdotes. I felt like a prospector: if only, I thought, I could
sink my probe with enough precision, up would gush the stuff
to make us both some real money. The times were right, I
became more certain than ever, for *An Old Man Remembers the
Jazz Age*.

But Harry was harder to draw out than I'd anticipated.
When next I broached the topic—it was a Friday evening, and
the sunset was gorgeous—he spoke again of his angel. He was
relaxed and affable, I remember, and I humored him. "You mean

metaphorically he was an angel, Harry," I said. "You mean he was a very good man."

"Oh, no," said Harry, turning toward me. "No, he was not a good man at all!" The armchairs were, as usual, facing the windows, angled only slightly toward each other, so we sat as if piloting some great craft into the darkling sky. "But he was a real angel, absolutely authentic."

"Who was he, Harry?"

"His name," said Harry, "was Anson Havershaw." He sat forward and peered at me. "You do want to hear the story?" he said. "I should hate to bore you."

When was it, precisely, that I began to take Harry's angel seriously? I suppose there was something in the tale that caught my imagination immediately. He described to me how, as a very young man, and fresh from Harvard, he had glimpsed across the floor of an elegant New York speakeasy a man who bore a striking resemblance to himself. "An uncanny physical likeness," said Harry. "Perfectly extraordinary." He had lost sight of the man, and spent an hour looking for him, without success. He returned to the speakeasy night after night; a week later he saw him again. He introduced himself. The other was Anson Havershaw, a wealthy and sophisticated young dandy, "a much more polished character than I," said Harry, "and he recognized the similarity between us at once; it amused him. He asked me to lunch with him the following day at the Biltmore, and said that we should become friends."

All light had faded from the sky by this point. There was a long pause. "Well, we did become friends," said Harry at last, "very good friends indeed. Oh, enough, Bernard!" He was sitting with one long leg crossed over the other, ankles sockless, his left hand clutching his right shoulder and his gaze fixed on the distant spire, which glittered in the darkness like a dagger. All the tension, all the vitality seemed suddenly to drain out of him. He sat there deflated and exhausted. The room was by this time full of shadows, and Harry was slumped in his armchair like a corpse. The exertion involved in his flight of memory seemed to have sharpened the foul smell that clung to him, for the perfume could no longer mask it at all. I moved quietly to the door. "Call me," I said, "when you want to continue." A hand flapped wearily from the arm of the chair. I left him there, alone in the shadows.

"It was some weeks later, when we were on terms of intimacy," said Harry, when next we met, "that Anson first invited me to his house. The front door was opened by his valet, an Englishman called Allardice. He showed me into Anson's dressing room and left me there.

"I settled myself to wait. After a few minutes Anson entered in a silk dressing gown of Chinese design, followed by Allardice. He greeted me warmly and asked if Allardice could get me anything; then he told me to talk to him while he dressed—or rather, while Allardice dressed him."

A long pause here; Harry's fingers were kneading the arm of the chair. Then he began to speak quickly and warmly. "Anson stepped up to the glass and slipped the gown from his shoulders; he stood there quite naked, with one foot advanced and turned very slightly outwards, and his fingers caught lightly on his hips. How tall and slender, and hairless he was! And white, Bernard, white as milk!"

Harry at this point sat up quite erect in his armchair and lifted a hand to sketch Anson's figure in the air before him.

"He had a neck like the stem of a flower," he said softly, "and narrow shoulders; and his chest was very flat, and very finely nippled, and merged imperceptibly into a belly punctuated by the merest suggestion of a navel. He stood before the glass and gazed at himself with all the impersonal admiration he might have expended on a piece of fine porcelain or a Ming vase, as though he knew he was quite beautiful, and suffered no impulse to humility on the point . . ."

Harry turned to me and held out his glass. There were pearls of perspiration on his forehead, and his smell was very bad. I gave him more gin. "Then," he went on, "he had me come close and examine his body. There was a slight flap of skin midway between his hipbones, and believe me, Bernard, a flap is all it was; there was no knot to it. It was"—Harry groped for words—"vestigial! It was . . . decorative!"

Silence in that gloom-laden and incense-reeking room.

"I asked him what he was. 'I have not your nature,' he said quite simply. 'I am of the angels.'"

Harry's gaze shifted back to the open window. "The dressing proceeded," he whispered, "and when Anson looked upon his final perfection, Allardice came forward with a flower for his buttonhole—an orchid, I think it was; and then at last the hush and reverence were banished. 'Come, Harry,' he cried, and together we glided down the stairs, with Allardice, close behind, intent upon the flurry of instructions Anson was giving him with regard to the evening. I was, I suppose, utterly mystified, and utterly intoxicated by this time, for I followed him; I followed him like a shadow . . ."

Harry fell silent again. His hand was still lifted in the air, and trembling, as he stared out of the window. As for myself, I felt suddenly impatient of this talk. These, I said to myself, are nothing but the gin-fired fantasies of a maudlin old queen. I muttered some excuse and left; Harry barely noticed.

There comes a day, in the ripe maturity of late summer, when you first detect a suggestion of the season to come; often as subtle as a play of evening light against familiar bricks, or the drift of a few brown leaves descending, it signals imminent release from savage heat and intemperate growth. You anticipate cool, misty days, and a slow, comely decadence in the order of the natural. Such a day now dawned; and my pale northern soul, in its pale northern breast, quietly exulted as the earth slowly turned its face from the sun. This quickening of the spirit was accompanied, in my relationship with Harry, by disillusion and withdrawal. Oddly enough, though, I spoke of his angel to no one; it was as though I'd tucked it into some dark grotto of my brain, there to hold it secret and inviolate.

The murder victim of Avenue C, ran the prevailing theory, was a double-crosser involved in a major drug deal. The nastiness was presumed to be a warning to others not to make the same mistake. The garbage men went out on strike for three days, but a settlement was reached before things really began to go bad, and the trucks were soon rolling again—stinking ripely and clouded with insects, noxious monsters trumpeting and wheezing through the midnight streets. The one that serviced my block was called *The Pioneer*, and on the side of it was painted a covered wagon rumbling across some western prairie. When I found myself downwind of *The Pioneer*, I thought, unkindly, of Harry.

It was at around this time that I began to toy with the notion of a historical novel about heretics. I'd chanced upon a gnostic tale in which Satan, a great god, creates a human body and persuades a spirit called Arbal-Jesus to project his being into it for a few moments. Arbal-Jesus complies with Satan's seemingly innocent request, but once inside the body he finds himself trapped, and cannot escape. He screams in agony, but Satan only laughs; and then mocks his captive by sexually violating him. Arbal-Jesus' only consolation is that another spirit accompanies him in the body, and guarantees his release. That spirit is Death.

But then the brief taste of fall vanished, and the heat returned with greater ferocity than ever. On my way out one morning I met Harry. "Bernard," he said, "why do I never see you now?" I felt guilty. He looked rather more seedy than usual; his jaw was stubbled with fine white hairs, and traces of dried blood adhered to his nostrils. His bony fingers clutched my arm. "Come down this evening," he said. "I have gin." Poor old man, I thought, lonely and shabby, scraping about in two rooms after all these years . . . why does he still cling to the raft?

I knocked on Harry's door around seven. All was as usual—the smells, the gin, the Chrysler Building rising like a jeweled spearhead against the sky, and upon Harry's wall the crucifix shining in the shadows of the fading day. Poor old Harry; I sensed immediately he wanted to continue with his story, but was holding back out of deference to me. I felt compelled to reopen the subject, though not simply out of courtesy to an old man's obsession. I had been thinking some more about this shadowy figure, the beautiful, decadent Anson Havershaw, he of the milk-white flesh and the nonexistent navel, and about Harry's cryptic but no doubt carnal relationship with him. It was, I felt, a most bizarre fiction he had begun to weave about a man who, I presumed, had in fact actually existed, and indeed might still be alive.

So Harry began to talk. He described how Anson swept him into a summer of hectic and dazzling pleasures, of long nights, riotous and frenzied, when all of America seemed to be convulsed in a spasm of fevered gaiety, and the two of them had moved through the revels like a pair of gods, languid, elegant, twin souls presiding with heavy-lidded eyes over the nation's binge. That summer, the summer of 1925, Harry often found himself leaving Anson's house in the first light of dawn, still in evening clothes, and slipping into the welcome gloom of St. Ignatius Loyola on Park Avenue. "You wouldn't know it, Bernard," he said; "they tore it down in 1947. A lovely church, Gothic Revival; I miss it . . . at the early Mass it would be lit only by the dim, blood-red glow from the stained-glass windows, and by a pair of white candles that rose from gilded holders on either side of the altar and threw out a gorgeous, shimmering halo . . . The priest I knew well, an ascetic young Jesuit; I remember how his pale face caught the candlelight as he turned to the congregation—the whole effect was so strangely beautiful, Bernard, if you had seen it you would understand the attraction Catholicism held for so many of us . . . it was the emotional appeal, really; disciplined Christianity we found more difficult to embrace . . ."

Harry rambled on in this vein for some minutes, his eyes on the spire and his fingers curled about his glass. My own thoughts drifted off down parallel tracks, lulled comfortably by his voice. As a raconteur Harry was slow and fastidious; he composed his sentences with scrupulous care and lingered indulgently over his more graceful phrases. "I doubt I would have done well in business," he was saying, inconsequentially; "I just haven't the kidney for it. One needs strong nerves, and I was always much too effete. Anson used to say that the world was a brothel, and he was right, of course. So where is one to turn? I can tell you where I turned: straight into the arms of Mother Church!" He swallowed the rest of his gin. "But that's another story, and forgive me, Bernard, I seem to be digressing again. All this happened so very long ago, you see, that I tend to confuse the order in which things occurred . . .

"There are two questions, Bernard, that have to be addressed to an angel. One concerns his origins; the other, his purpose."

At these words I began to pay active attention once more. This angel business was, of course, nonsense; but I had come to suspect that something rather fantastic, or even perverse, might lie behind it.

"About his origins I could learn almost nothing," Harry continued. "People said he arrived in New York during the last year of the first war; he had apparently been raised in Ireland by his mother, who was from Boston and had married into an obscure branch of the Havershaws of Cork, an eccentric family, so they said; but then, you see, well-born Europeans with cloudy origins have always been drifting into New York, and so long as their manners and their money are adequate—particularly the latter—they're admitted to society and no one's very bothered about where they've come from. We are, after all, a republic."

Boston! At the mention of Boston an idea suddenly occurred to me. Harry was old Boston, this I knew, and I wondered whether this angel of his might be nothing more than an elaborate sexual disguise. Anson Havershaw, by this theory, was simply an alter ego, a detached figment of Harry's neurotic imagination, a double or other constructed as a sort of libidinal escape valve. In other words, Harry transcended his own guilty carnality by assuming at one remove the identity of an angel—this would explain the physical resemblance between the two, and the contradictory themes of hedonism and spirituality; what Catholic, after all, lapsed or otherwise, could ever believe the body was a temple in which nothing was unclean? I watched Harry smiling to himself, and his expression, in the twilight, and despite the patrician dignity of the nose, seemed suddenly silly, pathetic.

"And his purpose?" I said drily.

"Ah." The pleasure slowly ebbed from his face, and he began to make an unpleasant sucking noise with his dentures. "Who knows?" he said at last. "Who knows what an angel would be doing in a century like this one? Maybe he was just meant to be an angel for our times." There was a long pause. "Immortal spirit burned in him, you see . . . Sin meant nothing to him; he was pure soul. This was his tragedy."

"His tragedy?"

Harry nodded. "To be pure soul in an age that would not believe its existence." He asked me to give him more gin. I was feeling very irritable as I poured his gin.

We sat there, Harry and I, in silence, he no doubt contemplating these spurious memories of his, while I wondered how soon I could decently escape. Harry had taken from his pocket a small jade compact and was powdering his face with rapid, jerky movements, his eyes averted from me so I had only the beaky profile. "Pure soul," he repeated, in a murmur, "in an age that would not believe its existence."

"What happened to him?" I said wearily.

"Oh," he replied, snapping shut the compact, "I lost sight of him. I believe he came to a bad end; I believe he was sent to prison."

"No he wasn't."

Harry looked at me sharply. There was, for the first time in our relationship, a genuinely honest contact between us. All the rest had been indulgence on his part and acquiescence on mine. "Am I so transparent?" he said. "I suppose I must be. Dear Bernard, you're angry with me."

I rose to my feet and moved to the window and stared into the night. "I don't think Anson Havershaw ever existed," I said. "There was instead a man consumed with guilt who created a fairy story about angels and spirits in order to conceal certain truths from himself." Why, I thought, do old drunks always choose me to tell their stories to?

"I haven't told you the complete truth," said Harry.

"There was no Anson Havershaw," I said.

"Oh there was, there was. There is," said Harry. A pause. Then: "There was no Harry Talboys."

I turned. This I was not prepared for.

"I am Anson Havershaw."

I laughed.

He nodded. "I shall show you," he said, and rising to his feet, he began laboriously to remove his jacket, and then to unbutton his shirt.

In the middle of Harry's ceiling was a fixture into which three light bulbs were screwed. A short length of chain hung from it; Harry pulled the chain, and the room was flooded with a harsh raw light. Beneath his shirt, it now became apparent, he wore a garment of some sort of off-white surgical plastic. Slowly he removed his shirt. The plastic, which was quite grubby, encased him like a sleeveless tunic from his upper chest to a line somewhere below the belt of his trousers. It was fastened down the side by a series of little buckles, and a very narrow fringe of dirty gauze peeped from the upper edge, where the skin was rubbed to an angry rash. Harry's arms were the arms of a very old man, the flesh hanging from the bone in loose white withered flaps. He smiled slightly, for I suppose I must have been gazing with horrified curiosity at this bizarre corset of his. I was standing close to the incense, and as Harry fumbled with the buckles I brought the censer up under my nose; for the smell rapidly became very bad indeed. He dropped his trousers and underpants. The corset extended to his lower belly, forming a line just above a hairless pubis and a tiny, uncircumcised penis all puckered up and wrinkled in upon itself. He loosed the final straps; holding the corset to his body with his fingers, he told me gently that I must not be shocked. And then he revealed himself to me.

There was, first of all, the smell; a wave of unspeakable foulness was released with the removal of the corset, and to defend my senses I was forced to clamp my nostrils and inhale the incense with my mouth. Harry's flesh had rotted off his lower ribs and belly, and the clotted skin still clinging to the ribs and hipbones that bordered the hole was in a state of gelatinous putrescence. In the hole I caught the faint gleam of his spine, and amid an indistinct bundle of piping the forms of shadowy organs. I saw sutures on his intestines, and the marks of neat stitching, and a cluster of discolored organic vessels bound with a thin strip of translucent plastic. He should have been dead, and I suppose I must have whispered as much, for I heard him say that he could not die. How long I stood there gazing into his decaying torso I do not know; at some point I seemed to become detached from my own body and saw as if from high up and far away the two figures standing in the room, the flowers and the crucifix

between them, myself clutching the censer and Harry standing with his opened body and his trousers at his ankles. It took
long enough, I suppose, for the full horror of his condition to
be borne home to me. This is what it means to be an angel, I
remember thinking, in our times at least: eternal life burned
in him while his body, his temple, crumbled about the flame.
Out there in the hot night the city trembled with a febrile life
of its own, and somewhere a siren leaped into sudden desolate
pain. All I saw then was a young man standing in the corner of
a shabby room watching an old man pull up his trousers.

As I write this it is late January, and very cold outside. Snow
lies heaped in filthy piles along the edge of the sidewalk, and
the Chrysler Building is a bleak gray needle against a thickening
winter afternoon sky. The men from the men's shelter huddle
in the doorways in the Bowery, selling cigarettes from off the
tops of plastic milk crates, and the smell of incense still per-
vades the lower floors of the building. I can't help thinking of
him as Harry—it seems somehow to suit him better. He asked
me to write an account of our friendship, I wouldn't otherwise
have done it; writing seems futile now. Everything seems futile,
for some reason I don't fully understand, and I keep wondering why any of us cling to the raft. The one consolation I can
find is the presence of that other spirit traveling with us in the
body—a consolation denied my rotting friend downstairs, whoever, whatever, he is.

River of Names

Dorothy Allison

At a picnic at my aunt's farm, the only time the whole family ever gathered, my sister Billie and I chased chickens into the barn. Bille ran right through the open doors and out again, but I stopped, caught by a shadow moving over me. My cousin, Tommy, eight years old as I was, swung in the sunlight with his face as black as his shoes—the rope around his neck pulled up into the sunlit heights of the barn, fascinating, horrible. Wasn't he running ahead of us? Someone came up behind me. Someone began to scream. My mama took my head in her hands and turned my eyes away.

Jesse and I have been lovers for a year now. She tells stories about her childhood, about her father going off each day to the university, her mother who made all her dresses, her grand-mother who always smelled of dill bread and vanilla. I listen with my mouth open, not believing but wanting, aching for the fairy tale she thinks is everyone's life.

"What did your grandmother smell like?"

I lie to her the way I always do, a lie stolen from a book. "Like lavender," stomach churning over the memory of sour sweet and snuff.

I realize I do not really know what lavender smells like, and I am for a moment afraid she will ask something else, some ques-tion that will betray me. But Jesse slides over to hug me, to press her face against my ear, to whisper, "How wonderful to be part of such a large family."

I hug her back and close my eyes. I cannot say a word. I was born between the older cousins and the younger, born in a pause of babies and therefore outside, always watching. Once, way before Tommy died, I was pushed out on the steps while everyone stood listening to my Cousin Barbara. Her screams went up and down in the back of the house. Cousin Cora brought buckets of bloody rags out to be burned. The other cousins all ran off to catch the sparks or poke the fire with dogwood sticks. I waited on the porch making up words to the shouts around me. I did not understand what was happening. Some of the older cousins obviously did, their strange expressions broken by stranger laughs. I had seen them helping her up the stairs while the thick blood ran down her legs. After a while the blood on the rags was thin, watery, almost pink. Cora threw them on the fire and stood motionless in the stinking smoke.

Randall went by and said there'd be a baby, a hatched egg to throw out with the rags, but there wasn't. I watched to see and there wasn't; nothing but the blood, thinning out desperately while the house slowed down and grew quiet, hours of cries growing soft and low, moaning under the smoke. My aunt Raylene came out on the porch and almost fell on me, not seeing me, not seeing anything at all. She beat on the post until there were knuckle-sized dents in the peeling paint, beat on that post like it could feel, cursing it and herself and every child in the yard, singing up and down, "Goddamn, goddamn, that girl . . . no sense . . . goddamn!"

I've these pictures my mama gave me—stained sepia prints of bare dirt yards, plank porches, and step after step of children—cousins, uncles, aunts; mysteries. The mystery is how many no one remembers. I show them to Jesse, not saying who they are, and when she laughs at the broken teeth, torn overalls, the dirt, I set my teeth at what I do not want to remember and cannot forget.

We were so many we were without number and, like tadpoles, if there was one less from time to time, who counted? My maternal great-grandmother had eleven daughters, seven sons; my grandmother, six sons, five daughters. Each one made at least six. Some made nine. Six times six, eleven times nine. They went on like multiplication tables. They died and were not missed. I come of an enormous family and I cannot tell half their stories. Somehow it was always made to seem they killed themselves: car wrecks, shotguns, dusty ropes, screaming, falling out of windows, things inside them. I am the point of a pyramid, sliding back under the weight of the ones who came after, and it does not matter that I am the lesbian, the one who will not have children.

I tell the stories and it comes out funny. I drink bourbon and make myself drawl, tell all those old funny stories. Someone always seems to ask me, which one was that? I show the pictures and she says, "Wasn't she the one in the story about the bridge?" I put the pictures away, drink more, and someone always finds them, then says, "Goddamn! How many of you were there anyway?"

I don't answer.

Jesse used to say, "You've got such a fascination with violence. You've got so many terrible stories."

She said it with her smooth mouth, that chin nobody ever slapped, and I love that chin, but when Jesse spoke, my hands shook and I wanted nothing so much as to tell her terrible stories.

So I made a list. I told her: that one went insane—got her little brother with an iron; the three of them slit their arms, not the wrists but the bigger veins up near the elbow; she, now she strangled the boy she was sleeping with and got sent away; that one drank lye and died laughing soundlessly. In one year I lost eight cousins. It was the year everybody ran away. Four disappeared and were never found. One fell in the river and was drowned. One was run down hitchhiking north. One was shot running through the woods, while Grace, the last one, tried to walk from Greenville to Greer for some reason nobody knew. She fell off the overpass a mile down from the Sears, Roebuck warehouse and lay there for hunger and heat and dying.

Later, sleeping, but not sleeping, I found that my hands were up under Jesse's chin. I rolled away, but I didn't cry. I almost never let myself cry.

Almost always, we were raped, my cousins and I. That was some kind of joke, too.

"What's a South Carolina virgin?"

"'At's a ten-year-old can run fast."

It wasn't funny for me in my mama's bed with my stepfather, not for my cousin, Billie, in the attic with my uncle, not for Lucille in the woods with another cousin, for Danny with four strangers in a parking lot, or for Pammie who made the papers. Cora read it out loud: "Repeatedly by persons unknown." They stayed unknown since Pammie never spoke again. Perforations, lacerations, contusions, and bruises. I heard all the words, big words, little words, words too terrible to understand. DEAD BY AN ACT OF MAN. With the prick still in them, the broom handle, the tree branch, the grease gun . . . objects, things not to be believed . . . whiskey bottles, can openers, grass shears, glass, metal, vegetables . . . not to be believed, not to be believed.

Jesse says, "You've got a gift for words."

"Don't talk," I beg her, "don't talk." And this once, she just holds me blessedly silent.

I dig out the pictures, stare into the faces. Which one was I? Survivors do hate themselves, I know, over the core of fierce self-love, never understanding, always asking, "Why me and not her, not him?" There is such mystery in it, and I have hated myself as much as I have loved others, hated the simple fact of my own survival. Having survived, am I supposed to say something, do something, be something?

I loved my Cousin Butch. He had this big old head, pale thin hair, and enormous, watery eyes. All the cousins did, though

Butch's head was the largest, his hair the palest. I was the dark-headed one. All the rest of the family seemed pale carbons of each other in shades of blond, though later on everybody's hair went brown or red and I didn't stand out so. Butch and I stood out then—I because I was so dark and fast, and he because of that big head and the crazy things he did. Butch used to climb on the back of my Uncle Lucius's truck, open the gas tank and hang his head over, breathe deeply, strangle, gag, vomit, and breathe again. It went so deep, it tingled in your toes. I climbed up after him and tried it myself, but I was too young to hang on long, and I fell heavily to the ground, dizzy and giggling. Butch could hang on, put his hand down into the tank and pull up a cupped palm of gas, breathe deep and laugh. He would climb down roughly, swinging down from the door handle, laughing, staggering, and stinking of gasoline. Someone caught him at it. Someone threw a match. "I'll teach you."

Just like that, gone before you understand.

I wake up in the night screaming, "No, no, I won't!" Dirty water rises in the back of my throat, the liquid language of my own terror and rage. "Hold me. Hold me." Jesse rolls over on me; her hands grip my hipbones tightly.

"I love you. I love you. I'm here," she repeats.

I stare up into her dark eyes, puzzled, afraid. I draw a breath in deeply, smile my bland smile. "Did I fool you?" I laugh, rolling away from her. Jesse punches me playfully, and I catch her hand in the air.

"My love," she whispers, and cups her body against my hip, closes her eyes. I bring my hand up in front of my face and watch the knuckles, the nails as they tremble, tremble. I watch her for a long time while she sleeps, warm and still against me.

James went blind. One of the uncles got him in the face with homebrewed alcohol.

Lucille climbed out the front window of Aunt Raylene's house and jumped. They said she jumped. No one said why.

My uncle Matthew used to beat my Aunt Raylene. The twins, Mark and Luke, swore to stop him, pulled him out in the yard one time, throwing him between them like a loose bag of grain. Uncle Matthew screamed like a pig coming up for slaughter. I got both my sisters in the tool shed for safety, but I hung back to watch. Little Bo came running out of the house, off the porch, feet first into his daddy's arms. Uncle Matthew started swinging him like a scythe, going after the bigger boys, Bo's head thudding their shoulders, their hips. Afterward, Bo crawled around in the dirt, the blood running out of his ears and his tongue hanging out of his mouth, while Mark and Luke finally got their daddy down. It was a long time before I realized that they never told anybody else what had happened to Bo.

Randall tried to teach Lucille and me to wrestle. "Put your hands up." His legs were wide apart, his torso bobbing up and down, his head moving, constantly. Then his hand flashed at my face. I threw myself back into the dirt, lay still. He turned to Lucille, not noticing that I didn't get up. He punched at her, laughing. She wrapped her hands around her head, curled over so her knees were up against her throat.

"No, no," he yelled. "Move like her. He turned to me. "Move." He kicked at me. I rocked into a ball, froze.

"No, no!" He kicked me. I grunted, didn't move. He turned to Lucille. "You." Her teeth were chattering but she held herself still, wrapped up tighter than bacon slices.

"You move!" he shouted. Lucille just hugged her head tighter and started to sob.

"Son of a bitch," Randall grumbled, "you two will never be any good."

He walked away. Very slowly we stood up, embarrassed, looked at each other. We knew.

If you fight back, they kill you.

My sister was seven. She was screaming. My stepfather picked her up by her left arm, swung her forward and back. It gave. The arm went around loosely. She just kept screaming. I didn't know you could break it like that.

I was running up the hall. He was right behind me. "Mama! Mama!" His left hand—he was left-handed—closed around my throat, pushed me against the wall, and then he lifted me that way. I kicked, but I couldn't reach him. He was yelling, but there was so much noise in my ears I couldn't hear him.

"Please, Daddy. Please, Daddy. I'll do anything, promise. Daddy, anything you want. Please, Daddy."

I couldn't have said that. I couldn't talk around that fist at my throat, couldn't breathe. I woke up when I hit the floor. I looked up at him.

"If I live long enough, I'll fucking kill you."

He picked me up by my throat again.

"What's wrong with her?"

"Why's she always following you around?"

Nobody really wanted answers.

A full bottle of vodka will kill you when you're nine and the bottle is a quart. It was a third cousin proved that. We learned what that and other things could do. Every year there was something new.

You're growing up. My big girl.

There was codeine in the cabinet, paregoric for the baby's teeth, whiskey, beer, and wine in the house. Jeanne brought home MDA, PCP, acid; Randall, grass, speed, and mescaline. It all worked to dull things down, to pass the time.

Stealing was a way to pass the time. Things we needed, things we didn't, for the nerve of it, the anger, the need. You're growing up, we told each other. But sooner or later, we all got caught. Then it was When Are You Going to Learn?

Caught, nightmares happened. "Razorback desperate," was the conclusion of the man down at the county farm where Mark and Luke were sent at fifteen. They both got their heads shaved, their earlobes sliced.

What's the matter, kid? Can't you take it?

Caught at sixteen, June was sent to Jessup County Girls' Home where the baby was adopted out and she slashed her wrists on the bedsprings.

Lou got caught at seventeen and held in the station downtown, raped on the floor of the holding tank.

Are you a boy or are you a girl?

On your knees, kid, can you take it?

Caught at eighteen and sent to prison, Jack came back seven years later blank-faced, understanding nothing. He married a quiet girl from out of town, had three babies in four years. Then Jack came home one night from the textile mill, carrying one of those big handles off the high-speed spindle machine. He used it to beat them all to death and went back to work in the morning.

Cousin Melvina married at fourteen, had three kids in two

and a half years, and welfare took them all away. She ran off with a carnival mechanic, had three more babies before he left her for a motorcycle acrobat. Welfare took those, too. But the next baby was hydrocephalic, a little waterhead they left with her, and the three that followed, even the one she used to hate so—the one she had after she fell off the porch and couldn't remember whose child it was.

"How many children do you have?" I asked her.

"You mean the ones I have, or the ones I had? Four," she told me, "or eleven."

My aunt, the one I was named for, tried to take off for Oklahoma. That was after she'd lost the youngest girl and they told her Bo would never be "right." She packed up biscuits, cold chicken, and Coca-Cola, a lot of loose clothes, Cora and her new baby, Cy; and the four youngest girls. They set off from Greenville in the afternoon, hoping to make Oklahoma by the weekend, but they only got as far as Augusta. The bridge there went out under them.

"An Act of God," my uncle said.

My aunt and Cora crawled out down river, and two of the girls turned up in the weeds, screaming loud enough to be found in the dark. But one of the girls never came up out of that dark water, and Nancy, who had been holding Cy, was found still wrapped around the baby, in the water, under the car.

"An Act of God," my aunt said. "God's got one damn mean sense of humor."

My sister had her baby in a bad year. Before he was born we had talked about it. "Are you afraid?" I asked.

"He'll be fine," she'd replied, not understanding, speaking instead to the other fear. "Don't we have a tradition of bastards?"

He was fine, a classically ugly healthy little boy with that shock of white hair that marked so many of us. But afterward, it was that bad year with my sister down with pleurisy, then cystitis, and no work, no money, having to move back home with my cold-eyed stepfather. I would come home to see her, from the woman I could not admit I'd been with, and take my infinitely fragile nephew and hold him, rocking him, rocking myself.

One night I came home to screaming—the baby, my sister, no one else there. She was standing by the crib, bent over, screaming red-faced, "Shut up! Shut up!" With each word her fist slammed the mattress fanning the baby's ear.

"Don't!" I grabbed her, pulling her back, doing it as gently as I could so I wouldn't break the stitches from her operation. She had her other arm clamped across her abdomen and couldn't fight me at all. She just kept shrieking.

"That little bastard just screams and screams. That little bastard, I'll kill him."

Then the words seeped in and she looked at me while her son kept crying and kicking his feet. By his head the mattress still showed the impact of her fist.

"Oh no," she moaned, "I wasn't going to be like that. I always promised myself." She started to cry, holding her belly and sobbing. "We an't no different. We an't no different."

Jesse wraps her arm around my stomach, presses her belly into my back. I relax against her. "You sure you can't have children?" She asks. "I sure would like to see what your kids would turn out to be like."

I stiffen, say, "I can't have children. I've never wanted children."

"Still," she says, "you're so good with children, so gentle.

I think of all the times my hands have curled into fists, when I have just barely held on. I open my mouth, close it, can't speak. What could I say now? All the times I have not spoken before, all the things I just could not tell her, the shame, the self-hatred, the fear; all of that hangs between us now—a wall I cannot teardown.

I would like to turn around and talk to her, tell her . . . "I've got a dust river in my head, a river of names endlessly repeating. That dirty water rises in me, all those children screaming out their lives in my memory, and I become someone else, someone I have tried so hard not to be."

But I don't say anything, and I know, as surely as I know I will never have a child, that by not speaking I am condemning us, that I cannot go on loving her and hating her for her fairy-tale life, for not asking about what she has no reason to imagine, for that soft-chinned innocence I love.

Jesse puts her hands behind my neck, smiles and says, "You tell the funniest stories."

I put my hand behind her back, feeling the ridges of my knuckles pulsing.

"Yeah," I tell her. "But I lie."

How Soft, How Sweet

Suzanne Gardinier

It is 1958 and snowing in Syracuse and my mother is transferring lumps of wet clothes from a washer to a dryer in a laundromat. The room is warm, windows beaded with steam, her coat, wool scarf, and mittens in a heap on a chair. Seated on a dryer next to the one my mother fills is my father, in loafers and a baggy suit jacket, reading aloud from *Dr. Zhivago*. It's the paperback copy they bought each other for Christmas. They have been married eleven days. For my mother the sound of my father's voice reading about the vast Russian winter and doomed love sounds like something from a movie: richer than her own voice, when she asks for more quarters or for him to repeat something, larger, more passionate and assured. It is the voice of the world, and as he reads she imagines him reeling out of Korean bars when he was in the army, or running the car he had as a kid into the pumps of the town gas station in a shower of windshield glass and blood. His strength is in his voice, she thinks, and listens intently, hoping it can be absorbed.

He reaches for an inside jacket pocket and a silver flask that was his father's flashes in his palm. He takes a long pull, holding the book open with his other hand, then leans toward my mother over the whirling circle of their clothes, offering the whiskey. This is a secret between them, there is no one else in the laundromat (no woman in sneakers folding sheets alone, no children bickering over dropped change, no old man asleep with no hat or overcoat), and the smell of the whiskey, its smoky taste, the effortless waves of confidence it brings, are funny to them, exhilarating, not essential. They laugh and the flask disappears, back to its place next to my father's heart, and his voice rises, breaks, giggles, recovers, keeps on. For an instant the gesture and the adolescent laugh remind my mother of her own father. With a flush of embarrassed affection she flicks the memory away.

When they supper together in the early dark they sit on the same side of the kitchen table in the tiny veterans' housing complex apartment, knees touching, feet close to a leased space heater, the snow falling more thickly outside. My father carves and forks slices of meatloaf from the crusted glass loaf pan, clanks portions of steaming mashed potatoes into their plates, and will not let my mother help, although she has prepared the meal. He spreads her paper napkin across her thighs, snaps the caps off their first bottles of beer and holds his in the air, proposing a toast.

His gaze leaps between her eyes and her lips, and he wants to tell her how much he loves her, how she has taken his crabbed, soiled life in her hands and unfolded it, smoothed it clean, how wondrous it is that she has let him touch her everywhere and not been ashamed. He has no words for this, and pauses, grinning, feeling the intense heat against the toes of his loafers and the cold of the beer bottle creeping to his wrist, desire gathering in his mouth and chest and groin, as it does at this time every night. She holds her bottle just above the tabletop, eyes fixed on his face—the miracle of beard grown from cheeks smooth that morning, the mouth eager for her in a way she loves and fears—and waits for what she expects from him always: words, to lift her from her constricted self, the way the smell of pipe in his sweater does, or the look of his name and photograph on identification cards.

"To winter!" he says, too loudly, "to cold, to shivers, to ten below zero!" His words are beginning to blur a little. He leans to kiss her neck and speaks into her skin. She is startled at the heat of his face against her, and at the shrill alarm of fear that clangs wildly inside at his blurred voice and his kisses, his knees now between hers. It is all so new, and yet oddly familiar. Not understanding, she closes her eyes and travels away from the clanging fear, so she can let him take her into the cold bedroom, under heavy layers of comforters, the meal and even the beer left unattended, although she can taste them on his breath.

She remembers sitting on her father's lap as he read her stories in his smooth tenor voice, eating crackers and Liederkranz cheese, his blunt fingers turning the pages, catching crumbs between them. As my father kisses her he can feel her escape, and he holds her more tightly, unfastens her clothes, trying to locate her and keep her close. Naked, he covers her with the length of his body, carefully supporting his weight with his arms, trying to prevent her departure. The effort arouses him, and as he pushes into her he thinks, *this will keep her, with this I will find her,* and listens desperately for signs for her presence, her pleasure. She is puzzled that he doesn't understand, that without the escape none of this would be possible; but she has no words for this, and can only allow a few sharp intakes of breath and a few moments' response from her hips to seep past her determined control, because she knows how this matters to him. Deep inside she tightens around him, and marvels at his fevered climb, his explosion. Then he is still, sad, far away. It's too hot, and she flings a sheaf of covers aside.

"I want to make children with you," he says into the dark, now on his back beside her, invisible and brave. Instantly he knows the words are not right, and searches for a joke, but only the crude and unfit come to mind. He wonders why she consented to marry him, and sees clearly ahead the narrow path he must walk to protect his good fortune. His body's ripples of pleasure ebb.

She is thrilled at what he has said, and contemptuous at the same time—how bald he is, how foolishly unprotected— and doesn't understand that doubleness. Again she travels, sits beside her father in his Chevy, on the way to Fort Dix to break her engagement to another man. He is there to protect her in case of trouble. On the seat between them in a snap-jawed box lies the ring. Suddenly she is worried that there is something effete about the way he holds the steering wheel, something weak in his posture or his jaw. What if something happens? Will he be enough? Panic races its fingers up her legs.

My father shreds his thoughts in search of words to redeem himself. The silence grows unbearable to him. Finally he tries her name: "Barbara?" he asks. "Barbara?"

Years later, when she is trying to move his leaden, unconscious body from the front walk to their bed, or when he lines up my brothers to be beaten, she will touch in her mind my father's declaration and his two soft questions as if they are a candle flame, and she must pass her fingers through to test herself, to see if she is still alive. But now his eyes are intelligent, still his own, and his hipbones rise on either side of his cock delicately, covered by only the thinnest sheath of skin. There is nothing about him of the heavy, clumsy drunk, the bully, the cold destroyer. Next to her he is all nervous hope and adoration. The sheets are warm with it. She curls against him and burrows her fingers into the hair on his chest.

Relieved, he encircles her with his arm and sleeps. As his breathing deepens she wonders why she feels so little, why she can't share his eagerness, his shudders, his awkward testimonies of love. She has always known she is beautiful; her father has told her this since before she can remember. Yet her body feels like someone else's. As she lies there with her head on my father's chest she admits for several seconds that it feels like a prison, in which she must serve out the term of her life. She touches her fingertips to her face. In this shelter I begin.

Secretary

Mary Gaitskill

The typing and secretarial class was held in a little basement room in the Business Building of the local community college. The teacher was an old lady with hair that floated in vague clouds around her temples and Kleenex stuck up the sleeve of her dress for some future, probably nasal purpose. She held a stopwatch in one old hand and tilted her hip as she watched us all with severe, imperial eyes, not caring that her stomach hung out. The girl in front of me had short, clenched blond curls sitting on her thin shoulders. Lone strands would stick straight out from her head in cold, dry weather.

It was a two-hour class with a ten-minute break. Everybody would go out in the hall during the break to get coffee or candy from the machines. The girls would stand in groups and talk, and the two male typists would walk slowly up and down the corridor with round shoulders, holding their Styrofoam cups and looking into the bright slits of light in the business class doors as they passed by.

I would go to the big picture window that looked out onto the parking lot and stare at the streetlights shining on the hoods of the cars.

After class, I'd come home and put my books on the dining room table among the leftover dinner things: balled-up napkins, glasses of water, a dish of green beans sitting on a pot holder. My father's plate would always be there, with gnawed bones and hot pepper on it. He would be in the living room in his pajama top with a dish of ice cream in his lap and his hair on end. "How many words a minute did you type tonight?" he'd ask.

It wasn't an unreasonable question, but the predictable and agitated delivery of it was annoying. It reflected his way of hoarding silly details and his obsessive fear I would meet my sister's fate. She'd had a job at a home for retarded people for the past eight years. She wore jeans and a long army coat to work every day. When she came home, she went up to her room and lay in bed. Every now and then she would come down and joke around or watch TV, but not much.

Mother would drive me around to look for jobs. First we would go through ads in the paper, drawing black circles, marking X's. The defaced newspaper sat on the dining room table in a gray fold and we argued.

"I'm not friendly and I'm not personable. I'm not going to answer an ad for somebody like that. It would be stupid."

"You can be friendly. And you are personable when you aren't busy putting yourself down."

"I'm not putting myself down. You just want to think that I am so you can have something to talk about."

"You're backing yourself into a corner, Debby."

"Oh, shit." I picked up a candy wrapper and began pinching it together in an ugly way. My hands were red and rough. It didn't matter how much lotion I used.

"Come on, we're getting started on the wrong foot."

"Shut up."

My mother crossed her legs. "Well," she said. She picked up the "Living" section of the paper and cracked it into position. She tilted her head back and dropped her eyelids. Her upper lip became hostile as she read. She picked up her green teacup and drank.

"I'm dependable. I could answer an ad for somebody dependable."

"You are that."

We wound up in the car. My toes swelled in my high heels. My mother and I both used the flowered box of Kleenex on the dashboard and stuck the used tissue in a brown bag that sat near the hump in the middle of the car. There was a lot of traffic in both lanes. We drove past the Amy Joy doughnut shop. They still hadn't put the letter Y back on the Amy sign.

Our first stop was Wonderland. There was a job in the clerical department of Sears. The man there had a long disapproving nose, and he held his hands stiffly curled in the middle of his desk. He mainly looked at his hands. He said he would call me, but I knew he wouldn't.

On the way back to the parking lot, we passed a pet store. There were only hamsters, fish and exhausted yellow birds. We stopped and looked at slivers of fish swarming in their tank of thick green water. I had come to this pet store when I was ten years old. The mall had just opened and we had all come out to walk through it. My sister, Donna, had wanted to go into the pet store. It was very warm and damp in the store, and smelled like fur and hamster. When we walked out, it seemed cold. I said I was cold and Donna took off her white leatherette jacket and put it around my shoulders, letting one hand sit on my left shoulder for a minute. She had never touched me like that before and she hasn't since.

The next place was a tax information office in a slab of building with green trim. They gave me an intelligence test that was mostly spelling and "What's wrong with this sentence?" The woman came out of her office holding my test and smiling. "You scored higher than anyone else I've interviewed," she said. "You're really overqualified for this job. There's no challenge. You'd be bored to death."

"I want to be bored," I said.

She laughed. "Oh, I don't think that's true."

We had a nice talk about what people want out of their jobs and then I left.

"Well, I hope you weren't surprised that you had the highest score," said my mother.

We went to the French bakery on Eight-Mile Road and got cookies called elephant ears. We ate them out of a bag as we drove. I felt so comfortable, I could have driven around in the car all day.

Then we went to a lawyer's office on Telegraph Road. It was a receding building made of orange brick. There were no other houses or stores around it, just a parking lot and some taut fir trees that looked like they had been brushed. My mother waited for me in the car. She smiled, took out a crossword puzzle and focused her eyes on it, the smile still gripping her face.

The lawyer was a short man with dark, shiny eyes and dense immobile shoulders. He took my hand with an indifferent aggressive snatch. It felt like he could have put his hand through my rib cage, grabbed my heart, squeezed it a little to see how it felt, then let go. "Come into my office," he said.

We sat down and he fixed his eyes on me. "It's not much of a job," he said. "I have a paralegal who does research and leg-work, and the proofreading gets done at an agency. All I need is a presentable typist who can get to work on time and answer the phone."

"I can do that," I said.

"It's very dull work," he said.

"I like dull work."

He stared at me, his eyes becoming hooded in thought. "There's something about you," he said. "You're closed up, you're tight. You're like a wall."

"I know."

My answer surprised him and his eyes lost their hoods. He tilted his head back and looked at me, his shiny eyes bared again. "Do you ever loosen up?"

The corners of my mouth jerked, smilelike. "I don't know." My palms sweated.

His secretary, who was leaving, called me the next day and said that he wanted to hire me. Her voice was serene, flat and utterly devoid of inflection.

"That typing course really paid off," said my father. "You made a good investment." He wandered in and out of the dining room in pleased agitation, holding his glass of beer. "A law office could be a fascinating place." He arched his chin and scratched his throat.

Donna even came downstairs and made popcorn and put it in a big yellow bowl on the table for everybody to eat. She ate lazily, her large hand dawdling in the bowl. "It could be okay. Interesting people could come in. Even though that lawyer's probably an asshole."

My mother sat quietly, pleased with her role in the job-finding project, pinching clusters of popcorn in her fingers and popping them into her mouth.

That night I put my new work clothes on a chair and looked at them. A brown skirt, a beige blouse. I was attracted to the bland ugliness, but I didn't know how long that would last. I looked at their gray shapes in the night-light and then rolled over toward the dark corner of my bed.

My family's enthusiasm made me feel sarcastic about the job—about any effort to do anything, in fact. In light of their enthusiasm, the only intelligent course of action seemed to be immobility and rudeness. But in the morning, as I ate my poached eggs and toast, I couldn't help but feel curious and excited. The feeling grew as I rode in the car with my mother to the receding orange building. I felt like I was accomplishing something. I wanted to do well. When we drove past the Amy Joy doughnut shop, I saw, through a wall of glass, expectant construction workers in heavy boots and jackets sitting on vinyl swivel seats, waiting for coffee and bags of doughnuts. I had sentimental thoughts about workers and the decency of unthinking toil. I was pleased to be like them, insofar as I was.

I returned my mother's smile when I got out of the car and said "thanks" when she said "good luck."

"Well, here you are," said the lawyer. He clapped his short, hard-packed little hands together and made a loud noise. "On time. Good morning!"

He began training me then and continued to do so all week. No interesting people came into the office. Very few people came into the office at all. The first week there were three. One was a nervous middle-aged woman who had an uneven haircut and was wearing lavender rubber children's boots. She sat on the edge of the waiting room chair with her rubber boots together, rearranging the things in her purse. Another was a fat woman in a bright, baglike dress who had yellow in the whites of her wild little eyes, and who carried her purse like a weapon. The last was a man who sat desperately turning his head as if he wanted to disconnect it from his body. I could hear him raising his voice inside the lawyer's office. When he left, the lawyer came out and said, "He is completely crazy," and told me to type him a bill for five hundred dollars.

Everyone who sat in the waiting room looked random and unwelcome. They all fidgeted. The elegant old armchairs and puffy upholstered couch were themselves disoriented in the stiff modernity of the waiting room. My heavy oak desk was an idiot standing against a wall covered with beige plaster. The brooding plants before me gave the appearance of weighing a lot for plants, even though one of them was a slight, frondy thing.

I was surprised that a person like the lawyer, who seemed to be mentally organized and evenly distributed, would have such an office. But I was comfortable in it. Its jumbled nature was like a nest of available rags gathered tightly together for warmth. My first two weeks were serene. I enjoyed the dullness of days, the repetition of motions, the terse, polite interactions between the lawyer and me. I enjoyed feeling him impose his brainlessly confident sense of existence on me. He would say, "Type this letter," and my sensibility would contract until the abstractions of achievement and production found expression in the typing of the letter. I was useful.

My mother picked me up every day. We would usually stop at the A&P before we went home to get a loaf of white French bread, beer and kielbasa sausage for my father. When we got home I would go upstairs to my room, take off my shirt and blouse, and throw them on the floor. I would get into my bed of jumbled blankets in my underwear and panty hose and listen to my father yelling at my mother until I fell asleep. I woke up when Donna pounded on my door and yelled, "Dinner!"

I would go down with her then and sit at the table. We would all watch the news on TV as we ate. My mother would have a shrunken, abstracted look on her face. My father would hunch over his plate like an animal at its dish.

After dinner, I would go upstairs and listen to records and write in my diary or play Parcheesi with Donna until it was time to get ready for bed. I'd go to sleep at night looking at the skirt and blouse I would wear the next day. I'd wake up looking at my ceramic weather poodle, which was supposed to turn pink, blue or green, depending on the weather, but had only turned gray and stayed gray. I would hear my father in the bathroom, the tumble of radio patter, the water, the clink of a glass being set down, the creak and click as he closed the medicine cabinet. Donna would be standing outside my door, waiting for him to finish, muttering "shit" or something.

Looking back on it, I don't know why that time was such a contented one, but it was.

The first day of the third week, the lawyer came out of his office, stiffer than usual, his eyes lit up in a peculiar, stalking way. He was carrying one of my letters. He put it on my desk, right in front of me. "Look at it," he said. I did.

"Do you see that?"

"What?" I asked.

"This letter has three typing errors in it, one of which is, I think, a spelling error."

"I'm sorry."

"This isn't the first time either. There have been others that I let go because it was your first few weeks. But this can't go on. Do you know what this makes me look like to the people who receive these letters?"

I looked at him, mortified. There had been a catastrophe hidden in the folds of my contentment for two weeks and he hadn't even told me. It seemed unfair, although when I thought about it I could understand his reluctance, maybe even embarrassment, to draw my attention to something so stupidly unpleasant.

"Type it again."

I did, but I was so badly shaken that I made even more mistakes. "You are wasting my time," he said, and handed it to me once again. I typed it correctly the third time, but he sulked in his office for the rest of the day.

This kind of thing kept occurring all week. Each time, the lawyer's irritation and disbelief mounted. In addition, I sensed something else growing in him, an intimate tendril creeping from one of his darker areas, nursed on the feeling that he had discovered something about me.

I was very depressed about the situation. When I went home in the evening I couldn't take a nap. I lay there looking at the gray weather poodle and fantasized about having a conversation with the lawyer that would clear up everything, explain to him that I was really trying to do my best. He seemed to think that I was making the mistakes on purpose.

At the end of the week he began complaining about the way I answered the phone. "You're like a machine," he said. "You sound like you're in the Twilight Zone. You don't think when you respond to people."

When he asked me to come into his office at the end of the day, I thought he was going to fire me. The idea was a relief, but a numbing one. I sat down and he fixed me with a look that was speculative but benign, for him. He leaned back in his chair in a comfortable way, one hand dangling sideways from his wrist. To my surprise, he began talking to me about my problems, as he saw them.

"I sense that you are a very nice but complex person, with wild mood swings that you keep hidden. You just shut up the house and act like there's nobody home."

"That's true," I said. "I do that."

"Well, why? Why don't you open up a little bit? It would probably help your typing."

It was really not any of his business, I thought.

"You should try to talk more. I know I'm your employer and we have a prescribed relationship, but you should feel free to discuss your problems with me."

The idea of discussing my problems with him was preposterous. "It's hard to think of having that kind of discussion with you," I said. I hesitated. "You have a strong personality and . . . when I encounter a personality like that, I tend to step back because I don't know how to deal with it."

He was clearly pleased with this response, but he said, "You shouldn't be so shy."

When I thought about this conversation later, it seemed,

on the one hand, that this lawyer was just an asshole. On the other, his comments were weirdly moving, and had the effect of making me feel horribly sensitive. No one had ever made such personal comments to me before.

The next day I made another mistake. The intimacy of the previous day seemed to make the mistake even more repulsive to him because he got madder than usual. I wanted him to fire me. I would have suggested it, but I was struck silent. I sat and stared at the letter while he yelled. "What's wrong with you!"

"I'm sorry," I said.

He stood quietly for a moment. Then he said, "Come into my office. And bring that letter."

I followed him into his office.

"Put that letter on my desk," he said.

I did.

"Now bend over so that you are looking directly at it. Put your elbows on the desk and your face very close to the letter."

Shaken and puzzled, I did what he said.

"Now read the letter to yourself. Keep reading it over and over again."

I read: "Dear Mr. Garvy: I am very grateful to you for referring . . ." He began spanking me as I said "referring." The funny thing was, I wasn't even surprised. I actually kept reading the letter, although my understanding of it was not very clear. I began crying on it, which blurred the ink. The word "humiliation" came into my mind with such force that it effectively blocked out all other words. Further, I felt that the concept it stood for had actually been a major force in my life for quite a while.

He spanked me for about ten minutes, I think. I read the letter only about five times, partly because it rapidly became too wet to be legible. When he stopped he said, "Now straighten up and go type it again."

I went to my desk. He closed the office door behind him. I sat down, blew my nose and wiped my face. I stared into space for several minutes, every now and then dwelling on the tingling sensation in my buttocks. I typed the letter again and took it into his office. He didn't look up as I put it on his desk.

I went back out and sat, planning to sink into a stupor of some sort. But a client came in, so I couldn't. I had to buzz the lawyer and tell him the client had arrived. "Tell him to wait," he said curtly.

When I told the client to wait, he came up to my desk and began to talk to me. "I've been here twice before," he said. "Do you recognize me?"

"Yes," I said. "Of course." He was a small, tight-looking middle-aged man with agitated little hands and a pale scar running over his lip and down his chin. The scar didn't make him look tough; he was too anxious to look tough.

"I never thought anything like this would ever happen to me," he said. "I never thought I'd be in a lawyer's office even once, and I've been here three times now. And absolutely nothing's been accomplished. I've always hated lawyers." He looked as though he expected me to take offense.

"A lot of people do," I said.

"It was either that or I would've shot those miserable blankety-blanks next door and I'd have to get a lawyer to defend me anyway. You know the story?"

I did. He was suing his neighbors because they had a dog that "barked all goddamn day." I listened to him talk. It surprised me how this short conversation quickly restored my sensibility. Everything seemed perfectly normal by the time the lawyer came out of his office to greet the client. I noticed he had my letter in one hand. Just before he turned to lead the client away, he handed it to me, smiling. "Good letter," he said.

When I went home that night, everything was the same. My life had not been disarranged by the event except for a slight increase in the distance between me and my family. My behind was not even red when I looked at it in the bathroom mirror.

But when I got into bed and thought about the thing, I got excited. I was more excited, in fact, than I had ever been in my life. That didn't surprise me, either. I felt a numbness; I felt that I could never have a normal conversation with anyone again. I masturbated slowly, to put off the climax as long as I could. But there was no climax, even though I tried for a long time. Then I couldn't sleep.

It happened twice more in the next week and a half. The following week, when I made a typing mistake, he didn't spank me. Instead, he told me to bend over his desk, look at the typing mistake and repeat "I am stupid" for several minutes.

Our relationship didn't change otherwise. He was still brisk and friendly in the morning. And, because he seemed so sure of himself, I could not help but react to him as if he were still the same domineering but affable boss. He did not, however, ever invite me to discuss my problems with him again.

I began to have recurring dreams about him. In one, the most frequent, I walked with him in a field of big bright red poppies. The day was brilliant and warm. We were smiling at each other, and there was a tremendous sense of release and goodwill between us. He looked at me and said, "I understand you now, Debby." Then we held hands.

There was one time I felt disturbed about what was happening at the office. It was just before dinner, and my father was upset about something that had happened to him at work. I could hear him yelling in the living room while my mother tried to comfort him. He yelled, "I'd rather work in a circus! In one of those things where you put your head through a hole and people pay to throw garbage at you!"

"No circus has that anymore," said my mother. "Stop it, Shep."

By the time I went down to eat dinner, everything was as usual. I looked at my father and felt a sickening sensation of love nailed to contempt and panic.

The last time I made a typing error and the lawyer summoned me to his office, two unusual things occurred. The first was that after he finished spanking me he told me to pull up my skirt. Fear hooked my stomach and pulled it toward my chest. I turned my head and tried to look at him.

"You're not worried that I'm going to rape you, are you?" he said. "Don't. I'm not interested in that, not in the least. Pull up your skirt."

I turned my head away from him. I thought, I don't have to do this. I can stop right now. I can straighten up and walk out. But I didn't. I pulled up my skirt.

"Pull down your panty hose and underwear."

A finger of nausea poked my stomach.

"I told you I'm not going to fuck you. Do what I say."

The skin on my face and throat was hot, but my fingertips were cold on my legs as I pulled down my underwear and panty hose. The letter before me became distorted beyond recognition. I thought I might faint or vomit, but I didn't. I was held up by a feeling of dizzying suspension, like the one I have in dreams where I can fly, but only if I get into some weird position.

At first he didn't seem to be doing anything. Then I became aware of a small frenzy of expended energy behind me. I had an impression of a vicious little animal frantically burrowing dirt with its tiny claws and teeth. My hips were sprayed with hot sticky muck.

"Go clean yourself off," he said. "And do that letter again."

I stood slowly, and felt my skirt fall over the sticky gunk. He briskly swung open the door and I left the room, not even pulling up my panty hose and underwear, since I was going to use the bathroom anyway. He closed the door behind me, and the second unusual thing occurred. Susan, the paralegal, was standing in the waiting room with a funny look on her face. She was a blonde who wore short, fuzzy sweaters, and fake gold jewelry around her neck. At her friendliest, she had a whining, abrasive quality that clung to her voice. Now, she could barely say hello. Her stupidly full lips were parted speculatively.

"Hi," I said. "Just a minute." She noted the awkwardness of my walk, because of the lowered panty hose.

I got to the bathroom and wiped myself off. I didn't feel embarrassed. I felt mechanical. I wanted to get that dumb paralegal out of the office so I could come back to the bathroom and masturbate.

Susan completed her errand and left. I masturbated. I retyped the letter. The lawyer sat in his office all day.

When my mother picked me up that afternoon, she asked me if I was all right.

"Why do you ask?"

"I don't know. You look a little strange."

"I'm as all right as I ever am."

"That doesn't sound good, honey."

I didn't answer. My mother moved her hands up and down the steering wheel, squeezing it anxiously.

"Maybe you'd like to stop by the French bakery and get some elephant ears," she said.

"I don't want any elephant ears." My voice was unexpectedly nasty. It almost made me cry.

"All right," said my mother.

When I lay on my bed to take my nap, my body felt dense and heavy, as though it would be very hard to move again, which was just as well, since I didn't feel like moving. When Donna banged on my door and yelled "Dinner!" I didn't answer. She put her head in and asked if I was asleep, and I told her I didn't feel like eating. I felt so inert, I thought I'd go to sleep, but I couldn't. I lay awake through the sounds of argument and TV and everybody going to the bathroom. Bedtime came, drawers rasped open and shut, doors slammed, my father eased into sleep with radio mumble. The orange digits on my clock said 1:30. I thought: I should get out of this panty hose and slip. I sat up and looked out into the gray, cold street. The shrubbery on the lawn across the street looked frozen and miserable. I thought about the period of time a year before when I couldn't sleep because I kept thinking that someone was going to break into the house and kill everybody. Eventually that fear went away and I went back to sleeping again. I lay back down without taking off my clothes, and pulled a light blanket tightly around me. Sooner or later, I thought, I would sleep. I would just have to wait.

But I didn't sleep, although I became mentally incoherent for long, ugly stretches of time. Hours went by; the room turned gray. I heard the morning noises: the toilet, the coughing, Donna's hostile muttering. Often, in the past, I had woken early and lain in bed listening to my family clumsily trying to organize

itself for the day. Often as not, their sounds made me feel irra-
tional loathing. This morning, I felt despair and a longing for
them, and a sureness that we would never be close as long as
I lived. My nasal passages became active with tears that didn't
reach my eyes.

My mother knocked on the door. "Honey, aren't you going
to be late?"

"I'm not going to work. I feel sick. I'll call in."

"I'll do it for you, just stay in bed."

"No, I'm going to call. It has to be me."

I didn't call in. The lawyer didn't call the house. I didn't go in
or call the next day or the day after that. The lawyer still didn't
call. I was slightly hurt by his absent phone call, but my relief
was far greater than my hurt.

After I'd stayed home for four days, my father asked if I wasn't
worried about taking so much time off. I told him I'd quit, in
front of Donna and my mother. He was dumbfounded.

"That wasn't very smart," he said. "What are you going to
do now?"

"I don't care," I said. "That lawyer was an asshole." To everyone's discomfort, I began to cry. I left the room, and they all
watched me stomp up the stairs.

The next day at dinner my father said, "Don't get discour-
aged because your first job didn't work out. There're plenty of
other places out there."

"I don't want to think about another job right now."

There was a disgruntlement all around the table. "Come
on now, Debby, you don't want to throw away everything you
worked for in that typing course," said my father.

"I don't blame her," said Donna. "I'm sick of working for
assholes."

"Oh, shit," said my father. "If I had quit every job I've had on those grounds, you would've all starved. Maybe that's what I should've done."

"What happened, Debby?" said my mother.

I said, "I don't want to talk about it," and I left the room again.

After that they may have sensed, with their intuition for the miserable, that something hideous had happened. Because they left the subject alone.

I received my last paycheck from the lawyer in the mail. It came with a letter folded around it. It said, "I am so sorry for what happened between us. I have realized what a terrible mistake I made with you. I can only hope that you will understand, and that you will not worsen an already unfortunate situation by discussing it with others. All the best." As a P.S. he assured me that I could count on him for excellent references. He enclosed a check for three hundred and eighty dollars, a little over two hundred dollars more than he owed me.

It occurred to me to tear up the check, or mail it back to the lawyer. But I didn't do that. Two hundred dollars was worth more then than it is now. Together with the money I had in the bank, it was enough to put a down payment on an apartment and still have some left over. I went upstairs and wrote "380" on the deposit side of my checking account. I didn't feel like a whore or anything. I felt I was doing the right thing. I looked at the total figure of my balance with satisfaction. Then I went downstairs and asked my mother if she wanted to go get some elephant ears.

For the next two weeks, I forgot about the idea of a job and moving out of my parents' house. I slept through all the morning noise until noon. I got up and ate cold cereal and ran the dishwasher. I watched the gray march of old sitcoms on TV. I worked on crossword puzzles. I lay on my bed in a tangle of quilt and fuzzy blanket and masturbated two, three, four times in a row, always thinking about the thing.

I was still in this phase when my father stuck the newspaper under my nose and said, "Did you see what your old boss is doing?" There was a small article on the upcoming mayoral elections in Westland. He was running for mayor. I took the paper from my father's offering hands. For the first time, I felt an uncomplicated disgust for the lawyer. Westland was nothing but malls and doughnut stands and a big ugly theater with an artificial volcano in the front of it. What kind of idiot would want to be mayor of Westland? Again, I left the room.

I got the phone call the next week. It was a man's voice, a soft, probing, condoling voice. "Miss Roe?" he said. "I hope you'll forgive this unexpected call. I'm Mark Charming of *Detroit Magazine*."

I didn't say anything. The voice continued more uncertainly. "Are you free to talk, Miss Roe?"

There was no one in the kitchen, and my mother was running the vacuum in the next room. "Talk about what?" I said.

"Your previous employer." The voice became slightly harsh as he said these words, and then hurriedly rushed back to condolence. "Please don't be startled or upset. I know this could be a disturbing phone call for you, and it must certainly seem intrusive." He paused so I could laugh or something. I didn't, and his voice became more cautious. "The thing is, we're doing a story on your ex-employer in the context of his running for mayor. To put it mildly, we think he has no business running for public office. We think he would be very bad for the whole

Detroit area. He has an awful reputation, Miss Roe—which may not surprise you." There was another careful pause that I did not fill.

"Miss Roe, are you still with me?"

"Yes."

"What all this is leading up to is that we have reason to believe that you could reveal information about your ex-employer that would be damaging to him. This information would never be connected to your name. We would use a pseudonym. Your privacy would be protected completely."

The vacuum cleaner shut off, and silence encircled me. My throat constricted.

"Do you want time to think about it, Miss Roe?"

"I can't talk now," I said, and hung up.

I couldn't go through the living room without my mother asking me who had been on the phone, so I went downstairs to the basement. I sat on the mildewed couch and curled up, unmindful of centipedes. I rested my chin on my knee and stared at the boxes of my father's old paperbacks and the jumble of plastic Barbie-doll cases full of Barbie equipment that Donna and I used to play with on the front porch. A stiff white foot and calf stuck out of a sky-blue case, helpless and pitifully rigid.

For some reason, I remembered the time, a few years before, when my mother had taken me to see a psychiatrist. One of the more obvious questions he had asked me was, "Debby, do you ever have the sensation of being outside yourself, almost as if you can actually watch yourself from another place?" I hadn't at the time, but I did now. And it wasn't such a bad feeling at all.

Wrong

Dennis Cooper

When Mike saw a pretty face, he liked to mess it up, or give it drugs until it wore out by itself. Take Keith, who used to play pool at the Ninth Circle. His crooked smile really lights up the place. That's what Mike heard, but it bored him. "Too obvious."

Keith was a kiss-up. Mike fucked him hard, then they snorted some dope. Keith was face first in the toilet bowl when Mike walked in. Keith had said, "Knock me around." But first Mike wanted him "dead." Not in the classic sense. "Passed out."

Mike dragged Keith down the hall by his hair. He shit in

Keith's mouth. He laid a whip on Keith's ass. It was a grass skirt once Mike dropped the belt. Mike kicked Keith's skull in before he came to. Brains or whatever it was gushed out. "That's that."

José was Keith's friend. Now that Keith wasn't around he moved in. Mike said okay *if* they'd fist fuck. José's requirement was drugs: speed, coke, pot, the occasional six-pack. "Oh, and respect, of course."

"Great stuff," José whispered. Mike shrugged. "Too fem," he thought, putting a match to José's pipe. José had hitchhiked from Dallas. He had a high-pitched voice, wore a gold crucifix on a chain. "Typical Mexican shit."

José slipped on a dress. Pink satin, ankle length, blue sash. He put on makeup. *"Mamacita!"* Mike fisted "her" on the window ledge. "She" dangled over the edge. Mike shook "her" off his wrist. "She" fell four stories, broke "her" neck.

Steve had blond hair, gloomy eyes, and chapped lips. "He should be dead," Mike thought. He liked the kid's skin, especially on his ass. Sick white crisscrossed with gray stretch marks. Mike liked how lost it became in pants, like the bones in an old lady's face.

Mike knocked a few of Steve's teeth out. He'd called Mike "a dumb fuck." That night Mike kicked in Steve's ribs and tied him up for the night. They fell asleep around four. By morning Steve was cold, eyes open, blue face. Mike dressed and took off.

He walked home. He thought of offing himself. "After death, what's left?" he mumbled. He meant "to do." Once you've killed someone, life's shit. It's a few rules and you've already broken the best. He had a beer at the Ninth Circle.

He picked up Will on the street. "Snort this." Mike tore Will's shorts off and slapped his ass. "Shit in my mouth," Mike said. Will did. It changed the way Mike perceived him. Will was a real person, not just a fuck. Mike let him hang out.

Will's body came into focus. It wasn't bad: underweight, blue eyes, a five o'clock shadow. Beauty had nothing to do with it. Mike could see what he was looking at. But he got used to the sight. One night he strangled Will to be safe.

The night was rough: wind, rain, chill. Mike walked from Will's place on West Tenth to Battery Park, chains clinking each step. He stared out at the Hudson. He put a handgun to his head. "Fuck this shit." His body splashed in the river, drifted off.

Morning came. Cops kicked Will's door in, found his corpse. Will's friends got wind of it, phoned one another up. Down river tourists were standing around on a dock looking bored. One girl pulled down on her mom's skirt and pointed out. "What's that?"

George looked out at the Hudson. He saw a dead body. He shot the rest of his roll of film, then milled around with the other tourists. Guides led them back to the bus. It was abuzz with the idea of death, in grim or joking tones. George listened, his feelings somewhere between the two.

The World Trade Center was not what he'd hoped. It wasn't like he could fall off. Big slabs of glass between him and his death. No matter where he turned his thoughts were obvious. The city looked like a toy, a space-age forest, a silvery tray full of hypodermics. He wanted one fresh perception, but . . .

Wall Street was packed with gray business suits. Seeing the trading floor, he thought first of a beehive, then of the heart attacks those guys would get. It was like watching a film about some other time and place, very far back and relegated to books.

George took off his clothes. He lay on the bed. "Where you from?" It was his roommate, a Southerner, judging by the accent. "West." "Of what?" the man asked. "This," and George turned his back. The Southerner shook his head. "Not worth it," he thought.

That night George walked through the West Village. "I'm tired of sleeping with *that*," a man sneered as they crossed paths. The guy was chatting to some friend of his, but he eyed George's ass. Hearing this, George felt as cold as the statue he'd touched at the Met last night. A boy was playing the lute when art froze him stiff.

The Ninth Circle was packed. Hustlers in blue jean vests, businessmen in all the usual suits. George leaned against the bar lighting a cigarette. "What's up pal?" It was his roommate's voice. "Not much," George thought, but they talked.

Lights out. Dan's cock was minuscule, so George agreed to be fucked. Dan spread the asscheeks and sniffed. George did his best to relax. He thought of ovens with roasts cooking in them. He knew his ass smelled more rancid than them, but maybe that was the point.

George thought of home. It was a white stucco, one story. His room was paneled in oak. He never aired it out. It reeked of BO, smoke, and unlaundered sheets. The smell was clinically bad, but he loved the idea that he'd had such an impact on something outside himself.

George didn't want to be held while he slept. He never got enough rest as it was. No lover could comprehend that. To them a hug was an integral act. George felt pinned down by one, too pressed to squeeze back. "Don't." Dan sighed and moved off.

George dreamed in bursts. Little picturesque plots. Casts

of peripherals refocused, brought to the fore in a world he'd backed into unknowingly. He saw himself floating dead in the Hudson; Dan held a knife to his throat in an alley; the room caught fire and he went up in smoke.

Dan thought of love as defined by books, cobwebbed and hidden from view by the past. Too bad a love like that didn't actually exist. In the twentieth century one had to fake it. He put his cheek on the boy's ass and seemed to sleep. He couldn't tell if he was or not. Then he did.

George sat on a park bench feeding some birds what was left of his sandwich. He drew a handful of postcards from one jacket pocket. They were all cityscapes, what friends and folks would expect. Bums limped by begging for change. Their clothes were falling off. George turned his palms up. "Die," he said under his breath.

"Dear Philippe, New York makes sense. I fit right in. I'm sitting under a bunch of trees. They'd be great if bums weren't dying all over the place. Everything you said was right. I'm going back to the hotel now to take a nap. Anyway, George."

"Dear Dad, The trip's going great. We're in New York for the weekend, then up to Boston, then the ride back to L.A. The man I'm sharing a room with reminds me of you. He's nice, from the South. Don't touch a thing in my room. I'll be home in two weeks. Love, George."

"Dear Sally, I thought about you today as I walked forty blocks to a pretty park. My legs are used to it. They sell marijuana in stores here. I bought a bag for ten bucks. I'm smoking it as I write. Out of room. Be seeing you in a while. Love, George."

"Dear Santa Claus, For Christmas I want a penthouse in New York, one in L.A., and one someplace in Europe. I've been a good boy, plus . . ." George ripped the card in half. "Duh," he said, giggling at himself.

"Dear Dennis, I think I miss you most of all. What's-her-name said that to Ray Bolger, right? Yesterday I saw the top of what's on this card. Today I'm off on my own. Tonight I'll hit the bars. Hope you're great. See you, George."

George headed toward the hotel. His calves ached. Times Square was spooky; too many junkies out, pissed eyes way back in their heads. The hotel lobby felt homey. Dan was out. George kicked his shoes off, snoozed a bit.

The Ninth Circle was packed. George downed three beers in no time. One man was cute, but his haircut resembled a toupee. Another stood in an overhead light, too sure of its effect. His expression was "perfect." Between them George would have chosen the latter, depending on who else showed up.

Fred's loft was spacious, underfurnished. Track lighting bleached out its lesser points. George got the grand tour. "This is the bed, of course. This is a painting by Lichtenstein. Amusing, yes? And these are the torture devices I mentioned." George saw a long table lined with spiked dildos, all lengths of whips, three branding irons, sundry shit.

To George it looked like a game. Whether it wound up that way or not was beside the point. Handcuffs clicked shut in the small of his back. Electrical tape sealed his lips. Black leather shorts made him feel sort of animal-esque.

George fantasized that his father was hugging him. He didn't know why. It had something to do with a gesture that couldn't be downgraded or reinterpreted, made into some half-assed joke. Someone who made him feel this all important must be intrigued at least.

It started out with a spanking. Slaps to the face, which George wasn't so wild about. His asshole swallowed in something's enormity simply enough. More slaps. Fred's breaths grew worse, a kind of storm knocking down every civilized word in its path.

George was hit on the head. "Shit!" Again. This time he felt his nose skid across one cheek. His forehead caved in. One eye went black. Teeth sputtered out of his mouth and rained down on his chest. He died at some point in that.

George was across the loft watching himself kick. The sight was slightly blurred like the particulars in a dream sequence. He saw a club strike his face. It was unrecognizable. His arms and legs slammed the tabletop like giant crudely made gavels.

George had a lump in his throat. He wondered why, if he was still alive, he should feel shit for that too-garish wreck of himself. "But that's the beauty of dead kids," he thought. "Everything they ever did seems incredibly moving in retrospect."

He watched until his old body was such a loss that each indignity was simply more of the same. So he looked down at his current form. He was a hologram, more or less. "Too much!" he thought. He tried to walk. It was a snap, like bounding over the moon.

So this was death. "Hey, not bad," he thought. He inhaled slowly and slid without incident through the steel door. Descending the stairs was exactly like falling down them, liberated and discombobulating, a drug hallucination without the teeth grinding.

He walked west, sometimes right down the middle of streets, cars plowing through him. He strolled through shoppers, amused by the idea that he was just part of the air to them, at best a breeze they'd write off to earth's natural forces.

Seeing a husband and wife, the male of which he'd have been

quite attracted to during his life, he followed them up a rickety staircase, through their front door. Jeff, as the wife called him, hit the head. George watched him shit, loved the dumb look on his face, but was driven back into the street by the subsequent stench.

Now what? He took a leisurely stroll to the river, down Christopher Street. The piers were decrepit. One was completely decapitated. A few rotten pylons stuck out of the water. George felt an odd emotional attachment to them.

He sat on a bench. The dawn felt terrific. He warmed slightly like fog just before it burned off. He thought of movies he'd loved where the ghosts of dead men were big jokes, mere plot twists, a sort of stab in the dark.

Who would have thought it was true? All those old ladies in New England mansions were far more sane than their distended eyes would have had one believe. "One," he muttered. He'd always hated when people used "one" in conversation. But it was the right term for him now.

He stared out at the brownish river. It was the first time he'd thought about water's solidity. If he were to hurl himself in, would he break into millions of molecules? Or would he, like Jesus Christ, land on his feet? "Interesting prospect," he thought, but he couldn't chance it.

He walked slowly up West Street past several leather bars he would have liked to check into, but he was tired. Sure, he could crash out wherever he liked, see whichever cute rock star nude, fly to London for nothing. But he'd get bored of the voyeur bit before he knew it. Then what?

George thought of things that had haunted him during his life: A staircase that, after turning a corner, led to a brick wall. B&W photos of great buildings destined to be dusty heaps. A human face that had turned into just one more mudslide from heaven.

The hotel loomed in the distance. Its neon sign blinked out VACANCY. "An appropriate place for myself or what's left of me," George thought. He headed for its rococo, checking the faces of hapless pedestrians for his reflection. But they stared straight ahead, not realizing.

George passed through the door of room 531. Dan lay on the single bed nearest the window, writing a postcard, probably to the wife he'd been complaining about on the previous night. His face seemed peaceful, but maybe it was the light: low, grayish.

George liked Dan, though "liked" was too clear a word. "Something" had drawn George to him. It had to do with Dan's fatherliness, George thought. That was a much bigger turn-on than tight jeans on tanned, over-exercised guys. His ideal man was a little bushed around the eyes.

George hadn't spoken all day. He felt a tightness inside his throat. "Dan?" he croaked, "I know you don't hear me, but if you can sense me in any way tug on your left ear." George waited. Dan continued to scratch out what George had no doubt were inanities.

"Okay, I feel a little like somebody telling some guy in a coma I still care, but here goes. I don't really know you, but I feel attached to you, even though you're not exactly an individual. You're more a type, which makes me some kind of aesthete, I guess, and you the real work of art, not that I buy all your bullshit.

"We had sex. I let you fuck me. That was the hot part, but though it's hard to admit, all the hugging and shit is what I really liked. To be held tight by a person who's had me . . . well it's one thing to shake hands and chat awkwardly about art, and something else to be fucked then respected.

"I used to think that if lovers got wind of my shit I'd be 'too realistic,' in their words. I kept rolling onto my back, clenching my ass when sucked off so the stink couldn't get out. I had this weird idea that there was something wrong under my looks, not just gory stuff.

"Then some guy ate out my ass and asked for a second date. Since that night I've tried to shrug off each fear in turn. Now I'm dead. It figures no one's around to appreciate or make bad jokes about my 'passing on,' as you'd probably call it.

"I wanted love. Sure, I was attracted to sex-crazed types, their faces so overcome by the need for me it was as though leers were sculpted right into their skulls and their skin was just draped over bone like a piece of cloth. But I was a stupid jerk.

"This part is meant for my father's ears. I've felt more than you thought or I'm able to spit out. My moods were really mysterious, even to me, which makes them not worth the time to you, no matter how long you stared in my 'great eyes' last night."

George felt faint and teetered slightly. He wished he had a banana, something with sugar to pep him up, but he imagined he couldn't eat, that food would perch in his waist like a caged canary, or drop with a thump to the carpet.

Dan filled the postcard and lay back. George could just make it out. "Dear Fran," it began. He didn't notice his name in the scribbles. It was a simple tale: Empire State Building, good view, dinner at Lüchow's, Love, Dan. P.S. I wish [unintelligible] tonight.

Was George beginning to fade away? He wasn't sure. So

much depended on the right light. "Umm, this may be it," he mumbled. He hadn't meant to lower his voice. "Shit," and he started to tremble. "I like you. What can I say? Or not you, but you're all I have.

"I blew it." He blended into the afternoon. Outside the window a car honked. Inside the room a man's watch ticked. Dan stood and scratched his ass. He put the card in his shirt pocket. He had a faraway look in his eyes as he lit his cigarette.

From
After Delores

Sarah Schulman

1988

I was on my second one, staring at the still blinking leftover Christmas lights when a female voice came to me from the other side of the bar. It started as a tickle in my ear and then, for a second, I thought someone had the sense to record a quiet rap song, but when she got so close I could see her reflection in my ice, I realized that a real person was talking to me. A blonde.

"Hey," she said, pulling up a barstool. "You want to buy a phone machine for ten dollars?"

We drank for a while until the girl asked if I wanted to see the machine. I was tired and needed to talk so I just decided to tell her the truth.

"I can't. I have to give Priscilla Presley back her gun."

"Do you have to do it right now?"

"I guess it can wait. I'll show it to you if you want to see it, but we have to go to the bathroom."

"No thanks, I've seen guns before. You look kinda sad."

"I am sad."

Somebody played Patsy Cline on the jukebox and that made me even sadder, but in a pleasurable melancholy way, not a painful Delores-type way.

"Look," she said in adolescent earnest as I watched her recite from memory. "You have the possibility to make your life beautiful, but possibility is not forever and it's not immediate. Know what I mean?"

"Who told you that?"

"Charlotte. That's my girlfriend. So, you want to see the machine or not?"

I paid the check, rang Pris's buzzer one more time but still no answer.

"She's probably live at Caesar's Palace," I muttered.

"What?"

"Never mind. Let's go see the machine."

First, though, the girl had to call her friend who was getting an abortion the next day to see if she needed her to go along or not. It was the last cold night in March and the wind was blowing dark and ugly. She used the pay phone on the corner as I huddled in the doorway with a cigarette and tried to push away the tiredness.

"You got your period!" she shrieked. "That's great!"

The girl seemed only five or six years younger than me but she was from a whole different generation. She wore those black tights and black felt mini-skirt and oversized shirt that everybody wore. Her hair was cut short on one side and long on the other with blonde added to the tips. My head was still in the sixties. The only thing that happened in the last two decades that made any sense to me at all was Patti Smith. When Patti Smith came along even I got hip, but then she went away.

"How did she schedule an abortion without a pregnancy test?" I asked, following her little leather cap and one dangling earring.

"I don't know but she got her period. Isn't that great?"

She started walking east and then more east until it was too east. *There I go again*, I thought, *being old-fashioned*. The idea that Avenue D is off-limits was a thing of the past. Now white people can go anywhere.

"Where are we going?"

"Charlotte's place. That's my lover. I have the key."

"How did you know it was okay to come out to me so quickly?" I asked.

"Easy. Charlotte taught me the trick. She says that if you're talking to a woman and she looks you in the eye and she really sees you and listens to what you have to say, then you know she's gay. It works every time."

"Charlotte sounds like a pretty unusual person," I said.

"Yeah," the girl answered, not noticing the cold men in thin jackets staring silently as we passed by. "Only she's married . . . to a woman, you know, named Beatriz. I stay at her place sometimes when they've got gigs out of town. Charlotte's an actress. I'm gonna be one too. Beatriz is a director. They're different."

Our conversation was the only sound on the street and her part of it was much too loud.

"It's funny having Charlotte's key. It's like an older person."

"How old is she?"

"Thirty-eight. My father's forty. Why do older people always have keys?"

"Because older people have apartments. They're not moving around staying different places. They know where they live."

"Let's get some beer," she said heading for the yellow light of a bodega presiding over the steely emptiness of Avenue C. I watched the Spanish men watching her. She was so young. She had no wrinkles on her face and wore a childish blue eyeliner passing for sophistication.

"Let's get a quart bottle of Bud and a small bottle of Guinness and mix it. It's not too bad."

I handed her two dollars over the stacks of stale Puerto Rican sweets and shivered. Even the apartment was cold.

"We make love here in the afternoons when Beatriz is away. Charlotte says she likes the smell of young flesh. She says it smells like white chocolate. Old flesh smells like the soap you use in the morning until it's really old and then it starts to rot. My grandmother used to smell that way but I loved her so it smelled good. One time Charlotte and I came up here and an old man passed us on the stairs. '*I hate that smell*,' Charlotte said. '*It's weak and worse than garbage.*' But I loved it because it reminded me of my grandmother. When you love someone they always smell good. Want to hear a record?"

She was smoking Camels without filters and playing albums by groups I had never heard of.

"Listen to this version of 'Fever.' It's Euro-trash, you know,

French New Wave? Instead of the word *fever* she says *tumor*.
'Tumor all through the night.'"

We sat and listened. My Punkette sprawled out on the floor.
Me, freezing in the only chair.

"That was great," she said, pouring more beer. "Let's hear it
again."

Her hands were short and white with badly painted black
nails.

"I'm so in love with Charlotte," she said.

"How do you know?" I asked.

"Well, she's strong and she's a good lover. You think I'm
young but I know the difference. Plus she has good information
about life. Like, you know what she told me? She told me to tell
all my secrets but one. That way you invest in the world and
save a little something for yourself."

She grabbed on to one of the longer strands of her hair and
started splitting the split ends.

"I know that she and Beatriz love each other and I'm trying
hard to see it from Beatriz's point of view so that someday we can
all be friends. But for now I don't mind seeing her afternoons,
I guess. I have to work mostly nights anyway. Just a couple of
lunches. I go-go dance in New Jersey. Told you that, right? On
New Year's Eve I was so coked up after work and wanted to spend
the night with her so badly that I wandered into the Cubby Hole
at four-thirty in the morning and they still made me pay."

She had drunk all the beer by that time and smoked all her
cigarettes. I gave her some of mine.

"Thanks. There was this yuppie girl there talking to me and
I was so desperate I would have gone home with her but she
didn't ask. Charlotte encouraged me to take that job, dancing.
It's not too bad. Want to see my costume?"

She went into the next room to change and I started smoking. It was so cold, I had on a sweater and two blankets and was still chattering.

"Okay," she shouted from behind the door. "Now, sing some tacky disco song."

"Bad girl," I sang. "Talking 'bout a bad, bad girl."

Then she came go-going in in her little red sparkle G-string and black high heels. Her breasts were so small that she could have been a little girl showing off her first bikini. She bit her lip, trying to look sexy but she just looked young. I segued into the next song.

"Ring my bell-ll-ll, ring my bell. My bell. Ding a ling a ling."

"Sometimes they hold up twenties," she said, still dancing. "But when I boogie over to take them they give me singles instead. 'Sorry honey.'"

Then I saw her eyes. They were smart. They were too smart for me.

"Charlotte says there's a palm at the end of the mind and it's on fire. What does that mean?"

And I thought *this kid can get anything she wants, anything.*

She saw me staring at her eyes and she got scared all of a sudden, like she was caught reaching into her daddy's wallet.

"I've never done that for someone I respected before."

Those breasts, I thought. *How could anyone make love to those breasts? There's nothing there. Nothing at all.*

"Do you think Charlotte will leave her? What do you think?"

"You really believe in love, don't you?" I said.

She looked up at me from her spot on the floor, totally open.

"I don't know what you want from me," I said. "I'm the last person in New York City you should be asking about relationships."

"Do you think she'll leave her?"

Then I realized she saw something special in me. She trusted me. And I was transformed suddenly from a soup-stained waitress to an old professor. We were sitting, not in a Lower Eastside firetrap but before a blazing hearth in a wood-lined brownstone. Charlotte was my colleague and Punkette, her hysterical mistake.

"Look, sometimes you have to cheat on your wife and sometimes you have to go back to her."

I looked into her eyes again. They were really listening.

"Maybe you'll get what you want," I said. "But you'll have to be patient."

And suddenly I wanted her so badly. I wanted to throw off the blankets and be vulnerable again, to roll on the rug with a little Punkette in a red G-string and I wanted to show her a really good time. Nostalgia.

Work

Denis Johnson

I'd been staying at the Holiday Inn with my girlfriend, honestly the most beautiful woman I'd ever known, for three days under a phony name, shooting heroin. We made love in the bed, ate steaks at the restaurant, shot up in the john, puked, cried, accused one another, begged of one another, forgave, promised, and carried one another to heaven.

But there was a fight. I stood outside the motel hitchhiking, dressed up in a hurry, shirtless under my jacket, with the wind crying through my earring. A bus came. I climbed aboard and sat on the plastic seat while the things of our city turned in the windows like the images in a slot machine.

Once, as we stood arguing at a streetcorner, I punched her in the stomach. She doubled over and broke down crying. A car full of young college men stopped beside us.

"She's feeling sick," I told them.

"Bullshit," one of them said. "You elbowed her right in the *gut*."

"He did, he did, he did," she said, weeping.

I don't remember what I said to them. I remember loneliness crushing first my lungs, then my heart, then my balls. They put her in the car with them and drove away.

But she came back.

This morning, after the fight, after sitting on the bus for several blocks with a thoughtless, red mind, I jumped down and walked into the Vine.

The Vine was still and cold. Wayne was the only customer. His hands were shaking. He couldn't lift his glass.

I put my left hand on Wayne's shoulder, and with my right, opiated and steady, I brought his shot of bourbon to his lips.

"I was just going to go over here in the corner and nod out," I informed him.

"I decided," he said, "in my mind, to make some money."

"So what?" I said.

"Come with me," he begged.

"You mean you need a ride."

"I have the tools," he said. "All we need is that sorry-ass car of yours to get around in."

We found my sixty-dollar Chevrolet, the finest and best thing I ever bought, considering the price, in the streets near my apartment. I liked that car. It was the kind of thing you could bang into a phone pole with and nothing would happen at all.

Wayne cradled his burlap sack of tools in his lap as we drove out of town to where the fields bunched up into hills and then dipped down toward a cool river mothered by benevolent clouds.

All the houses on the riverbank—a dozen or so—were abandoned. The same company, you could tell, had built them all, and then painted them four different colors. The windows in the lower stories were empty of glass. We passed alongside them, and I saw that the ground floors of these buildings were covered with silt. Sometime back a flood had run over the banks, cancelling everything. But now the river was flat and slow. Willows stroked the waters with their hair.

"Are we doing a burglary?" I asked Wayne.

"You can't burgulate a forgotten, empty house," he said, horrified at my stupidity.

I didn't say anything.

"This is a salvage job," he said. "Pull up to that one, right about there."

The house we parked in front of just had a terrible feeling about it. I knocked.

"Don't do that," Wayne said. "It's stupid."

Inside, our feet kicked up the silt the river had left there. The watermark wandered the walls of the downstairs about three feet above the floor. Straight, stiff grass lay all over the place in bunches, as if someone had stretched them there to dry.

Wayne used a pry bar, and I had a shiny hammer with a blue rubber grip. We put the pry points in the seams of the wall and started tearing away the Sheetrock. It came loose with a noise like old men coughing. Whenever we exposed some of

the wiring in its white plastic jacket, we ripped it free of its connections, pulled it out, and bunched it up. That's what we were
after. We intended to sell the copper wire for scrap.

By the time we were on the second floor, I could see we were
going to make some money. But I was getting tired. I dropped
the hammer and went to the bathroom. I was sweaty and thirsty.
But of course the water didn't work.

I went back to Wayne, standing in one of two small empty
bedrooms, and started dancing around and pounding the walls,
breaking through the Sheetrock and making a giant racket,
until the hammer got stuck. Wayne ignored this misbehavior.

I was catching my breath. I asked him, "Who owned these
houses, do you think?"

He stopped doing anything. "This is my house."

"It is?"

"It was."

He gave the wire a long, smooth yank, a gesture full of
the serenity of hatred, popping its staples and freeing it into the
room.

We balled up big gobs of wire in the center of each room,
working for over an hour. I boosted Wayne through the trap-
door into the attic, and he pulled me up after him, both of us
sweating and our pores leaking the poisons of drink, which
smelled like old citrus peelings, and we made a mound of white-
jacketed wire in the top of his former home, pulling it up out
of the floor.

I felt weak. I had to vomit in the corner—just a thimbleful
of grey bile. "All this work," I complained, "is fucking with my
high. Can't you figure out some easier way of making a dollar?"

Wayne went to the window. He rapped it several times with
his pry bar, each time harder, until it was loudly destroyed. We

threw the stuff out there onto the mud-flattened meadow that came right up below us from the river.

It was quiet in this strange neighborhood along the bank except for the steady breeze in the young leaves. But now we heard a boat coming upstream. The sound curlicued through the riverside saplings like a bee, and in a minute a flat-nosed sports boat cut up the middle of the river going thirty or forty, at least.

This boat was pulling behind itself a tremendous triangular kite on a rope. From the kite, up in the air a hundred feet or so, a woman was suspended, belted in somehow, I would have guessed. She had long red hair. She was delicate and white, and naked except for her beautiful hair. I don't know what she was thinking as she floated past these ruins.

"What's she doing?" was all I could say, though we could see that she was flying.

"Now, that is a beautiful sight," Wayne said.

On the way to town, Wayne asked me to make a long detour onto the Old Highway. He had me pull up to a lopsided farmhouse set on a hill of grass.

"I'm not going in but for two seconds," he said. "You want to come in?"

"Who's here?" I said.

"Come and see," he told me.

It didn't seem anyone was home when we climbed the porch and he knocked. But he didn't knock again, and after a full three minutes a woman opened the door, a slender redhead in a dress printed with small blossoms. She didn't smile. "Hi," was all she said to us.

"Can we come in?" Wayne asked.

"Let me come onto the porch," she said, and walked past us to stand looking out over the fields.

I waited at the other end of the porch, leaning against the rail, and didn't listen. I don't know what they said to one another. She walked down the steps, and Wayne followed. He stood hugging himself and talking down at the earth. The wind lifted and dropped her long red hair. She was about forty, with a bloodless, waterlogged beauty. I guessed Wayne was the storm that had stranded her here.

In a minute he said to me, "Come on." He got in the driver's seat and started the car—you didn't need a key to start it.

I came down the steps and got in beside him. He looked at her through the windshield. She hadn't gone back inside yet, or done anything at all.

"That's my wife," he told me, as if it wasn't obvious.

I turned around in the seat and studied Wayne's wife as we drove off.

What can be said about those fields? She stood in the middle of them as on a high mountain, with her red hair pulled out sideways by the wind, around her the green and grey plains pressed down flat, and all the grasses of Iowa whistling one note.

I knew who she was.

"That was her, wasn't it?" I said.

Wayne was speechless.

There was no doubt in my mind. She was the woman we'd seen flying over the river. As nearly as I could tell, I'd wandered into some sort of dream that Wayne was having about his wife and his house. But I didn't say anything more about it.

Because, after all, in small ways, it was turning out to be one of the best days of my life, whether it was somebody else's dream or not. We turned in the scrap wire for twenty-eight dollars—each—at a salvage yard near the gleaming tracks at the edge of town, and went back to the Vine.

Who should be pouring drinks there but a young woman whose name I can't remember. But I remember the way she poured. It was like doubling your money. She wasn't going to make her employers rich. Needless to say, she was revered among us.

"I'm buying," I said.

"No way in hell," Wayne said.

"Come on."

"It is," Wayne said, "my sacrifice."

Sacrifice? Where had he gotten a word like sacrifice? Certainly I had never heard of it.

I'd seen Wayne look across the poker table in a bar and accuse—I do not exaggerate—the biggest, blackest man in Iowa of cheating, accuse him for no other reason than that he, Wayne, was a bit irked by the run of the cards. That was my idea of sacrifice, tossing yourself away, discarding your body. The black man stood up and circled the neck of a beer bottle with his fingers. He was taller than anyone who had ever entered that barroom.

"Step outside," Wayne said.

And the man said, "This ain't school."

"What the goddamn fucking piss-hell," Wayne said, "is that suppose to mean?"

"I ain't stepping outside, like you do at school. Make your try right here and now."

"This ain't a place for our kind of business," Wayne said, "not inside here with women and children and dogs and cripples."

"Shit," the man said. "You're drunk."

"I don't care," Wayne said. "To me you don't make no more noise than a fart in a paper bag."

The huge, murderous man said nothing.

"I'm going to sit down now," Wayne said, "and I'm going to play my game, and fuck you."

The man shook his head. He sat down too. This was an amazing thing. By reaching out one hand and taking hold of it for two or three seconds, he could have popped Wayne's head like an egg.

And then came one of those moments. I remember living through one when I was eighteen and spending the afternoon in bed with my first wife, before we were married. Our naked bodies started glowing, and the air turned such a strange color I thought my life must be leaving me, and with every young fiber and cell I wanted to hold on to it for another breath. A clattering sound was tearing up my head as I staggered upright and opened the door on a vision I will never see again: Where are my women now, with their sweet, wet words and ways, and the miraculous balls of hail popping in a green translucence in the yards?

We put on our clothes, she and I, and walked out into the town flooded ankle-deep with white, buoyant stones. Birth should have been like that.

That moment in the bar, after the fight was narrowly averted, was like the green silence after the hailstorm. Somebody was buying a round of drinks. The cards were scattered on the table, face up, face down, and they seemed to foretell that whatever we did to one another would be washed away by liquor or explained away by sad songs.

Wayne was a part of all that.

The Vine was like a railroad club car that had somehow run

itself off the tracks into a swamp of time where it awaited the blows of the wrecking ball. And the blows really were coming. Because of Urban Renewal, they were tearing up and throwing away the whole downtown.

And here we were, this afternoon, with nearly thirty dollars each, and our favorite, our very favorite, person tending bar. I wish I could remember her name, but I remember only her grace and her generosity.

All the really good times happened when Wayne was around. But this afternoon, somehow, was the best of all those times. We had money. We were grimy and tired. Usually we felt guilty and frightened, because there was something wrong with us, and we didn't know what it was; but today we had the feeling of men who had worked.

The Vine had no jukebox, but a real stereo continually playing tunes of alcoholic self-pity and sentimental divorce. "Nurse," I sobbed. She poured doubles like an angel, right up to the lip of a cocktail glass, no measuring. "You have a lovely pitching arm." You had to go down to them like a hummingbird over a blossom. I saw her much later, not too many years ago, and when I smiled she seemed to believe I was making advances. But it was only that I remembered. I'll never forget you. Your husband will beat you with an extension cord and the bus will pull away leaving you standing there in tears, but you were my mother.

Debbie's Barium Swallow

Laurie Weeks

Take pity on meat!
—Gilles Deleuze

Buildings or spinal columns shoot up from the pavement to sway clacking around a girl. Debbie, for this was her name, found herself one day walking like a friendly ghost through this forest of vertebrae. She's a disoriented T-cell obeying commands from a nervous system driven by a mean brain, and all of Debbie's instructions more or less consist of the same signal which is DEBBIE GET A JOB. What is happening to me, a girl thinks, walking to her job. No one touches her flesh so her flesh is made of air.

Though she's wearing an attractive dress patterned with duck hunters in fur earmuffs, Debbie feels like an exposed tooth nerve throbbing across the sidewalk. Oxygen in the city is composed of chemicals designed to make you feel kind of funny; you walk through the streets bathed and breathing in this corporate substance and suddenly your body's awash in loss and grief. Only your job can numb this anguish. Thank you jesus, Debbie thinks, for giving me such fast typing skills. Internal sirens signal the uncoupling of her nervous system from her brain: now your mind's an engine running on the abstract fuel of cash, now your fingertips have fused to the keyboard and the distant mechanism of your body fishtails away into the vacuum between circuits.

This girl Debbie stands sweating and smoking cigarettes in the urine fog of the subway. How would it be to have a girl like Debbie's arteries dilate around you in a slow red rush of velvet drapes? How would it feel to tune Debbie's body into a swollen receptacle made of hot corpuscles like a wet fleshy bed where you could screamingly discharge your rage and fear and then relax? I'm a girl but I pretend I'm a guy pushing in and out of you. I watched your body walking down the sidewalk, guys knew who you were. I put my hands on your body you were underneath my hands. Girls never end and that's their beauty; shoot one down and one even younger pops up in her place.

Flashback: Debbie wading through the frigid air, on her way to Mrs. Seaman's first-grade class. The vast gray sidewalk a blown beach shooting out electric water from the reservoirs nearby giving off a hum. The rancid smoke of bodies rises from the schoolhouse chimneys far away above the stunted trees. Tenderly a crossing guard like an orderly guides her to the playground.

Debbie joins the other small ghosts in a game of Double Dutch, but her bones and musculature swarm with lead and heavy water and her bewildered frame can't possibly decipher the whispering equation of twin whips and cement. Disentangling herself, she carries herself across the schoolyard to a corner where Jay Marks sits feverishly against a tree, his pointed face and hairless eyes swivelled toward a line of yellow dogs slathering outside the metal fence. Do you love me, Jay? Debbie whispers and Jay rubs the pebbles with his feet, his knees and eyes closing in a shiver of assent, his tongue swelling out black from the cavern of his teeth, a gentle maggoty fluid pouring from his nose.

A girl like Debbie doesn't walk out of nowhere to appear before you somnolent in a body she wears around herself like a brace, as mesmerizing as a sugarcube soaked in LSD; she comes at you from an angular black garden of instruments and appliances and mechanical shapes, a neighborhood awash in the radiation from TeeVee. At any given moment Debbie's tongue will swell into a gag because she finds it impossible to "say what she means," as if she shelters in her mouth a deadly totem, a lump of evidence secreted by her cells, a byproduct of her saturation in those atmospheric chemicals and metals which crave her flesh as much as you or I.

5:45 A.M. Smoking cigarettes and stoned in the park beneath a moist pink tissue of sky. A little bird is singing in the steamy morn and Debbie he wants to be your friend. Debbie hasn't slept for days and she doesn't have any hunger, just some blood and its taste in her mouth. Her body holding the cigarette is invisible to her. She can sense its vast presence like a phantom limb, with its maddening nonspecific itches and low-grade clamour for attention, but when she tries to situate it in the park to calm it down her body is absent and she can't make it move. Maybe if she picks up a novel she'll find her own body somewhere deep inside. A slur of drool and cookie oozes from Debbie's mouth.

I, Debbie, nigger faggot cunt crippled by my sawed-off dick, was once a baby who wanted nothing more than to recount humorous anecdotes to the little bees and dinosaurs inhabiting my crib but I was transformed before the age of one, even, into a truncated dream girl projected on the landscape by the powerful brain of a fitful male sleeper, a captain of industry and finance and medical research obsessed with carving order out of chaos. One morning I, Debbie, woke from my deep lengthy sleep to find myself throwing up into a bowl of Captain Crunch. One morning I, that's me, Debbie Brown, woke up to find myself a bit of liquid data trickling down from the computer burns inside someone's thigh.

Every day, walking to the bank or job or doctor, Debbie says just one foot before the other, then there you'll be. She tries to visualize her body as she walks, but it's a weak signal fading in and out. Something will happen today, Debbie thinks, this day is waiting just for me. Here is the flourescent hallway and your life throbbing in your eyes, here is the machine glittering with its jewels & light, mocking laughter squealing in from the circuits, and here is the park, a fluttery unsurrounded place where a girl can take her lunch. As she dabbles her feet in the bubbles of a fountain, Debbie hums to herself the hit single "Me and you and a dog named Boo, travelin' and-a livin' off the land." What is pain, she wonders, while her body chatters loosely in its dress or brace like a mouthful of ruined teeth. Windchimes drift on the air like fillings from extracted molars, and language, a black food, fills up your mouth.

Dear Debbie, says the inter-office memo. Security reports that you seem to be making more trips to the lavatory than are absolutely necessary. As you know, federal law prohibits the installation of surveillance cameras in the actual lavatories themselves, so of course we can do nothing but speculate about your activities once you have disappeared from the visual field of the hall cameras into the ladies' room which as noted earlier you seem to do with a peculiar frequency. Debbie, of course we realize you may have a medical problem but we found no deviant symptomology of this nature in your current medical records. Dr. Joe Gannon the company physician informs us that the average or normal female employee will excrete 2-5 times between the hours of 9 A.M. and 5 P.M. There are of course only spotty statistics on the frequency of excretion during the noon hour as many female employees perform their eliminative functions elsewhere in venues such as a restaurant, department store, or—perhaps not unlike yourself Debbie—a park. At any rate Debbie, security reports that you make on the average between 16-24 visits per day to the lavatory which is considerably higher than the maximum average, even if we allow for the excessive consumption of fluids which we've noted you seem prone to at your work station. Therefore Debbie we're certain you'll understand our request that you visit Nurse Georgette Hawkins of Dr. Gannon's office on the 13th floor no later than 4 P.M. today for a urinalysis. On a happier note Debbie you're still in the running for Employee Lady of the Month for which you could receive a solid oak plaque with a gold Emblem of Excellence affixed near your name.

A little girl's pussy is so mild. When you're six years old it's just a thing you have, a dolphin's friendly smile. There came a day for Debbie at the age of seven when she lay with her book "Little Women" in a beam of sunlight on the carpet. Her disposition had the charm and color of a Gummy Bear, she was content as a little frog, burbling along through the book's merry stream, when she came up short against the sensual buildup of a young girl's lingering illness, and ultimately the sentence which contained the climax, or death of the girl—a wavery, blurred stem of a girl, Beth, drowning in her sickbed beneath the milky light of dawn. And suddenly in Debbie's body a new gland activated to flood her limbs with a feverish fluid, and the place between her legs went liquid with heat and fear and pleasure as thick as the circulating streams of blood coiled inside her, looping their lazy way through her arms and legs, their red currents ferrying Debbie's body toward that final day in the future when her flesh will collapse inward to be extinguished in the gravitational crush of her own black hole. In young Debbie's cunt a deadly new steam began to gather.

Last night Debbie snorted heroin, Special K, and cocaine, plus she was drunk. Her faggot friends dressed her up in a leisure suit and big red wig and took her to the disco. She stood grooving on the dance floor, loose, relaxed, slave to the rhythm but for mysterious reasons completely paralyzed. Prior to blacking out, she looked up to observe her left eye dangling in a cloud of smoke over by the mirrorball. Around 5 A.M., she came to her senses in midair, slamming faster than the speed of sound down a long corridor of utter emptiness from her loft bed to the floor, startling Mimi the cat awake from a nightmare of crafty rodents. That didn't hurt at all, Debbie thought as she picked herself up and staggered to the bathroom. In the sick red light coming from the mirror she saw her faggot pals had painted her lips in a heart shape and drawn red hearts on her cheeks. She looked like a blow-up doll for men.

In the deserted street outside, a garbage truck rumbling by like a tank triggers for Debbie another neural shift. Remote vacuum of the sleeping neighborhood where young Debbie lay incubating in her girlish bedroom, sleepless at 3 A.M. A vulnerable time for adolescent insomniacs and in the absence of other stimulii the cold military harmonies of a semi truck shifting gears fused itself to the erotic channels of her nervous system. Am I the only girl awake in this town? she would wonder on those cold western nights when she waited for the dad to walk into her room with a shotgun. The truck, with its secret cargo of chemicals designed to produce metastasis once the workers or sheep have outlived their usefulness, accelerated to vaporize beyond the city limits. Tossing on her white sheets Debbie watched the radium stars swing by her suburban window hour after hour; from the stars' vantage point Debbie in her nightgown appeared no doubt to be a small piece of pork sizzling behind an oven door.

There's a guy named Benny Lymphoma tracking Debbie from his post with the IRS. Last night Benny woke up like he does every night soaking in a sweat produced by what he thinks of as his "African" dream. A dream where you have the steamy swollen body of a girl, where you're floating in a state of arousal toward a hot magnetic core. Everything around you is fertile, molten, black and indistinct. Your body has erupted in a febrile slur of rash and slow-moving fluids. You're Benny Lymphoma but you're a girl. Around you the black planet steams, loses its definition, melts into uncontrollable hallucination and permeates the moistened barrier of your skin. Your bloodstream slips its channel to flow into the air. When Benny Lymphoma puts his penis in a girl, hot convulsive horror shudders up his spine and emerges from his tongue in a gush of shame that tastes like blood.

Lately every time it occurs to Debbie to play with herself her body inflates with despair so profound it annihilates her desire; the advancing sexual rush withdraws like film in reverse, so that the stem of Debbie's body seals itself off from her caresses: Debbie's own torso has snubbed her. When her eyes open every morning she's cradled alone in a strange bed, she shudders in the milky light of dawn. Somewhere else a palm runs across a young girl's nipple, you only have to think the phrase "young girl" to yourself and your body will react, the young girl's lips part her legs part Debbie shuts her eyes against the glare. A wave of pain like electrocution surges through her muscles.

Debbie is coughed from the subway's warm esophagus to find herself blinking beneath a freeway, concrete girders pushing up from the ground like tibias discharged from a grave. "SIMPLY SONOGRAM" THIS WAY, says a sign with an arrow. ONE MILE. Debbie needs medical tests quite a lot, because a) she keeps discovering new symptoms of disease, and b) she doesn't trust her body, especially since she can barely find it, so she needs trained professionals to provide a steady stream of diagnoses, not to mention actual photos to monitor and document the cunning vicissitudes of her insides.

Sometimes Debbie feels as if her body is a moist vat incubating a brood of young, holographic Debbies, each one a nodule of fear; that her body cavities are host to a whirling circus of dismembered coltish legs, knees decomposed to jelly; that her skin is a sac filled with blood spilling from a little girl's disembodied, raging mouth; that the girl's scalp drifts through this red fluid trailing long hair like a squid; that the floating body parts of this girl who was Debbie are walled in by adult Debbie's pulsing organs emitting the crimson worldbeat of sirens.

Whenever God or whatever, Satan, Daddy lifts my skirt like he does at the slightest whim, Mommy the grim nurse takes a sample and drains off your fluids to replace them with a paralyzing potion like curare. What words can Debbie use for this secret procedure? It's as if her strangled impulses to speak or scream circulate, mischievous protons, with increasing friction through her limbs and, finding no outlet, soundlessly detonate, their seething shrapnel searing new wounds, points of entry, receptors, into the surface of her cells. Diseased souls of the world can now dissolve in Debbie's hair like creme rinse and enter her body through her scalp—fertilizing her cells with their own nerves, producing a serum of dread that leaks through her tissues, causing them to swell.

Will she ever wake up, wonders Debbie as she strolls beneath the freeway, from this long dreamy state or zone of exile where she crawls and shakes with fever in the toxic dirt? Crawling one knee before the other and spindly vultures wheel in the bleached sky above your head. One knee before the other every day, inching from 34th St. to 35th, a node-shaped blip traveling from sector to sector on the grid, crawling back to your job in the distant skyline of white buildings dominated by a hospital's authoritative, soothing facade.

When she was younger Debbie liked an angular harsh zone far from any town, because in the chill space there was room for her anguish and desire. What had she been since birth if not a wet receptive nerve bundle pulsing in rhythm to the vibration of magnetic rays and microwaves beaming at her from the TeeVee and electrical transformers surrounding the house? Her nervous system was irradiated with the sexuality of radar and toxins so she grew up to find herself responsive to vistas suggestive of exile, waste products in decay beneath a solar glare, and alien force-fields of any type. Debbie would stand by herself brooding in the desert or other desolate western landscape, adopting a sensual and moody pose in the presence of rusting machinery, abandoned factories, and power substations, feeling as if the emotional substance secreted by her glands was leaching into the atmosphere to recompose as a poetic iron carcass, oxidizing like Debbie beneath a frigid, corrosive tongue of wind.

Standing outside a prison now in her new urban setting, Debbie thinks The Mystery Is Gone, and a surge of excitement runs through her veins like a cold electric current; a naked bulb hangs in her chest where her heart was; steel bars compose her ribcage; and behind the prison fence Debbie senses a throbbing, sullen populace that wants to be her friend. As she leans against the chain link fence, an ambulance flashes past, a smear of red in the infected air. The white sky bulges like an eyeball swivelled back in someone's head. Bits of virus cultured by the prison medical staff for testing on the inmates are released periodically from smokestacks into the bruised tissues of the sky. The membranes lining Debbie's mouth and nose and throat are colonized instantly by spores and Debbie knows the prison grows inside her, composed of the cells of her tissue.

Giovanni's Apartment

Sam D'Allesandro

He follows me all the way from the bus station to my neighborhood. It is late, almost no one out. When I turn around I can't see him but I know he's there. I can hear the click of his shoes against the sidewalk. I pass an old lady asleep in a doorway with a small gray cat. From the enormous pile of Macy's bags its green eyes blink up at me, offended and unfriendly, before returning to sleep. Cats used to come up to me. That seems to be happening less and less lately. All the dogs and cats I run into seem to be on a tighter schedule and have more of a destination mapped out than I do. I've been feeling more alone than when I first moved here and didn't know anybody. Now I know some people. That means I have less of an excuse to feel lonely but do anyway.

The feeling doesn't go away when, near the liquor store, a prostitute in spike heels and a big hairdo follows me for a block. Her smile turns venomous as we reach the intersection and I still haven't said yes. "Well, if you're not interested you could at least go to the liquor store and buy me a bottle of wine. Didn't your daddy ever teach you how to treat a lady, little boy?" She serves up that "little boy" with plenty of extra snide. I like her flair for the dramatic.

"Thunderbird 2000, that's all I want, baby." She's back to the sexy voice she used when she first approached me. As I get closer to the intersection it nosedives into a grating, threatening whine: "Quit being such a piss ant. You don't want to be a piss ant all your life, do you?" I guess this barrage must have worked on someone for her to put so much effort into it, but I'm already blasé about anything anybody might say to me late at night around here.

In the middle of the next block I realize I can still feel him behind me, following in the distance. Even when I can't hear him I know he's there. I can feel him wanting me. As the gap between us gets smaller I start to feel what he wants to do to me. The whole hot scenario flashes through my mind, then starts to drop down through the rest of my body. A shivering wave of equal parts excitement and terror moves through my insides. I check to make sure the outside stays cool, stiffening all my muscles, especially my face. Guys like me mistakenly think that masks the vulnerability beginning to bubble up inside.

A block later he's ten steps behind me. "Are you gonna turn

around and look at me?" The voice is low and quiet. It cements me to the square of sidewalk I'm standing on. I feel his eyes boring into the back of my head, making their way through a messy jumble of hair, skin, and tissue to an ugly unguarded place where thoughts are plainly visible. He stares at my fear and indecision like a grocery list. He's going shopping in there. I'm embarrassed to have him get behind my facade so easily, but there's nothing I can do about it. He's already inside where, at the moment, I'm nothing but a whirring mass of confusion and desire. He can see what's going to happen, what's possible with me. He can see which of the things he wants he can get.

Since I've been told to do so, in effect, I turn. I'm already giving him what he wants but that was going to happen anyway. I know that now, as my eyes check him out in nervous darts and jumps. You could make a picture out of the pattern my eyes follow as they scan his face, connecting from one point of inter-est to another, like a dot-to-dot drawn in by a hyperactive child. I mentally do so. The design hovers about an inch in front of his face for a moment.

That's the only way I can really get a good look at him, dis-connecting the face and putting the image slightly outside so I can see it without getting caught. So I can look at it, recognize what it means to me, and then there's a feeling of giving into it as the picture hovers in front of him, slips away, and sinks back into the face it came from. He's solid again, 3-D and threaten-ing. There's the hint of a smile on his lips.

I first saw that smile, that face, in a beautiful black-and-white film. When I mention it sometime later, he says he did it as a favor for a friend. He was never in another. The film lasts about forty minutes. In it he's almost a mannequin, his expression blank and unchanging as if it were painted on stone. He never speaks, although he's in almost every frame. The camera follows him as he walks all over a city. Which city isn't clear, as all the sites that could have distinguished it are left out. Dark and decaying urban neighborhoods, deserted blocks of apartment buildings, corner bars with tiny twenty-year-old neon signs, stores shut and barred. Everything looks fairly normal, fairly sinister.

He's wearing a gray suit, or one that looks gray in black-and-white. It's just rained and the pavement's slick and shiny. The only sound besides '50s jazz is the scrape and click of his shoes, snatches of disembodied voices drifting out from bars, a whoosh of tires against wet street in the distance. He moves through dark alleys, finally stopping at a door he seems to know. He knocks and, when a man comes to the door, he stabs him.

This is my first glimpse of Giovanni. It's the image I see in my head as we walk toward his apartment. I can't say whether I'm more attracted to the Giovanni walking beside me or the Giovanni/killer from the film. For me, so far, they're one and the same. I've actually spent more time observing the killer in the film than I have the flesh-and-blood person.

Over me washes a warm flush of fear and fascination with the possibility of my own violent demise. I think of the film, how easy it seemed to him. I imagine a few possibilities and prepare to die.

When he asks me my name, I stupidly shoot back, "Why do you want to know?" Instantly I wish I could grab the words back out of the air. Instead they hover there, naked and embarrassing, like a bad child I can't disassociate myself from. I watch him give an invisible mental snort, then drop the whole thing as if it hadn't happened. It's not really important to his plan, after all. So I give up and tell him.

We're still walking in my direction. I haven't had to make any turns yet that would show I'm leaving my route for his. From time to time a near-meaningless sentence falls out of my mouth.

"It's cold out tonight."

"Yeah, real cold."

He participates like a bad actor reading lines. We both know it's not necessary. Its main purpose—that of alleviating my nervousness—doesn't seem to be working. Besides, small talk sounds pretty silly when you put it alongside the thoughts running just beneath—both of us imagining a nakedness in the other we so far can't confirm. I know one thing he doesn't want—the me I appear to be to my friends. He wants a different me, naked and sweating and out of control, any iota of facade dissolved. And that's exactly what I needed. Even I know that now.

Inside my head I'm already beginning to imagine that I might be in love with him even as we're walking toward his apartment, toward his bed, his body. I'm already starting to see him as a warm, slightly frightening oasis against the backdrop of cold, dirty pavement, trash and leering car lights. Still walking, I watch the comparatively tiny practical portion of me tell the romantic side to shut up since it doesn't even know the guy.

The pickup was that unremarkable. I was easy, but I had to be. I was a lonely, horny, walking bundle of need. I probably left a trail of the stuff on the sidewalk behind me like a snail slick. And everything about him worked: big enough, dark enough, demanding enough. There was no choice involved.

The bedroom had black walls. Red light coming from a lava

lamp on the floor made it a warm and luscious hell. A fat mattress on a low platform was the only furniture I could see. I
was alone: Giovanni had gone into the other room for something. As I lay down it was like sinking into a dream, deeper and
deeper, until I disappeared into the bed. The red light turns to
black. I sink in deeper still and my thoughts slow until almost
motionless, until they begin to drown in heavy waves of bar-
biturate-like nothingness. Everything dissolves: me, the room,
my mind. All my anxiety from meeting Giovanni slips away
leaving me in sleepy comfort. I only want to stay there, deep
in soothing folds of darkness and ready to sleep like a child in a
warm bed on a winter night.

When I resurface he's standing over me, naked, watching.
His skin is drenched in the red light, glowing with it. I reach my
arms up toward his. We stay in this picture for some moments
as he savors the exquisite little gulf between my gesture and
his body. When he moves an inch closer, my hand runs slowly
down his velvet belly, over the red-liquid skin, and I draw him
to me. Then he kills me and revives me three times.

A month later he's everything. Everything about him is too
good: the body, the apartment, the silence. The calm he puts
inside of me like one long continuation of the feeling I had
sinking into his mattress that first night—that was just a small
taste of what Giovanni could be for me. Something important,
primal, needed. He treated the animal side of me with the same
care and nourishing a mother lavishes on a baby.

Now I remember that actually I'd taken some codeine on my
way home that night. I was looking for a little induced calm.
Things hadn't been going so well and I needed to make my
mind shut up for a while. But I forgot about that until sometime later, attributing all the dreaminess of the first night to

Giovanni's effulgence. By then he was installed inside me—the ultimate drug, effectively filling my bloodstream, warm and soothing; the thing that I wanted and knew I wanted. I loved knowing for a change.

I'm now thirty days old, all a continuation of that first night— hot bath, dream without end, big fat death of the outside world. He used sex as a means of communicating. I need sex as a way to get into heaven. I didn't know exactly what I wanted, and what I needed I got.

He told me he had to be touching me in some way all night, or he couldn't sleep: an arm slung across my back, a leg twisted together with one of mine, a hand on my hip. Most of all he liked me curled into his furry gut, the smaller curve of my body swallowed by his larger one. Together we formed one large womb providing a safety neither of us possessed on our own. Not so completely, at least. I was shocked to think he needed me. I was willing to let him have whatever I had that he might want, but I wasn't sure what that might be. My attributes are invisible to me. The beauty he sees in me is different from that which I think of owning. He was falling in love with a person I didn't know and I was that person.

I stayed in the apartment for thirty-two days without leaving. I was swallowed. Day and night happened only indoors. The first day I almost made the conscious decision to take the day off, but it was more like I just didn't want to go to work; then I didn't go the next day, then never went again. It wasn't a good job anyway. The first morning, as he was leaving, he came back into the bedroom—dressed now in the gray '40s suit from the film, or one like it—leaned down, kissed me, and said, "Stay here, okay?" I remember lying in bed in the dark room and spotting the black telephone in the corner, with an answering machine attached. Its red-and-green blinking lights lit up a tiny portion of the darkness, maybe six inches square, reminding me of a miniature airport landing strip. I watched the little reds and greens for a long time, enjoying the warm dark, thinking about calling in, too lazy to get up, then too unconcerned. Then I never thought about the phone again for thirty-two days.

The living room was sunny and warm most of the day, sun streaming in through the windows. They looked out onto the interior of a block of houses and apartment buildings, the part where all the backyards meet inside the block. If I tired of sunbathing on the floor, I could go to the window and look out. Flowers, trees, dirt, garbage, a child's swing set but no child, two women having coffee at an iron table. I couldn't be bored. When even this simple panorama was too much for me to take in, I'd return to the bare symmetry of the sun-drenched floor. Even here the grain of the wood could fascinate or overwhelm me into shutting my eyes for a dreamless float. It's all I wanted. Something had happened to me, I knew, but I didn't know what and I didn't really care to know. It was something I'd needed for as long as I could remember, only I'd never known what or how to get it. Somehow Giovanni was making it happen, was giving me the life I'd never had.

I lay on the floor as if it were a beach. The bedroom was always red and dark, each color dissolving into the other, always night—deep, black, and empty. That's the way I felt. It felt good. A lot fell away: my anxiety, my fear, my job, my apartment, my possessions, my need to create an existence. A new existence had already been created; all I had to do was slip into it. I started to feel alive again. My old life stripped away like dead skin. I abandoned everything that had happened before

I met Giovanni. It disappeared. I was sick of carrying history around. If it had gotten me anywhere it was to Giovanni, and now that I was here I didn't need to know how it had happened. Sex was a way to forget. Each night, each time he killed me and revived me, a little more of my past slipped away, leaving me free to be happy for perhaps the first time ever. I loved the emptiness. I felt clean for the first time since I was born.

Giovanni let me do all this: stay in the apartment for thirty-two days; sunbathe on the living room floor all afternoon; drown in the red-black night of the bedroom; empty out, die, and revive three times each night. He let me do this because I wanted to. His only demand was for me to do as I wanted in the hope that it would always lead me back to him. I owned him now. I used sex to become exactly what he wanted. That was how I had captured him. I was his property now. He used sex to become exactly what I needed. We were deforming into Siamese twins.

As a child, I needed everything. I couldn't get anything from just being me. I couldn't masturbate. I couldn't sleep alone, I couldn't make decisions. I was a body looking for a schedule or set of instructions. I didn't know exactly what I should be wanting: I only knew how to be unsettled with what was happening around me but with no clue as to how to change that into something more satisfying.

I had one unbreakable routine. I sat around until no one was looking and then walked out the door. I kept walking until I somehow stopped: zombie-ing across intersections without looking, continuing over lawns, through vacant lots, housing-tract construction sites, shopping malls. If I hit a wall, I'd pivot like a robot and start in a new direction. I wasn't going anywhere in particular—I didn't care about destination. I wasn't thinking, I was just walking. I didn't know what else to do. At the time my actions seemed involuntary, now I'm not so sure. Of course I'd be tracked down eventually. It all depended on how much of a head start I had.

During the spanking with the spatula that always followed, I'm told that I stared blankly into space. And why not? After all, I hadn't been trying to be bad. It was out of my control. When the other kids on the block got bored, they found a new game or made a nuisance of themselves. I was different. I was ready to go out and find whatever seemed to be calling me out of the little house, away from my Tinkertoys and the two-toned TV set. It didn't matter if I found it. I was just a tourist at heart, a lost soul accidentally born on the wrong continent and trying to find my way back to Paris, a three-year-old sex slave looking for a master.

On the thirty-third day I went out—I was now thirty-three days old—the sidewalk felt like rubber, like a thin membrane floating on water. I wasn't sure I could move out of the way if someone came toward me. I wasn't sure I could speak. Staying in a quasi-controlled environment for thirty-two days has nothing to do with being outside. I was sure I couldn't have forgotten how to live outside the apartment but the sidewalk still felt like rubber.

I walked to the "dime store." Nothing there cost a dime. Even a #2 pencil was fifteen cents. I bought a package of small adhesive shapes that were made to glow in the dark after a light's been shone on them. The woman who sold them to me was a dwarf with blonde hair. She wore thick platform shoes to make her four inches taller. Even so, she still only came up to the level of my belly. As she rang up my

purchase I suddenly had a paranoid vision of standing there blankly, unable to count out the money—like a three-year-old child. Indeed, as I lifted a handful of change toward her, most of it slid out of my hand and scattered onto the worn linoleum. She said, "Whoopsie daisy," the way my grandmother used to, the tone warm and meaningless, designed to make me feel more a victim of gravity than just plain clumsy. Her name was Mary. As she stooped to help me pick it up, I introduced myself and invited her to dinner the next night.

When she arrived the next night I was still on a high stool gluing the glowing shapes to the bedroom ceiling. I was making the Milky Way. Here I was God. I could recreate the star world any way I wanted.

Settling onto the bed below me, Mary kicked off her shoes, flipped her hair back out of her face, and told me she didn't usually accept dinner invitations from people she didn't know. "I have to be a little careful about people, being so small, but somehow I had a good feeling about you. I'm psychic, you know. I can usually trust my instincts about people. And you know what I thought about you? I thought, this guy doesn't need me for anything, he just wants company for dinner. A person who doesn't need you to be anything for them can be a good friend to have. So here I am. Actually I'm not as superstitious as this probably makes me sound. Besides, I never turn down a dinner invitation."

Far below me I could see her lying on the bed and talking. She looked even smaller than the day before. Without her shoes, her legs curled underneath her. For two hours she gave me suggestions about where to put the small glowing shapes, how a nebula should look, what parts of the Milky Way needed more filling in. From my perch I thought, *she certainly seems to*

know a lot about stars, she's a good person to have around at a time like this. I could take her suggestions or not, she didn't seem to care. She kept on giving advice either way, another trait that reminded me of my grandmother.

"How about a supernova over there. No, more to the right. A little more . . . right there. Perfect."

I lay down on the bed with her and we turned out the lights. The blackness above became a sky, a black heaven with a thousand dots of green-white light, as if somehow I had covered the ceiling in a black sheet full of tiny pinholes and then shone a bright light above it. The room had changed, but then again it hadn't. It was still the black night it had always been, only more so. The feeling of sinking still soothed me. We lay on the bed for three hours. I told Mary about having not left the apartment for thirty-two days. She told me about her childhood.

Giovanni sat in the living room reading. Later the three of us ordered out for Chinese and watched David Letterman. Billy Idol was being interviewed, only he wouldn't answer any of the questions. He had his leather shirt open to the waist and kept sliding his hand inside to play with his nipples. Mary and Giovanni found this slightly shocking for TV. I didn't. Then Mary said goodnight and went home. Giovanni took me into the bedroom and killed and revived me three times under the stars. Afterward, he told me he loved me for making the bedroom into heaven. I loved him for making my body into heaven. It was now thirty-four days since Giovanni followed me. I was the same number of days old. Then I fell asleep and dreamed about Mary.

Here's part of what Mary told me that first night. Two days after her father tried to kill himself, her mother put her two children into the car and drove to the beach. Mary was five

years old. The Santa Ana Freeway was bumper to bumper and it took hours to get there, hot and boring. The radio in the old Chevy was irritating with static but left on anyway, the same jingle repeating a hundred times: "One block Main Street, Santa Ana Freeway, Stanley's Chevrolet!" Other than that, no one said a word.

The Huntington Pier is long, old, and high above the water when you get out to the end. The three of them walk very slowly. The whole day seems as if it's happening in slow motion. Mary's mother wears a pink suit, something like the one Jackie Kennedy would make famous two years later in Dallas. In fact her mother looks something like Jackie Kennedy: dark shoulder-length hair, pink suit, medium high heels. Her face is beautiful and tense. They walk to the end of the pier and stand for a long time, not talking. Mary's mother holding each of their hands, one of them on either side. She's thinking. Anyone could tell. She's standing at the end of Huntington Pier where the water is very deep and the fishermen catch sand sharks and the barnacles on the pilings are said to be razor sharp.

Mary thinks about the one death she's already seen. She went fishing with her father and saw a girl jump off the pier here. The girl drowned. That day, her father stood, holding her hand, as they watched the Coast Guard cutter fish the body out of the water and bring it up to the aid station on the pier. Mary's thinking about that as she stands and watches the seagulls fight over little bits of bait and fish gut.

When she talks about that day now, her Jackie-on-the-pier story, she's got it down to one basic sentence: "There were gulls, fish smells, sun, a little breeze, and my mother in her pink suit holding her two children by the hands." One basic sentence for a scene that's flashed through her mind hundreds of thousands of times. "I understand what happened. I just don't know what it means.

"When my father came out of the hospital a year later, he rented a hotel room and stayed there for six days. He killed himself with a mixture of valium, Gordon's gin, and hypothermia. He passed out in a tub of cold water and his body temperature dropped until he died. When I was older, and my mother told me how he'd done it, I imagined him frozen from the inside out. She said his heart just stopped beating."

This is the story Mary told me the first night she came over, one day after I met her and thirty-four days after I met Giovanni.

The only people I know now are Giovanni—the man who followed me—and Mary. I never told anyone where I'd moved. I never went back to my old place; I didn't want anything there. Everything I needed was here. About the third day, Giovanni asked me if I needed anything from my old place. We were sitting at the little dinette table in the tiny room full of windows between the kitchen and the living room. I was wearing his plaid shirt. "No, nothing," I said. "I mean, you don't have a cat or anything?" *No*, I thought back, remembering, *I don't*. Dino was dead. I shook my head. "Good." That was the end of it.

I was still wearing Giovanni's clothes, only now it didn't seem like I was wearing someone else's clothes. Now they were just our clothes. That sounds silly, but the fact is we were both wearing them, every day. I never returned any of the phone calls to those friends that found out where I'd moved to. I let the machine talk instead. They were not my friends anymore. They were friends of someone they remembered me to be that I wasn't anymore, or maybe never had been. I'd never had that many friends anyway. Now as I moved about the apartment every other day or so the phone rang three times, then the message went off, then a maybe distantly familiar voice might say my name, leave a number, and hang up. As time went on this happened less and less.

On Sundays the three of us took Mary's one-eyed, no-tail dog, Barney, for walks in the park, or sometimes a picnic. Tuesday nights we'd go to Charlie's to watch Giovanni shoot pool. I loved holding the shiny glass balls in my hands. Sometimes I'd slip one in Mary's purse when no one was looking and take it home. Mary would roll her eyes at the theft in a slight bit of disapproval, then say nothing and walk out. In a way she was as attracted to the pool balls as I was, delighting in the growing collection. Mary attracted things anyway, all sorts of things, accumulating and stacked into her upstairs apartment over the dime store. Giovanni and I had almost nothing. Gio liked it spare, minimal, clean. A big pile of colored pool balls sat in one corner of the living room.

Coming into the kitchenette area one day, Mary spotted her mother languishing with coffee at the metal dinette table. Occasionally she brushed the hair out of her eyes with her hand. She was reading a stack of colorful magazines and smoking a cigarette. The effect was stunning, the style and positioning of the elements in the pose an almost unbelievably glamorous combination, so self-absorbed, so eloquently casual. A perfect laziness. "Maybe she's eating a little square pan of fudge with a spoon," Mary told me. "I can't recall." For a long time after this we steal cigarettes from the neighbors' house and lay them out with a magazine on the dinette, hoping to entice Mary's mother to repeat her impressive carelessness.

Sitting at the kitchen table, smoking a cigarette, with the latest issue of *Vanity Fair,* I try to imitate the way Mary remembered her mother looking that day. I drink more coffee. I try slumping more. I take another drag on my Salem, but her study in coolness escapes me. I'm a million miles from the image, from the experience I'm after. Maybe the magazine isn't trashy enough to make me not care about anything, to induce the total laziness. I wonder if possibly a hangover Mary never knew about is supposed to be part of the scene. Maybe it's the missing pan of fudge that's keeping the whole attitude from solidly setting in.

At some point, Giovanni decided the apartment had become too cluttered and he systematically began removing things, maybe one every other day. At first I hardly noticed. I didn't really know where these things went until one day Barney and I stumbled over our portable TV outside. I guess Giovanni had been putting the stuff out on the sidewalk free for anyone who wanted it. *That's Gio*, I thought to myself. I picked up the little TV and took it to Mary's. I had the key.

After a while there was nothing left in the apartment except the mattress in the bedroom, the lava lamp on the floor next to it, the dinette in the kitchen, and the Saturn chair in the living room. I didn't mind so long as he didn't throw out anything Mary had brought over. Next, the few things left started moving from room to room. One day the mattress was in what used to be the bedroom, then in the living room, maybe in the dining room a week later. As the mattress moved, the dinette and Saturn chair usually moved too. The rooms didn't really have names any more, except the bathroom. They were all just empty spaces. Boxes. I had to look each day to see where things were, but that wasn't too hard since there weren't many things and I wasn't doing anything but reading the paper and walking Barney anyway. I never asked him why he was doing it. He wanted to.

Then one day I realized that the phone no longer worked. It had been so long since it rang that I'd stopped thinking about it. I'd always let the machine answer anyway since the only one I wanted to talk to besides Giovanni was Mary, and she never called, she just came over. Or left a note. "Come by the store." I don't know when it stopped working.

Slowly I began to realize that Giovanni no longer had any friends besides Mary and me. At least not any that would come over. He always had before. I guess he spent so much time with us now they had just fallen away.

At first this bothered me a little. I didn't really know what was going on but I didn't want to ask. I wanted to just let him go through whatever it was he was doing. After all, he'd let me do whatever I wanted without question, as long as I was still there for him. I stopped thinking about it and listened to the radio more. At first I was bored. Then I stopped wanting to do anything else. Then it became satisfying. Listening to the radio seemed to be what I was supposed to do, so I was doing it.

I went out less and less, not wanting to move away from the radio on the living room floor. Giovanni took over some of Barney's walks. The rest of the time Barney would sunbathe with me on the living-room floor. He was old. Mostly he just slept or else listened to the radio too. I could tell he liked certain songs more than others. Chaka Khan was his favorite.

By this time Gio and I thought I must be going a little crazy again. Except for occasional short walks with Barney, I was going into another thirty-two-day hibernation. I was the one going crazy since the only thing I wanted to do was listen to the radio. Giovanni wasn't crazy for taking all the furniture out of the apartment and never speaking. I was crazy for living in an apartment that had no furniture with someone who never spoke.

We still made love every night. Amazing, terrific killings and resurrections, night after night. Those were the only sounds we made with each other. It was the only exercise I got. I could feel my legs and back and arms stretching, feel air coming into my comatose lungs. For the first time all day we'd be really looking at each other, our lips brushing, not able to get enough of each other, petting hair and arms and stomachs as if each of us were a little baby with the mother he totally loves and who totally loves him more than anyone else in the world. We were using sex to be together. Once in a while, at these times, I would whisper his name, just to make sure I still had it.

I lived on coffee and cereal. That's all I would eat. Plus a big bowl of vitamins left by the bed for me each morning with a note that said, "Eat these." Giovanni must be the one leaving them, but I was asleep so I don't know for sure. This went on for I don't know how long. Maybe if I'd felt I was in jail I'd have made marks on the wall to count off the days but I didn't so I didn't. Giovanni now took Barney for all of his walks. The front door was unlocked but I wasn't sure if there was a world beyond it anymore or, if so, what kind of world it was. I knew there must be a world that Giovanni went out into every day, but I wasn't sure that I could do the same. I pictured it as a membrane that you had to try and walk through. If it accepted you, you reached another place outside the apartment. If not, it bounced you back hard onto the floor, leaving you dazed and feeling something was wrong. Inside the apartment nothing was wrong. It was my world, the warm living-room floor and the soft radio. Perfect. Everything just as it should be. I ate my vitamins, had coffee

and cereal, petted Barney, followed the sunny spots on the floor
around the living room, listened to the radio, and made love at
night.

One night Barney woke me up to show me a mouse in his water
dish. Apparently it had tried to get a drink, fell in, and drowned.
Barney and I lay down on the cool linoleum and looked at the
little mouse body for a long time. Then Barney fell asleep.

From where I lay I could see the dinette table where Mary and
I had worked so hard at recreating the smoking-Jackie image
her mother had once evoked: silver legs, mosaic surface of grays
and dirty rose, metallic chairs covered in metal-deck vinyl. I
think those chairs were the only furniture Giovanni ever spent
money on. A big sculpture of Barney made out of insulating
wire hung above the table. I made that, a long time ago it now
seems. If you follow the wire Barney to the ceiling, and let
your eye travel down and around the bend of the doorframe
into the kitchen, you come to a yellowed and grease-spattered
de Kooning print, the shiny paper now dull and thick. It's an
ad for his Grand Palais show in Paris, 1979: a woman with
blonde hair and two big eyes, one bigger than the other, one
set higher than the other. She could be Mary. In the painting
you can't tell how tall she is. A series of slashing lines and
scribbles takes your eyes down to enormous breasts, barely
covered by what looks like a pink cocktail dress, down past
the triangular crotch with the extra line accents, past the type
that actually advertises the show, to the white slick of the
refrigerator.

My eyes stop when they get to the messy patchwork of newspaper clippings that Mary and I put up with the little black
magnets she stole from the dime store. Off to one side is a lime
green religious tract that an old lady once handed me on the

street. I lie on the cold linoleum listening to the refrigerator hum and Barney sleeping and go over and over the words:

> *You probably had a normal childhood. No major worries; no struggle for existence. And there were some high points: the first job; courtship and marriage; a new home; the first child.*
>
> *But now days pass by in monotony. So you shop aimlessly or watch TV or find hobbies. Some try divorce or alcohol. But nothing is solved.*
>
> *You see the neighbors in the same rut. There's no future except routine, then old age. Then death. And that's scary!*

I was still lying there with Barney when Mary came in. It was just starting to get light. She'd used her key, not wanting to wake us. She'd just got back and couldn't wait to see Barney. Mary didn't say a word about finding me naked on the kitchen floor, she just leaned down (which wasn't very far for her) and kissed me on the cheek. Sleepy Barney suddenly jumped up and started dancing around her, his toenails making a racket of little clicking sounds on the linoleum, snuffling and snorting and making whining noises as Mary petted him.

"Go get your clothes, and we'll take Barney for a walk. How's Gio?"

"He's okay."

"What happened to all the furniture? Never mind. Your TV's sitting on my coffee table. At least you still have the Saturn chair and the dinette. My God, I've got to be able to sit down somewhere when I come visit."

"Mary . . ."

"You know what I wanted to do? I wanted to come in this

morning, see Barney, and then crawl into bed with you and Gio. I missed you guys so much. You'd have been so surprised. I don't know, though, I might not have had the guts. I've never even seen Gio naked. Wait a minute, yes I have, that night I brought over the martinis and he was in the tub so we went in and sat around drinking martinis. That was so fun. How could I forget it. I even told my mother about that. I told her all about you two."

Barney trotted along in front of us sniffing invisible things of apparent importance. He hardly ever looked up; his eyes were always glued to the two inches of ground in front of his nose. It was cold out, leaves on the path. I hadn't realized that in the last forty-nine days the seasons had begun to change. It seemed like summer the last time I was out. Perhaps knowing I hadn't spoken in a while, Mary did all the talking, rattling on, jumping from one subject to another, then back to a previous one. When she really got going, you had to know Mary pretty well to follow. When Giovanni first met her, he'd ask me later what she was talking about. I'd tell him how she got to topic K from topic Z, and what K had to do with H, and how she got to H from A. Once you got to know Mary's mind, how quickly it moved, you learned to follow. You had to adopt her logic. If I'm around Mary all day I sometimes notice that I'm starting to think and sound like her. That means no one else will be able to follow me except Mary and Giovanni. Maybe Barney—I'm not so sure about him. But they're the only ones I talk to anyway.

I'm thinking about this as we walk and Mary continues to rattle. She hardly stops for a breath, occasionally reaching—she doesn't need to stoop—to give Barney a pat. After forty-eight days in the apartment, the streets are almost unbearably beautiful. I finally manage to speak, wedging in when Mary takes a breath. I tell her about Barney waking me up to show me the mouse in his water dish.

"He'll never drink out of that dish again. He's like that. Once he found a cricket swimming in his old dish and that was it. He never went near it again. Too bad, that Yogi Bear dish was pretty cute too."

Then I tell her about Giovanni throwing out all the furniture except the Saturn chair. Mary laughs and when I say "No, I'm really kind of concerned," she stops walking and takes both my hands.

"Listen, that's just Gio. He needs a change once in a while. He goes to work five days a week. He likes his work but gets a little freaked playing Mr. 9-to-5 sometimes, that's all. Didn't you ever think he maybe needed to do something to compete with your spells? He loves you. If you go crazy he'll take care of you for the rest of your life. And it's not just a physical thing— all that killing and reviving you talk about—it's deeper. He's not a talker. He just wants to feel it and do it. He doesn't say it, he shows it. And that's pretty great. So don't worry. The apartment's beautiful empty, you have to admit—good floors, good light. It'll fill up again. I'll fill it, slowly so as not to cause a stir, one thing at a time. My place is so crammed I've got to farm the stuff out somewhere. Besides, I'm giving up my storage bin at U-Haul. I'm sick of paying the damn rent on it."

I didn't even know Mary had a storage bin. Then she lowers the boom. She thinks it's time for me to get a job. Her words send a stinging sensation of violent fear up my spine to my head. A shiver runs through my brain, vibrates off the top of my head, and is gone.

"Just something part-time, no big deal. I'll help you find something in the neighborhood to start with." The fact is Mary already knows of a job opening at the place where we buy our coffee. This seems perfect to her because the hours wouldn't conflict with our morning visits. And we'd also be able to get free coffee. Mary, in her own way, always thinks things out logically.

"But what about *The Flintstones* in the afternoon?"

"Come on, I think we've seen enough of those to last a lifetime. Really, don't you think you're ready for this? I do. You can't do thirty-two days in this apartment again." (I didn't tell her it had actually been forty-eight by this time, more or less.) "You needed to do that, that's okay, but now you're through it. Let's face it, it's time, sweetie."

Unbelievably I somehow found all this making some kind of vague sense. I quietly began mulling over the image in my mind, picturing myself behind the coffee-store counter, wearing one of their dark green aprons, measuring out fresh beans into the grinder. In my mind, the other people who worked there seem pretty hip. And the place always smells good. Mary took my silence as a good sign and shut up for a while.

By the time we get back to the apartment, Giovanni's gone and I've pretty much snapped out of my forty-eight-day torpor. It happened that fast. I show Mary the tract on the fridge that possessed me the night before.

"Hmm, maybe we should drop that from the collection. It gives me the creeps."

The espresso pot's already rumbling on the stove. This causes Barney to retreat into the other room as usual. Once we're settled in at the dinette with our coffee, Mary begins again:

"You know she's not coming out this time, my mother. Our Jackie doesn't look too good. By the time I got there she'd already gone back into the hospital. I went in and—you know, she's not really our Jackie anymore at all. She's lost a lot of weight. She's got about four inches of gray roots showing. Almost white. In the last six months she's aged about ten years. Somehow she got old. Somehow I didn't think that would ever happen.

"She was asleep. I sat with her a long time. Then she woke up and we talked for a while. She's pretty weak but she was really happy to see me. She asked about you and Barney and Gio. When it was time to go I told her not to worry, she'd be out in a couple of days. She said, 'No, honey, not this time. I'm going to die soon, Mary. If I get out I won't get out for long.'

"I'm going back down in two weeks, after I get things squared away here. Will you come down with me, at least for a while? She wants to meet you. I told her about us reenacting the Jackie-at-the-dinette scene and she thought that was hysterical. I've got to go. She doesn't need me, it's not that, she's still the totally self-contained phenomenon she always was. It's just—I don't know, she's the one I always wanted to be. I want to see her a little more before she's finished being perfect."

Giovanni comes too, and Barney. For the weekend. Then I have to get back to start my new job. It's only part-time. Giovanni looks on it as an amusing experiment. He really doesn't care if I do it, he just wants me to do what I want to do. But I'm ready, and Mary wants me to do it. She made me promise to at least give it a try. I also have the job of painting her apartment while she's gone. I suspect it's just a ploy to keep me busy. She's going to give me $200 and I'll buy Giovanni a VCR for Christmas. Then we can all watch *The Flintstones* and *Our Miss Brooks* reruns at night. Except Tuesdays, cheap beer night, Gio's pool night.

Lust

Susan Minot

Leo was from a long time ago, the first one I ever saw nude. In the spring before the Hellmans filled their pool, we'd go down there in the deep end, with baby oil, and like that. I met him the first month away at boarding school. He had a halo from the campus light behind him. I flipped.

Roger was fast. In his illegal car, we drove to the reservoir, the radio blaring, talking fast, fast, fast. He was always going for my zipper. He got kicked out sophomore year.

By the time the band got around to playing "Wild Horses," I had tasted Bruce's tongue. We were clicking in the shadows on the other side of the amplifier, out of Mrs. Donovan's line of vision. It tasted like salt, with my neck bent back, because we had been dancing so hard before.

Tim's line: "I'd like to see you in a bathing suit." I knew it was his line when he said the exact same thing to Annie Hines.

You'd go on walks to get off campus. It was raining like hell, my sweater as sopped as a wet sheep. Tim pinned me to a tree, the woods light brown and dark brown, a white house half hidden with the lights already on. The water was as loud as a crowd hissing. He made certain comments about my forehead, about my cheeks.

We started off sitting at one end of the couch and then our feet were squished against the armrest and then he went over to turn off the TV and came back after he had taken off his shirt and then we slid onto the floor and he got up again to close the door, then came back to me, a body waiting on the rug.

You'd try to wipe off the table or to do the dishes and Willie would untuck your shirt and get his hands up under in front, standing behind you, making puffy noises in your ear.

He likes it when I wash my hair. He covers his face with it and if I start to say something, he goes, "Shush."

For a long time, I had Philip on the brain. The less they noticed you, the more you got them on the brain.

My parents had no idea. Parents never really know what's going on, especially when you're away at school most of the time. If she met them, my mother might say, "Oliver seems nice" or "I like that one" without much of an opinion. If she didn't like them, "He's a funny fellow, isn't he?" or "Johnny's perfectly nice but a drink of water." My father was too shy to talk to them at all unless they played sports and he'd ask them about that.

The sand was almost cold underneath because the sun was long gone. Eben piled a mound over my feet, patting around my ankles, the ghostly surf rumbling behind him in the dark. He was the first person I ever knew who died, later that summer, in a car crash. I thought about it for a long time.

"Come here," he says on the porch.

I go over to the hammock and he takes my wrist with two fingers.

"What?"

He kisses my palm then directs my hand to his fly.

Songs went with whichever boy it was. "Sugar Magnolia" was Tim, with the line "Rolling in the rushes / down by the riverside." With "Darkness Darkness," I'd picture Philip with his long hair. Hearing "Under My Thumb" there'd be the smell of Jamie's suede jacket.

We hid in the listening rooms during study hall. With a record cover over the door's window, the teacher on duty couldn't look in. I came out flushed and heady and back at the dorm was surprised how red my lips were in the mirror.

• • •

One weekend at Simon's brother's, we stayed inside all day with the shades down, in bed, then went out to Store 24 to get some ice cream. He stood at the magazine rack and read through *MAD* while I got butterscotch sauce, craving something sweet.

I could do some things well. Some things I was good at, like math or painting or even sports, but the second a boy put his arm around me, I forgot about wanting to do anything else, which felt like a relief at first until it became like sinking into a muck.

It was different for a girl.

When we were little, the brothers next door tied up our ankles. They held the door of the goat house and wouldn't let us out till we showed them our underpants. Then they'd forget about being after us and when we played whiffle ball, I'd be just as good as they were.

Then it got to be different. Just because you have on a short skirt, they yell from the cars, slowing down for a while, and if you don't look, they screech off and call you a bitch.

"What's the matter with me?" they say, point-blank.

Or else, "Why won't you go out with me? I'm not asking you to get married," about to get mad.

Or it'd be, trying to be reasonable, in a regular voice, "Listen, I just want to have a good time."

So I'd go because I couldn't think of something to say back

that wouldn't be obvious, and if you go out with them, you sort of have to do something.

I sat between Mack and Eddie in the front seat of the pickup. They were having a fight about something. I've a feeling about me.

Certain nights you'd feel a certain surrender, maybe if you'd had wine. The surrender would be forgetting yourself and you'd put your nose to his neck and feel like a squirrel, safe, at rest, in a restful dream. But then you'd start to slip from that and the dark would come in and there'd be a cave. You make out the dim shape of the windows and feel yourself become a cave, filled absolutely with air, or with a sadness that wouldn't stop.

Teenage years. You know just what you're doing and don't see the things that start to get in the way.

Lots of boys, but never two at the same time. One was plenty to keep you in a state. You'd start to see a boy and something would rush over you like a fast storm cloud and you couldn't possibly think of anyone else. Boys took it differently. Their eyes perked up at any little number that walked by. You'd act like you weren't noticing.

The joke was that the school doctor gave out the pill like aspirin. He didn't ask you anything. I was fifteen. We had a picture of him in assembly, holding up an IUD shaped like a T. Most girls were on the pill, if anything, because they couldn't handle a diaphragm. I kept the dial in my top drawer like my mother and thought of her each time I tipped out the yellow tablets in the morning before chapel.

• • •

If they were too shy, I'd be more so. Andrew was nervous. We stayed up with his family album, sharing a pack of Old Golds. Before it got light, we turned on the TV. A man was explaining how to plant seedlings. His mouth jerked to the side in a tic. Andrew thought it was a riot and kept imitating him. I laughed to be polite. When we finally dozed off, he dared to put his arm around me, but that was it.

You wait till they come to you. With half fright, half swagger, they stand one step down. They dare to touch the button on your coat then lose their nerve and quickly drop their hand so you—you'd do anything for them. You touch their cheek.

The girls sit around in the common room and talk about boys, smoking their heads off.

"What are you complaining about?" says Jill to me when we talk about problems.

"Yeah," says Giddy. "You always have a boyfriend."

I look at them and think, As if.

I thought the worst thing anyone could call you was a cock-teaser. So, if you flirted, you had to be prepared to go through with it. Sleeping with someone was perfectly normal once you had done it. You didn't really worry about it. But there were other problems. The problems had to do with something else entirely.

• • •

Mack was during the hottest summer ever recorded. We were renting a house on an island with all sorts of other people. No one slept during the heat wave, walking around the house with nothing on which we were used to because of the nude beach. In the living room, Eddie lay on top of a coffee table to cool off. Mack and I, with the bedroom door open for air, sweated and sweated all night.

"I can't take this," he said at three A.M. "I'm going for a swim." He and some guys down the hall went to the beach. The heat put me on edge. I sat on a cracked chest by the open window and smoked and smoked till I felt even worse, waiting for something—I guess for him to get back.

One was on a camping trip in Colorado. We zipped our sleeping bags together, the coyotes' hysterical chatter far away. Other couples murmured in other tents. Paul was up before sunrise, starting a fire for breakfast. He wasn't much of a talker in the daytime. At night, his hand leafed about in the hair at my neck.

There'd be times when you overdid it. You'd get carried away. All the next day, you'd be in a total fog, delirious, absent-minded, crossing the street and nearly getting run over.

The more girls a boy has, the better. He has a bright look, having reaped fruits, blooming. He stalks around, sure-shouldered, and you have the feeling he's got more in him, a fatter heart, more stories to tell. For a girl, with each boy it's as though a petal gets plucked each time.

• • •

Then you start to get tired. You begin to feel diluted, like watered-down stew.

Oliver came skiing with us. We lolled by the fire after everyone had gone to bed. Each creak you'd think was someone coming downstairs. The silver loop bracelet he gave me had been a present from his girlfriend before.

On vacations, we went skiing, or you'd go south if someone invited you. Some people had apartments in New York that their families hardly ever used. Or summer houses, or older sisters. We always managed to find someplace to go.

We made the plan at coffee hour. Simon snuck out and met me at Main Gate after lights-out. We crept to the chapel and spent the night in the balcony. He tasted like onions from a submarine sandwich.

The boys are one of two ways: either they can't sit still or they don't move. In front of the TV, they won't budge. On weekends they play touch football while we sit on the sidelines, picking blades of grass to chew on, and watch. We're always watching them run around. We shiver in the stands, knocking our boots together to keep our toes warm, and they whizz across the ice, chopping their sticks around the puck. When they're in the rink, they refuse to look at you, only eyeing each other beneath low helmets. You cheer for them but they don't look up, even if it's a face-off when nothing's happening, even if they're doing drills before any game has started at all.

● ● ●

Dancing under the pink tent, he bent down and whispered in my ear. We slipped away to the lawn on the other side of the hedge. Much later, as he was leaving the buffet with two plates of eggs and sausage, I saw the grass stains on the knees of his white pants.

Tim's was shaped like a banana, with a graceful curve to it. They're all different. Willie's like a bunch of walnuts when nothing was happening, another's as thin as a thin hot dog. But it's like faces; you're never really surprised.

Still, you're not sure what to expect.

I look into his face and he looks back. I look into his eyes and they look back at mine. Then they look down at my mouth so I look at his mouth, then back to his eyes then, backing up, at his whole face. I think, Who? Who are you? His head tilts to one side.

I say, "Who are you?"

"What do you mean?"

"Nothing."

I look at his eyes again, deeper. Can't tell who he is, what he thinks.

"What?" he says. I look at his mouth.

"I'm just wondering," I say and go wandering across his face. Study the chin line. It's shaped like a persimmon.

"Who are you? What are you thinking?"

He says, "What the hell are you talking about?"

Then they get mad after, when you say enough is enough. After, when it's easier to explain that you don't want to. You wouldn't dream of saying that maybe you weren't really ready to in the first place.

Gentle Eddie. We waded into the sea, the waves round and plowing in, buffalo-headed, slapping our thighs. I put my arms around his freckled shoulders and he held me up, buoyed by the water, and rocked me like a sea shell.

I had no idea whose party it was, the apartment jam-packed, stepping over people in the hallway. The room with the music was practically empty, the bare floor, me in red shoes. This fellow slides onto one knee and takes me around the waist and we rock to jazzy tunes, with my toes pointing heaven-ward, and waltz and spin and dip to "Smoke Gets in Your Eyes" or "I'll Love You Just for Now." He puts his head to my chest, runs a sweeping hand down my inside thigh and we go loose-limbed and sultry and as smooth as silk and I stamp my red heels and he takes me into a swoon. I never saw him again after that but I thought, I could have loved that one.

You wonder how long you can keep it up. You begin to feel as if you're showing through, like a bathroom window that only lets in grey light, the kind you can't see out of.

They keep coming around. Johnny drives up at Easter vaca-tion from Baltimore and I let him in the kitchen with everyone sound asleep. He has friends waiting in the car.

"What are you, crazy? It's pouring out there," I say.

"It's okay," he says. "They understand."

So he gets some long kisses from me, against the refrigerator, before he goes because I hate those girls who push away a boy's face as if she were made out of Ivory soap, as if she's that much greater than he is.

The note on my cubby told me to see the headmaster. I had no idea for what. He had received complaints about my amorous displays on the town green. It was Willie that spring. The headmaster told me he didn't care what I did but that Casey Academy had a reputation to uphold in the town. He lowered his glasses on his nose. "We've got twenty acres of woods on this campus," he said. "If you want to smooch with your boyfriend, there are twenty acres for you to do it out of the public eye. You read me?"

Everybody'd get weekend permissions for different places, then we'd all go to someone's house whose parents were away. Usually there'd be more boys than girls. We raided the liquor closet and smoked pot at the kitchen table and you'd never know who would end up where, or with whom. There were always disasters. Ceci got bombed and cracked her head open on the banister and needed stitches. Then there was the time Wendel Blair walked through the picture window at the Lowes' and got slashed to ribbons.

He scared me. In bed, I didn't dare look at him. I lay back with my eyes closed, luxuriating because he knew all sorts of expert angles, his hands never fumbling, going over my whole body, pressing the hair up and off the back of my head, giving an extra hip shove, as if to say *There*. I parted my eyes slightly, keeping the screen of my lashes low because it was too much to look at him, his mouth loose and pink and parted, his eyes looking through my forehead, or kneeling up, looking through my throat. I was ashamed but couldn't look him in the eye.

• • •

You wonder about things feeling a little off-kilter. You begin to feel like a piece of pounded veal.

At boarding school, everyone gets depressed. We go in and see the housemother, Mrs. Gunther. She got married when she was eighteen. Mr. Gunther was her high school sweetheart, the only boyfriend she ever had.

"And you knew you wanted to marry him right off?" we ask her.

She smiles and says, "Yes."

"They always want something from you," says Jill, complaining about her boyfriend.

"Yeah," says Giddy. "You always feel like you have to deliver something."

"You do," says Mrs. Gunther. "Babies."

After sex, you curl up like a shrimp, something deep inside you ruined, slammed in a place that sickens at slamming, and slowly you fill up with an overwhelming sadness, an elusive gaping worry. You don't try to explain it, filled with the knowledge that it's nothing after all, everything filling up finally and absolutely with death. After the briskness of loving, loving stops. And you roll over with death stretched out alongside you like a feather boa, or a snake, light as air, and you . . . you don't even ask for anything or try to say something to him because it's obviously your own damn fault. You haven't been able to—to what? To open your heart. You open your legs but can't, or don't dare anymore, to open your heart.

• • •

It starts this way:

You stare into their eyes. They flash like all the stars are out. They look at you seriously, their eyes at a low burn and their hands no matter what starting off shy and with such a gentle touch that the only thing you can do is take that tenderness and let yourself be swept away. When, with one attentive finger they tuck the hair behind your ear, you—

You do everything they want.

Then comes after. After when they don't look at you. They scratch their balls, stare at the ceiling. Or if they do turn, their gaze is altogether changed. They are surprised. They turn casually to look at you, distracted, and get a mild distracted surprise. You're gone. Their blank look tells you that the girl they were fucking is not there anymore. You seem to have disappeared.

Pretending to Say No

Bruce Benderson

I'm not shitting you, man, and why should I be? She came, she came to our house! No, really, the buzzer rings and I tell myself, I'm not answering that shit cause if somebody wants to see me they call first. I only answer that bell when I know who it is! But the bell keeps ringing and ringing and Tito, that's my uncle trying to sleep, says, Answer the fucking bell and tell them if they touches it one more time I'm going to blow 'em away! Me in my drawers yet. Who's going to run downstairs five flights to give 'em that message? So I press the buzzer, listen for the door and shouts, You got the wrong place whoever you fucking are, stop leaning on that bell unless you want to get blown away! Let me in, a white-lady voice calls up the stairwell, It's me, Nancy Reagan.

No shit, man. It was the President's wife coming to see us. So I ask Tito, Quick, you know Nancy Reagan? 'Cause since he got involved with those Colombians and started to deal the crack he has contact with some very swift people. They got limousines and everything. And he half asleep saying, Sure, I used to fuck her but her ass was too tight. No, I says, the President's wife.

Yes, it's the President's wife, comes the white-lady voice right at the door this time, Would you please open up for a minute? And my uncle, hearing it too, sits right up in the bed: I gonna knock that damn fool head right off those shoulders if you brought that white drag queen up here, what's her name. No, I says, I didn't tell no drag queen to come up here! I didn't bring no drag queen up here except maybe once. And it was Tito got me to know them, always running crack for him to this bar near the Deuce, and some of those queens, really, listen, if you was standing right next to one of them you might think she was real.

So I walk real quiet to the door, on tippytoes, and take a good look through the peephole. It's a white lady for sure, it ain't no drag queen. For one things this one's too old, and real skinny. She's not wearing no coat and she's got a red dress on. What you want? I call through the door. I just want to come in for a moment, she says and sticks her hand in her purse, pulls out bills and waves them at the peephole. She got money, I tell my uncle. Oh shit, says he, some white bitch coming in the middle of the night to buy crack. But don't let her in now, say I ain't got none. Come back tomorrow, I call through the door. Please, she says. We ain't got nothing, lady, go away.

Then she starts banging on the door real loud, louder than Mr. T. can hit a door, so my uncle gets really pissed and telling China Sue his Chinese chick that he in bed with, Mama, you roll yourself up in this quilt here, and cover your head, ok? 'cause I going to open the door, and he went and got the shotgun. Ok, he goes. Now when I give the sign, you throw the door open, one, two, three, go! He aims the gun and I throw open the door. Wait! goes the white lady, don't do it! I come as a friend. I ain't going to shoot you if you moves your ass out this building now, lady, I ain't got no scotty and I don't want no trouble from the super. Hear me, please, for a second, says she. Who sent you here? says Tito. I just rang any bell. What you doing that for? I need help . . . Now wait a minute, lady, if I let you in, what you going to do? I'll even pay you. She waves the bills at us again, and the top one at least, well that's a twenty. Tito keeps the gun on her but motions with his shoulder. Get in here and put the money on the table.

Nancy Reagan gives a sigh of relief, comes in and puts the money on the table. Tito picks it up. Now what else you got in that purse? Give it here. Oh there's no need for that, she says, your kindness will be rewarded. I've just come from Odyssey House. Do you know what that is? The drug program? I says. Nancy Reagan smiles and at that moment I know it's her.

So I tell Tito, Yo, Man, this ain't no crack head, this be Nancy Reagan. Tito looks at her close and says, C'mon, man, I told you before if you be bringing those drag queens here from the Deuce you got to tell me first. You can't trust a drag queen, they into stealing and acting like some kind of grand lady, that's what they are all about. Now you got to go 'cause I don't want my nephew hanging out with drag queens.

Yo, man, this ain't a drag queen, you be making a big mistake.

Tito takes another look at her and then he calls Suzy. Tito trusts her about some things. So China Sue comes out and Tito says, Suzy, this a drag queen? Oh my god, Suzy goes, and runs back to the bedroom and puts a sheet on.

So Tito puts down the gun and he kind of bows to her and says, How you doin', Nancy Reagan?

Not so well, says she, since you ask. Maybe you happened to watch TV tonight? Yeah, I did, says Tito, what that got to do with it? Well, says Nancy, didn't you notice what happened to me? Oh, I saw it, pipes up Sue, coming back with the sheet wrapped around her. You were at the drug program and you put your arm around this little black kid and he told the TV audience how he used to take angel dust and how much you helped him? Nancy Reagan listens real careful to every word China Sue says, and then looks her straight in the eye and says, Is that *all* you saw?

Yes, Mrs. Reagan, you were wonderful, oh, and then you said that this was only one of many young lives that had almost been ruined by the insanity of drugs. But tell me, dear, Nancy says, was it all in closeup? I don't know. Well, would anybody happen to have a needle? Nancy says. Tito's mouth drops open, my eyes bug out. And a little bit of thread? Nancy goes on. You see when the reporters left and I went into the ladies' room, I bent down to fix my hose and saw that the hem of my dress had come undone. In front. And here we were supposed to go right on to a midnight supper to discuss the fund-raiser and I was stuck in the ladies' room with a sagging hem. So I went out another entrance hoping to find somebody who could help me fix the thing before I had to face another reporter. I was so terribly embarrassed, I just couldn't go back, and when I realized there wasn't anywhere to find a needle and thread this time of night, I panicked and began ringing doorbells and now I'm at wit's end . . .

She keeps going on like that while she parks her ass right at our kitchen table, and puts her purse down so I can take a good look at it. Genuine alligator. Well, I says to myself, too bad I didn't noticed that before, Nancy Reagan, when I was trying to figure was you shitting us.

So I go over to her, and real polite and everything says, You want a Bud? I'd love one, says Nancy. Well give her a glass, barks Tito. A glass will not be necessary, Nancy tells him.

Don't you worry, goes China Sue, I can fix that hem for you pronto. Tito, you got any thread? It'll have to be scarlet, says Nancy, or at least a magenta. She puts her hand to her ears to see if both earrings is still there and takes a swallow of beer.

Tito starts running all over the place, opening drawers, cursing, and slamming 'em shut, looking for thread. And I am wishing I'd cleaned up like he wanted me to before China Sue come over so's the place wouldn't look so bad.

Nancy Reagan takes a good look around, checks the place out. Well, look at you, I keep thinking. Here's the First Lady of our country, but she ain't wearing no diamonds or Gucci and not even one gold chain. Shit, if I had her money I'd be wearing ten gold chains and mink-lined Adidas.

So where are your parents this evening? she asks. Oh, they's out, I answer quick. Out to dinner. And will they be back soon? Nancy says, looking at the lipstick on her beer can and covering it up with her hand. Carlos ain't got no parents, Suzy pipes up. Everybody has parents, Nancy sasses back. So Suzy wraps the sheet over her head and ranks, Well he don't, what you think a that? and Nancy stares up at the wall.

What about him, anyway? I says to my uncle, talking about

my father. He dead or what? He ain't dead, he in jail, says Tito.
You know that. And what does your father do? Nancy goes on,
like Tito didn't say nothing. Construction, I tell her. But I lives
with my uncle. Uncle here don't mind my staying here long's I
clean up before he brings girls over. And I do all the laundry for
the both of us too.

Well how about your little sister, says Nancy, can't she help
out too? You mean Suzy? That ain't a sister. Can't you see she
Chinese? She's Tito's wife. Carlos, shut your mouth! Suzy hol-
lers, laughing. They ain't married and shit, I goes on, she's just
his woman. And how old a woman is she? is Nancy's next dig.
Fourteen, I says. But I'm eighteen. I got ID. You want to see it?
I get up to get the proof I bought at Playland but Nancy starts
waving me down.

Now don't you start giving me that kind of questioning shit
in my own house, First Lady, Tito says, trying to sound polite. I
wouldn't do it if I was in yours. Nancy pulls a mean face at him
and grabs for the alligator purse, she opens it up. I'm really glad
to have met all of you, she tells us in a sweet ho-voice. Did you
find the thread? If I did I would a told you, says Tito, getting
pissed. That's strange, she says in a voice gone all cold, that you
don't have any, and she keeps looking through that purse. Come
to think of it they said on television something about her having
a gun in there.

Fiddlesticks! she says all of a sudden. Don't tell me I forgot
that beeper? Now how am I ever going to get in touch with
Jim? She snaps the purse shut loud and Suzy jumps and starts
laughing again. The two of them acting so spooky, it's starting
to scare the daylights out of me.

Who's this Jim? Tito'd like to know. We don't want no Jim
up here. Jim's my bodyguard, and he's a perfectly lovely fellow,

Nancy tells him. Yeah? You got a bodyguard? I says. She just gives me a look like don't put me on, dude. Shit, I goes on, I bet he gots some fresh weapons, I mean since you rule the country he can get his hands on just about anything. We don't rule the country, Nancy says, and starts looking bullets at me. Hold on a minute, I says to myself, and if she do got a gun in there? So I tell her how sorry I am about opening the door in my drawers. I really didn't know you was deciding to come and see us. And anyway, we got plenty of beer, why don't I put a little music on. That's sweet of you, she thanks me, and this time it's that same hooker's voice. Go ahead and do what you usually do.

So I put something mellow on. It's got a good beat. And before I know it I start relaxing and forget all about that we got the First Lady sitting right here. Tito and Suzy are maxing too. Come here, baby, he tells the Chi-nee. They snuggle up and bug out on each other, 'cause to tell the truth they was very high when they went to bed. Suzy got these problems in her pussy, she went to the hospital twice but they didn't do nothing. They said it was some kind of miscarriage and they sent her home stuffed up with Kotex but still bleeding. That was yesterday, I think, and since it hurt so much Tito give her all the crack she wants, he even put a little bit in her pussy. It was more than the hospital would do.

Finally I says, Nancy, you comfortable? I can call you that, right? Oh yes, she says, and I'm comfortable, but Ron must be worried. You mean the President, I says. No, she says, I mean Ron, Jr., my son. He was with me tonight. Then damn right, I agree with her. Like if I thought some drug addict at Odyssey House was to fuck with my mother or my sister I would be getting my gun already, they would not be alive today. You must care a lot about your mother and sister, she says. Yeah, I'm a family man. You want to see a picture of my baby girl? You mean a picture of your girlfriend? she says. No, I says, my little baby girl, she's a cute little thing. But weren't you just telling me about your girlfriends? says Nancy. I didn't tell you about no girlfriends, I says. Tito the only one brings girls up here, that why I got to clean the house up for him. I don't trust fooling around with no girls anymore. You never know who they been with. They all sick.

Sick? asks Nancy, and she starts playing with that hem again. Well, I says, I know this girl lost all her weight. They says she got the AIDS. Had these terrible headaches in the hospital. They wanted to cut her head open but she wouldn't let them. She left in the middle of the night 'cause they said they wouldn't let her out.

The First Lady lets go of that hem. The poor girl! she starts shouting at me. Yo, wait a minute, I tells her. I know rich people got delicate stomachs. But it ain't my fault. Me and my uncle are helping her out all the time. Anytime she wants to get high, we get her some dope 'cause we be willing to protect this dude that supplies it.

Oh, but this is terrible, terrible, says Nancy, like a little chick all of a sudden instead of an old lady. This is so terrible that I can't believe what you're saying is true. You are giving heroin to an AIDS victim. Well, yeah, I says, we are doing what we can because we are good people. We try to help out when we can. If I have my facts straight, she lays on me, drug abuse can give that awful disease to people. No shit, I says, you mean we're making her get more sick?

Just a minute, Tito interrupts, and he lets go of China Sue. Every time we get her high she thanks us and telling us how much better she is feeling. But that's only temporary, Nancy shoots back, you're killing her. We won't do it no more, Suzy promises. But the First Lady has already got a whole different look on her face, a bright idea. Write a letter to me, at the White House. A letter? says Tito. Well I ain't going to sign it. We're going to make certain this young girl gets help, says Nancy, that's all. You mean you got something that will make her feel better? I says. And she nods. It's all the lady will tell us and it sounds mysterious. Probably something only she can get hold of.

So I am worrying how am I going to write this letter when the worst thing happens. Because the doorbell starts to ring again. I keep making like it's not, but whoever it is is leaning on it like the First Lady did before. And the more it rings the madder Tito is getting. Until finally he starts calling out my name: Carlos, c'mere! And I go over and he shouts in my ear, Go downstairs and get rid of you-know-who!

That's when I realize I still got just my shorts on and run into the bedroom red as a beet. I start pulling on my pants quick so I can get down there and get rid of her before she gets inside the building—'cause I know who it be! But I know it's too late too, 'cause, someways, she is always getting in this building. I can hear those heels, then her calling through the door, Carlos, Carlos honey, open up!

Don't you answer that fucking door! Tito hisses at me, but she hears him and shouts back, What's a matter, you got a girl in there?

So Nancy grabs her purse quick and stands up. What's going on? she says loud, which is what we didn't need. All you ever do is lie to me! comes through the door, and Wait till I get my hands on you! Oh, says Nancy, even louder, Look at the trouble I'm causing after you were so nice. Young lady! Don't worry, I am not his girlfriend, I'm Nancy Reagan!

Bitch! comes the answer through the door, I'm Diana Ross! So Nancy gets right up and opens the door and says, You see? I'm not his girlfriend.

Well, it's this black queen comes up here sometimes. Calls herself Chaka Con, like the singer. She gives Nancy the onceover and can't believe her eyes. Honey, that drag is so convincing! But do you really want to look that old? Connie, shut up, says China Sue, this is the First Lady. Hmm, hmm, says Con, looks like the Last Lady to me.

Connie comes over to sit on my lap. Whatever got into me, thinking you was cheating on me. I take back everything I said.

Chaka, you got to leave, Tito tells her. I just finished saying to Carlos that he got to ask me first before he bring a drag queen up here. But instead of getting up, Connie gets mad. No queens, huh. Then what she doing here?

Connie, I tells her, this is Nancy Reagan for real. Ok, says Connie, it's a big world out there, and anybody can be anything they want. Nancy Reagan's got class and I can see somebody wanting to do her drag, if they can afford it. I ain't complaining. Now I'm black so I want to be Chaka or Sheila E., but if I was white, I'd probably want to do Farrah Fawcett or somebody.

What you want here tonight? growls Tito. Ok, I'll get to the point. I come to get a ten but I only got five and I can bring the rest to you tomorrow. I don't sell that stuff no more, says Tito. What's a matter with you, says Connie, you know you can trust me. I really want to get high, baby. I'll make it worth you while. Both a you.

Chaka Con licks her lips and looks at Tito, then at me.

Me and Tito try to give the First Lady a look like what is this queen talking about, but Nancy has turned into some kind of statue. Maybe she has slipped a Valium. Chaka starts looking her up and down. What you doing here, honey? I ripped my dress, says Nancy. This isn't the girl you were telling me about, is it? Oh no, First Lady, I swears, this one don't take no dope.

Chaka Con takes in Nancy's purse. Oooh, look at that! It's just like the one Nancy was carrying on TV tonight. Where'd you get it and how you know she was gonna have it tonight? You come here to cop, girl? Why else would a white queen with an expensive purse come all the way down here? Come on, honey, share with your sisters, I'll give you five and you give me a rock.

So all of a sudden Nancy gets this look in her eyes like something dawned on her. No, that ain't it either, how can I explain it? It's like maybe that is happening somewhere in her head but then she deciding to show that to us. And slow like a statue with a motor in it she turns to me and says, *So that's what's going on.*

Tito hops up fast. After all this is the President's wife. You going to believe any nigger drag queen come in here out of the street, Mrs. Reagan? he says.

The Con hops up too. Wait a minute, dudes, what is going on here? I demand to know! Who is this queen and why is she making everybody so jumpy?

Chaka Con, says China Sue, I am trying to tell you! This is the First Lady! She come here to get her hem sewn.

So Chaka walks right up to the First Lady and looks into her face. And then she takes a good look at the hands and the shoe size too, and says. Holy Shit, you're her! And she grabs hold the First Lady's hand, says, Mrs. Reagan, I didn't know, will you ever forgive me? I have admired you for such a long time. All my girlfriends love you.

It's perfectly all right, says the First Lady. I know you didn't know.

Chaka Con grabs a mirror out of her purse, checks herself out fast and throws it back in. Have you, have you known these folks long? she asks. We just met tonight, Nancy tells her. Umm, excuse me for asking, but in that purse, would you happen to have a needle and thread? No, honey, I mean Mrs. Reagan, I don't, says Connie like some kind of lady, I do all my sewing at home. In fact I am known as quite a seamstress. If you like, I will send my address to the White House and you can drop by for alterations anytime you please.

But Nancy gets a deep-freeze look in her eyes again, I never seen such a hard look, and gives a long sigh that everybody can hear, before she says, How kind of you to offer. Now who expected her to say that after that look and that sigh? But I need help now, she goes on, and drops her head and covers up her face with her hands. You can hear a pin drop.

Suzy is looking down at her feet, 'cause she don't want to see the First Lady that way. Me, I keep quiet. Finally Chaka says, Listen, now buck up, lady, c'mon now, I mean you are the First Lady, you ain't supposed to be crying like that over one silly little hem. Now cut it out, will you. You got responsibilities.

It's easy for you to say, Nancy whimpers, you don't know what it's like. Nobody does. So Chaka Con gets up and puts her hand on the First Lady's shoulder. Mrs. Reagan, Mrs. Reagan child, you stop that crying now. And the First Lady says. Well, we have feelings too.

Can I ask you something? Chaka says. You want me to get that needle and thread for you? Same color as the dress you're wearing? That would be ever so kind of you, the First Lady mumbles through her fingers.

Then don't you worry, Mrs. Reagan, croons Connie, but— uh, well there ain't no stores open now, oh I mean I could get you some black thread—the First Lady shivers a little when she says this to her—but to match your color, well I'm going to have to go all the way up to 128th Street, to a friend's a mine . . .

Nancy looks up. Then you'd better hurry. Do you need cab fare? Well, the cab costs a lot, I hate to ask you for that, child, says Chaka Con. But already Nancy is opening that purse and all of us kind of leaning over to peek inside.

How much do you need? says Nancy.

How much do I need? How much do I need? says Chaka. Mrs. Reagan, I got lots of needs. See this wig? See these shoes, see this dress? Well, the wig costs money, the shoes costs money, and the dress costs money. You know how it is, don't you. I been looking for a job. I sure hope I find one tomorrow. Because, you know, I'm not like those other niggers out there. How I look, the kind of image I have, well, that's important to me. I can't stand people don't take care a themselves. People who let themselves go and ain't got no respect for themselves. They make me sick, you know what I mean? They lying in their own shit, they expect other people to carry the load for them and then's they don't appreciate it when's they do! And I don't want to be one of those people. I mean it's hard for all of us, ain't it? All I need is just a little headstart, things is bad now but all I need is just a little push to get me going 'cause I got plans. And once I get going nothing can stop me. What you got in that purse there, anyways?

Nancy shuts that purse fast. You—you got a weapon in there? Connie says, and she looks up at Tito and swallows. Don't believe everything you read in the papers, Nancy sneers. I didn't mean nothing by that, Mrs. Reagan. Now listen, you want me to get that needle and thread for you?

The First Lady's eyes kind of go dim. I suppose so, she says. Well, gimme a hundred dollars, says Con.

Nancy starts to freeze up again but makes a big effort. She looks real hard at Chaka Con and she starts to blink a whole lot. I pay it back to you, says Chaka. So Nancy goes back in that purse and takes out two fifty-dollar bills, hands 'em to the Con. Tito, Chaka says, can I talk to you for a minute? But what about the thread? Nancy says. Oh I'm going right out, child, lickety-split.

Chaka gets up and gallops into the bathroom.

So now me and Suzy are sitting there alone with the First Lady, and Suzy is just looking down at her feet and finally says, I got to get a drink of water, and trots away too. And I'm left there staring at Nancy so after a minute I says excuse me too and go in the bathroom too. And Tito is just now lighting up that pipe and Chaka Con got it stuck between her lips. But when she sees all these folks and only one little rock in there, she says, C'mon, load it up, I want a king-size toke.

So we begin to get high, and 'cause Tito has really packed that pipe up, after two tokes my head is rushing like you wouldn't believe. So when we hear Nancy banging on that door, we look at each other and bursts out laughing. But finally Tito says, Well we got to go out there. And ones of us got to go find that thread for her. And that'll be you, right, Chaka Con? And Connie looks at him and says, Unh, unh, baby. I'm the one got us this money to pay for all this shit, I ain't going nowhere. So Tito says, Carlos, you got to go and find that thread. And I tell him, I'm too stoned. So we decide that we going to tell her that Chaka just remembered that friend she thought she had on 128th Street ain't there no more, she made a big mistake. And if she asks us for the money back, we only give her twenty because she owes us the rest for letting her chill out here. 'Cause wouldn't the kind of hotel that she would go to cost even more?

So we go out there together and tell the First Lady just how it has to be. And everybody is waiting for her to get shit-faced mad and call that bodyguard to come back here. You can imagine how surprised we are then when Nancy don't get mad at all. She just sits there, with that alligator purse in her skinny lap and her knobby hands folded on top of it. Life has its slaps in the face, she says, I'd be the first to admit that. So Tito tells her no hard feelings but some folks don't find it so easy to get by. And Nancy answers him back, I've seen more than you can probably imagine. And Suzy says to her, But First Lady, I thought you was living in some kind of wonder dream. And Nancy Reagan looks her straight in the eye and says, Well, the dream I am living, that fairy-tale dream that I wake up to each morning, in which I am lying next to the kindest, bravest, and most understanding—and I suppose the most powerful—man in the world, well that dream came true for me but I had to work for it. Lord knows I worked to make that dream come true. And looking around me at you, I see these bright, young shining faces. Sure they have suffered a lot already, but they still are alive and burning and aching with the desire to have the things they should have.

And then she says, Do you know what? I've got a funny feeling. Call it an intuition, but you and you and you and you, you'll have that dream someday. And that's why it is such a joy to look into your eager young eyes and see the power to make it happen . . .

Well, I didn't hear the rest of what Mrs. Reagan was saying, 'cause suddenly my head started to float. It was like—well it was like we are always going to movies me and Tito and my friends. It's all we ever do 'side from getting high. Now here comes the part where the basketball player kid who up to now

is the underdog meets some older person making him realize
that he can make it too. It's the part we all like the best, but we
never knew nobody who was going to do that in real life. I mean
somebody who could really say that to us. So it was a great high.
And suddenly that nervous skinny old lady sitting there got
changed into some kind of holy lady. Or a queen. Yeah, that's
it, a queen holding out this wand, and each time she points it at
somebody everything goes all right. You gonna be rich now. Or
maybe that's not it. But it is like you going to be rich and have
everything you want.

But the most bugged-out thing of all, that's when I look over
and see Connie and she's crying. I can hardly hear her but she is
saying that, O, Nancy, you came to visit us and we done treated
you horrible, girl, we showed you no respect, you know what I
be doing with that money you gave me already, I—

Hush! Says Nancy. There is no need. I don't need the thread
any more because the experience I have had here is a million
times more fulfilling than any press conference or TV camera. I
will go back to Odyssey House and tell them about this experience. Nancy stands up and it's like a ray of sun shining on us,
and she says, Would you mind if I used your bathroom?

So Nancy gets up and goes to the bathroom. And we keep
sitting there saying nothing. I look at Tito, and China Sue, and
Chaka Con, and I see changed people. Nobody can talk.

Then we start to hear it. I guess I was the first one. Plop plop
plop. And I realize I can hear the First Lady. And Tito looks up
and so does Chaka Con and China Sue, and we look into each
other's eyes, and finally I says it, because I know that's what we
all thinking. Wouldn't it be fresh if we could get a look at the
First Lady taking a dump?

So one by one we all get up and tiptoe toward the bathroom

door to peer through the crack, to watch the First Lady drop her load. She's got her dress all bunched up and held out in front of her, and the panty hose are just kind of shoved down at her ankles. I don't know but I expected the First Lady to roll them panty hose down. And then she reaches for the paper—and if you thought about it—well wouldn't the First Lady take just a few squares at a time and put them on top of each other all neat so that the edges matched? Well this one just grabbed the end of the roll and yanked. But then something else happened, and I don't know if I want to tell you about it. But ok, I will, and what happened then was, instead of lifting the edge of her ass off the seat and wiping, the First Lady stood up. And when she did, it knocked us all on our ass, because the biggest cock you've ever seen flipped out the top those panty hose.

Well at first it was like a punch in the gut. I mean, being stoned and all, we couldn't get over it—that the First Lady wasn't no lady. But finally Chaka Con gets enough breath and says, Child, child, child, you mothafucka, you pulled the wool over our eyes. And the First Lady yanked up the panty hose and pulled off her wig and came out laughing, big, loud, low laughs, laughs I heard before. And Tito, who can hardly get his breath neither, manages to cuff me on the head, gasping, You fool, didn't I tell you it was a drag queen. And then still laughing, everybody goes to punch Brand X, 'cause that's who it was. This drag queen Brenda from the Deuce. They call her Brenda X or Brand X most the time. And Tito still gasping, I knew it all along, and Brand X laughing and laughing and saying, Like hell you did, and going to grab that crack pipe, saying, Give me that shit, 'cause I am the one who paid for it. And Suzy laughing and saying, No you wasn't, it was Nancy Reagan. And where'd you get that kind of money, girl, Chaka Con is saying. You wouldn't believe the sick trick from Washington, says Brand X, gave me five hundred to put on this drag so he could pretend he was fucking Nancy Reagan. And then the pipe starts going around and our heads fill up with smoke and the First Lady shrinks away, right back to TV size.

A Real Doll

A.M. Homes

I'm dating Barbie. Three afternoons a week, while my sister is at dance class, I take Barbie away from Ken. I'm practicing for the future.

At first I sat in my sister's room watching Barbie, who lived with Ken, on a doily, on top of the dresser.

I was looking at her but not really looking. I was looking, and all of the sudden realized she was staring at me.

She was sitting next to Ken, his khaki-covered thigh absently rubbing her bare leg. He was rubbing her, but she was staring at me.

"Hi," she said.

"Hello," I said.

"I'm Barbie," she said, and Ken stopped rubbing her leg.

"I know."

"You're Jenny's brother."

I nodded. My head was bobbing up and down like a puppet on a weight.

"I really like your sister. She's sweet," Barbie said. "Such a good little girl. Especially lately, she makes herself so pretty, and she's started doing her nails."

I wondered if Barbie noticed that Miss Wonderful bit her nails and that when she smiled her front teeth were covered with little flecks of purple nail polish. I wondered if she knew Jennifer colored in the chipped chewed spots with purple magic marker, and then sometimes sucked on her fingers so that not only did she have purple flecks of polish on her teeth, but her tongue was the strangest shade of violet.

"So listen," I said. "Would you like to go out for a while? Grab some fresh air, maybe take a spin around the backyard?"

"Sure," she said.

I picked her up by her feet. It sounds unusual but I was too petrified to take her by the waist. I grabbed her by the ankles and carried her off like a Popsicle stick.

As soon as we were out back, sitting on the porch of what I used to call my fort, but which my sister and parents referred to as the playhouse, I started freaking. I was suddenly and incredibly aware that I was out with Barbie. I didn't know what to say.

"So, what kind of a Barbie are you?" I asked.

"Excuse me?"

"Well, from listening to Jennifer I know there's Day to Night Barbie, Magic Moves Barbie, Gift-Giving Barbie, Tropical Barbie, My First Barbie, and more."

"I'm Tropical," she said. I'm Tropical, she said, the same way a person might say I'm Catholic or I'm Jewish. "I came with a one-piece bathing suit, a brush, and a ruffle you can wear so many ways," Barbie squeaked.

She actually squeaked. It turned out that squeaking was Barbie's birth defect. I pretended I didn't hear it.

We were quiet for a minute. A leaf larger than Barbie fell from the maple tree above us and I caught it just before it would have hit her. I half expected her to squeak, "You saved my life. I'm yours, forever." Instead she said, in a perfectly normal voice, "Wow, big leaf."

I looked at her. Barbie's eyes were sparkling blue like the ocean on a good day. I looked and in a moment noticed she had the whole world, the cosmos, drawn in makeup above and below her eyes. An entire galaxy, clouds, stars, a sun, the sea, painted onto her face. Yellow, blue, pink, and a million silver sparkles.

We sat looking at each other, looking and talking and then not talking and looking again. It was a stop-and-start thing with both of us constantly saying the wrong thing, saying anything, and then immediately regretting having said it.

It was obvious Barbie didn't trust me. I asked her if she wanted something to drink.

"Diet Coke," she said. And I wondered why I'd asked.

I went into the house, upstairs into my parents' bathroom, opened the medicine cabinet, and got a couple of Valiums. I immediately swallowed one. I figured if I could be calm and collected, she'd realize I wasn't going to hurt her. I broke another

Valium into a million small pieces, dropped some slivers into
Barbie's Diet Coke, and swished it around so it'd blend. I figured if we could be calm and collected together, she'd be able
to trust me even sooner. I was falling in love in a way that had
nothing to do with love.

"So, what's the deal with you and Ken?" I asked later after
we'd loosened up, after she'd drunk two Diet Cokes, and I'd
made another trip to the medicine cabinet.

She giggled. "Oh, we're just really good friends."

"What's the deal with him really, you can tell me, I mean, is
he or isn't he?"

"Ish she or ishn' she," Barbie said, in a slow slurred way,
like she was so intoxicated that if they made a Breathalyzer for
Valium, she'd melt it.

I regretted having fixed her a third Coke. I mean if she o.d.'ed
and died Jennifer would tell my mom and dad for sure.

"Is he a faggot or what?"

Barbie laughed and I almost slapped her. She looked me
straight in the eye.

"He lusts after me," she said. "I come home at night and he's
standing there, waiting. He doesn't wear underwear, you know.
I mean, isn't that strange, Ken doesn't own any underwear. I
heard Jennifer tell her friend that they don't even make any for
him. Anyway, he's always there waiting, and I'm like, Ken we're
friends, okay, that's it. I mean, have you ever noticed, he has
molded plastic hair. His head and his hair are all one piece. I
can't go out with a guy like that. Besides, I don't think he'd be
up for it if you know what I mean. Ken is not what you'd call
well endowed . . . All he's got is a little plastic bump, more of
a hump, really, and what the hell are you supposed to do with
that?"

She was telling me things I didn't think I should hear and all the same, I was leaning into her, like if I moved closer she'd tell me more. I was taking every word and holding it for a minute, holding groups of words in my head like I didn't understand English. She went on and on, but I wasn't listening.

The sun sank behind the playhouse, Barbie shivered, excused herself, and ran around back to throw up. I asked her if she felt okay. She said she was fine, just a little tired, that maybe she was coming down with the flu or something. I gave her a piece of a piece of gum to chew and took her inside.

On the way back to Jennifer's room I did something Barbie almost didn't forgive me for. I did something which not only shattered the moment, but nearly wrecked the possibility of our having a future together.

In the hallway between the stairs and Jennifer's room, I popped Barbie's head into my mouth, like lion and tamer, God and Godzilla.

I popped her whole head into my mouth, and Barbie's hair separated into single strands like Christmas tinsel and caught in my throat nearly choking me. I could taste layer on layer of makeup, Revlon, Max Factor, and Maybelline. I closed my mouth around Barbie and could feel her breath in mine. I could hear her screams in my throat. Her teeth, white, Pearl Drops, Pepsodent, and the whole Osmond family, bit my tongue and the inside of my cheek like I might accidently bite myself. I closed my mouth around her neck and held her suspended, her feet uselessly kicking the air in front of my face.

Before pulling her out, I pressed my teeth lightly into her neck, leaving marks Barbie described as scars of her assault, but which I imagined as a New Age necklace of love.

"I have never, ever in my life been treated with such utter disregard," she said as soon as I let her out.

She was lying. I knew Jennifer sometimes did things with Barbie. I didn't mention that once I'd seen Barbie hanging from Jennifer's ceiling fan, spinning around in great wide circles, like some imitation Superman.

"I'm sorry if I scared you."

"Scared me!" she squeaked.

She went on squeaking, a cross between the squeal when you let the air out of a balloon and a smoke alarm with weak batteries. While she was squeaking, the phrase *a head in the mouth is worth two in the bush* started running through my head. I knew it had come from somewhere, started as something else, but I couldn't get it right. *A head in the mouth is worth two in the bush*, again and again, like the punch line to some dirty joke.

"Scared me. Scared me. Scared me!" Barbie squeaked louder and louder until finally she had my attention again. "Have you ever been held captive in the dark cavern of someone's body?"

I shook my head. It sounded wonderful.

"Typical," she said. "So incredibly, typically male."

For a moment I was proud.

"Why do you have to do things you know you shouldn't, and worse, you do them with a light in your eye, like you're getting some weird pleasure that only another boy would understand. You're all the same," she said. "You're all Jack Nicholson."

I refused to put her back in Jennifer's room until she forgave me, until she understood that I'd done what I did with only the truest of feeling, no harm intended.

I heard Jennifer's feet clomping up the stairs. I was running out of time.

"You know I'm really interested in you," I said to Barbie.

"Me too," she said, and for a minute I wasn't sure if she meant she was interested in herself or me.

"We should do this again," I said. She nodded.

I leaned down to kiss Barbie. I could have brought her up to my lips, but somehow it felt wrong. I leaned down to kiss her and the first thing I got was her nose in my mouth. I felt like a St. Bernard saying hello.

No matter how graceful I tried to be, I was forever licking her face. It wasn't a question of putting my tongue in her ear or down her throat, it was simply literally trying not to suffocate her. I kissed Barbie with my back to Ken and then turned around and put her on the doily right next to him. I was tempted to drop her down on Ken, to mash her into him, but I managed to restrain myself.

"That was fun," Barbie said. I heard Jennifer in the hall.

"Later," I said.

Jennifer came into the room and looked at me.

"What?" I said.

"It's my room," she said.

"There was a bee in it. I was killing it for you."

"A bee. I'm allergic to bees. Mom, Mom," she screamed. "There's a bee."

"Mom's not home. I killed it."

"But there might be another one."

"So call me and I'll kill it."

"But if it stings me I might die." I shrugged and walked out. I could feel Barbie watching me leave.

I took a Valium about twenty minutes before I picked her up the next Friday. By the time I went into Jennifer's room, everything was getting easier.

"Hey," I said when I got up to the dresser.

She was there on the doily with Ken, they were back to back, resting against each other, legs stretched out in front of them.

Ken didn't look at me. I didn't care.

"You ready to go?" I asked. Barbie nodded. "I thought you might be thirsty." I handed her the Diet Coke I'd made for her.

I'd figured Barbie could take a little less than an eighth of a Valium without getting totally senile. Basically, I had to give her Valium crumbs since there was no way to cut one that small.

She took the Coke and drank it right in front of Ken. I kept waiting for him to give me one of those I-know-what-you're-up-to-and-I-don't-like-it looks, the kind my father gives me when he walks into my room without knocking and I automatically jump twenty feet in the air.

Ken acted like he didn't even know I was there. I hated him.

"I can't do a lot of walking this afternoon," Barbie said. I nodded. I figured no big deal since mostly I seemed to be carrying her around anyway.

"My feet are killing me," she said.

I was thinking about Ken.

"Don't you have other shoes?"

My family was very into shoes. No matter what seemed to be wrong my father always suggested it could be cured by wearing a different pair of shoes. He believed that shoes, like tires, should be rotated.

"It's not the shoes," she said. "It's my toes."

"Did you drop something on them?" My Valium wasn't working. I was having trouble making small talk. I needed another one.

"Jennifer's been chewing on them."

"He doesn't have anything to hide," I said. "He has tan molded plastic hair, and a bump for a dick."

"I never should have told you about the bump."

I lay back on the bed. Barbie rolled over, off the pillow, and rested on my chest. Her body stretched from my nipple to my belly button. Her hands pressed against me, tickling me.

"Barbie," I said.

"Umm Humm."

"How do you feel about me?"

She didn't say anything for a minute. "Don't worry about it," she said, and slipped her hand into my shirt through the space between the buttons.

Her fingers were like the ends of toothpicks performing some subtle ancient torture, a dance of boy death across my chest. Barbie crawled all over me like an insect who'd run into one too many cans of Raid.

Underneath my clothes, under my skin, I was going crazy. First off, I'd been kidnapped by my underwear with no way to manually adjust without attracting unnecessary attention.

With Barbie caught in my shirt I slowly rolled over, like in some space shuttle docking maneuver. I rolled onto my stomach, trapping her under me. As slowly and unobtrusively as possible, I ground myself against the bed, at first hoping it would fix things and then again and again, caught by a pleasure/pain principle.

"Is this a water bed?" Barbie asked.

My hand was on her breasts, only it wasn't really my hand, but more like my index finger. I touched Barbie and she made a little gasp, a squeak in reverse. She squeaked backwards, then stopped, and I was stuck there with my hand on her, thinking about how I was forever crossing a line between the haves and the have-nots, between good guys and bad, between men and animals, and there was absolutely nothing I could do to stop myself.

Barbie was sitting on my crotch, her legs flipped back behind her in a position that wasn't human.

At a certain point I had to free myself. If my dick was blue, it was only because it had suffocated. I did the honors and Richard popped out like an escape from maximum security.

"I've never seen anything so big," Barbie said. It was the sentence I dreamed of, but given the people Barbie normally hung out with, namely the bump boy himself, it didn't come as a big surprise.

She stood at the base of my dick, her bare feet buried in my pubic hair. I was almost as tall as she was. Okay, not almost as tall, but clearly we could be related. She and Richard even had the same vaguely surprised look on their faces.

She was on me and I couldn't help wanting to get inside her. I turned Barbie over and was on top of her, not caring if I killed her. Her hands pressed so hard into my stomach that it felt like she was performing an appendectomy.

I was on top, trying to get between her legs, almost breaking her in half. But there was nothing there, nothing to fuck except a small thin line that was supposed to be her ass crack.

I rubbed the thin line, the back of her legs and the space between her legs. I turned Barbie's back to me so I could do it without having to look at her face.

Very quickly, I came. I came all over Barbie, all over her and a little bit in her hair. I came on Barbie and it was the most horrifying experience I ever had. It didn't stay on her. It doesn't stick to plastic. I was finished. I was holding a come-covered Barbie in my hand like I didn't know where she came from.

Barbie said, "Don't stop," or maybe I just think she said that because I read it somewhere. I don't know anymore. I couldn't listen to her. I couldn't even look at her. I wiped myself off with a sock, pulled my clothes on, and then took Barbie into the bathroom.

At dinner I noticed Jennifer chewing her cuticles between bites of tuna-noodle casserole. I asked her if she was teething. She coughed and then started choking to death on either a little piece of fingernail, a crushed potato chip from the casserole, or maybe even a little bit of Barbie footie that'd stuck in her teeth. My mother asked her if she was okay.

"I swallowed something sharp," she said between coughs that were clearly influenced by the acting class she'd taken over the summer.

"Do you have a problem?" I asked her.

"Leave your sister alone," my mother said.

"If there are any questions to ask we'll do the asking," my father said.

"Is everything all right?" my mother asked Jennifer. She nodded. "I think you could use some new jeans," my mother said. "You don't seem to have many play clothes anymore."

"Not to change the subject," I said, trying to think of a way to stop Jennifer from eating Barbie alive.

"I don't wear pants," Jennifer said. "Boys wear pants."

"Your grandma wears pants," my father said.

"She's not a girl."

My father chuckled. He actually fucking chuckled. He's the only person I ever met who could actually fucking chuckle.

"Don't tell her that," he said, chuckling.

"It's not funny," I said.

"Grandma's are pull-ons anyway," Jennifer said. "They don't have a fly. You have to have a penis to have a fly."

"Jennifer," my mother said. "That's enough of that."

I decided to buy Barbie a present. I was at that strange point where I would have done anything for her. I took two buses and walked more than a mile to get to Toys R Us.

Barbie row was aisle 14C. I was a wreck. I imagined a million Barbies and having to have them all. I pictured fucking one, discarding it, immediately grabbing a fresh one, doing it, and then throwing it onto a growing pile in the corner of my room. An unending chore. I saw myself becoming a slave to Barbie. I wondered how many Tropical Barbies were made each year. I felt faint.

There were rows and rows of Kens, Barbies, and Skippers. Funtime Barbie, Jewel Secrets Ken, Barbie Rocker with "Hot Rockin' Fun and Real Dancin' Action." I noticed Magic Moves Barbie, and found myself looking at her carefully, flirtatiously, wondering if her legs were spreadable. "Push the switch and she moves," her box said. She winked at me while I was reading.

The only Tropical I saw was a black Tropical Ken. From just looking at him you wouldn't have known he was black. I mean, he wasn't black like anyone would be black. Black Tropical Ken was the color of a raisin, a raisin all spread out and unwrinkled. He had a short afro that looked like a wig had been dropped down and fixed on his head, a protective helmet. I wondered if black Ken was really white Ken sprayed over with a thick coating of ironed raisin plastic.

I spread eight black Kens out in a line across the front of a row. Through the plastic window of his box he told me he was hoping to go to dental school. All eight black Kens talked at once. Luckily, they all said the same thing at the same time. They said he really liked teeth. Black Ken smiled. He had the same white Pearl Drops, Pepsodent, Osmond family teeth that

Barbie and white Ken had. I thought the entire Mattel family must take really good care of themselves, I figured they might be the only people left in America who actually brushed after every meal and then again before going to sleep.

I didn't know what to get Barbie. Black Ken said I should go for clothing, maybe a fur coat. I wanted something really special. I imagined a wonderful present that would draw us somehow closer.

There was a tropical pool and patio set, but I decided it might make her homesick. There was a complete winter holiday, with an A-frame house, fireplace, snowmobile, and sled. I imagined her inviting Ken away for a weekend without me. The six o'clock news set was nice, but because of her squeak, Barbie's future as an anchorwoman seemed limited. A workout center, a sofa bed and coffee table, a bubbling spa, a bedroom play set. I settled on the grand piano. It was $13.00. I'd always made it a point to never spend more than ten dollars on anyone. This time I figured, what the hell, you don't buy a grand piano every day.

"Wrap it up, would ya," I said at the checkout desk. From my bedroom window I could see Jennifer in the backyard, wearing her tutu and leaping all over the place. It was dangerous as hell to sneak in and get Barbie, but I couldn't keep a grand piano in my closet without telling someone.

"You must really like me," Barbie said when she finally had the piano unwrapped.

I nodded. She was wearing a ski suit and skis. It was the end of August and eighty degrees out. Immediately, she sat down and played "Chopsticks."

I looked out at Jennifer. She was running down the length of the deck, jumping onto the railing and then leaping off, posing like one of those red flying horses you see on old Mobil gas signs. I watched her do it once and then the second time, her foot caught on the railing, and she went over the edge the hard way. A minute later she came around the edge of the house, limping, her tutu dented and dirty, pink tights ripped at both knees. I grabbed Barbie from the piano bench and raced her into Jennifer's room.

"I was just getting warmed up," she said. "I can play better than that, really."

I could hear Jennifer crying as she walked up the stairs.

"Jennifer's coming," I said. I put her down on the dresser and realized Ken was missing.

"Where's Ken?" I asked quickly.

"Out with Jennifer," Barbie said.

I met Jennifer at her door. "Are you okay?" I asked. She cried harder. "I saw you fall."

"Why didn't you stop me?" she said.

"From falling?"

She nodded and showed me her knees.

"Once you start to fall no one can stop you." I noticed Ken was tucked into the waistband of her tutu.

"They catch you," Jennifer said.

I started to tell her it was dangerous to go leaping around with a Ken stuck in your waistband, but you don't tell someone who's already crying that they did something bad.

I walked her into the bathroom, and took out the hydrogen peroxide. I was a first aid expert. I was the kind of guy who walked around, waiting for someone to have a heart attack just so I could practice my CPR technique.

"Sit down," I said.

Jennifer sat down on the toilet without putting the lid down. Ken was stabbing her all over the place and instead of pulling him out, she squirmed around trying to get comfortable like she didn't know what else to do. I took him out for her. She watched as though I was performing surgery or something.

"He's mine," she said.

"Take off your tights," I said.

"No," she said.

"They're ruined," I said. "Take them off."

Jennifer took off her ballet slippers and peeled off her tights. She was wearing my old Underoos with superheroes on them, Spiderman and Superman and Batman all poking out from under a dirty dented tutu. I decided not to say anything, but it looked funny as hell to see a flat crotch in boys' underwear. I had the feeling they didn't bother making underwear for Ken because they knew it looked too weird on him.

I poured peroxide onto her bloody knees. Jennifer screamed into my ear. She bent down and examined herself, poking her purple fingers into the torn skin; her tutu bunched up and rubbed against her face, scraping it. I worked on her knees, removing little pebbles and pieces of grass from the area.

She started crying again.

"You're okay," I said. "You're not dying." She didn't care. "Do you want anything?" I asked, trying to be nice.

"Barbie," she said.

It was the first time I'd handled Barbie in public. I picked her up like she was a complete stranger and handed her to Jennifer, who grabbed her by the hair. I started to tell her to ease up, but couldn't. Barbie looked at me and I shrugged. I went downstairs and made Jennifer one of my special Diet Cokes.

"Drink this," I said, handing it to her. She took four giant gulps and immediately I felt guilty about having used a whole Valium.

"Why don't you give a little to your Barbie," I said. "I'm sure she's thirsty too."

Barbie winked at me and I could have killed her, first off for doing it in front of Jennifer, and second because she didn't know what the hell she was winking about.

I went into my room and put the piano away. I figured as long as I kept it in the original box I'd be safe. If anyone found it, I'd say it was a present for Jennifer.

Wednesday Ken and Barbie had their heads switched. I went to get Barbie, and there on top of the dresser were Barbie and Ken, sort of. Barbie's head was on Ken's body and Ken's head was on Barbie. At first I thought it was just me.

"Hi," Barbie's head said.

I couldn't respond. She was on Ken's body and I was looking at Ken in a whole new way.

I picked up the Barbie head/Ken and immediately Barbie's head rolled off. It rolled across the dresser, across the white doily past Jennifer's collection of miniature ceramic cats, and *boom* it fell to the floor. I saw Barbie's head rolling and about to fall, and then falling, but there was nothing I could do to stop it. I was frozen, paralyzed with Ken's headless body in my left hand.

Barbie's head was on the floor, her hair spread out underneath it like angel wings in the snow, and I expected to see blood, a wide rich pool of blood, or at least a little bit coming out of her ear, her nose, or her mouth. I looked at her head on the floor and saw nothing but Barbie with eyes like the cosmos looking up at me. I thought she was dead.

"Christ, that hurt," she said. "And I already had a headache from these earrings."

There were little red dot/ball earrings jutting out of Barbie's ears.

"They go right through my head, you know. I guess it takes getting used to," Barbie said.

I noticed my mother's pin cushion on the dresser next to the other Barbie/Ken, the Barbie body, Ken head. The pin cushion was filled with hundreds of pins, pins with flat silver ends and pins with red, yellow, and blue dot/ball ends.

"You have pins in your head," I said to the Barbie head on the floor.

"Is that supposed to be a compliment?"

I was starting to hate her. I was being perfectly clear and she didn't understand me.

I looked at Ken. He was in my left hand, my fist wrapped around his waist. I looked at him and realized my thumb was on his bump. My thumb was pressed against Ken's crotch and as soon as I noticed I got an automatic hard-on, the kind you don't know you're getting, it's just there. I started rubbing Ken's bump and watching my thumb like it was a large-screen projection of a porno movie.

"What are you doing?" Barbie's head said. "Get me up. Help me." I was rubbing Ken's bump/hump with my finger inside his bathing suit. I was standing in the middle of my sister's room, with my pants pulled down.

"Aren't you going to help me?" Barbie kept asking. "Aren't you going to help me?"

In the second before I came, I held Ken's head hole in front of me. I held Ken upside down above my dick and came inside of Ken like I never could in Barbie.

I came into Ken's body and as soon as I was done I wanted to do it again. I wanted to fill Ken and put his head back on, like a perfume bottle. I wanted Ken to be the vessel for my secret supply. I came in Ken and then I remembered he wasn't mine. He didn't belong to me. I took him into the bathroom and soaked him in warm water and Ivory liquid. I brushed his insides with Jennifer's toothbrush and left him alone in a cold-water rinse.

"Aren't you going to help me, aren't you?" Barbie kept asking.

I started thinking she'd been brain damaged by the accident. I picked her head up from the floor.

"What took you so long?" she asked.

"I had to take care of Ken"

"Is he okay?"

"He'll be fine. He's soaking in the bathroom." I held Barbie's head in my hand.

"What are you going to do?"

"What do you mean?" I said.

Did my little incident, my moment with Ken, mean that right then and there some decision about my future life as queerbait had to be made?"

"This afternoon. Where are we going? What are we doing? I miss you when I don't see you," Barbie said.

"You see me every day," I said.

"I don't really see you. I sit on top of the dresser and if you pass by, I see you. Take me to your room."

"I have to bring Ken's body back."

I went into the bathroom, rinsed out Ken, blew him dry with my mother's blow dryer, then played with him again. It was a boy thing, we were boys together. I thought sometime I might play ball with him, I might take him out instead of Barbie.

"Everything takes you so long," Barbie said when I got back into the room.

I put Ken back up on the dresser, picked up Barbie's body, knocked Ken's head off, and smashed Barbie's head back down on her own damn neck.

"I don't want to fight with you," Barbie said as I carried her into my room. "We don't have enough time together to fight. Fuck me," she said.

I didn't feel like it. I was thinking about fucking Ken and Ken being a boy. I was thinking about Barbie and Barbie being a girl. I was thinking about Jennifer, switching Barbie and Ken's heads, chewing Barbie's feet off, hanging Barbie from the ceiling fan, and who knows what else.

"Fuck me," Barbie said again.

I ripped Barbie's clothing off. Between Barbie's legs Jennifer had drawn pubic hair in reverse. She'd drawn it upside down so it looked like a fountain spewing up and out in great wide arcs. I spit directly onto Barbie and with my thumb and first finger rubbed the ink lines, erasing them. Barbie moaned.

"Why do you let her do this to you?"

"Jennifer owns me," Barbie moaned.

Jennifer owns me, she said, so easily and with pleasure. I was totally jealous. Jennifer owned Barbie and it made me crazy. Obviously it was one of those relationships that could only exist between women. Jennifer could own her because it didn't matter that Jennifer owned her. Jennifer didn't want Barbie, she had her.

"You're perfect," I said.

"I'm getting fat," Barbie said.

Barbie was crawling all over me, and I wondered if Jennifer knew she was a nymphomaniac. I wondered if Jennifer knew what a nymphomaniac was.

"You don't belong with little girls," I said.

Barbie ignored me.

There were scratches on Barbie's chest and stomach. She didn't say anything about them and so at first I pretended not to notice. As I was touching her, I could feel they were deep, like slices. The edges were rough; my finger caught on them and I couldn't help but wonder.

"Jennifer?" I said, massaging the cuts with my tongue, as though my tongue, like sandpaper, would erase them. Barbie nodded.

In fact, I thought of using sandpaper, but didn't know how I would explain it to Barbie: *you have to lie still and let me rub it really hard with this stuff that's like terry-cloth dipped in cement.* I thought she might even like it if I made it into an S&M kind of thing and handcuffed her first.

I ran my tongue back and forth over the slivers, back and forth over the words "copyright 1966 Mattel Inc., Malaysia" tattooed on her back. Tonguing the tattoo drove Barbie crazy. She said it had something to do with scar tissue being extremely sensitive.

Barbie pushed herself hard against me, I could feel her slices rubbing my skin. I was thinking that Jennifer might kill Barbie. Without meaning to she might just go over the line and I wondered if Barbie would know what was happening or if she'd try to stop her.

We fucked, that's what I called it, fucking. In the beginning Barbie said she hated the word, which made me like it even more. She hated it because it was so strong and hard, and she said we weren't fucking, we were making love. I told her she had to be kidding.

"Fuck me," she said that afternoon and I knew the end was coming soon. "Fuck me," she said. I didn't like the sound of the word.

Friday when I went into Jennifer's room, there was something in the air. The place smelled like a science lab, a fire, a failed experiment.

Barbie was wearing a strapless yellow evening dress. Her hair was wrapped into a high bun, more like a wedding cake than something Betty Crocker would whip up. There seemed to be layers and layers of angel's hair spinning in a circle above her head. She had yellow pins through her ears and gold fuck-me shoes that matched the belt around her waist. For a second I thought of the belt and imagined tying her up, but more than restraining her arms or legs, I thought of wrapping the belt around her face, tying it across her mouth.

I looked at Barbie and saw something dark and thick like a scar rising up and over the edge of her dress. I grabbed her and pulled the front of the dress down.

"Hey big boy," Barbie said. "Don't I even get a hello?"

Barbie's breasts had been sawed at with a knife. There were a hundred marks from a blade that might have had five rows of teeth like shark jaws. And as if that wasn't enough, she'd been dissolved by fire, blue and yellow flames had been pressed against her and held there until she melted and eventually became the fire that burned herself. All of it had been somehow stirred with the lead of a pencil, the point of a pen, and left to cool. Molten Barbie flesh had been left to harden, black and pink plastic swirled together, in the crater Jennifer had dug out of her breasts.

I examined her in detail like a scientist, a pathologist, a fucking medical examiner. I studied the burns, the gouged-out area, as if by looking closely I'd find something, an explanation, a way out.

A disgusting taste came up into my mouth, like I'd been

sucking on batteries. It came up, then sank back down into my stomach, leaving my mouth puckered with the bitter metallic flavor of sour saliva. I coughed and spit onto my shirt sleeve, then rolled the sleeve over to cover the wet spot.

With my index finger I touched the edge of the burn as lightly as I could. The round rim of her scar broke off under my finger. I almost dropped her.

"It's just a reduction," Barbie said. "Jennifer and I are even now."

Barbie was smiling. She had the same expression on her face as when I first saw her and fell in love. She had the same expression she always had and I couldn't stand it. She was smiling, and she was burned. She was smiling, and she was ruined. I pulled her dress back up, above the scar-line. I put her down carefully on the doily on top of the dresser and started to walk away.

"Hey," Barbie said, "aren't we going to play?"

Days Without Someone

Dodie Bellamy

Day One

Hieroglyphs litter my computer screen . . . where's the story? Maybe it's over my shoulder—I turn my head back: a messy bed the pillows angled against one another, forming a V or the head of an arrow *pointing at me* . . . the lack not just of Ryder but of both our bodies. I swivel in my office chair to better study these vanished others those two naked forms on the bed rolling about from pillow to pillow, silent and in slow motion like some corny

film, gauze filter over the lens a mysterious source of sunlight
shiny moments glinting in little star bursts . . .

Ryder's gone to Barcelona for twelve days, an eternity considering we've been dating less than two months. My own ass
is as good as anything, I suppose, to remember him by . . .
tender, burning from the inside out *in daylight an invasion
incongruous as Magritte's locomotive* . . . last night I wrote my
love all over him: purple bruises with a flourish of red fila-
ments *frayed nerves*. How's he going to hide that from his
wife?

*Writing has always been more sexual than sex, the sustained
arousal of never quite getting it right.*

A bit of post-orgasmic conversation returns to me:

Me: And he lived to tell about it.
Ryder: Who would he tell?
Me: He tells the sunset.

He'd certainly never tell a homo sapiens. I like to imagine
Ryder flying all the way to Spain just to confess to a Mediter-
ranean sunset—it's so Marguerite Duras. Reminded of Ryder, I
underline a passage from *Blue Eyes, Black Hair*:

She looks at him. It's inevitable. He's alone and
attractive and worn out with being alone. As alone
and attractive as anyone on the point of death.

A married man who drinks by himself and sleeps on the
couch. I tell myself I'm better off outside his life, his tortured
take on the mundane.

Day Two

Stuffed in my mailbox a postcard mailed from Oakland the day he left. His words are elegant and black. A large passage is written over a smear of white-out . . . with the tip of a butter knife I scrape it away. A corroded message slowly emerges—I can't make out every word but the subject matter is clearly Freud on cryptography, how it reveals the inner man. Ryder knew I'd excavate his secret—so well has he trained me in the labyrinthine pleasures of the hidden *pulling away from the toll booth Ryder says softly but firmly "I thought you were going to abuse me." I know this is a code but for what? Tentatively I pat his thigh, fumble with a shirt button . . . yes? . . . no? . . . then the waistband his zipper parts as easily as his lips and I bow my head to the inevitable . . . over the Golden Gate Bridge, down the endless expanse of Lombard Street . . . Ryder won't let me see where I'm going, my cheek brushing denim my mouth full of cock. From the waist up he's a model citizen of the road, observing the speed limit, smiling at fellow motorists at stoplights as he murmurs "Oh wow" or "This is great."*

My lover has lips as round and swollen as life preservers, but they don't make me feel very safe.

Slits of world peek through Levelor blinds—Ryder's out there, maneuvering his way through a foreign tongue. The distance is inconceivable: thousands of miles, a handspan in an atlas. Is Spain any farther from San Francisco than Oakland? I'm used to living in his absence *the imperceptible accrual of appetite . . .* burnishing my favorite tender moments like worry stones, I superimpose them on the daily, try to survive their unavoidable dilution. Does Ryder flicker through these words like a summoned ghost—or am I driving him even farther away with my insomniac urge to reinvent him *no wife, willing to slay dragons, etc.* no wonder I'm always surprised when he's through the door—suddenly—rubbing his erection against me, all pleasure, or apologizing with tears in his eyes.

Day Three

The head of his penis is unbelievably soft, velvet without the nape. Right now, nothing about him seems very believable *he is flying far above me in the ink-colored sky unreachable a concept bereft of input.* I should have asked him for something—something funky of his, to wear. One unseasonably warm afternoon he left a sweater here—I hardly knew him but I pulled it over my naked breasts—the sleeves hanging to the tips of my fingers were his hands holding me down, the rough brown wool his chest, his back *sheathed in his molecules I felt positively amniotic* . . . after I came I wiped the collar between my legs. And the magic worked—we were lovers in a couple of weeks. When I told him my ritual he wore the sweater to work the next day, idiotically smiling to himself, my secretions a necklace about his fine German throat.

His Lou Reed cassette, a prison novel by Albertine Sarrazin, a magazine from San Diego: Ryder clings to the things he loaned me *these fragments I have shored against my ruins.* High-strung and schmaltzy I play "Classic Film Scores for Bette Davis"—a CD he bought in admiration of my intelligence and drama, the large gestures with which I snub him at parties. If he lit two cigarettes in his mouth at once, he knows I wouldn't laugh . . . graciously I take what he offers, suck the moist tip with a broad jerky movement *let's not ask for the moon* Ryder likes to point out the constellations, the brown stars in my iris, Venus, Orion.

He was always telling me how "good" I looked. But sitting here at the keyboard in a flannel bathrobe without Ryder to look at me, do I look like anything at all? There's not an inch of me he hasn't licked—some residue of him must linger, an astral impression radiating from my body pink smeared with yellow trailing off into the atmosphere *his skin smells of soap, his hair like cherries* at public events he blankly wavers beside the Mrs.—how do I pull off casual with this man who just that morning stuck his tongue up my ass, I strain to look past those pale eyes instead of burrowing *why can't I grab those adorable touchables that compose his person* with perfect aim we graze arms or hips slipping one another a sly grin—an eyewitness probably wouldn't even notice.

Day Four

Ryder says we're Paolo and Francesca, a damnation so beautiful it made Dante weep. I'll never understand the ease he can come to . . . then walk away from . . . such pleasure. I am humbled before this love of mine—beyond hopeless, a love with no consequences, no returns . . . devoid . . . I've always been this way: either not there or too eager. My writing like grave worms moves in on Ryder destroying his last grasp on corporeality. I sense his spirit yearning for something to embody: the stiff daguerreotypes of my memory, a brace clamped to his neck for these unreasonable exposures: Ryder ravishing my armpit, his penis probing one orifice after another and then my thighs my breasts anything that can be clenched, Ryder brushing a lock of my hair across his lower lip, holding my hand through his colorful glove. I'm growing antsy with this script of the remembered, nothing but theme and variation—I want to defile him, rearrange his history as easily as my hairdo. Ryder is a red brick wall. Before him a man in a brown suit is upside down in midair, having fallen from Ryder's window—the artist has drawn the man's scream very clumsily so that his mouth looks like Howdy Doody's, giving an unintentional comic air to the impending squash. Ryder as the red brick wall is impassive through all this.

The writing won't let me be—I have to keep pen and paper beside my bed—it sneaks up on me in the middle of the night. Then leaves.

Day Five

The world encroaches . . . Ryder grows tiny, crushed with immensity—like the end of *The Incredible Shrinking Man* when the infinitesimal merges with the infinite and we know we're not watching any ordinary Hollywood schlock but a slice of Deep Meaning. Still, Ryder won't be eradicated. At work, strolling down the fluorescent beige corridor, from the gleam at my feet stream ghosts of grooves engraved from the strain of heavy machines that look inside people. Above me to the right, a blue disk embossed with a stylized white female *the moon—or a biscuit of sky* as I make him coffee Ryder's still wearing his denim jacket he lifts up the back of my nightgown pulls me to him biting my lips his cold hands cupping my bare ass—this memory inflicts a pang of arousal, a cramp in the groin, painful as anything futile or lost.

Nina Simone on the jukebox, two glasses of red wine on a table the size of a crossword puzzle. Someone who isn't Ryder sits facing me, with blue eyes, black hair—a spectre from Marguerite Duras. As he leans forward his chest seems to swallow the table, he says, "The only thing I have under my wings are shadows." Occasionally his large hand wanders across a bit of my body: a stray I could easily fuck with affection, then walk away from. Ryder is off drinking margaritas with his wife *there is nothing in our situation to remain faithful to.*

Day Six

Desire for Ryder has burnt off with the fog. I am left with a hollow of mysterious origin, a curiosity towards this object of my recent relentless attentions. Late at night the phone turns tensile, surreal, an implement aliens use in their sex experiments: his wife just a room away, Ryder begins to masturbate through the receiver *"I'm going to tighten my hand around your throat so you can't move and then I'm going to stick my . . ."* Across the bay I self-consciously whisper, "I'd like that." He's amazed at the volumes of cum sprayed across his belly, scoops some up with a finger and eats it. How could this person be so kinky, yet have such a sweetness, a cleanness about him, something very Cranach . . . beneath his dewy skin that fine chiselled bone straining . . . he asks me to squeeze his nipples, hovers above me a bright ecstatic angel eyes closed biting his lower lip, he quietly throws his head back then slowly brings it down chin to chest then back up again: this come shot is precise, yet flattened and blurred like a color xerox of a collage; as I type it a frenetic neighbor stomps above my head. Sex, no matter how fondly recalled, comes across so generic. Only the spurts of conversation between gasps and undulations intrigue me, the way he calls me "Babe" when he's excited—nursing my neck or shoulder he reaches up nibbles my earlobe and sighs, "Anything you want, Babe," and I feel cheap in a way I want to go on forever.

Day Seven

Red grease floats atop the warm soapy water—clank of stainless steel and chipped saucers—my hands crinkle to pale prunes as Lou Reed warbles Ryder's favorite refrain *I break into a million pieces and fly into the sun* . . . who needs this solar glare when there's the ocean . . . we lingered in the shadow of the coastal highway, the salty breeze cooling my exposed genitalia. "Suck my cock," yelled a man we couldn't see, exiling us to the beach . . . small birds scuttled along the wet sand as if animated by Disney . . . the onrushing waves left soap suds at our feet with an overtone of *TV commercial or environmental disaster.* Ryder reached under my black silk overcoat, under my skirt, his forefinger twirling pubic curls—the shore was scattered with city dwellers their features surprisingly distinct beneath the full moon—before their eager nocturnal eyes I felt like a potboiler, the kind of book read by people who shop at Walgreen's *let's fly into the sun let's fly anywhere these beachcombers can't see.* Rinsing a handful of silverware I think *I'd forgotten that I could live without him: in my bed, on the phone—next to him everything else seemed bland and disconnected—last night, falling asleep I looked into the shutter of a camera a giant mechanical iris spiraled closed, blocking out the light, blocking out Ryder. Maybe I should call it quits maybe I should wipe my dirty fingers across this page, have his bastard baby.*

His eyes are the color of my coffee cup he has two hands tendons form deep ridges on the top of his feet: a minefield of camouflage: if his wife sees through my writing I may never see him again. His name's not Ryder, he's not in Spain really: encoded in my language Ryder remains disembodied as he is from my life. His corpse walks in Barcelona—it is beet red beneath a peeling nose and baseball cap.

A huge phallic monster burrowed under the ground shooting up tentacles that grabbed townspeople sucking them into its gaping vagina dentata maw, but I didn't find much depth in the story—last night, walking home from the movies, I was assaulted by Ryder's presence, a sadness as surprising and intense as a cold spot in a haunted house *just when I thought I was getting rid of him* a few hours later he sent me a package in my dream—on the outside of the bubble envelope he wrote, "I hope you're missing me as much as I miss you." I opened it eagerly, hoping the thick wad of paper inside was a letter. But it was just a survey Ryder had filled out concerning his hotel service and his knowledge of local history. Is he worth all this attention? He's off having a Club Med adventure with Mrs. Wonderful while I sit here with time, and more time. A couple of nights ago I walked up to the passenger side of a car he was sitting in—he leaned through the window and kissed me. Then the car sped away and I had to live in a commune with some hippies.

Day Eight

Desire that giant burrowing nematode sneaks up and grabs me. Rattling my chest, Ryder's wormy laugh. He has me. All the places he's been . . . in relation to my body *it's well past the halfway point* he fucked me sideways while I fucked his mouth with my right hand he sucked so hard I thought the flesh was going to fall away like well-cooked chicken—he said he was coming at both ends one long vibrating tunnel . . . what's inside . . . what's out . . . the hair on his ass grates against my tongue . . . when I lick him there I'm leaving more than saliva behind: sibilants . . . fricatives . . . a layer of soul . . . Resurrected from Barcelona and this text, will he emerge weatherbeaten but no worse for wear—or will he have irrevocably turned . . . I removed the belt from my robe and tied his wrists to the bedstead—do whatever you want with me, he said, make it hurt *he wanted to be pliable, pliable as absence* . . . beyond a few entries in my diary, the gush of a school girl, I never could write about Ryder *I was silenced before the undefinable thingness of his lips, his hands, his cock, all the insistent anatomical components . . . then he left and the words rushed in like vultures, picking away, redefining . . .*

Day Nine

I am aching. I am alone. If only I could give a bourgeois patina of meaning to this. Something French: "Pleasure is the creation of the mind, the body can't do anything without it." I'm lying on my stomach and Ryder is fucking me from behind—it feels pretty good, though I don't take his efforts seriously—I wriggle my bladder into the optimal position, patiently anticipating My Turn—then abruptly the flesh of my vagina crystallizes *the unsuspected is inevitable there is no stopping*—and when it does happen I raise up on my arms and cry out. This is an ideal state of discourse—unmediated, with a totally receptive audience. Ryder, how could you throw me into this solitary confinement? Here on the inside we call it the "hole." I'm distressed by this lack of feedback. This silence. I jump out a window *wheeling around for one second which is long and good, a century* my foot breaks with the impact so I crawl on knees and elbows, dragging this useless lump to the highway *I am oozing mud, thorns scratch me at random from bushes—another century goes by, I can't recognize anything*—then I hear the air brakes, the slam of a door, boot-sized footprints—"Monsieur Le Truckdriver," I plead, "I'm a prisoner of love, the dark side of someone's double life. Please, will you sneak me to Paris!"

Eagerly he licks his cum from my mouth: I want to bring the reader this close to writing.

"Dear William Gibson:

"Right now I'm reading *Blue Eyes, Black Hair.* I'm afraid that Marguerite Duras is going to destroy my style—I find myself wanting to do all this frou-frou shit that I don't like even when she does it. I've been working on this prose thing about longing and absence, what it's like to experience a person who is not there. Sitting here at my MacPlus, I wonder about my main character—is he a sort of entity haunting the screen—*where* does he exist? Since I've so recently read *Mona Lisa Overdrive*, I'm reminded of cyberspace, how cyberspace is your metaphor for desire and longing, the way we spend most of our time away from the loved/coveted person, and are frustrated by our unrealistic wish to have them with us instantly on demand. In cyberspace we can relive heightened emotional/sexual states otherwise lost to us just by their being transitory—at the end of *Mona Lisa Overdrive*, Angie becomes not a physical bride, but a bride to her lover's imagination. I'm hesitant about responding to your writing because you must have responses to your writing up the wazoo."

Day Ten

Maybe the reader is my lover in some sense that I'm too literal to understand. Into a barely imaginable future I try to project this erotic reader, an incubus complete with organs that function and hands to hold my pages. This image isn't any more satisfying than if I were to tape an obscene message for my phone machine *sorry I'm not home right now but I'm hot for your* . . . it just isn't the same as having a body on the other end of the line, the bona fide heavy breathing.

Ryder, where are you? Wrap your phone cord around your cock. Remember me.

I betrayed my writing for Ryder—for six weeks I did nothing but fuck and get emotional. When he was aroused, Ryder turned monosyllabic, which really did it for me. I'd be chattering away and all he'd say was, "Yeah," his voice low and raspy, urgent as a wet tongue in my ear. Passion did a quick dissolve and I waxed silent as Ryder filled the frame, became the frame: his body, his emanations. "Yeah."

Now writing is taking its revenge. The present tense won't stick to Ryder—narrative has thrust him finally, irretrievably IN THE PAST. The tendons there are so pronounced his feet look webbed—I used to run my fingers in the fissures that extend from toes to ankle, daydreaming of roads carved between mountains, of running away. He said that entering me was going home—but what's home, Ryder—the couch in the living room, where you spend the night, depressed, when your friends leave? When he looked at his house through my eyes, he claimed his things look interesting. From the little I saw of them, his things were simple, mostly secondhand, suggesting a lower socio-economic status than his own. One night while I sucked his toes and he sucked mine, we somehow managed to fuck at the same time, a sort of elongated 69 pivoting on his cock. I turned my head and smiled at him, said, "This is very Kama Sutra." "You're right," he answered, "But what would they call it . . . something like 'turkey clawing under bright moon.'" We laughed until he fell out of me.

Ryder's flown into the sun and my heart is in a window display in North Beach—a valentine of dried roses and grass, it looks like a wreath you'd see on a pet's grave.

Day Eleven

How can I go on writing about desire when it has vanished. I've mutated to *neuter*. But isn't inconstancy the essence of desire? When you least suspect, it rushes up on you leaving soap suds at your feet. Before I'd ever touched him I wanted Ryder dearly— just the thought of him would get me wet. Once I had his body I was no longer moved by the idea, but by the thing itself.

I can't stand my own impenetrability—do I love do I hunger? Perhaps the chain reaction is still possible but hidden, and only Ryder can supply the missing ingredient, the lightning bolt that zaps the new Prometheus to life. *Or—maybe it's all been a dream, a very small and savage dream.* Maybe his eye contact hypnotized me, leaning so close his breath flushed my cheek, peering *into* me. He learned every dot in my iris—maybe he used them to navigate his way to my soul. He stole it. And then he went to Barcelona, carelessly tossing it back at me.

All I can imagine saying upon his return is, "I don't know, Ryder, you feel so alien."

Duras: "A swell surged up to the wall of the house but fell

back at his feet as if to avoid him; it was fringed with white and alive, like writing." Alive, yes, but at whose expense? I ache for the innocents who try to befriend me. Bloodthirsty and iridescent, writing sucks the marrow from the unsuspecting then sits back picking its teeth with a rib. Poor Ryder never had a chance *do what you want with me, he said*—now he totters along the shore, his tortured features barely recognizable: a body pink and bloated from fermenting gasses—his pale eyes plead—but the damage has already been done. I've seen enough movies to not touch him—the slightest pressure of my hand would upset the delicate biochemical balance. A heap of dust or something more gooey collapsing at my feet, not even a shell would I be left with.

Day Twelve

A shifting, a readiness—fear—my body is a mold waiting for plastique. In just a few hours he'll be near enough to know . . .

My mind is clear, clear as the night we parked in Marin overlooking the bay. There in the front seat of his car Ryder first made me come. He marvelled, the witness to a miracle—or, a child with a toy that finally works. I teased, "Ryder, it's a normal body function." The Golden Gate Bridge filled the windshield, gold and gleaming. "The tower of Camelot," Ryder said. Craning his neck up at the heavens—boyish—he pointed out Orion, only visible in the Northern Hemisphere, only in winter. We huddled together, our clothes still undone, watching the crescent moon blink through wisps of clouds, and I thought to myself *this is happiness.*

The last time I kissed Ryder he was in a doorway, leaving. I stood on my toes to get closer and breathed, "I'll immortalize you." There's something Faustian about this story. I can invoke his name, his personality, but my loving descriptions of his body are bloodless, as though I were parroting another author. I remember his penis was friendly—just like him. But that's it. If I touch him again will it merely feel awkward . . . or good as a first time?

Late this evening Ryder returns and this memoir will be over.

Writing versus life—is the one flight, the other hot pursuit? I don't remember. I once was a nerdy high school girl with nothing much else to do than lie on her twin bed filling a spiral notebook with poems of isolation and black curtains *a vulnerability so coddled it grew sentient.*

If this were a modernist novel, in the end I suppose I'd choose Life. The phone rings after midnight. A man's voice on the line, urgent and impossible. He doesn't identify himself, implores, "Can I come over I need to see you. Right now!" Without missing a beat I chirp back, "Well, Babe—what are you waiting for?"

Spiral

David Wojnarowicz

1

Back near the monitor the blazing light of the hand jerking the hardened dick is creating a blind spot to the right
of it in the room and I can just about make out some sil-
houetted shape of a guy in shorts and shirt opened, knowing
this because as he moves from dick to dick his shirt floats like
a curtain billowing into no light and disappearing again and
he's got a baseball cap on. I'm moving into this blind spot to

watch and he's on his knees sucking some kid's prick. There's
an old man in the darkest shadows his flesh is a bland color just
a dead white, emptied of blood and he seems afraid of the light
keeps shifting weight from one foot to the other in a squatting position at some point the sucking guy has his back to the
old man and he's leaning over the ledge to get another guy's
prick in his mouth and the old man takes a large hand and peels
the guy's shorts down in a slow motion insistence and soon
has his tongue planted firmly between the guy's cheeks. The
guy starts rolling his ass in the air in circular motions and
continues sucking the prick of the stranger before him. The
old guy is lapping away like a puppy with a bowl of milk
and I'm standing there in the darkness and there's a stream
of water or something snaking across the floor and the pale
glow of faces staring towards us at the monitor that I can only
see sideways and on the angled screen is a pair of eyes looking dreamily up at the owner of a fat dick that's slowly sinking
down his throat. A man enters the basement and walks over in
my general direction momentarily blinded by the monitor and
he runs into me before his eyes adjust, instead of backing up he
reaches out and pulls me into a hug his arms muscled and hard
and his embrace is squeezing air from my lungs. I rub my hands
over the surface of his body his clothes and an almost indiscern-
ible dampness to his shirt his body hard as wood his lips grazing
my neck his hand pulling my head down so that he can softly
bite the nape of my neck dragging his tongue around to my ear
up and down the lines of my throat and my fingers are loosening his belt and my hands slip through his open zipper into all
that warmth inside his underwear and down under his balls and
his hand is on the back of my neck on my shoulders and he's
pushing and I'm sinking down slow into a crouching position

and from there slipping my hands beneath the edge of his white T-shirt and the T-shirt is tight and he's beginning to sweat his body generating intense heat and my mouth is opening and I'm licking under his balls the length and head of his dick is falling across the bridge of my nose resting against my eyelids and one of my hands swings up to wipe across my mouth to collect spit and then falls to my cock and I'm slicking it up with spit creating a random rhythm while licking at the base of his dick his hands are in my hair moving around cradling the base of my skull. As I stand back up I'm losing myself in the pale cool color of his flesh in the shadows and he takes my head in his hands and pulls my face close to his gaze and I realize he's one of those guys that you know absolutely that if you'd met him twenty years earlier you both could have gone straight to heaven but now mortality has finally marked his face. He was really sexy though; he was like a vast swimming pool I wanted to dive right into.

2

All I can remember was the beautiful view and my overwhelming urge to puke. I was visiting my friend in the hospital and realizing he was lucky. Even though he was possibly going blind he did get the only bed in the room that had a window and a view. Sixteen floors up overlooking the southern skies as all the world spins into late evening. It was a beautiful distance to drift in but I still wanted to throw up. There among the red and yellow clouds drifting behind the silhouettes of the skyline was the overwhelming smell of human shit. It was the guy in the next bed; all afternoon he'd been making honking sounds like a suffocating goose. He was about ninety years old and I only got a glimpse of him and saw that they'd strapped an oxygen mask over his leathered face and when he screamed it sounded like a voice you'd hear over a contraption made of two tin cans and a piece of wire. Calling long distance trying to get the operator. Someone in charge. Someone in authority. Someone who could make it all stop with a pill, a knife, a needle, a word, a kiss, a smack, an embrace. Someone to step in and erase the sliding world of fact.

3

This kid walks into my sleep he's maybe seventeen years old stretches out on a table says he's not feeling well. He may be naked or else wearing no shirt his hands behind his head. I can see a swollen lump pushing under the skin of his armpit. I place my hands on his stomach and chest and try to explain to him that he needs to be looked at by a doctor. In the shadows of this room in the cool blue light the kid, a very beautiful boy, looks sad and shocked and closes his eyes like he doesn't want to know or like somehow he can shut it all out.

Later some guy appears in the place. He has an odd look about his face. He tries to make it known that he knows me or someone close to me. He leans in close has flat dull eyes like blue silvery coins behind his irises. I think it is the face of death. I get agitated and disturbed and want to be left alone with the kid. Try to steer him away to some other location. He disappears for a moment and then reappears in the distance but far away isn't far enough. I turn and look at the kid on the table he looks about ten years old and water is pouring from his face.

4

Two blocks south there is a twenty story building with at least three hundred visible windows behind which are three hundred tiny blue television screens operating simultaneously. Most of them are tuned to the same stations you can watch the patterns of fluctuating light pop out like in codes. Must be the war news. Twenty seconds of slow motion video frames broadcasting old glory drifting by in the bony hands of white zombies, and half the population ship their children out on the next tanker or jet to kill and be killed. My friend on the bed never watches his tv. It hangs anchored to the wall above his bed extended over his face and on the end of a gray robotic-looking arm. If he bothered to watch the tv he would see large groups of kids in the saudi desert yakking about how they were going to march straight through to baghdad, find a telephone booth and call home to mom and dad. Then he'd see them writing out their wills on the customary government-supplied short forms. Or maybe he'd catch the video where the commanding instructor holds up a land mine the size of a frisbee and says, if you step on one of these there won't be nothing left of you to find . . . just red spray in the air. Or the fort dix drill sergeant out of view of the rolling cameras, when ya see those towel-heads . . .

But my friend is too weak to turn the channels on other people's deaths. There is also the question of dementia, an overload of the virus's activity in his brain short-circuiting the essentials and causing his brain to atrophy so that he ends up pissing into the telephone. He sees a visitor's face impaled with dozens of steel nails or crawling with flies and gets mildly concerned. Seeing dick cheney looming up on the television screen with that weird lust in his eyes and bits of brain matter in the cracks of his teeth might accidentally be diagnosed as dementia. I catch myself just as all this stomach acid floods up into my throat, run out to the hallway to the water fountain.

5

It's a dark and wet concrete bunker, a basement that runs under the building from front to back. There is one other concrete staircase that is sealed off at the top by a street grate and you can hear the feet of pedestrians and spare parts of conversations floating down into the gloom. At a midpoint in the room you can do a 360-degree slow turn and see everything; the shaky alcoves built of cheap plywood, a long waist-high cement ledge where twenty-three guys could sit shoulder to shoulder if forced to, the darkened ledge in the back half hidden by pipes and architectural supports, and the giant television set. It's one of the latest inventions from japan, the largest video monitor available and it is hooked into the wall, then further encased in a large sheet of plexiglass in order to prevent the hands of some bored queen from fucking with the dials and switching the sex scenes to *Let's Make A Deal*. The plexi is covered in scratches and hand prints and smudges and discolored streaks of body fluids. At the moment the images fed from a vhs machine upstairs are a bit on the blink. When the original film was transferred it was jumping the sprockets of the projector and now I'm watching images that fluctuate strobically up and down but only by a single centimeter. Each body or object or vista or close-up of eye, tongue, stiff dick, and asshole is doubled and vibrating. Kind of pretty and psychedelic and no one is watching it anyway. There is a clump of three guys entwined on the long ledge. One of them is lying down leaning on one elbow with his head cradled in another guy's hand. The second guy is feeding the first guy his dick while a third guy is crouching down behind him pulling open the cheeks of his ass and licking his finger and poking at its bull's-eye. The shadows cast by their bodies cancel out the details necessary for making the vision interesting or decipherable beyond the basics. One of the guys, the one who looks like he's praying at an altar, turns and opens his mouth wide and gestures towards it. He nods at me but I turn away. He wouldn't understand. Too bad he can't see the virus in me, maybe it would rearrange something in him. It certainly did in me. When I found out I felt this abstract sensation, something like pulling off your skin and turning it inside out and then rear-ranging it so that when you pull it back on it feels like what it felt like before, only it isn't and only you know it. It's some-thing almost imperceptible. I mean the first minute after being diagnosed you are forever separated from what you had come to view as your life or living, the world outside the eyes. The calendar tracings of biographical continuity get kind of screwed up. It's like watching a movie suddenly and abruptly going in reverse a thousand miles a minute, like the entire landscape and horizon is pulling away from you in reverse in order to spell out a psychic separation. Like I said, he wouldn't understand and besides his hunger is giant. I once came to this place fresh from visiting a friend in the hospital who was within a day or two of death and you wouldn't know there was an epidemic. At least forty people exploring every possible invention of sexual ges-ture and not a condom in sight. I had an idea that I would make a three minute super-8 film of my dying friend's face with all its lesions and sightlessness and then take a super-8 projector and hook it up with copper cables to a car battery slung in a bag over my shoulder and walk back in here and project the film onto the dark walls above their heads. I didn't want to ruin their evening, just wanted maybe to keep their temporary worlds from narrowing down too far.

6

The old guy is still honking away when I get back to the room. There are tiny colored lights wobbling through the red threads of dusk and I'm trying to concentrate on them in order to avoid bending over suddenly and emptying out. I've been trying to fight the urge to throw up for the last two weeks. At first I thought it was food poisoning but slowly it was civilization. Everything is stirring this feeling inside me, signs of physical distress, the evening news, all the flags in the streets, and the zombie population going about its daily routines. I just want to puke it all out like an intense projectile. I sidetrack myself by concentrating on the little lights at dusk; imagining one of them developing a puff of smoke in its engines and plummeting to the earth among the canyon streets. Any event would help. The nurse finally shows up and behind the curtains I hear the sounds of a body thumping, the sounds of cloth being rolled up, of water splashing, and the covers being unfurled and tucked. Finally she leaves taking the smell of shit with her in a laundry cart. My friend wakes up and starts weeping; he's hallucinating that he can't find something that probably never existed. I understand the feeling just like I understand it when he sometimes screams that he hates healthy people. A senate group was in new york city recently collecting information on the extent of the epidemic and were told that in the next year and a half there will be thirty-three thousand homeless people with AIDS living in the streets and gutters of the city. A couple of people representing the policy of the city government assured the senators that these people were dying so fast from lack of health care that they were making room for the others coming up from behind; so there would be no visible increase of dying homeless on the streets. Oh I feel so sick. I feel like a human bomb tick tick tick.

7

I had an odd sleep last night. I felt like I was lying in a motel room for hours half awake or maybe I was just dreaming that I was half awake. In some part of my sleep I saw this fat little white worm, a grub-like thing that was no bigger than a quarter of an inch. When I leaned very close to it, my eye just centimeters above it, I could see every detail of the ridges of its flesh. It was a meat eater. The worm had latched onto something that looked like a goat fetus. It had large looping horns protruding from its head. The whole thing was white, fetal in appearance, its horns were translucent like fingernails. The grub was beginning to eat it and I pulled it off. It became very agitated and angry and tried to eat my fingers. I threw it onto the ground but there was yet another one and it was crawling toward some other fetal looking thing. I smacked it really hard. Picked it up and threw it down but my actions didn't kill it. My location was a wet dark hillside around dawn or dusk with a little light drifting over the landscape. Looking around I realized that the entire contents of a biology lab or pet shop had been dumped on the ground. Maybe I had stolen everything. There were big black tarantulas, all sorts of lizards, some small mammals and

bugs and frogs and snakes. At some point a big black tarantula was crawling around, blue-black and the size of a catcher's
mitt. It made a little jump like it had seized something. I looked
closely and saw it was eating an extraordinarily beautiful monitor lizard, a baby one. The spider didn't scare me; my sense of
anxiety came from mixing the species. They all seemed to have
come from different countries and were now thrown accidentally together by research or something. I pushed at the spider,
picked it up and tried to unfasten its mandibles from the belly of
the lizard. Someone else was with me; I handed them the spider
and said, Take it somewhere else or put it in something until I
figure out what I'm doing. The person threw the spider on the
ground in a rough manner. I said, don't do that, you'll kill it. If
you drop a tarantula from a height higher than five inches its
abdomen will burst.

8

Fevers. I wake up these mornings feeling wet like something
from my soul, my memory is seeping out the back of my head
onto the cloth of the pillows. I woke up earlier with intense
nausea and headache. I turned on the television to try to get
some focus outside my illness. Every station was filled with half-
hour commercials disguised as talk shows in which lowgrade tv
actors and actresses talk about how to whiten your investment
earnings or shake the extra pounds from your bones. I am convinced I am from another planet. One station had a full close-up
of a woman's face, middle-aged, saying, People talk about a sensation they've experienced when they are close to death in which
their entire lives pass before their eyes. Well, you experience a

similar moment when you are about to kill someone. You look at that person and see something in the moment before you kill him. You see his home, his family, his childhood, his hopes and beliefs, his sorrows and joys; all this passes before you in a flash. I didn't know what she was making these references for.

The nausea comes back. I try a new position on the bed with some pillows and slip back into sleep. I'm walking through this city not really sure where or why. I've got to piss really bad and go down this staircase of a subway or a hotel. (Architecture grows around my moving body like stone vegetation.) I find this old bathroom, mostly metal stalls and shadows like the subway station toilets of my childhood. I could sense sex as soon as I walked in, the moist scent of it in the yellow light and wet tiles and concrete. I go into this stall and pull out my dick and start pissing into the toilet. A big section of the stall's divider is peeled away and I see this guy in his late teens early twenties jerking off watching me. When I finish I reach through the partition and feel his chest through his shirt. He zips up and comes around into my stall and closes the door and leans against it his hands on his thighs. I unzip his trousers and peel them down to his knees. I roll up his shirt so I can play with his belly. When his pants are down at his knees I notice a fairly large wound on one of his thighs, lots of scrapes and scratches on his body. The wound does something to me. I feel vaguely nauseous but he is sexy enough to dispel it. He pulls down his underwear and leans back again like he wants me to blow him. I crouch and slowly start licking under the base of his prick. The wound is close to my eye and I notice this series of red and green and yellow wires, miniature cables looping out of it. There are two chrome cables with sectioned ribs pushing under the sides of flesh. Then this blue glow coloring the air above the wound. I stop licking and look closer and see it is a miniature monitor, a tiny black and white television screen with an even tinier figure gesticulating from a podium in a vast room. There is the current president, smiling like a corpse in a vigilante movie, addressing the nation on a live controlled broadcast; the occasion is an enormous banquet in washington, a cannibal banquet attended by heads of state and the usual cronies; kirkpatrick and her biological warfare husband. The pope is seated next to buckley and his sidekick buchanan. Oliver north is part of the entertainment and he squats naked in a spotlight in the center of the ballroom floor. A small egg pops out of his ass and breaks in two on the floor. A tiny american flag tumbles out of the egg waving mechanically. The crowd breaks into wild applause as whitney houston steps forward to lead a rousing rendition of the star spangled banner. I wake up in a fever so delirious i am in a patriotic panic. Where, where the fuck at five in the morning could i run and buy a big american flag. My head hurts so bad i have to get out of bed and stand upright in order to ease the pressure. I go to the bathroom and finally throw up. I come back into the room, yank open the window and lean out above the dark empty streets and scream: THERE IS SOMETHING IN MY BLOOD AND IT'S TRYING TO FUCKING KILL ME.

9

I still fight the urge to puke. I've been fighting it all week. Whenever I witness signs of physical distress I have to fight the urge to bend over at the waist and empty out. It can be anything. The bum on the corner with festering sores on his face. It could be the moving skeleton I pass in the hall on the way in. Some guy with wasting syndrome and cmv blindness who is leaning precariously out his wheelchair in the unattended hallway searching in sightlessness for something he's lost. He's making braying sounds. What he's looking for is beneath the wheels of his chair. A tiny teddy bear with a collegiate outfit sewn to its body and a little flag glued to its paw. I pick it up and notice it has saliva and food matter stuck in its fur and i wonder if this is what civilization boils down to. I place it in the guy's hands and he squeals at me, his eyes a dull gray like the bellies of small fish. I have to resist that urge to puke. It's upsetting but i realize i'm only nauseated by my own mortality.

My friend on the bed is waking. The hospital gown has pulled along his torso in the motions of sleep revealing a blobby looking penis and schools of cancer lesions twisting around his legs and abdomen. He opens his eyes too wide a couple of times and I hand him a bunch of flowers. I see double, he says. Twice as many flowers, I say.

10

Sometimes I come to hate people because they can't see where I am. I've gone empty, completely empty and all they see is the visual form; my arms and legs, my face, my height and posture, the sounds that come from my throat. But I'm fucking empty. The person I was just one year ago no longer exists; drifts spinning slowly into the ether somewhere way back there. I'm a Xerox of my former self. I can't abstract my own dying any longer. I am a stranger to others and to myself and I refuse to pretend that I am familiar or that I have history attached to my heels. I am glass, clear empty glass. I see the world spinning behind and through me. I see casualness and mundane effects of gesture made by constant populations. I look familiar but I am a complete stranger being mistaken for my former selves. I am a stranger and I am moving. I am moving on two legs soon to be on all fours. I am no longer animal vegetable or mineral. I am no longer made of circuits or disks. I am no longer coded and deciphered. I am all emptiness and futility. I am an empty stranger, a carbon copy of my form. I can no longer find what I'm looking for outside of myself. It doesn't exist out there. Maybe it's only in here, inside my head. But my head is glass and my eyes have stopped being cameras, the tape has run out and nobody's words can touch me. No gesture can touch me. I've been dropped into all this from another world and I can't speak your language any longer. See the signs I try to make with my hands and fingers. See the vague movements of my lips among the sheets. I'm a blank spot in a hectic civilization. I'm a dark smudge in the air that dissipates without notice. I feel like a window, maybe a broken window. I am a glass human. I am a glass human disappearing in rain. I am standing among all of you waving my invisible arms and hands. I am shouting my invisible words. I am getting so weary. I am growing tired. I am waving to you from here. I am crawling around looking for the aperture of complete and final emptiness. I am vibrating in isolation among you. I am screaming but it comes out like pieces of clear ice. I am signaling that the volume of all this is too high. I am waving. I am waving my hands. I am disappearing. I am disappearing but not fast enough.

Ceremonies

Essex Hemphill

I stood before him grinning, my undershorts and pants were down around my knees. I trembled and panted as he stroked me. After weeks of being coaxed and teased to come by, I had finally succumbed to George's suggestions. I had sneaked up to the store very early that morning, before it opened, after my mother left for work.

The sexual hunger that would eventually illuminate my eyes began then. I was a skinny little fourteen-year-old Black boy, growing up in a ghetto that had not yet suffered the fatal wounds and injuries caused by drugs and Black-on-Black crime.

My neighborhood, my immediate homespace, was an oasis of strivers. A majority of the families living on my block owned their homes. My sexual curiosity would have blossomed in any context, but in Southeast Washington, D.C., where I grew up, I had to carefully allow my petals to unfold. If I had revealed them too soon they would surely have been snatched away, brutalized, and scattered down alleys. I was already alert enough to know what happened to the flamboyant boys at the school who were called "sissies" and "faggots." I could not have endured then the violence and indignities they often suffered.

George was at least thirty years older than I, tall, and slightly muscular beneath his oversized work clothes which consisted of khakis, a cotton short-sleeved shirt, and a white apron. He wore black work boots similar to those of construction workers. Many of the boys in the neighborhood teased him viciously, but I hadn't understood before the morning he and I were together just what motivated them to be cruel and nasty by turn. At that time, I didn't know that George had initiated most of the boys I knew and some of their older brothers, one by one, into the pleasures of homo sex.

Only months before my visit to him that April morning, I had roamed the parking lot of a nearby country bar—my adolescent desire drove me out there one night, and one night only—discreetly asking the predominately white patrons if they would let me suck their dicks for free. My request was never fulfilled because I believe the men were shocked that I would so boldly solicit them. I was lucky no one summoned the police to come for me. I was lucky I wasn't dragged off to some nearby wooded area and killed.

George was a white man. My initiation into homo sex was guided by the hands of a white man. The significance of this in a racial context was not lost on me, but it wasn't a concern strong enough to check my desire. For weeks George had whispered he wanted to suck my dick. Catching me alone in the store or responding to my request for a particular product, he would quickly serve me, seizing the opportunity to whisper in my ear. *And I was listening.*

Eventually I went to the store on pretense, requesting something I knew they wouldn't have, such as a specific brand of soap or floor wax, just so he would wait on me and whisper. If we had been caught when we finally began fucking, the law would have charged him with molesting and sodomizing me as a minor because of my age, but the law would not have believed that I wanted him to suck my dick. I wanted him to touch me. I wanted to fuck his ass. I, willingly, by the volition of my own desires, engaged in acts of sexual passion, somewhat clumsily, but nonetheless sure of my decision to do so.

When George liberated his equally swollen cock from his pants it sprang out engorged with blood and fire. The head of it was deep pink in color. I was startled to see that the hair surrounding it was as red as the hair on his head.

George again lowered himself to eye level with my cock and drew me into his mouth once more. It was hard to tell which of us was enjoying the cock sucking more. Suddenly, he pulled his mouth off my wet shaft, got up off his knees and hurried to the front of the store. He promptly returned with a short stack of grocery bags, newspapers, and a small jar of Vaseline.

"You're gonna fuck me." It wasn't a statement or a command from him, it was a fact neither of us could turn away from.

After spreading the newspaper and bags on the floor behind

the deli counter to create a makeshift paper pallet, George opened the Vaseline, scooped out some with his index finger, and pushed it up into his asshole. He turned his back to me so I could see the pink entrance of his anus being penetrated by the steady in and out motion of his finger. My dick was so hard I thought it would break into a thousand pieces of stone around our feet. The lips of his asshole kissed and sucked his finger as he pushed it in and out, in and out. After thoroughly greasing his asshole, George then scooped out more Vaseline and smeared it all over my dick.

"Ahh! Ahh!" I sighed out in pleasure.

"Yeah, you're ready," he said approvingly, stroking me a few times more. Guided by George, who had now laid down upon the pallet and beckoned me to climb on, my cock, led by his hand, entered his ass in one smooth penetration. I didn't know at that moment that I would mount him all summer, night and day, and pour my adolescence into him. I would lie to get away from home and friends to be with him. I learned then that sneaking, ducking, and hiding were key components of a homo sex life simply because of the risk of exposure and the often devastating consequences.

I continued to visit George early in the morning before the store opened, fucking him at the back of the store behind the deli counter on bags and newspapers. I fucked him at his house at the end of his work day while his mongrel dog sat and watched us. From the spring through the late summer of 1971, George was the focus of my sexuality. He was the veracity of my sexual desire.

As it would turn out, I became his sole sex partner for that brief summer. I have often speculated that perhaps among all of the homeboys who passed through his hands, I was the one *wanting* to learn more. George knew this, and to the extent that he could exploit my youth for his pleasure, I allowed myself to be exploited and fondled and sucked, because l wanted this, too. I wanted him. I didn't come back to the store and tease him and curse him as did the other boys who had fucked him. I didn't demand money as some did. After their orgasms they resented him, but what they really resented was the recognition of their own *homo* sexual desire.

I kept silent about our activities. I would dare not say that we were in love. I wasn't sure I loved myself at fourteen, but I knew that my dick got hard for George. Never once did I give any thought to the possibility that I might be committing some sin I would be punished for in hell. Sin was the furthest thing from my consciousness. Hell was all around me in the ghetto of my adolescence.

My dick did not fall off in his mouth. I did not turn green from kissing him. I didn't burst into flames during our orgasms, nor did he. In fact, during orgasm, I often called out Jesus' name, which seemed appropriate for warding off such evil as I might have imagined we were committing. If anything, I was most concerned about being caught by my buddies or his co-workers. To this day I'm convinced the other fellas didn't know that I, too, was being initiated by George. Our group identity and rapport did not allow for this kind of discussion or candor to occur.

I regret that we were never able to talk about our visits to George. I regret, too, that we were not able to sexually explore one another in the same way that we allowed George to explore us. Ours was truly a fragile, stereotypical Black masculinity that would not recognize homo desire as anything but perverse and a deviation from the expected "role" of a man.

The ridicule we risked incurring would have condemned us to forever prove our "manhood" or succumb to being the target of a hatred that was, at best, a result of hating *self* for desiring to sexually touch the flesh of another male.

At fourteen, I was astute enough to know my mouth should not reveal any desire that would further endanger me. There was no "older" brother at home to stand watch over my blossoming manhood. There was no father there, either. I was solely responsible for myself—the eldest sibling, the eldest son. Neither of those absences is an explanation for my sexual identity. Only nature knows the reason why.

During that same summer that George introduced me to homoeroticism, my public acceptance as "one of the boys" was severely challenged. The night is so clear to me. It was mid-August, sultry, humid, August, and the anticipation of returning to school was in the air. My buddies, Tommy, Tyrone, Leon, Peanut, and Kevin, we were all across the street from my house talking with some of the older boys—David, George, Doug, Wayne, Kenny, and Leon's brother, Crip.

My mother's bedroom was located at the front of our house and her windows faced out to the street. Her windows were open because there was no air conditioning in the house at that time. The night breeze was as much relief as we could hope for from the oppressive Washington summers.

Across the street from my house, on Douglas's and Kenny's front porch, we were talking about everything from sports to girls. It was the typical conversation of males in various stages of adolescence. We all shined in the streetlights that beat down on our variously muscular frames burnished by the summer sun. Our conversation rose and fell, exerting its brashness and bravado against the night, kicking around in our heads, drawing us into laughter and silence by turns, as we listened to stories of pussy conquests, petty scams, and recent ass kickings. The conversation was dominated by the older boys, who by turn tried to impart fragments of street warrior knowledge to us. We were sitting and standing, absorbing all this, relaxing our tough postures, allowing a communal trust to put us at ease and make us glib and attentive.

Crip was standing. I was sitting. It happened that from where I sat I could eye his crotch with a slight upward shift of my eyes. Well, one of the times that I peeked, Crip caught me. I would soon discover that I had cruised into very dangerous territory. Lulled by the conversation, I had allowed myself to become intoxicated on the blossoming masculinity surrounding me. I might as well have been shooting semen from wet dreams straight into my veins for the high I was on in this gathering of males.

Instantly, Crip jumped forward and got in my face. "I see you looking at my dick!" he hurled at me. I felt as though he had accused me of breaking into his house and violating his mother. Immediately, all conversation ceased and all eyes focused on me and Crip.

"Do you wanna suck my big, Black dick, muthafucka?" he demanded, clutching his crotch and moving up into my face. "Do you, nigga?"

Thank God my instincts told me to stand up. It was this defensive posture that perhaps saved me from an *absolute* humiliation, but my "No" was weak.

"Well why are you looking at my dick? Is you a freak? You must wanna suck it. Are you a faggot? You can suck it, baby," he mockingly cooed, still clutching what was more than a handful of cock.

The fellas were laughing and slapping palms all around by this time. I was becoming visibly angry but I had still uttered nothing more than a meek "No" to his challenge. I then remembered my mother's bedroom windows; they were open; she must have heard him.

The laughter began to die down. The sexual tension in the air was palpable enough to be slapped around. Crip's attitude changed for the worse.

"You shouldn't be looking at a muthafucka's dick unless you plan to suck it," he sneered. It now seemed that all along he had been bellowing at me, so I was even more convinced my mother had heard him.

"Are you funny, nigga?" he asked, deadly serious, which elicited more raucous laughter from the fellas.

"No," I said, attempting to put more conviction in my voice. Crip was but an inch or two taller than me, and a pretty Black male. He carried beauty as agilely as some Black men carry footballs and basketballs and pride. I was surely attracted to him, but to even have hinted at that would have cost me more than the humiliation I endured that night.

So there we stood, me surrounded by gales of laughter punctuated by his booming voice, and all the time, in the back of my mind, I believe my mother was listening, in shock, hearing my humiliation. To her credit, if she overheard this she never confronted me with it.

Crip finally ended his tirade. The conversation resumed its boisterous, brash bravado. Shortly thereafter, I excused myself from the fellas, crossed the street, locked the door behind me, and cried myself to sleep in my bed. It would not be the last time I would cry myself to sleep because a male had inflicted me with emotional pain. It would not be the last time I would lock the door behind me and go to my bed alone, frightened of my sexuality and the desires I could not then speak of or name as clearly as I could articulate the dangers.

My sexual encounters with George ceased several weeks before summer vacation ended. In retrospect, I believe I stopped visiting him at the store and at his home as a direct result of the humiliation I suffered from Crip. I must have thought it would only be a matter of time before we would be discovered. Whatever my reasons, my refusal to engage in any more sex bewildered George. He continued to coax me to climb up on his back, but could no longer be seduced. He enticed me with money but I refused that, too. When I was sent to the store by my mother, I would go two blocks out of the way to another convenience store just to avoid the longing I recognized in his eyes, a longing that was partially stoked by my mutual desire. I would later discover that such a longing inhabits the eyes of many homosexuals, particularly those who believe themselves to be unable to come out of the closet.

The school year resumed itself uneventfully. The only change, other than those occurring because of puberty, was the increasing burden of carrying a secret. I was learning to live with it safely hidden away, but for how long? It was surely danger-ous knowledge. There was no one I could tell about my sexual adventures with George. There was no previous reference of intimacy to compare to sex. I continued nurturing my desire in the long nights of my adolescence, quietly masturbating in my bed as my younger brother slept above on the upper bunk.

Black male adolescent survival in a ghetto context made me realize the *necessity* of having a girlfriend, a female I could be seen walking home after school. It would be my luck to date girls who were "good," girls who were not going to experiment with sex beyond kissing and fondling, and even that was often only tolerated at a minimum if tolerated at all.

I was not the kind of male to force the issue of going all the way sexually. For me, it was enough to have a cover for my *true* desires, and that's what these girl were—covers. But I treated them with respect. They were girl *friends* more often than not.

I had the opportunity to have sex with one of the girls I dated. She agreed to skip school with me one day. We hid out at her house, our mutual motive: sex. After a long morning of petting and kissing the big moment arrived. We stumbled to her bedroom along an unfamiliar path that frightened and excited us. I was nervous because I expected her mother or father or one of her siblings to walk in and catch us.

In our adolescent nakedness we were beautiful, but if caught, we would have been seen as *being ugly*. We were sixteen and fifteen and ripe with curiosity and desire. Her skin was honey gold, smooth, so soft to my touch. Her breasts were full and sweet, the nipples brown and swollen by my tongue. Her hair was plaited in thick braids that coiled atop her head like snakes. We were both virgins. Nothing in our timid sex education classes at school or our evasive discussions at home had prepared us for walking into her bedroom to face our beautiful nakedness.

I believe we both felt we had to go through with the act because we had gone so far. In my mind, George appeared, but that was *different*. He had not instructed me about girls or young women. No one had. I kept hearing the older boys scat about breaking the cherry, but there was no cherry hanging between her legs when I looked. What was there was wet and warm to my fingers.

She laid so still on her bed. I knelt above her, fondling her breasts, kissing her, imagining these must be the things to do to seduce her. Neither of us spoke. As our breathing escalated I grabbed my cock and guided the head toward her vagina. She opened her legs to show me the mouth that was there, wet and waiting. Sunlight poured over us. Sweat bathed our bodies. We were straining ourselves to break rules we were taught not to break. We exerted ourselves against everything we were told not to do.

I pressed my head against the wet mouth. I pushed. She pulled away. I inched forward. Pushed. She pulled away again.

"Am I hurting you?" I asked nervously.

"Yes," she said softly.

"We don't have to do this," I assured her, saying this more for my comfort rather than her own. *I* didn't want to be doing this, after all.

"But I want to," she said. "I want to do this. It will make you—it will make *us* happy."

I rose up off her body. "Maybe this isn't the right time," I said. Looking down at her, I then realized how lovely she was and how little I knew of her. How little she *really* knew of me. I thought of George and a tingle stirred in my loins. I realized I didn't desire penetrating her. I was doing this for my reputation. I thought I needed to walk away with a bloody sheet to prove what—that I could break a hymen? I had no thought about consequences. There was no condom to prevent pregnancy, no pills being taken that I knew of. We were entangled in limbs we couldn't name, dry-throated, sweaty, pursuing different objectives in the afternoon bed we had stolen. My erection slowly fell. I lowered myself onto her again and kissed her lightly on the lips.

"We should probably get dressed," I encouraged her. "Someone might come home soon." That was the last and only time we were naked together. Not long after, we stopped seeing each other romantically.

A year later, she began dating an older boy around school. We saw each other less often, and then one day I saw her in a maternity blouse. I believe she finished school—I'm not sure— but by that time she wasn't my concern. I was seeing another "good girl," walking her home, holding her hand, pretending I was consumed by love—safe, by all appearances, from being identified as a faggot.

Robin

Eileen Myles

Rightaway I'd like to separate this Robin from all Robins you or I have ever known. This Robin I am about to tell you about is not someone that any of us know. She is somebody I found and I would like to tell her secret.

I call her Robin because she is red and black and angular and resembles a bird in her speed and in her cruelty. I fell in love with her briefly, last year. I'm just not in love with her anymore but there's this residue.

She was sort of a famous junkie, which I thought was pretty

exotic, never having been particularly involved with heroin, having had a taste here and there—I was at an art event a couple of years ago and a friend dragged me to the dinner afterwards and Robin entertained our end of the table with a story about how she had been busted for dealing dope, but instead of going to jail she informed on somebody else. She knew that she would die in jail, she knew she couldn't take it. I was appalled and thrilled by her coldness. She spoke carefully, slowly, halting, choosing her words . . . how is it that junkies talk, very ornate, piercing and hollow and obviously this girl was a prince. A dead one. She smelled of flowers, she smiled at me when she got up to leave. I'm so glad you're here she said intensely like I was the only soul in the room, or a soul who had a soul like hers.

I knew Robin had a girlfriend. Historically, they were kind of merged. My friends who used to do heroin said Robin 'n Babe as if it were one word. Babe played in a band, played till all the band members were so strung out that they were no band. By then Robin 'n Babe were an item so they teamed up and Robin sold drugs and Babe did them and they held sort of an elite junkie salon for a few years. Robin knew everyone in New York. Everyone on that trendy glamour junkie circuit. She wanted to write, had been doing so for years. In notebooks, in between experiences I guess. I think I had what Robin wanted and vice versa.

One day I was in her apartment and I found myself touching her leg. Her apartment was nice. Actually it was Babe's. It was hard to unravel where one stopped and the other began— It was Babe's bombed-out junkie rock star haven and Robin moved in when Babe kicked Lulu, the old girlfriend, out. Lulu died of AIDS. She wound up hooking on 3rd Avenue after they kicked her out of the band because she was so bad. The lives of drunks and druggies is such a treacherous moral landscape with avalanches and peaks and nasty pitfalls. Robin moved in and cleaned house, eventually at some point of successful drug dealing had extensive carpentry work done, the apartment had modernesque divides, shelves for aeons of rock star clothes and shoes, millions of records and Robin's little dealing room lined with scales and books. There she sat with her extraordinary stark white-face, a weirdly shaped skull, kind of cubist and long, with raven-ish black hair. I adored her because she was a masque. This, combined with her sensibility, literary and scrupulous, made her essentially Aquarian to me, an endless revolving door.

Just before I put my hand on her leg I had asked about her and Babe. I was making an honest woman of myself. We're roommates she said in her voice that was of the air, tentative yet treacherous. Actually, she leaned forward stretching her arms down to her pointed toes. "I don't really know. We don't really talk about it. Babe is not disposed to discuss anything so abstract as our relationship. She is not . . ." She sighed, thinking the better of continuing. "I don't know what she's doing." "Honesty," her face telegraphed. Robin had a deep morality of which she never spoke, but she communicated its breadth and its depth, by her protective pauses. You knew she was a good person because she held back at moments of deepest revelation. She did not spill, and I always felt that to push her a bit would be sloppy and expose my own lack of a system of conduct.

So I put my hand on this woman who smelled so good. Her fragrance was coming my way. When we smell a person's perfume we think that we're smelling their essence, their identity somehow. The body has to be there for the perfume to stick to, but when they're gone it's the perfume that we know. I've forgotten its name. I asked her once.

Some kind of sexy thirties jazz was on the stereo. I knew I was in her house now, not Babe's. The design was hers, but the ornaments were Babe's. Babe's paintings and the guitars and record collection. She had made a home for Babe, kind of a mother or a wife. I found that so hot to discover an ex-heroin dealer in the middle of the art world who was really a good woman, once I told her that—I couldn't believe how hokey it sounded and by her silence I knew she was horrified. I bet she wanted to break the silence of our affair just to tell Babe some of the stupid things I said.

Okay well if this is all right I put my hand on her leg. It seemed seductive enough. I'm really attracted to you I said. The feeling is mutual she replied. Soon we were half-dancing half making out in the middle of the room and it was really hot, I mean she had a hard desperate mouth, her hands were up my shirt and I was feeling her ass. All my instincts were on target in the particular way I felt like a bow and arrow nocked, then release.

Soon we were on the bed, ripping our pants off and this was when I began to feel in the middle of their relationship because you knew you were going wild in the precise same place where a couple woke each morning and looked at that painting, Babe's.

I think this is going to be a problem she said. She got up and sat on the chair, lit up a cigarette. A move I regard as "womanning" me—I've felt it before. It's the gesture of a torn, or badly married, man.

Well, are you going to tell Babe. Yes, I'm quite certain we are due to have a conversation about this, among other things. She bit each syllable as she spoke. Robin had to go to work, she was a cook, a neat transformation for a dealer, though actually she was a cook first, that's how she started dealing drugs. Cooking in all of Ricky Mountain's restaurants. Even sold him the drugs he'd OD'd on legend says, though Robin says it's not true. And she was the one who told me the legend. Someone else got him those. It was weird she said to have your boss coming in the kitchen to buy from you. They always came to me, she said of her connections. It was never something I decided to do. They knew I could help them, she said.

So she went to work, pretty wonderful, all vulnerable and pink. The pretty Robin. One of many. I guess I went home. I went running down in the park by the East River. I needed to stretch out my feelings that were really making me crazy and all furled & unfurled.

We had a date the next day at 4. I don't know how I tolerated my home, I think I was working or something, some piece of writing, but I stopped at three to let feeling build, and then it was 4:15, 4:30 I was out of my mind. Quarter of 5 she called. Where are you! Well I'm out doing a few errands. It took a little longer than I thought. Are you coming over? *Well* I had *thought* I would *still* do *that*, but it is pretty late. She was almost needling me off the phone. Yeah, c'mon I said. Up the stairs came this angry woman who I sometimes thought resembled Elizabeth Taylor or Keith Richards and sometimes when she was really nice, Donovan. Frozen and mean in a white jacket coming up my steps. Hello, I said, holding the door. I was no longer in fun-affair with vulnerable married woman. In one day that was already over. She sat in her white jacket on the small orange couch. Do you want a drink? I had automatically stored exactly what she had served me from her refrigerator the day before. I was glad she said no because I would have been ashamed to reveal what a copy-cat I was. Raspberry Soho Cola. Your furniture is not very comfortable she said.

I feel nervous I confided nervously teetering over the counter that faced the itchy couch. "*Why* do *you* feel nervous, would it make you feel better to tell me?" These quiet utterances thundered like the I Ching. What a jerk I am. I never wanted to go to hell, but I thought I could date the devil. "I feel funny." Do you want to go up on the roof I asked. No I don't. Why would I want to go up on the roof? This is awful. I have invited a wolf into my home. I went over and started knocking into, touching, kissing the wolf. It was the only thing I could think of doing. C'mere get up I huskily growled. Where are we going she whispered. Tamed. Over there. I pointed at the bed. My goal from the day before was to get our clothes completely off, that kind of sex. I was trying to get her shoes off, to be sort of sexy/servile but I was so awkward she pulled her weird green '70s rock star boot back to herself and started untying. Behold the skinny body I loved. I was revolted but addicted.

Momentarily, she acted as if she intended to really ravage me, but it was a phoney growl. She didn't know how. I must fuck Robin. That was my job. She had the largest . . . cunt, vagina I have ever stuck my finger in. It was big red and needy. I stuck two three fingers in and fucked her and fucked her. I've always received complaints that I was rough but I felt like I could have been shoving a stick up this woman, a branch. Her ass was up in the air, it was April and the trees were still pretty bare and I looked through the black rusty cross-hatched window gates of my East Village apartment and I felt detached and I fucked and fucked her with my hand, and twisting her nipples. She moaned and growled with pleasure. Such a woman, I have never met such a horny animal nor have I ever so distinctly serviced a woman before. Do you want my fist inside you. Anything she shrieked, anything.

So this is my late winter stolen landscape. Robin's hungry

butt bobbing in front of my window next to my desk where I write. I felt my home, myself, violated by this animal. I couldn't stop. This must be what faggots do. The inside of her pussy was hot and warm, it did, it did feel like a live animal. I put my fingertip to her butt-hole but there didn't seem to be any magic there. I was getting bored. Wanna come up on me. I wanted to be underneath—her pussy on my mouth. Sure, anything. I had no way of framing her true repertoire with these kind of replies. I suspected she had done everything in the past, or on the other hand maybe she was a liar.

Here it comes, the salty hairy organ, the slippery wet thing with a hard pearly center, jammed in my face. I started licking and sucking like crazy. I am wild for the sensation of having my face covered and dominated, almost smothered by a cunt. She was happy. It all seemed one to her, then a great groan and buckets of wet acrid fluid flooded into my mouth, splashing down my cheeks and onto my pillow. Initially I surmised she had come in some new way, but it was pee and now I had drank it for the first time. I swallowed some, but then no I don't really want to drink piss. I wiped the edges of my mouth and then kissed her. I think she said I'm sorry but grinned at me wiping my face. Do you have any music she said. Take a look—the tapes are on the refrigerator. I lay on the bed, fascinated by the acrid taste of piss, yet horrified at the inadequacies of my tape collection. Da, *duh-duh*, Da, *duh-duh* came the opening notes of "Kimberly" and Robin walked naked across the length of my apartment like she was the real Patti Smith.

I think we tried to cram more into her pussy for a while after that and she gave my lips a quick swipe with her mouth, but I really suspected that was not her cup of tea. Because she was not a lesbian, nothing like that.

Do you have a towel? Actually I didn't. Or I didn't have a clean towel and I didn't want to give her mine, out of a desire not to insult one of us. Finally I gave her a facecloth. I guess a towel's a towel. I didn't know what was going on. I've got to meet my girlfriend she explained. Today she had a girlfriend. A blow to the stomach, received in silence of course. I'm going out too I said. Well then come on, come with me to meet her. I did something in the kitchen sink, brushed my teeth, but I was feeling demolished.

Outside I unlocked my bike—"No, you know . . . I'm just going to ride off." She gave me a giant devil grin. Thanks she jeered. What am I going to do I thought as I rode off. There were millions of other ways to get laid but I chose this one. She called me a couple of days later. I explained how rotten I felt. I would never want to cause you pain she assured me. I felt mildly cauterized but Ouch. Actually what kept running through my mind was that an alley cat had run in and pissed all over my apartment. I went to see her at work on Saturday. She wore a mustard colored shirt. She was beautiful. She resembled Donovan. She was sulking in the sunlight. She had to start cooking. Come back later she said as she went in. I bumped into her that night at a party. I ignored her. She looked angry and flipped out. Babe was there. I feel like committing suicide a friend of mine confided to Babe. I feel like committing homicide Babe replied. I left town, stayed with Mary, David's sister at the beach.

Robin started calling me a few weeks later. I didn't return the calls and then I did. I felt strong. I was over her. She called me from work. Come see me she begged. I'm going to a memorial service I told her. But I haven't eaten yet. Come here she said. She made me the most delicious burritos. Fabulous. I could taste them all through the service, a room full of old friends of a man I hardly knew. I knew his lover. I liked him a lot. I hugged Roberto and left. Outside the church I unlocked my bike thinking about Robin. I got home and the phone rang. I must be crazy she said but I'm working a double shift but I can't stop thinking about you. Can I come over. She walked into my arms as she closed the door. It was the most delicious sex, her fingers jabbing inside of me so far up, I just felt I had grown so much larger inside just to accommodate her touch, just to take that woman inside of my stomach. I can't believe I'm going back to work now. I went to an opening and just smirked and felt so well fucked and aching.

It went like that, rattle-trap like a bad machine for many months. I told her I didn't want to see her anymore. I told her I just wanted to see her for coffee. We fucked, and I regretted it. The sex seemed to get wilder and wilder and in the midst of it she'd say: hope you've gotten over your desire to call this a relationship. I hope you've gotten over your desire to publicize this.

About a year later I'm watching leaves drop off the branches of some different trees and the leaves landing among the branches themselves. I can't really remember exactly what she said or anything quite like it. I only know in the midst of passion she would always betray me like pleasure was a hook she used to throw me. I was just a poor fish. She didn't want me, she didn't want anyone to know about us, least of all Babe. She would invite me over to sleep in her home when Babe spent weekends on Fire Island and she'd call Babe and ask her if she was warm enough, and take her time and chuckle and have her relationship in front of me.

Once I woke up in the middle of the morning, maybe five, after dawn, it was blue and Robin was asleep and I lay there looking at Babe's painting. It got truer and truer to me, I

thought it was pretty good. Two little fiery creatures, little cray-
ons of color, one connected to something below the frame of the
painting—really anchored and attached and the other, brighter,
was floating in space. The anchored one, obviously Robin, was
giving the other, Babe, a tongue lashing. Babe danced, immune,
and yet it was a child's painting, a defiant work. A slap against
her Mom. The reality of lying in their bed in the middle of
their life looking at their relationship was more than I could
bear. I had to move on—there may have been a little more but
not much.

They lived in Soho. The first time I met Robin for sex we
went to Rizzoli's. Then we saw some art. Big dark paintings that
looked like designer sheets. We picked up sandwiches—mine was
tuna, and we carried them home. I guess I don't regret not stopping at the sandwich. Once we did just have lunch and she told
me about going all the way to Thailand to cop. And she snorted
all the profits, her and Babe. Then someone passed the window
of the restaurant that we both knew and she practically ducked.
Later when I accused her of ducking she denied it. She carried
drugs on the airplane up that massive pussy.

Once after we stopped fucking we had a small honeymoon. I
went to visit her and it was late afternoon and it started to rain.
It got darker, naturally, and she showed me in great detail her
room. She had an extensive postcard collection, mostly from
Italy and the Far East. My therapist said she was probably a
classic narcissist and she couldn't love, not me anyhow but she
collected people too. She was not an artist. This is one way I
have of hurting her. She showed me an odd fan that looked like
a globe. She knew where you could get hundreds of these at one
time, they were intended for bankers—some place where you
couldn't rustle the papers too much. I guess it kept her room

cool when she dealt. All the rest of these fans were destroyed and now there were only a few and she had one of them here in her room. The titles of her books in her shelves didn't impress me. You could tell she still had her college books. I'm always shocked at what people haven't lost. There were pictures on her bulletin board of her and Babe going to one of Babe's gigs. Babe had weird makeup on and a cape, Robin just looked cool. She was. If I've ever met a cool woman in my life Robin was her.

Later she led me out to a round table in her front room and she told me about her early religious training and she went to Hebrew school. She was showing me her favorite spiritual book in the world something by Martin Buber. She read it very slowly, the smallest bite at a time, sometimes just a sentence. She had her head bent over that book and she looked like the sweetest Jewish boy, head bent in prayer. I fell in love with her again. I like the smell and taste of women's bodies. Sometimes I'm sure that's what I'm living for. But as for Robin I would like to make her drink piss. I know a boy who did it in high school. Somebody offered him twenty bucks to drink it the story goes. Did he drink it? Yes. I was about fifteen when I heard that story. His name was Frosty, he was from Lexington, and was the lead singer from a band that played all the local dances doing covers of the Rolling Stones. His big song was "I'm Alright." He would stoop down at the foot of the stage and his lip would curl up and it was heavenly. He was our Rolling Stone. I was amazed when I heard he drank piss. It was a new kind of spirituality I had begun to hear about. Humiliation. But this anger it has brought me makes me think I've done it wrong. She went to California for a week, rented a red car and discovered it was me she loved now. Not Babe. Too late. Now I sit in this incredible silence. I don't know why.

The Cat Who Loved La Traviata

Jaime Manrique

Nothing seemed to have changed in Times Square, and I found the familiar squalor somehow reassuring. As usual at this time of day, shoeless Muslims knelt on green towels, praying to Mecca in front of subway posters for Broadway shows. Squatting on the stairs leading to the street, begging aggressively for quarters, was the same woman I had seen for months, with the same shrinking baby, wrapped in a bunch of grimy rags. Nearby, bored cops chatted idly, petting their police dogs.

Forty-second Street was thick with a Sunday crowd of black

and Latino teenagers looking for cheap thrills. Mormon-looking tourists with cameras strolled, sticking close together while taking in the scene. They were offered sex of all kinds, pot, Colombian coke, smack, hash, ecstasy, uppers and downers, designer drugs and, of course, crack.

It was one of those rare, mild late afternoons at the end of July when the air was like silk and Manhattan felt like an island. The multicolored neon marquees of the movie theaters advertised life-sized photographs of seminude porno stars in sexy poses. A naked man, looking stoned out of his mind, wandered out of a peep show. Halfway down the block, a young woman dressed in Salvation Army uniform and armed with a megaphone, was stationed under the awning of a sex palace, preaching to the depraved and indifferent denizens of Times Square. Two preppies stopped in front of her, swayed, twirled, wobbled on their feet and collapsed, overdosing on the sidewalk.

"You don't have to get high on drugs," the woman blared. "Jesus will get you high. You'll be so high on Jesus you'll never want to come down."

Waiting for the light to change at the corner of Forty-second and Eighth, I looked over my shoulder: the skyscrapers of midtown had bloomed. The Chrysler building caught the reflection of the setting sun; its silver top reminded me of a minaret crowned with a long, shimmering sword. Crossing Eighth, I saw the sky beyond the Hudson, which looked as if all the nuclear reactors from Hoboken to Key West had exploded, setting the air afire. Yet the color was not that of natural combustion, but synthetic, like the orange of a hot burner on an electric stove.

I live on the west side of Eighth Avenue, above O'Donnell's Bar, between Forty-third and Forty-fourth Streets, an address formerly nicknamed The Minnesota Strip. The good old days had ended when the famous Greek restaurant The Pantheon closed due to lease problems. Since that time the short block—which comprises a Citibank at the corner of Forty-third, O'Donnell's Bar, the Pantheon building, a porno joint (Paradise Alley), a Gyro coffee shop, the Cameo (a beautiful old theater now turned XXX movie house), and a four-story building at the corner of Forty-fourth, formerly a whorehouse and now a shooting gallery—had been taken over by crack addicts, who conducted their business on the premises of Paradise Alley. Now I looked back with nostalgia to the days when young hookers (for all tastes) decorated the block around the clock . . . But wait a minute, not *that* young, I thought, standing on the east corner of Forty-third, as I spotted a tiny hooker standing in front of the door of my building. She looked about seven years old, maybe seven and a half. I had seen teenage hookers and hustlers, but this was a child. This was real depravity and decadence—no doubt a product of the crack epidemic. In spite of her spike heels, she barely reached the doorknob. She wore a vinyl miniskirt and red satin tank top. A pink plastic purse was strapped across her shoulder and her belly button was plugged with a blue stone. Her hair was streaked gold and punked-out. Long rhinestone earrings framed her cheeks and above the false eyelashes her eyelids were painted purple and sprinkled with gold glitter. Her tiny crimson lips were done in the shape of a heart. I stood in front of my door, open-mouthed, dangling the keys, waiting for her to move.

In her childish voice she said, "Want a date?"

I recoiled, aghast. Now she placed her baby hand on her hip and crossing one leg behind her knee she reclined lewdly against the wall. "Cheap blow job," she offered. I noticed now that her voice, though squeaky and reedy, had a sultry timbre. She was not a child—she was a midget hooker. I breathed a sigh of relief, "No, thank you," I said. "I live here."

She gave me a blank look, but made enough room for me to open the door. I ran up the stairs to my apartment on the fourth floor. I was worried about Mr. O'Donnell. The six months the vet had given him to live were over and even though Mr. O'Donnell seemed fine, I felt anxious when he was alone. Inside the apartment I set down my shopping bag and went to the closet to hang up my new suit. I was walking toward the living room calling Mr. O'Donnell's name when the phone rang.

"Santiago, is that you upstairs?" said Rebecca, my downstairs neighbor.

I picked up. "Hi, Rebecca. I just got here but I can't find Mr. O'Donnell."

"I'm so relieved it's you. I thought it might be a burglar. Mr. O'Donnell is down here with me."

"I'm coming down to get him. Is that okay?"

"Come on over. I'm so glad you're back."

Rebecca met me at her door. Her eyes were wide open, as if she had just had a major fright. Locking the door after I came in, she said, "Can I offer you a beer, iced tea, a glass of lemonade?"

"The lemonade sounds delish, but no thanks. Where's Mr. O'Donnell?" I looked around the room for him.

"I don't know whether we ought to disturb him right now. He's in my bedroom listening to side two of *La Traviata*."

Rebecca had discovered that Mr. O'Donnell would revive from his periodic bouts of listlessness by listening to Monserrat Caballe's rendition of Violeta. He'd lie still, smiling, his ears pricked up until the opera was over.

"Is he in bad shape?"

"I didn't want to call you at Lucy's, but when I went upstairs Saturday morning to feed him, he was more dead than alive. He refused his Kal Kan, so naturally I was worried. I went to Barkin' Fish for some catfish since he likes it so much. I practically had to force feed him, but he ate one fillet, a teensy bitty bit at a time."

"Should I take him to the hospital right now?" I said.

"Goodness gracious, Santiago. You're making me more nervous, and I'm already a shitty mess. I called the hospital and was told there's nothing we can do except make sure he takes his medicine with his meals. Today he's much better. He's been listening to *La Traviata* all day. This morning he refused to eat fish, so I gave him a container of pineapple yogurt. Wait till this side of the record is over and you can take him upstairs. He's as good as new, thanks to my ingenuity."

"I shouldn't have left him alone, but thank you so much, Rebecca."

"Will you stop feeling guilty about everything. I swear, Santiago, I'm going to start calling you the Honorary Jew. I took real good care of the kitty; Florence Nightingale couldn't have nursed him better. So, how's Lucy? Did you have a nice weekend?"

I gave Rebecca a much abridged and sanitized version of what transpired in Jackson Heights.

"Honey, it sounds like a Flannery O'Connor novel set in Queens," she observed. "It's the planets," she added philosophically. "As long as Pluto is aligned with Scorpio it's going to be bad."

Willing to blame it all on the stars, I said, "Oh yeah, and exactly how long is that going to last?"

"Seven years."

"Rebecca, I couldn't take seven years of this!"

"That's why I'm going away. I might as well enjoy myself while there's a chance."

Thinking she meant her upcoming vacation, I said, "I'd love to get away from here, if I could."

"Santiago, darling, I'm beginning to doubt this area is ever going to get any better. All this time I bought your theory that it was just a matter of time before Donald Trump moved in to redevelop Times Square."

"I agree with you, Rebecca," I said, conceding defeat. "Donald Trump can't solve his own problems nowadays, much less ours. If only they closed Paradise Alley it would be okay. It wasn't all that bad when it was just hookers."

"The hookers were like girl scouts selling cookies compared to what's going on now," Rebecca said. "But I'm getting tired of calling the mayor's office and the midtown precinct and signing petitions. Somebody is getting paid a lot of money to keep that business open."

"Maybe we ought to go to the press with the story," I suggested. "A front page story in the *Post* would do it, I'm sure."

"Honey, I'm afraid nothing will get done until there's a massacre down there. By then I'll be a basket case. I tell you, if Francisco asks me to marry him, I'm saying *sí, sí*." She fanned herself with a letter.

"Is it a letter from Francisco?" I asked.

"Santiago," she said, "would you be a dear and do a little translating for me?"

"In that case I'll have some lemonade." I sat down and Rebecca went to the kitchen. Some months back, in a bookstore in Greenwich Village, Rebecca had met Francisco, a Venezuelan tourist and a hairdresser. Although she did not speak Spanish, nor Francisco English, they became lovers. After he returned to Caracas, I became the official translator of their correspondence. She entered the room and handed me a glass of cold lemonade.

"The weather's been so terrible, and the situation downstairs seems to be getting so much worse," she said in her melodramatic Alabamian twang, "that I declare I was ready to hang myself if something mighty good didn't happen to me soon. But there it was, in the mailbox, a letter from my beloved."

I took a sip of lemonade, cleared my throat and toasted to love. Striking a Cyrano de Bergerac pose, I pulled out the letter. It was written in Francisco's tiny gothic handwriting, which I had come to know so well. Rebecca sat very still and upright, holding in her lap her glass of lemonade. Her head thrust forward, her lips quivering, her aquamarine eyes wide open and gleaming; the intensity of her expression was almost frightening. I could have read the first paragraph blindfolded since it was always the same. "Dear Rebecca," I read. "I hope this finds you and your loved ones enjoying good health. God willing."

"Santiago, is that a South American convention of letter writing? He always says the same thing."

I ignored her and went on. "I was so happy to receive your last letter and to find out that you're doing well."

"Goodness gracious. He's so formal."

"Rebecca, my sweet, in case you haven't noticed, we South Americans are formal people. And now, shall I go on?" I asked, somewhat irked by her interruptions. She smiled for an answer. I continued with my translation. "I'm doing very well, thank God."

"Is that a South American thing, Santiago, to punctuate every sentence with God?"

I sipped my lemonade to control my temper. "Rebecca, don't be ridiculous."

"Well, better to have a Christian for a boyfriend than a druggie," she sighed.

Her reasoning escaped me, so I resumed my translation. "I've been incredibly busy lately, and I get to my apartment late at night, and I'm usually so tired that even though I want to sit down and write to you every night I fall asleep in spite of my good intentions." God is merciful, I thought. If he wrote to her like this every day, translating would become excruciating. May God keep him very, very busy.

"What is it? Bad news?"

"It's nothing," I said, and continued translating. "I have the most exciting piece of news. One of my clients has been elected Miss Caracas and she'll be representing our city in the Miss Venezuela competition. The girl is too divine for words, and very intelligent and has lots of personality, and I'm positively sure that she'll be elected Miss Venezuela and go on to represent our country in the Miss Universe Pageant. Can you imagine what that will do for my business?"

"I smell a franchise," Rebecca exclaimed.

I looked up in disbelief. "I didn't know you were into beauty pageants."

"Beauty pageants are one of the interests Francisco and I share. Is that the end of the letter?"

I shook my head and continued. "'In your last letter you mentioned wanting to visit me during your vacation. My humble abode is at your service, and I would be glad to receive you in my home.'"

"Glad? Is that what he says, Santiago? Are you sure?"

"Sorry. I would be *happy* to receive you in my home," I corrected myself.

"You know, Santiago, there is a difference. That's what's called a nuance of the English language."

"Even in the best translations something gets lost," I remarked, annoyed with her.

"Don't mind me, honey. Go on with the letter. You're doing beautifully. It always amazes me how well you do this sort of thing."

Predictably, the third paragraph referred to me. "All this part is about me, Rebecca. Do you want me to translate it also?"

"Would you, honey? I don't want to miss a single one of his words."

"Okay, here it goes: 'Please thank our dear friend Santiago for translating my letters. I hope everything is going well with him, and that he and Mr. O'Donnell are enjoying good health, God willing. I always include Mr. O'Donnell in my prayers and ask José Gregorio Hernández for a miracle.'"

"Who's that? Is it voodoo?"

"He may as well pray to Donald Duck," I said. "It might be more effective. José Gregorio isn't canonized, but he's Venezuela's national saint because he introduced the microscope to the country. And you want to know how smart he was? He was killed by the only automobile in Caracas at that time."

Rebecca frowned. "Well, it's real sweet and thoughtful of him, in any case."

"Yeah," I said. "It's real sweet of him. Now let me finish: 'I look forward to hearing from you soon, and I hope you're following my beauty tips and are taking good care of your hair and your lovely complexion. It's midnight now, and through my window I can see the moon illuminating the city below, and everything—the sensual breeze that comes from the Caribbean, the stars in the sky, the fires twinkling in the mountains—reminds me of you, my adored Rebecca. Love, Francisco.'"

"He's a poet," Rebecca said.

Folding the letter and handing it to her, I said, "He's a hairdresser."

"A hair stylist and a makeup artist," she corrected me, and started bragging about what a great lover Francisco was and how she had never met a man who cared so much about a woman's needs.

I studied her, marveling at the change in her appearance since she had met this paragon. Before, she dressed like a receptionist in a funeral parlor. Tonight, she wore stone studded sandals and her toenails were painted a lurid purple. She had on khaki shorts and a Banana Republic shirt that depicted lush vegetation in an apocalyptic red. She wore too much glossy lipstick and mascara and green eyeshadow, but her gold-streaked, new wave haircut was becoming. I was alarmed, though, by all the gold and silver loops marching up her ears. I closed my eyes and saw Rebecca going all the way, like the Orinoco Indians in Venezuela, and piercing her lips, her nostrils, her . . .

"Santiago," she said, awakening me from my reverie, "is it very hot down there in August?"

"I don't know. I told you, I was there in November. It was pleasant during the day and cool at night. You might want to take a couple of sweaters."

"It sounds heavenly," she purred.

"So you've made up your mind to go?"

"I got to get away from these crack people downstairs before I crack up myself. Besides, I'm ready for adventure. Of course,

I'm mighty apprehensive to be going there alone. I don't know what I'll do without you," she said, referring, I think, to my services as a translator.

I tried to reassure her. "Caracas is a cosmopolitan city. You'll have no problems communicating with the people."

"But, you know, Santiago. The truth is, when Francisco and I are together, we understand each other perfectly. Isn't that incredible?"

"I'll say. But you could learn Spanish too. It's an easy language to learn, unlike English."

"I purchased a dictionary, and I'm learning useful expressions: *Buenos días. Cómo esá usted?*"

"Your accent is perfect," I lied.

"Thanks, honey. When I come back to New York (that is, if Francisco doesn't ask me to marry him), I'll take some lessons. Thank you so much for translating the letter. You're an angel, Santiago."

"Anything for love," I said.

"I hope it happens to you too. You'll be transformed, sugar." Rebecca sat with the letter on her breasts, blissed out. I could read love printed large over her face. Her happiness was becoming too painful to bear. I noticed side two of *La Traviata* was over and got up. "The opera is over," I said. "I'm exhausted and I have to get up early in the morning."

Rebecca followed me into her bedroom. Mr. O'Donnell was hiding under the blankets. "Uh-oh, Rebecca," I uttered in mock alarm, playing one of his favorite games. "Where's the kitty? I don't see him! He escaped again! Help!"

Mr. O'Donnell remained still. I sat on the bed and touched the bulge he made under the sheets, quickly pulling my hand away. In the winter this game was safe, because he was covered by heavy blankets; but in the summer his teeth and nails would poke through the sheets. I placed one hand on his head and the other on his thigh, immobilizing him. He struggled a bit to free himself but then started to purr loudly.

"It's a wonder to me how he can purr and be vicious at the same time," Rebecca said.

I uncovered him—Mr. O'Donnell was now on his back, smiling.

"Hello, kitty," I said, scratching him under his ears. "It's time to go home." As I picked him up, he felt lighter, bonier, as if he had lost weight over the weekend. On the spot where he had been lying remained thick chunks of his hair. In the summer Mr. O'Donnell shed copiously, but the way he was shedding lately he'd soon go bald. As I ran my fingers over his stomach, I noticed his coat of hair had lost all luster. Overnight, Mr. O'Donnell had become old.

I thanked Rebecca for everything and said good night. Upstairs, I stored the *pasteles* in the fridge. The cassette with the coke was harder to dispose of. Since I didn't own a TV, much less a VCR, its presence anywhere in the apartment was conspicuous. I threw the plastic case in the trash and then emptied the cocaine into a glass jar. I left it next to the salt, sugar, flour, oats, etc.

Setting the alarm for 6 A.M., I undressed, lay down, and turned off the overhead light. Although I was exhausted by the events of the past few days, I could not fall asleep. I was well aware of the strange turns and twists my otherwise dull existence was taking. I had in my possession what looked like a pound of cocaine. My brain went into overdrive. I needed to get some sleep, though. I turned on the air conditioner and tried to relax. I said to myself, *Your brain is out to kill you, Santiago. Stop thinking; remember your brain wants you dead.* As the room cooled, I started to drift off. My eyelids felt heavy, as if they were glued. I thought of Caracas. Of huge, prehistoric leaves. And stars that had auras, like the moon. Of parks in which exquisite orchids nested in gigantic, emerald trees. And the smells: the tropical breeze scented with a million gardenias. And the Caribbean in the moonlight, silvery and smooth, and in the distance, riding shimmering seahorses, a chorus of mermaids serenading me with sensual, heartbreaking boleros.

I was hungry when I woke up around midnight. But I wanted something light, like yogurt or fruit, and there was nothing like that in the fridge. I splashed cold water on my face, combed my hair and went downstairs.

Both sides of Forty-third Street were lined with garbage bags, and the homeless huddled in front of the shops closed for the night. The after-theater crowd had dispersed and was replaced by the usual junkies, transvestites, and habitués of porno palaces.

I crossed Eighth Avenue and went into the *New York Times* building to get today's newspaper. Then I walked to the Korean fruit stand at the corner of Forty-third and Eighth. I picked a piece of watermelon, oranges, carrots, and yogurt. I pulled out a twenty dollar bill. The woman rang the items as she placed them in a bag.

"Twelve-fifty," she said.

For some time I had suspected this woman of overcharging me. Tonight I decided to confront her.

"How's that possible?" I asked, grabbing the twenty from her hand.

"Pay, please. Next," she said, staring at me impassively.

Looking over my shoulder, I saw other customers in the store but no one behind me. I began pulling the items out of the bag. "Let's add them up one by one," I said.

"Four oranges, two dollars," she said, a flash of anger or annoyance sparkling in her eyes.

"Four oranges at fifty cents a piece, that's two dollars—if my math is correct."

"Watermelon," she paused, then looking directly into my eyes, "three dollars."

"It sounds like a lot for a small piece of watermelon, but it's too hot, okay, and I don't feel like arguing. So that's a total of five dollars."

With one sweep of her hand she grouped together the remaining items. "Carrots and yogurt, five dollars. Ten dollars total. Sorry for mistake. Pay, please."

"This is outrageous," I exploded, realizing my suspicions had been correct all along. "Yogurt is ninety cents at the supermarket, and a bag of carrots forty cents."

"Then go to supermarket."

I found it unnecessary to inform her that supermarkets in our neighborhood closed well before midnight.

"No want to pay price, no take," was her fortune cookie advice.

"Fine," I said. "I'll just take the oranges. And the yogurt."

She rang these items. I gave her the twenty dollar bill.

"Sorry, no change."

"You had change just a minute ago."

The woman said something in Korean, I guess. Wondering which member of my family had been insulted, I prepared to call her a few names myself in Spanish when she turned and looked toward the back of the store. A man in a stained apron, looking like a cross between Gertrude Stein and a Sumo wrestler,

emerged from behind a bamboo curtain holding a head of lettuce in one hand and a butcher knife in the other. They engaged
in an animated conversation, and the man gave me a scorching
look. *Now Santiago*, I said to myself, *you don't want to engage in
combat with that creature.* I put my hand in my pocket and found
a ten dollar bill. "Here," I said, looking at the man. "I'm sorry.
It's this heat."

It was cooler now, but the humidity was unchanged and the
sky looked cottony and gray. Feeling crappy, I dragged my feet
on the sidewalk as I noticed several crack addicts milling excitedly in front of Paradise Alley, like hyenas around carrion. I
unlocked the door and was about to go in, when a sharp object
hit the middle of my spine.

"Don't move," a man's voice ordered me. "Just give me your
money." His hand went into my right pocket, then into the left
one where my money was. Thinking, *This is where he busts my
head and runs away*, I closed my eyes.

"Give him back the dough," another voice screeched.

I turned around; the mugger's face was inches away from
mine—these were eyes that hadn't seen straight in years. I
grabbed the gun and snatched the bills. Out of the corner of my
eye, I saw the midget hooker pressing a huge sparkling blade
against the man's crotch.

"Now beat it, fuckface, before the cops get your stupid ass,"
she ordered him.

The man reeled backward until he reached the street curb.
Pointing a finger at my rescuer he yelled, "You're dead, you
fucking freak!"

I pointed the gun at the mugger. "You heard the lady! Piss
off!"

The man ran across the street dodging the oncoming Eighth

Avenue traffic. At the corner of Forty-third, he stopped and screamed a bunch of obscenities and threats. People were looking in our direction.

The gun shook violently in my hand; I felt dizzy. "I don't know how to thank you," I said.

"Don't mention it," she said, folding the blade and hooking it to a garter under her skirt.

"Here," I said, offering her the gun.

She shuddered as if I had offered her a cobra. "Are you crazy? I don't want that thing, man. It's yours. Who knows how many dudes he's killed with it."

Passersby were approaching. Like a gangster, I stuck the gun between my pants and my belly.

"See you around. I got to try to score tonight." She started to walk away.

"Hey, listen," I called after her, feeling that I hadn't thanked her enough. "What's your name?"

"Hot Sauce," she said. "And yours?"

I told her.

"Well, San-ti-a-go, it's been fun meeting you. Any time you want it, I'll give you a good deal, babe," she said, pouting and blowing me a kiss before she swaggered into the surrounding nocturnal sleaze. From behind, she looked like a child playing femme fatale.

The gun burning against my skin, I shut the door and dashed up the stairs. I locked the door and paced the length of the apartment looking for a niche to hide the gun in. Finally, I settled for the toilet water tank. Tomorrow I'll wipe off the fingerprints before I ditch it in the Hudson, I thought. I was still shaking and feeling slightly hysterical but it was too late to call anyone, even Rebecca. I lay in bed and tried to read the *Times*, but my eyes wouldn't focus. I ate an orange. Tonight, I wished I had a TV set. My mother was right—it was un-American not to own a television. Mr. O'Donnell jumped onto my bed. I set the paper aside. "You don't know how lucky you are to be a cat," I said. His face was on top of mine, and his breath stank, but I remained still. One half of his face was white and the other half gray, and he had the long pinkish nose of a tropical rat. I stared into his eyes. The black pupils were surrounded by a greenish circle that grew agate toward the edges. His whiskers were long and thick like plastic toothpicks stuck on his snout. I scratched him between his ears and he started to purr. "Yes, yes, I know," I said. Burying his nose under my chin, he went to sleep lying on my chest, his enlarged heart thumping against mine.

From
Annotations

John Keene

Multeities, Disjunctions, Intense Polysemic Pleasures

By the autumn of his childhood they had abandoned their prefab in the ghetto for a ranch house in a suburb whose property values and lack of crime could boast of national renown. No one, you understand, carped at the size of the required down payment, since it was assumed that they would eventually own their own property. Ignorance is incapable of concealing itself. Out there many of the Blacks were

descended from the slaves or servants who had once managed those estates, so tensions were bound to abound when
the educational system finally integrated. Douglass School.
Few Negro families had settled land as far out as Red Bud,
though even Franklin and Jefferson Counties had shown a
minimal Black presence since well before the Civil War. This
unconcern with the questions of whether a "there" was there,
or of what this "there" consisted, remained unnamed until a
later encounter with what they were denouncing as "pragma-
tism." History has been kindest to the charming old German
quarter, where the wealthier or more committed ones had
hidden in their rathskellers those dark fugitives headed north
for freedom. Information, he first noticed, in a series of notes
that someone had inscribed in the narrow, running margin.
"Missouri Compromise." Out there then one never needed to
lock one's doors or speak to one's neighbors for weeks. Once
a week a man, bearing more than a minor resemblance to the
president whose name became a curseword, delivered orange
juice and grape drink and lemonade just as they had observed
in the movies. My address, Madras. Hush Puppies, bell-bot-
tom denims, a Bengal-striped shirt, though you refused to be
photographed in platforms. A fulvous swatch of velour that
tired the eyes, your sweater was the only one lighter than
your skin. "Dibs on your TootsieRoll" was all they had to
say to quash any attempts to deny them, so you broke it into
morsels as had been demonstrated on TV, and went home
without anticipating a "Thank you." Boys should not flap
their arms when they run down stairs, or cover their mouths
when they laugh, made less to correct a child's deportment
choices than to allay a parent's useless fears. "Though the
crust may be brown the bread is still white." Lacking any

real conception of evil, a child is prone to explore the limits of her will. He fought back but they laughed at him, so that he discovered his skill as jokester, but he kept in mind the example of Richard Pryor. Mode for Joe. The father eventually began to dwell on the numerous half-veiled jealousies this move and its aftermath induced. Often, he would speak of Captain Wendell O. Pruitt, and the other Tuskegee flyers, who had never been properly honored. Just remembering the treatment of all those distinguished Black airmen filled his eyes with tears of awe and bitterness. Benign neglect. Who stood and saluted when the flag flapped high, who sang the anthem without anger. Time is no equalizer. As you will recall she was a blond divorcée with two attractive kids, whom she appeared to love more dearly than she did the thought of them. Although working-class and Irish, they quickly ignited a friendship, which differed from what we had encountered in the city. Civility offers an acceptable way to evade the issues at hand. Name us anonymous. "Grumio erat coquus," he yelled out in earnest, to the consternation of a number of his classmates and the instructor. Chalk hurled at the head was the usual punishment, though kneeling while hoisting a dictionary was not unknown. My mind is the sandbox that my thoughts play in, or the court in which they exercise their claims to reason. Nine, the magic number. Quietly they strode through the grounds of the Eden Seminary, the thrill of actually being there far more compelling than anything they encountered therein. Reinhold Niebuhr. Accordingly, along with the doctrinal classes the Opus-Dei brothers offered scale-model construction; however, journalism more thoroughly captured his mood. By then it was the Bicentennial, and you were playing "John Henry" in the program at the Loreto-Hilton, which entailed memorizing a medley of songs, and learning how to swing an invisible hammer. Hurry up this way again. More the name of the Algonquin Golf Club where one caddied than any other identifiable aspect, and the waiting buckets of crawdads which made the traipse across the greens go more quickly. Of course, the city's importance had diminished progressively since the days when it had served as the gateway to the West, though one's perspective on this fact waxes as one gains distance from it. DeSoto. Having abandoned it for the far more sterile suburbs, they were drawn back to that laboratory of human interaction. Against closure. As a result those endlessly engaged in the quest for happiness usually constitute the unhappiest lot. Anthropology offers us among its many conclusions that boys throw a certain way, girls another.

Theses, Antitheses, A Welter of Theories

Trundling through the pass of bald maples across the valley of ice, he felt bound irrevocably to the outside world and to some inner, still aspiring self. Schneeblick, so blink now. Daylight, reflecting off the soundless frosts cape of the nursery, transformed his hands into two bars of franklinite. The early, wintry sunsets arrived, and then, although they waited, nothing. O soul, sublime subject of bodily subtraction, which the sky has entombed in all this whiteness. He cowered in fear of the implications of such thoughts, yet brazenly continued to think them. His mother nevertheless purchased two pairs of long johns which inevitably curled and shrank. These scaled the calves like spiders, forcing one to wrench until they reached the socks. Indifference is not the same as ambivalence, which proceeds from different situational premises. Joliet, Père Marquette. Most winters pinched the flesh like pincers, yet a few hacked through the bones like scythes. Often the ground glared back as would a freshly Windexed mirror, so that when he fell, breaking what the doctor termed a "coccyx," seven years of bad luck became part of the bargain. One loses 90 percent of one's body heat through the head, though most worry about the throat, feet, and limbs. "Where did you leave your gloves this time?" which kept us silent, praying against frostbite. Catch-a-girl, kiss-a-girl. One could still go tobogganing down the steeper part of Art Hill, but there were lesser hills much closer in the more historic parts of Webster, where the dauntless ones could sled or ski-board on a stolen trashcan top. On your back, in the snow, making angels the sun would summon. White swath. Summer they awaited for its bounty of trips and excursions, such as a return to Meramec Caverns or Silver Dollar City, now, from what he read, not far from where the Klan was presently headquartered. A cathode bath usually proves easier than self-immersion in a written text, thus did the ends of those evenings eddy through that small, trans-fixing screen. On the other hand, you noted at the Monet exhibit at the Art Institute of Chicago, which you attended with your classmates and the chaperone, that although paint-ing had once served as the transcriptor of the soul, it now mainly served to break the hold of mechanical reproduction. The effect is essentially Suric, or "Quranic" with the subject matter secular. What seized their interest without parallel was the spectacle of the soldier grinding with the half-asleep young woman, which they watched through the undraped hotel window, while their elders snored two rooms away. Boys view, voyeurs. Yet he persisted in his interpretation of the surface of the oil, or was it charcoal mixed with oil, since for something so thick and black that one can make little of it, appreciation becomes an effect rather than an immediate feeling of the picture, followed by a gradual perceptive glowing. A guide, unbidden. Now he sings, now he sobs. And so although the choice between competing options creates a thicket of perplexing problems, one still can envision that open meadow of narrative possibilities, as that New York poet of the process of makes clear in his expressively opaque treatise. "Stop where you are and do not move," the policemen yelled out in unison. Dizzy, however, he dropped to his frozen, grassy bed, which they disdained as "so much unnecessary drama." I'n-Shta-Heh. Mittened, parkaed, he etched the scene around him with a penknife on a board the reverend had discarded. Please read directions carefully before opening. Stripped bare of all life, all color, the outdoors seemed in mourning, so we crept towards the road on our tiptoes, cringing that our crunching might offend. Lester leaps in. They too were unable, remember, to categorize to their satisfaction the book of drawings, and went about dismissing them as the products of a "troubled" mind. Snowblink, now blink, see. One's thoughts are the goads that drive one's calf-like existence forward, strange, diaphanous gods reappearing day and night. Marronage. Seen properly as a field of multe-ities, characterized by the presence of so many disjunctions, one might learn to appreciate this experience if only for the intense polysemic pleasures that it offers. Worry later. And so it was at that time when you lacked any real notion of the "body" that your grandfather lay silent on his deathbed, cradling you in his still strong arms. Appalled, they refuse to believe that you have told, since they remember your vows of silence.

Literature as a Guide to the Life Lived, a Deliverance

On the template of night's sky they visually traced the constellations, which proved far more difficult to perform at home than they had witnessed at the planetarium. Thus, the worn yet lyric intensity of each evening's secret offering, what its occurrence might furnish beyond our small and sparsely lit furnace. Meate-chi-cippi. Lay teachers and priests, the latter becowled and armed with crisp, authentic British accents, appealed to the authority of the "Classical" European tradition, now besieged with conflict to the point of internal sedition, like so much once imparted by "masters." Samuel Clemens. Throughout the boys a spirit of ridicule, beneath a veneer of respect, but only later would they fathom the immensity of their debt to these ill-paid, beleaguered pedagogues. Meachum Park. In the classroom Homer, Cicero, Melville, Tennyson, Hemingway, and Mauriac, while on the sly you perused Onstott, Heinlein, and Walker, yet those that would forge your aesthetic center in those formative years were Joyce, Tagore, Faulkner, and Morrison. Oozing, seething magma of presence, what I represents. "Gee, that's interesting, I had never noticed any patterns there," to which our silence was as much disproof as concurrence. Their theories to explain all manner of matter, though no theory to explain this thirst for theories. In the laboratory at the famous midwestern university, he prepared slides and learned the rudiments of neuroanatomy, sometimes growing giddy from the fumes of the rarefying benzene. Whereupon the accident with the microtome, which they shied away from shaping into a lawsuit. "J'averterai Bill dès qu'il sera revenu," repeat it, to impress them. Ultimately although some tired of bandying about "Nigger Jim" or "pickanines" before him, most were reveling in the new climate of conservatism, which introduced far more subtle ways of impressing upon others one's social and economic superiority. Time had come to begin applying to college, the next step to which the aspirations of their class had most logically led. Please remove seal before opening. "Harvard don't keep on folks who can't pay or charm their way!" she cackled, her face a cracking, crackling lantern. Who would leave the city of one's birth without hesitation, lest one suffocate under the swaddle of so much past. Convogosa. The strain of our ruse quite rightly blinded us, until we lost sight of who we truly were. Many of them now worked at the post office, which had become such a trying job. One must, in other words, eventually come to terms with the provisional. According to the standards the images conveyed, your appearance was grotesquely disharmonic. High butt, narrow hips, broad shoulders, full lips. As a result you cut the cake or stollen into minuscule pieces, aiming to perfect yourself, yet deep down you knew the real reason behind your actions was to savor more fully each morsel. In this way a sense of economy developed, whose flip side became an inability to see the larger picture. "Happy Days." Now you must talk up our quarrel. It is foolish, the perceptive film theorist noted, for them to invoke post-modernity when as a people they appear to have been bypassed by the modern. Besides, dialogue has proven so woefully insufficient, though we continue to invest our energies in it. Your cognizance linked these as a chain of incidents, closer observation made clear their antecedents, but what you sought, like any artist, were the very events themselves. St. Louis Blues. Afterwards, we dispersed to our pre-appointed stations in society, with many becoming doctors, bankers, or mechanics. This naturally obviated the need for friendly contact or regular, intimate phone calls. Hindsight is often crueler than an unforgiving lover; perfidy is the knife that wounds far more deeply than others. The parents were still whispering something about those two, which lent this all an aura of shame. Always the desire to be loved formed the nucleus, about which other events and moments, positive, negative, or otherwise, whirred like the elementary particles. Some men, women, certain trees, bare certainties. Were these accounts, as was projected for this aesthetic project, selected and set down as carefully as tesseracts, the cumulative effect would approximate that of a living, dazzling, eighteen-panel mosaic. Given the general trends towards ignorance and indifference, however, no one thought to challenge his methods, let alone his motives. We took turns reciting poems by the Black Arts poets from one of those volumes now growing dusty on the godmother's bookshelves. "Man, you don't even know the scrapple from the apple, and you ain't gon' get that out no old dead cracker's book," our reply a prolonged, anguished stare into a portrait of life dissolving before us. Thus his musings, when written down, gradually melded, gathered shape, solidified like a well-mixed mâché, and thus, upon rereading them he realized what he had accomplished was the construction of an actual voice. The final dances of youth, dim incandescence. Willow weep for me. And so, patient reader, these remarks should be duly noted as a series of mere life-notes aspiring to the condition of annotations.

The Secrets of Summer

Bret Easton Ellis

I'm trying to pick up this ok-looking blond Valley bitch at Powertools and she's sort of into it but not drinking enough, only pretending to be drunk, but she goes for me; like they all do, and says she's twenty.

"Uh-huh," I tell her. "Right. You look really young," even though I know she can't be more than sixteen, maybe even fifteen if Junior is working the doors tonight and which is pretty exciting if you consider the prospects. "I like them young," I tell her. "Not too young. Ten? Eleven? No way. But fifteen?"

I'm saying. "Hey, yeah, that's cool. It may be jailbait, but so what?"

She just stares at me blankly like she didn't hear a word, then checks her lips in a compact and stares at me some more, asks me what a wok is, what the word "invisible" means.

I'm getting totally psyched to get this bitch back to my place in Encino and I even get a medium hard-on waiting for her while she's in the ladies' room telling her friends she's leaving with the best-looking guy here while I'm at the bar drinking red-wine spritzers with my medium hard-on.

"What are these little fellas called?" I ask the bartender, a cool-looking dude my age, wondering, gesturing toward the drink.

"Red-wine spritzers," he says.

"I don't want to get too drunk, though," I tell him while he pours a group of frat guys another round. "No way. Not tonight."

I turn and look out at everyone dancing on the dance floor and I think I banged the DJ about a million years ago but I'm not too sure and she's playing some god-awful nigger rap song and I'm getting hungry and want to split and then here the girl comes, all ready to go.

"It's the anthracite Porsche," I tell the valet and she's impressed. "This is gonna be great," I'm saying. "I'm totally jazzed," I tell her but trying not to seem too eager.

She plays some Bowie tape while we drive toward the Valley. I tell her an Ethiopian joke.

"What's an Ethiopian with sesame seeds on his head?"

"What's an Ethiopian?" she asks.

"A Quarter Pounder," I say. "That really cracks me up."

We get to Encino. I open the garage door with the garage opener.

"Wow," she says. "You've got a big house," and then, "You'll take me home afterwards, later?"

"Yeah. Sure," I say, opening a bottle of fumé blanc. "Some chicks are stupid but I like that in a fuck."

We go into the bedroom and she's wondering where all the furniture is. "Where's the furniture?" she whines.

"I ate it. Just shut up, pop in a coil and lay down," I mutter, pointing her toward the bathroom, and then, "I'll give you some coke afterwards," even though I don't say what afterwards means, don't even hint.

"What do you mean? A coil?"

"Yeah. You don't want to get pregnant, do you? End up giving birth to something awful. A monster? Some kind of beast? You want that?" I ask. "Jesus, even your abortionist would freak out."

She looks at the bed and then at me and then tries to open the door to the other room.

"No way." I stop her. "Not *that* room." I shove her toward the bathroom door. She looks at me, still pretending to be drunk, then goes in, closes the door. I actually hear her fart.

I turn the lights off, with a Bic, light candles I bought at the Pottery Barn last night. I take off my clothes, touching myself, already stiff, stretch out on the bed, waiting, starving now.

"Come on come on come on."

The toilet flushes, she uses the bidet and then she comes out, shoes in hand, and seems shocked to find me lying on the bed with this giant hard-on but she plays it cool. She doesn't want to do this and she knows she's way out of her league and she knows it's too late and this turns me on even more and I have to giggle and she takes her clothes off, asking "Where's the coke? Where's the coke?" and I say "After, after" and pull her toward me. She doesn't really want to fuck so she tries to give me head instead and I let her for a little while even though I cannot feel a thing, so then I start fucking her really hard, looking into her face when I'm coming and, like always, she freaks out when she sees my eyes, shiny black, and she sees the horrible teeth, the ruptured mouth (what Dirk thinks looks like "the anus of an octopus"), and I'm screaming on top of her, the mattress below us sopping wet with her blood and she starts screaming too and then I hit her hard, punching her in the face until she passes out and I carry her outside to the pool and by the light coming from underwater and the moon, high in Encino tonight, bleed her.

I meet Miranda at the Ivy on Robertson for a late supper and she's looking, in her own words, "absoloutly fabulous." Miranda is "forty," with jet-black hair pulled back tight, a jagged white streak running through it on the side, a pale-tan complexion and high, gorgeous cheekbones, teeth the color of lightning, and she's wearing an original hand-beaded velvet dress by Lagerfeld from Bergdorf Goodman she bought when she was in New York last week to bid on a water bottle at Sotheby's that eventually went for a million dollars and to check out a private fund-raising party for George Bush, which, according to Miranda, was "just smashing."

"Even though you're older than me by, like, twenty years, you always seem incredibly youthful," I tell her. "You are definitely one of my favorite people to hang out with in L.A."

Tonight we're on the patio and it's hot and we're talking quietly about how Donald is used rather promiscuously in a layout on linen suits in the August issue of *GQ* and how if you look very carefully at the model next to him you can see four tiny purple dots on his tan neck that the airbrusher missed.

"Donald is absoloutly wicked," Miranda says.

I agree and ask, "What's the definition of superfluous? Ethiopian after-dinner mints."

Miranda laughs and tells me that I'm wicked too and I sit back, sipping my limeade and Stoli, very pleased.

"Oh look, there's Walter," Miranda says, sitting up a little. "Walter, Walter," she calls out, waving.

I despise Walter—fiftyish, faggot-clone, agent at ICM whose main claim to fame in some circles is that he bled every person in the Brat Pack except Emilio Estevez, who told me one night at On the Rox that he wasn't into "Dracula and shit like that." Walter saunters over to our table, wearing a completely tacky Versace tuxedo, and he drones on about the screening at Paramount tonight and how this film will do $110 million domestic and that he played fucky with one of the film's stars even though the film is a piece of shit and he flirts shamelessly with me and I'm not impressed. He slinks off—"What a slime, what a homo," I mutter—and then it's only me and Miranda.

"So tell me what you've been reading, darling," she asks, after the N.Y. steaks, blood rare and extra au jus on the side, arrive and we both dig in. "By the way, this is"—she cocks her head, chewing—"delish," and then, "Oh, but what a headache."

"Tolstoy," I lie. "I never read. Boring. You?"

"I absoloutly love that Jackie Collins. Marvelous trash," she says, chewing, a dark line of juice dripping down her pale chin as she pops two Advil, washing them down with the cup of au jus. She wipes her chin and smiles, blinking rapidly.

"How's Marsha?" I ask, sipping a red-wine spritzer.

"She's still in Malibu with . . ." and now Miranda lowers her voice, mentions one of the Beach Boys.

"No way, dude," I exclaim, laughing.

"Would I lie to you, baby?" Miranda says, rolling her eyes up, licking her lips, polishing that steak off.

"Marsha for the longest time was only into animals, right?" I ask. "Cows? Horses, birds, dogs, pets, you name it, right?"

"Who do you think controlled the coyote population last summer," Miranda says.

"Yeah, I heard about that," I murmur.

"Baby, she would go to Calabasas, out to the stables, and bleed a fucking horse in thirty minutes flat," Miranda says. "I mean, holy shit, baby, things were getting ridiculous for a while."

"I personally cannot stand horses' blood," I'm saying. "It's way too thin, too sweet. Other than that, I can deal with just about anything, but only when I'm feeling gloomy."

"The only animal I cannot abide is a cat," Miranda says, chewing. "That's because so many of them have leukemia and lots of other poo-poo diseases."

"Dirty, filthy creatures." I shudder.

We order two more drinks and split another steak before the kitchen closes and then Miranda confides to me that she almost got herself into a gang bang the other night over at Tuesday's place with all these frat boys from USC.

"I'm, like, completely taken aback by this," I say. "Miranda, you can be so lousy." I drink the rest of the spritzer, which is a little too bubbly tonight.

"Darling, believe me, it was some kind of accident. A party. Lots of young gorgeous men." She winks, fingering a tall glass of Moët. "I'm sure you can guess how that turned out."

"You're just, like, wicked," I tell her, chuckling. "How did you extract yourself from the . . . situation?"

"What do you think I did?" she says teasingly, gulping down the rest of the champagne. "I sucked the living shit right out of them." She looks around the mostly empty patio, waves over to Walter as he steps into his limo with a girl who looks about six, and Miranda says, softly, "Semen and blood is a delightful combo, and do you know what?"

"I'm captivated."

"Those ridiculous USC boys loved it." She laughs, throwing her head back. "Lined up again and I of course was only too happy to please them again and they all passed out." She laughs harder and I'm laughing too and then she stops, looking up at a helicopter crossing the sky, a searchlight sending down a cone of white. "The one I liked lapsed into a coma." She looks sadly out onto Robertson at a small tumbleweed the valets are playing soccer with. "His neck fell apart."

"Don't be sad," I say. "It's been a delightful evening."

"Let's catch a midnight flick in Westwood," she suggests, eyes brightening at her own suggestion.

We go to the movies after dinner but we first buy two large raw steaks at a Westward Ho and eat them in the front row and I flirt with a couple of sorority girls, one of whom asks me where I got my vest, meat hanging from my mouth, and Miranda even bought napkins.

"I adore you," I tell her, once the previews start. "Because you've got the right idea."

I'm at another club, Rampage (but pronounce it French), and I find a pseudo-hot-looking Valley bitch and she seems really slow and stupid like she's completely stoned or drunk or something but she's got great tits and a pretty hot body, not too heavy, maybe a little too skinny, and basically her emptiness thrills me.

"I usually hate skinny chicks," I'm telling her. "But you look great."

"Skinny chicks suck?" she asks.

"Hey—that's pretty funny," I tell her.

"Is it?" she asks, slack, washed out.

"I'm into you anyway."

We take my car and drive over to the Valley, into Encino. I tell her a joke.

"What do you call an Ethiopian wearing a turban?"

"Is this a joke?"

"Q-tip," I say. "That really cracks me up. Even you must admit it's riotous."

The girl is too stoned to respond to the joke but she manages to ask, "Does Michael Jackson live around here?"

"Yep," I say. "He's a buddy."

"I'm really impressed," she says ungratefully.

"I only went to one party after the Victory tour and it was really shitty," I tell her. "I hate hanging out with niggers anyway."

"That's not exactly the nicest thing you could say."

"Mellow out," I groan.

In my room she's into it and we're fucking wildly and when she starts to come I begin to lick and chew at the skin on her neck, panting, slavering, finding the jugular vein with my tongue, and I start bleeding her and she's laughing and moaning and coming even harder and blood is spurting into my mouth, splashing the roof, and then something weird starts to happen and I get really tired and nauseous and I have to roll off her and that's when I realize that this girl is not drunk or stoned but that she's on some, as she puts it now, "way-out fucking drugs."

"Ecstasy? LSD? Is it smack?" I'm gagging.

She lies there silently.

"Oh Christ no," I say, feeling it. "It's . . . heroin," I croak. "Oh shit. Now I'm majorly tripping."

I roll off the bed onto the floor, naked, my head killing me, this poison cramping my stomach up, and I crawl toward the bathroom, and all the time this fucking drugged-out bitch who has snapped out of her stupor is now crawling along with me, squealing "Let's play let's play let's play you're a cowboy and I'm a squaw, got it?" and I growl at her, trying to scare her, showing her my teeth, the fangs, my horrible transformed mouth, my eyes black, lidless. But she doesn't freak out, just laughs, completely high. I finally make it to the toilet and on my back vomit up her blood in geysers and then pass out with the door closed, on the floor. I wake the next night, groggy, her blood dried all over my face and neck and chest. I wash it off in a long, hot shower with a loofah and then I walk into the bedroom. On the bed, written on a matchbook from California Pizza Kitchen, is her name and phone number and below that, "Had a *wild* time." I go to the other room, swallow some Valium, open up my coffin and take a little nap.

I wake up later, restless, still kind of weak, grateful for the new customized coffin I had this guy out in Burbank build for me: FM radio, tape cassette, digital alarm clock, Perry Ellis sheets, phone, small color TV with built-in VCR and cable (MTV, HBO). Elvira is the hottest-looking woman on TV and she hosts this horror-movie show on Sunday nights which is my favorite show on TV and I would like to meet Elvira one day and maybe one day I will.

I get up, take my vitamins, work out with weights while playing Madonna on CD, take a shower, study my hair, blond and thick, and I'm thinking about calling Attila, my hair-dresser, and making an appointment for tomorrow night and then I call and leave a message. The maid has come and cleaned, which she is supposed to do, and I have specified to her that if she ever tries to open the coffin I will take her two little children and turn them into a human tostada with extra lettuce and salsa and eat them, muchas gracias. I get dressed: Levi's, penny loafers, no socks, a white T-shirt from Maxfields, an Armani vest.

I drive over to the Sun 'n' Fun twenty-four-hour tanning parlor on Woodman and get ten minutes of rays, then head over to Hollywood to maybe visit Dirk, who is mostly into pretty boys, hustlers down on Santa Monica, in bars, at gyms. He likes chain saws, which are okay if you have your place soundproofed like Dirk does. I pass an alley, four parking lots, a 7-Eleven, numerous police cars.

It's a warm night and I pop open the sunroof, play the radio loud. Stop off at Tower Records and buy a couple of tapes, then it's to the twenty-four-hour Hughes on Beverly and Doheny and pick up a lot of steak in case I don't feel like going out next week because raw meat is okay even though the juice is thin and not salty enough. The fat chick at checkout flirts with me while I write a check for seven hundred and forty dollars—the only thing I bought is filet mignon. Stop off at a couple of clubs, places where I have a free pass or know the doormen, check out the scene, then drive around some more. Think about the girl I picked up at Powertools, the way I drove her to a bus stop on Ventura Boulevard, dropped her off, hoping she doesn't remember. I drive by a sporting goods store and think about what happened to Roderick and shudder, get queasy. But I take a Valium and soon I'm feeling pretty good, passing by the billboard on Sunset that says DISAPPEAR HERE and I wink over at two blond girls, both wearing Walkmen, in a convertible 450SL at a stoplight we're at and I smile back at them and they giggle.

And I start following them down Sunset, think about stopping
for maybe some sushi with them, and I'm about to tell them
to pull over when I suddenly see that Thrifty drugstore sign
coming up, the huge neon-blue lowercase *t* flashing off and
on, floating above buildings and billboards, the moon hanging
low behind, above it, and I'm getting closer to it, getting weak,
and I make this totally illegal U-turn, and still feeling sort of
sick but better the farther I get from it, my rearview mirror
turned down, I head over to Dirk's place.

Dirk lives in a huge old-style Spanish-looking place that was
built a long time ago up in the hills and I let myself in through
the back door, and walking through the kitchen, I can hear the
TV blaring up above. There are two hacksaws in a sink filled with
pink water and suds and I smile to myself, hungry. Whenever
I hear about some young guy on the news who was found near
the beach, maybe part of his body, an arm or a leg or a torso,
sucked clean in a bag near a freeway underpass, I have to whisper to myself, "Dirk." Take two Coronas out of the fridge and
run upstairs to his room, open the door and it's dark. Dirk's sitting on the couch, wearing a PHIL COLLINS T-shirt and jeans, a
sombrero on his head and Tony Lamas, watching *Bad Boys* on
the VCR, rolling a joint, and he looks full, a bloody towel in the
corner.

"Hey, Dirk," I say.

"Hey, dude." He turns around.

"What's going on?"

"Nothing. You?"

"Just thought I'd stop by, see how it's hanging." I hand him
one of the Coronas. He twists the top off. I sit down next to
him, pop mine open, throw my cap over at the bloody towel,

below a poster of the Go-Go's and a new stereo. A mound of damp bones stains the felt on a pool table, beneath it a bundle of wet Jockey shorts spotted violet and black and red.

"Thanks, guy." Dirk takes a swallow. "Hey"—he grins—"what's brown and full of cobwebs?"

"Ethiopian's asshole," I say.

"Right on." We slap high five.

On the patio, a bag filled with flesh, heavy with blood, hangs from a wooden beam and moths flutter around it, and when it drips they scatter, then regroup. Beneath that someone has strung white Christmas lights around a large thorny tumbleweed. A blond bat flaps its wings, repositions itself in the rafters above the bag of flesh and the moths.

"Who's that?" I ask.

"That's Andre."

"Hey Andre." I wave.

The bat squeaks a reply.

"Andre's got a hangover," Dirk yawns.

"Bummer."

"It takes a long time to pull someone's skull out of their mouth," Dirk's saying.

"Uh-huh." I nod. "Can I have a seltzer?"

"Can you?"

"Nice toucan," I say, noticing a comatose bird in a cage that hangs near the French doors that lead out to a veranda. "What's its name?"

"Bok Choy," Dirk says. "Hey, if you're gonna get a seltzer, make me a mimosa, will you?"

"Jesus," I whisper. "The things that toucan has seen."

"The toucan doesn't have a clue," Dirk says.

Body bags lie out by the Jacuzzi, lit candles surround the

steaming water, a reminder of relatives who will not be as anguished as they should be, a test they will not pass.

I go back downstairs, get a seltzer, make Dirk a mimosa, then we hang out, watch the movie, drink some more beer, look through worn copies of *GQ*, *Vanity Fair*, *True Life Atrocities*, smoke some pot, and that's around the time I can smell the blood, coming from the next room, so fresh it's pulsing.

"I think I have the munchies," I say. "I think I may go berserk."

Dirk rewinds the movie and we start watching it again. But I can't concentrate. Sean Penn keeps getting beat up and I get hungrier but don't say anything and then the movie's over and he turns the channel to HBO, where *Bad Boys* is on, so we start watching it again and we smoke some more pot and finally I have to stand up and walk around the room.

"Marsha's with one of the Beach Boys," Dirk says. "Walter called me."

"Yeah," I say. "I had dinner with Miranda at the Ivy the other night. Can you dig it?"

"Gnarly. I can dig it." He shrugs. "I haven't talked to Marsha since"—he stops, thinks about something, says, hesitantly—"since Roderick." He switches the channel, then back again.

No one mentions Roderick a whole lot anymore. Last year, Marsha and Dirk were supposed to have dinner with Roderick at Chinois and when they stopped by his place in Brentwood, they found, at the bottom of Roderick's empty swimming pool, a wooden stake (which was really a Wilson 5 baseball bat crudely whittled down) driven into the concrete near the drain, which had been all scratched up (Roderick prided himself on long, manicured claws), and gray-black sand and dust and chunks of ash were scattered in piles in one corner. Marsha and Dirk had taken the stake, which was slathered with Lawry's garlic powder, and burned it in Roderick's empty house, and no one has seen Roderick since.

"I'm sorry, man," Dirk says. "It scares the shit out of me."

"Aw, come on, dude, let's not talk about that," I say. "Come on."

"Righty-o, Professor." Dirk does his Felix the Cat impersonation, slaps his Wayfarers on and smiles.

I'm walking around the room now, in the dark, shouts coming from the TV, moving toward the door, the smell rich and very thick, and I take another deep breath and it's sweet too and definitely male. I'm hoping I'll be offered some but I don't want to act like a leech and I lean up against the wall and Dirk is talking about stealing pints from Cedars and I'm moving toward the door, stepping over the towel drenched with blood, trying casually to open it.

"Don't open that door, dude," Dirk says, his voice low, raspy, sunglasses still on. "Don't go in there."

I pull my hand away real quick, put it in my pocket, pretend I was never going to check it out, whistle a Billy Idol song that I can't get out of my head. "I wasn't gonna go in there, dude. Chill out."

He nods slowly, takes off the sombrero, switching to another channel, then back to *Bad Boys*. He sighs and flicks something off one of his cowboy boots. "He's not dead yet."

"No, no, I get it, dude," I tell him. "Just mellow out."

I go downstairs, bring up some more beer, and we smoke some more pot, tell some more jokes, one about a koala bear and one about black people, another about a plane crash, and then we watch the rest of the movie, basically not saying a lot, long pauses between sentences, even words, the credits are rolling and Dirk takes off his sunglasses, then puts them back on, and I'm stoned. He looks at me and says, "Ally Sheedy looks good beaten up," and then outside, like ritual, a storm arrives.

I'm hanging out at Phases over in Studio City and it's getting late and I'm with some young girl with long blond hair who could be maybe twenty who I first saw with some geek dancing to "Material Girl" and she's bored and with me now and I'm bored and I want to get out of here and we finish our drinks and go to my car and get in and I'm sort of drunk and don't turn on the radio and it's silent in the car as she rolls down her window and Ventura is so deserted it's still silent except for the air-conditioning and she doesn't say a word about how nice my car is and so I finally ask this bitch, while uselessly opening the sunroof to impress her, getting closer to Encino, "How many Ethiopians can you fit in a Volkswagen?" and I take a Marlboro out of my jacket, push the lighter in, smiling to myself.

"All of them," she says.

I pull the car over to the side of the road, tires screeching, and turn the engine off. I sit there, waiting. Somehow the radio got turned on and some song is playing but I don't know which song it is and the lighter pops up. My hand is trembling and I'm staring at her, leaning away, cigarette still in my hand. I think she asks what's going on but I don't even hear her and I try to compose myself and I'm about to pull out onto Ventura but then I have to stop and stare at her some more and, bored, she asks what are we doing? and I keep staring and then, very slowly, still holding the cigarette, push the lighter in, wait until it heats up, pops out, light the cigarette, blow the smoke out, looking at her still, leaning away, and then I ask very quietly, suspiciously, maybe a little confused, "Okay"—taking a deep breath—"how many

Ethiopians can you fit into a Volkswagen?" I don't breathe until I hear her answer. I watch a tumbleweed come out of nowhere and hear it graze the bumper of the Porsche.

"I told you all of them," she says. "Are we going to your place or, like, what is this?"

I lean back, smoke some of the cigarette, ask, "How old are you?"

"Twenty."

"No. Really," I say. "Come on. It's just the two of us. We're alone now. I'm not a cop. Tell the truth. You won't get in trouble if you tell the truth."

She thinks about it, then asks, "Will you give me a gram?"

"Half."

She lights a joint I mistake for a cigarette and she aims the smoke out the sunroof and says, "Okay, I'm fourteen. I'm fourteen. Can you deal with it? God." She offers me the joint.

"No way," I say, not taking it.

She shrugs. "Yes way." Another drag.

"No way," I say again.

"Yes way. I'm fourteen. I was bas-mitzvahed at the Beverly Hills Hotel and it was hell and I'll be fifteen in October," she says, holding in smoke, then exhaling.

"How did you get into the club?"

"Fake ID." She reaches into her purse.

"Did I actually mistake Hello Kitty for Louis Vuitton?" I murmur aloud, grabbing the purse, smelling it.

She shows me the fake ID. "Guess you did, genius."

"How do I know it's fake?" I ask. "How do I know you're not just teasing me?"

"Study it real careful. Yeah, I was born twenty years ago in 1964, uh-huh, *right*," she sneers. "Duh."

I hand it back to her. Then I start the car up again and, still looking over at her, pull onto Ventura Boulevard and start heading toward the darkness of Encino.

"All of them." I shudder. "Whew."

"Where's my gram?" she asks, then, "Oh look, a sale at Robinson's."

I light another cigarette.

"I usually don't smoke," I tell her. "But you're doing something weird to me."

"You shouldn't smoke." She yawns. "Those things'll kill you. At least that's what my hideous mother always said."

"Did she die from cigarettes?" I ask.

"No, her throat was slashed by some maniac," she says. "She didn't smoke." Pause. "Mexicans have basically raised me." Another pause. "Let me tell you, that is no fun."

"Yeah?" I smile grimly. "You think cigarettes will kill me?"

She takes another drag off her joint and then it's gone and I pull into the garage and then we're walking into the bedroom and everything's speeding up, where the night's heading is becoming clearer, and she checks out the house and asks for a large vodka on the rocks. I tell her beer is in the fridge and that she can get it the fuck herself. She pulls some kind of demented hissy fit and slouches into the kitchen, muttering, "Jesus, my father has better manners."

"You can't be fourteen," I'm saying. "No way." I'm taking off my tie and jacket, kicking my loafers off.

She walks back in with a Corona in one hand, a fresh j in the other. She's wearing too much makeup, these ugly white Guess jeans but she looks like most girls, waxy and artificial.

"You poor pitiful bitch," I murmur.

I lie down on the bed, kick back, my head resting on some bunched-up pillows, stare at her, reach down, adjust myself.

"You don't have any furniture?" she asks.

"I've got a fridge. I got this bed," I tell her, running my hand across designer sheets.

"Yeah. That's true. Boy, you sure have a point." She walks around the room, then over to the door near the end of the room, tries it, locked. "What's in there?" she asks, looking at the sunrise/sunset chart I clipped from the L.A. *Herald Examiner* for this week, Scotch-taped to the door.

"Just another room," I tell her.

"Oh." She looks at me, finally a little scared.

I pull my pants off, fold them, throw them on the floor.

"Why do you have so much, like . . ." She stops. She's not drinking the beer. She's looking over at me, confused.

"So much what?" I ask, unbuttoning my shirt.

"Well . . . so much meat," she says meekly. "I mean, there's so much meat in your refrigerator."

"I don't know," I say. "Because I get hungry? Because red snapper appalls me?" I put the shirt down, next to the pants. "Christ."

"Oh." She just stands there.

I don't say anything else, prop my head back up on the pillows. I ease my underwear off slowly and motion for her to come over here, to me, and she slowly walks over, helpless, with a full beer, a sliver of lime in its top, a joint that has gone out. Bracelets circling her wrist look like they are made from fur.

"Uh, listen, this is—this is gonna sound like totally bizarre," she stammers. "But are you . . ."

She's coming nearer now, toward me, floating, unaware that her feet aren't even touching the floor. I rise up, a huge erection on the verge of bursting jutting out in front of me.

"Are you, like . . ." She stops smiling. "Like, a . . ." She doesn't finish.

"A vampire?" I suggest, grinning.

"No—an agent," she asks seriously.

I clear my throat.

When I say no, I'm not an agent, she moans and I have her by the shoulders now and I'm taking her very slowly, calmly, to the bathroom and while I'm stripping her, throwing the ESPIRIT T-shirt aside, into the bidet, she keeps giggling, wasted, and asking, "Doesn't that sound weird to you?" and then finally her young perfect body is naked and she looks up into eyes that cloud over completely, black and bottomless, and she reaches up, weeping with disbelief, and touches my face and I smile and touch her smooth, hairless pussy and she says, "Just don't give me a hickey," and then I scream and jump on her and rip her throat out and then I fuck her and then I play with her blood and after that basically everything's okay.

I'm driving down Ventura tonight toward my psychiatrist's office, over the hill. I did a couple of lines earlier and "Boys of Summer" is blasting from the tape deck and I'm singing along with it, air-jamming at stoplights, passing the Galleria, passing Tower Records and the Factory and the La Reina theater, which will close soon, and past the new Fatburger and the giant Nautilus that just opened. I got a call from Marsha earlier, inviting me to a party in Malibu. Dirk sent me these ZZ Top stickers to put on the lid of my coffin and I think that's pretty tacky but I'll keep them anyway. I'm watching all these people in their cars tonight and I've been thinking a lot about nuclear bombs since I've seen a couple of bumper stickers complaining about them.

In Dr. Nova's office I'm having a hard time.

"What's going on tonight, Jamie?" Dr. Nova asks. "You seem . . . agitated."

"I have these images, man, no, these *visions*," I'm telling him. "Visions of nuclear missiles blowing this place away."

"What place, Jamie?"

"Melting the Valley, the whole Valley. All the chicks rotting away. The Galleria just a memory. Everything gone." Pause. "Evaporated." Pause. "Is that a word?"

"Wow," Dr. Nova says.

"Yeah, wow," I say, staring out the window.

"What will happen to you?" he asks.

"Why? You think that would stop me?" I ask back.

"What do you think?"

"You think a fucking nuclear bomb is gonna end all this?" I'm saying. "No way, dude."

"End all what?" Dr. Nova asks.

"We'll survive that."

"Who is we?"

"*We* have been here forever and *we* will probably be around forever too." I check my nails.

"What will *we* be doing?" Dr. Nova asks, barely paying attention.

"Roaming." I shrug. "Flying around. Looming over you like a fucking raven. Picture the biggest raven you've ever seen. Picture it looming."

"How are your parents, Jamie?"

"I don't know," I say and then, my voice rising toward a scream, "But I live the cool life and if you do not refill my prescription of Darvocet—"

"What will you do, Jamie?"

I consider my options, then calmly explain.

"I'll be waiting," I tell him. "I'll be waiting in your bed room one night. Or under the table of your favorite restaurant, mutilating your wittle foot."

"Is . . . this a threat?" Dr. Nova asks.

"Or when you take your daughter to McDonald's," I say, "I'll be dressed as Ronald McDonald or the Grimace and I'll eat her in the parking lot while you watch and quickly get fucked up."

"We've talked about this before, Jamie."

"I'll be waiting in the parking lot or in your daughter's schoolyard or in a bathroom. I'll be crouching in your bathroom. I'll follow your daughter home from school and after I play fucky with her I'll be crouching in your bathroom."

Dr. Nova just looks at me, bored, as if my behavior is explainable.

"I was in the hospital room when your father died of cancer," I tell him.

"You've mentioned this before," he says idly.

"He was rotting away, Dr. Nova," I say. "I saw him. I saw your father rotting away. I told all my friends your father died of toxic shock. That he stuck a tampon up his ass and left it there too long. He died screaming, Dr. Nova."

"Have you . . . killed anyone else recently, Jamie?" Dr. Nova asks, not too visibly shaken.

"In a movie," I say. "In my mind." I giggle.

Dr. Nova sighs, studies me, largely unassured. "What do you want?"

"I want to be in the backseat of your car, waiting, drooling—"

"I hear you, Jamie." Dr. Nova sighs.

"I want my Darvocet refilled or else I'm gonna be waiting beneath that lovely black-bottom pool of yours one night while you're out for a little midnight swim, Dr. Nova, and I'll pull veins and tendons out of your well-muscled thigh." I'm standing now, pacing.

"I'll give you the Darvocet, Jamie," Dr. Nova says. "But I want you here on a less irregular basis."

"I'm totally psyched," I say. "You're as cool as they come."

He fills out a prescription and then, while handing it to me, asks, "Why should I fear you?"

"Because I'm a tan burly motherfucker and my teeth are so sharp they make a straight razor seem like a butter knife." I pause. "Need a better reason?"

"Why do you threaten me?" he asks. "Why should I fear you?"

"Because I'm going to be that last image you ever see," I tell him. "Count on it."

I head toward the door, then turn back around. "Where's the place you feel safest?" I ask.

"In an empty movie theater," Dr. Nova says.

"What's your favorite movie?" I ask.

"*Vacation*, with Chevy Chase and Christie Brinkley."

"What's your favorite cereal?"

"Frosted Mini Wheats or something with bran in it."

"What's your favorite TV commercial for?"

"Bayer Aspirin."

"Who did you vote for last election?"

"Reagan."

"Define the vanishing point."

"You"—he's crying—"define it."

"We've already been there," I tell him. "We've already seen it."

"Who's . . . we?" He chokes.

"Legion."

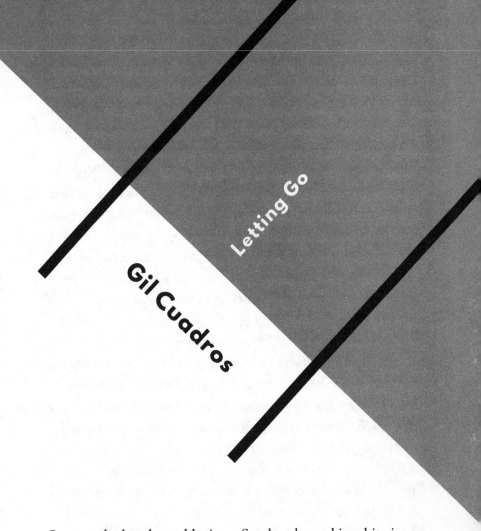

Letting Go

Gil Cuadros

I am on the beach a cold winter Sunday, dressed in white jeans, white t-shirt, white blazer. My feet are bare. The sand is unusually clean, shells are arranged in tribal patterns of the sun and moon, man and woman. I can't recall if these designs had appeared there with the tide or were there from when I arrived. I feel something move in my hand, which I grip tightly, a thick sea-worthy rope woven of twine. The length moves away from me like a kite's string. I can see the other end is tied to my old lover's foot in the wing tips he used to wear when he worked.

The soles have been worn down. My old lover's arms move spastically, as if holding his balance on a current I can't visualize. He looks down at me like I am the angel. We haven't had sex in over a year; he has been in this condition for quite a while.

My new lover, Rudy, is at my elbow, trying to pull me away with his usual arguments. We haven't had sex either. Not that Rudy hasn't tried, rubbing his crotch on the side of my leg, kneeling in front of me, unzipping my fly till I nearly fumble with the rope. Today he has been shopping, and is wearing the sheer white bathing suit he purchased. The trunks are skin tight, "Versace" runs along the waistband in bold black letters. Rudy turns around like a model, gold fleurs-de-lys are on each cheek of his ass.

There are moments when I want to get rid of this rope, having tested how many fingers I can actually let go of and still be able to manage the rope. The smaller fingers feel dead or asleep. As they curl open I can see cuts and bruises inside my palms. Rudy has brought astringent because he knows it will sting, and arnica because it can heal. I tell him that it doesn't hurt, but he refuses to hear that, insists that I should let go as he holds onto the rope himself. He says there are rolls of bandages he can wrap around my hands. I see through his deception. "How are you going to be able to hold the rope and bandage my hands?"

It's when I lose my temper that the priests come waltzing in. It has happened before. Their faces are drawn, skin and bones. The father today is particularly ugly, lesions cover what little flesh is exposed, his breath smells of shit and urine. He looks close in my face, says, "Son, it is time to let go, last rites, you need to live in the city of God." My old lover smiles, unaware of what is being said around me. He is so trusting. He has given Rudy and me his blessing, has thrown down what was left in his pockets, a brass lighter, copper coins as gifts to us. Rudy holds on to them, has buried them somewhere farther upshore.

I look where I believe the artifacts are buried and can see the sand rises in little dunes. I notice a head growing out of the sand, a young woman with long, black hair. My mother at sixteen. A young man follows her, reaches to hold her hand. By that simple touch, magic, I see her belly swell. There is pain in her eyes, regret for being so young. When I am born, my father dances with me in his arms, drunk. I smell his love. My mother pulls me away from him. He begins to strangle her, she won't leave. I want to ask her why, she slaps me. My neck feels broken and she continues to hit me. I grab her hand. I am now grown, masturbating every day in the bathroom, letting the water run to cover the sound. My mother is afraid of what I can do to her. I am sure of my strength, my ability to break her arm. That's when she tells me what a handsome boy I've become. My father turns his back on us, the muscles in his back are knotted. All he says is, "Faggot." My mother wants to hit me but cannot bring herself to do it. I see myself walk away from them alone.

It's like a mirror grazing over the sand, moving quickly to confront me. I try to have Rudy look at my life, but he is biting at my ear, blowing warm air into the canal. His fingertips are warm as they move over my body. I turn back to my image, now standing in front of me. Rudy says he is going to leave if I don't let go. As he moves away I gradually become colder. I hand the rope to my image, which he gladly accepts, seems to have strength I have lost. It is the first time I have ever released the rope and my hands feel strange and useless. Rudy is near, running down the beach. My image is being dragged into the ocean. I start running for Rudy, but I can't take my eyes off myself. I yell out my new lover's name. He stops. I look back and see my image drowning in the ocean, my old lover looks more like a dead fish floating in an aquarium. Rudy kisses me, says, "Today . . ." and can't complete his thought. The water has completely covered my image and the rope seems to have lost all tension. I return to Rudy, unsure that I love him or that I even want to be with him. I look down at my feet gliding over the sand, notice the cuffs of my pants have begun to fray, the threads twirl in the sea air and start to become twine.

Sight

Gil Cuadros

At first I think it must be the fires and the winds, miniscule ash floating through the air and into my eyes. Or the dry Santa Anas pushing down the hillsides, raising the temperature till moisture vanishes, making the edges of my eyes blood red. On the freeway, driving to my doctor, I see clouds of black smoke billowing off the mountains, strange aerial formations of crows and seagulls, twisting and turning like a swath of fabric falling in air. These are the signs, clues written in some ancient script, and I want to know what it all means. The doctor looks at me, her hair pulled back away from her face, as if she were asking, "Can't you read this language?" She is obviously frustrated, her fingers snap against each other, disbelief in their sounds. I must look ridiculous, sitting there, a smile across my mouth. She pulls out a model of a large eye the size of a bowling ball. She begins to disassemble the eye, the cornea, the retina, the optical nerve. I push the parts away from me; I can see that everything, everyone in her office has a glow around their bodies, some with colors more distinct, others thin and wavering. Even more unsettling, some people leave trails of light, a residue that takes a long time to dissipate. Occasionally a trail will curl upward, a large snake the color of ochre, poised as if ready to attack any nearby person. The doctor wants me to understand, says without this medication there is no hope; without this medication you are sure to lose all the sight that you have; the small discomfort you'll experience will be worth it compared to the alternative; what is one more drug to you? She is telling the truth, I can see it being said in the gold light that temporarily covers her body, can taste it under my tongue like a hazelnut liqueur. I tell her, "No, thank you." That is all I have to say and she starts shaking her head. The bones in her neck pop; she tells me I am foolish. By the time I near home, the drive has become more dangerous. My peripheral vision diminishes, the crest of my forehead, the crown of my head seems to ignite. My other senses revel in new-found power, guiding me through a maze of streets, using the scent of jacarandas and freshly cut, large-leaf philodendrons, the feel of bumps on the road, the dampness along my arm that means I've come into my underground parking space. People seem entranced with me as I step into the lobby of my apartment building; there is vague recognition but no recall of my name. I hear a few whisper,

"Who?" They look at me as one would a religious painting, a lamentation. I am temporarily blinded by the various colors spewing out from their bodies, can see one man is covered with nothing more than white static, while another woman has tendrils of bluish light connected to everyone she's near. For a moment the inside of my chest seems hollow. I smile briefly; by now I am used to people not recognizing me because of weight loss, the waste of my muscles, but this is different. An elderly woman holds the elevator for me, her arm braced against the closing door. A warm tingle runs down my throat, informs me that she is not well, some perceived similarity with myself. I face her and smell lavender, old wool, sweat like eucalyptus oil. Her hair is white, I know, but I see tumors instead, the stench of black rotted fruit, dappling her brain. Her heart is erratic and I feel as if it is my own and that I am the one who will fall soon. I want to touch her. I sense the elevator aching to lift us up. She is saying something to herself, I hear her say the word "God" with the warm buzz of bees and wooden flutes in her mouth. I feel my palm near her shoulder and her body begins to change, slippery as mercury. Now I can see an amber light emanating from her stomach, her head. She is unsure of why she feels better, but she takes it like a gift of inestimable worth. In my room I lie back, close and open my eyes and all is darkness. My ears hum, and the woolen blanket beneath my fingers seems unbearably rough. For a second I think I have fallen asleep, and now it is late, the street lights are turned off. Somewhere in the house, my roommate watches TV. Miles away I can sense my folks readying themselves for sleep, the rustle of their bedsheets, the sounds they make using the bathroom. My brother far away in another state begins to open a can of beer; I hear him spray the fluid across his hand. It used to make me sick, the thought of my family, but now I see it as a legacy I will not understand till much later. Through the window, a man watches me: he is white, bright as if a hundred candles were burning inside him. He sees that I am ready, calls more of his people to the window. At first I pretend not to know what he offers, can taste meat in my mouth, blood on my lips. There is no judgement on whatever I do; he is just there for me. Before I go, I want to tell my roommate what he needs to take to stay alive, the astragalus I have in my closet, this new experimental treatment out of Korea. I want to call my ex-lover and explain that I really understand why he had to leave me, his heart battered like bronze from all the other deaths in his life. I want my mother to know I know where all her anger comes from, and if I could just touch a certain spot on her body, near her breastbone, it would all be released, she would always be warm after that. But I have come to the end, thoughts of the world seem woven of thread, thinly disguised, a veil. I let the angels consume me, each one biting into my body, until nothing is left, nothing but a small glow and even that begins to perish.

Chain of Fools

Kevin Killian

Again I approach the Church, St. Joseph's at Howard and Tenth, south of Market in San Francisco. It's a disconcerting structure, in late Mission style, but capped with two gold domed towers out of some Russian Orthodox dream. I'm following two uniformed cops, in the late afternoon this October, we're followed by the sun as we mount the steps to the big brass doors and enter into the darkness of the nave. I see the pastor, Filipino, short and shambling, approach us from the altar, where two nuns remain, arranging fall flowers around the vestibule. I fall back while the cops detain the priest. They're passing him a sheaf of legal papers regarding the closing of the church, which has been damaged beyond repair by the earthquake of '89. Anger crosses the priest's handsome face, then he shakes the hands of the two policemen; all shrug as if to say, *shit happens*. I glance up at the enormous crucifix where the image of Christ is sprawled from the ugly nails. His slender body, a rag floating over his dick. His face, white in the darkened upper reaches of the Church. His eyes closed, yet bulging with pain. Again I bend my knee and bow, the body's habitual response. Across my face and upper torso I trace the sign of the cross, the marks of this disputed passage. I'm dreaming again—again the dreaming self asserts its mastery of all of time, all of space.

Late in the '60s Mom and Dad enrolled me in a high school for boys, staffed by Franciscans. I was a scrawny, petulant kid with an exhibitionist streak that must have screamed trouble in every decibel known to God or man. My parents had tried to bring me up Catholic, but as I see myself today, I was really a pagan, with no God but experience, and no altar but my own confusing body. In a shadowy antebellum building high on a hill above us, the monks rang bells, said office, ate meals in the refectory, drank cases of beer. In the halls of St. A—, bustling with boys, I felt like the narrator in Ed White's *Forgetting Elena*, marooned in a society I could hardly understand except by dumb imitation. In every room a crucifix transfixed me with shame: I felt deeply compromised by my own falsity. My self was a lie, a sham, next to the essentialism of Christ, He who managed to maintain not only a human life but a divine one too. He *was* God, the Second Person of the Trinity.

But I talked a good game, as any bright student can, and did my best to get out of my schoolwork, so I'd have more time to develop my homosexuality. I spent a year in French class doing independent study, reading *Gone with the Wind* in French, while the other students around me mumbled *"Je ne parle pas"* to an implacable friar. Presently I was able to convince the history teacher that reading *Gone with the Wind* in French should satisfy his requirements too. Then I could go home and confront my appalled parents by saying, "This is something I have to read for school."

Later on, when I was a senior and drunk all the time, a friend and I invented an opera, a collaboration between Flaubert and Debussy, set in outer space and ancient Rome, that we called *Fenestella*. George Grey and I flogged this opera through French class, music class, World Literature, etc. We recounted its storyline, acted out its parts, noted the influence of *Fenestella* on Stravinsky, Gide, etc, you name it. Our teachers slowly tired of Fenestella, but we never did. The heroine was an immortal bird—a kind of pigeon—sent by St. Valentine out into Jupiter to conquer space in the name of love—on the way to Jupiter she sings the immortal "Clair de Lune." I must have thought I too was some kind of immortal bird, like Fenestella, like Shelley's skylark. None of our teachers pointed out the unlikelihood of Flaubert (d. 1880) and Debussy (b. 1862) collaborating on anything elaborate. We had them quarrelling, reuniting, duelling, taking bows at La Scala, arguing about everything from *le mot juste* to the *Cathedrale Engloutée*. Nobody said a word, just gave us A's, praised us to the skies.

I had no respect for most of these dopes. In later life I was to pay the piper by dallying with several teens who had no respect for me. Nothing's worse than that upturned, scornful face, that throws off youth's arrogance like laser rays. When I was 16 I had the world by the tail. But in another light the world had already made me what I was, a blind struggling creature like a mole, nosing through dirt to find its light and food.

In religion class Brother Padraic had us bring in pop records which we would play, then analyze like poetry. It was a conceit of the era, that rock was a kind of poetry and a way to reach kids. Other boys, I remember, brought in "poetic" records like "All Along the Watchtower," "At the Zoo," "Chimes of Freedom." The more daring played drug songs—"Sister Ray," "Eight Miles High," "Sunshine Superman," or the vaguely scandalous—"Let's Spend the Night Together." When it was my turn I brandished my favorite original cast album—*My Fair Lady*—and played "Wouldn't It be Loverly." Now, that's poetry, I would say expansively, mincing from one black tile to a red tile, then sideways to a white tile, arms stretched out appealingly. After the bell rang a tall man dressed in black stepped out of the shadows between lockers and said, "Have you considered psychological counselling?" I should have been mortified, but I shook my head like a friendly pup and, with purposeful tread, followed him to his office. Then the office got too small for his needs and he drove me to what I soon came to think of as *our place*, down by the river, down by the weeds and waterbirds.

Getting in and out of a VW bug in those long black robes must have been a bitch. Funny I didn't think of that till later. It happened in front of my eyes but I didn't really notice. I was too—oh, what's the word—ensorcelled. He—Brother Jim—wasn't exactly good-looking, but he had something that made up for any defect: he'd taken that precious vow of celibacy, though not, he confided, with his dick. First I felt for it through the robes, then found a deep slit pocket I was afraid to slip my hand into. Then he laughed and lifted the robe over his legs and over most of the steering wheel. And down by the gas pedal and the clutch he deposited these awful Bermuda shorts and evocative sandals. And his underwear. His black robe made a vast tent, then, dark in the day, a tent I wanted to wrap myself up in and hide in forever, with only his two bent legs and his shadowy sex for company. So I sucked him and sucked him, Brother Jim.

"Why don't you turn around?" he asked. "Pull those pants all the way down, I like to see beautiful bodies." He made my knees wobble as he licked behind them. Wobble, like I couldn't stand up. On the wind, the scents of sand cherry and silverweed, the brackish river. The squawk of a gull. Scents that burned as they moved across my face, like incense. After a while he told me how lonely his life was, that only a few of the other monks were queers, there was no one to talk to. "You can talk to me," I told him, moved. Every semester he and the few other queer monks judged the new students like Paris awarding the golden apple. Some of us had the staggering big-lipped beauty that April's made from; some of us were rejected out-of-hand, and some of us, like me, seemed available. Then they waited till they felt like it, till they felt like trying one of us out.

He made me feel his . . . dilemma, would you call it? Boys, after all, are tricky because they change from week to week. You might fancy a fresh complexion: act right away, for in a month that spotless face will have grown spotted, or bearded, or dull. You might reject me because I have no basket, well, too bad, because by Christmas I'll be sporting these new genitals Santa brought me, big, bad and boisterous. This was Jim's dilemma—when you're waiting for a perfect boy life's tough. So they traded us, more or less. Always hoping to trade up, I guess.

"Don't trade me," I pleaded with him. "Oh never," he said, tracing the nape of my neck absently, while on the other side of the windshield darkness fell on a grove filled with oaks and wild hawthorn. "Never, never, never."

I wanted to know their names—who was queer, which of them—I *had* to know. He wouldn't say. I named names. How about the flamboyant arts teacher who insisted on us wearing tights, even when playing Arthur Miller? No. None of the effeminate monks, he told me, were gay. "They just play at it," he sneered. How about the gruff math teacher, who had been the protegé of Alan Turing and John van Neumann? If you answered wrong in class he'd summon you to his desk, bend you over his knee, and spank you. If you were especially dense you'd have to go to his disordered room in the evening and he'd penetrate you with an oily finger, sometimes two. "No," said Brother Jim, my new boyfriend. "Don't be absurd. None of those fellows are fags. You'd never guess unless I tell you." I told him I didn't really want to know, a lie, I told him I'd never done this with a man, a lie, I told him I would never tell another about the love that passed between us, a lie. And all these lies I paid for when June began and Jim got himself transferred to Virginia. But then another teacher stopped me in the hall. "Jim told me about your problem," he said, his glasses frosty, opaque. This was Brother Anselm. "He says you feel itchy round the groin area."

He's the one who took me to see *The Fantasticks* in Greenwich Village and bought me the record, "Try to Remember." If you're reading this, Anselm, try to remember that time in September when life was long and days were fucking mellow. As for you, Brother Jim, whatever happened to "never?" You said you'd "never" trade me, but when I turned 17 I was yesterday's papers. Thus I came to hate aging, to the point that even today I still pride myself on my "young attitude." Pathetic. I remember that our most famous alumnus was Billy Hayes, whose story was later made into a sensational film called *Midnight Express*. At that time he was mired in a Turkish prison for drug smuggling. We students had to raise funds for his legal defense, or for extra-legal terrorist acts designed to break him out. Students from *other* schools went door-to-door in elegant neighborhoods, selling chocolate bars to send their track teams to big meets, but we had to go around with jingling cans, asking for money for "The Billy Hayes Fund," and you know something, people gave! They didn't even want to know what it was, good thing too. Later when the film came out its vampy homoerotics gave me a chill. Later still, its leading man, Brad Davis, played *Querelle* in Fassbinder's film of the Genet novel. And even later still Davis died of AIDS and I conflated all these men into one unruly figure with a queer complaint against God.

Standing on the desert's edge, a man at the horizon, shaking a fist against an implacable empty sky.

At first I resented Jim and Anselm and the rest, their careless handling of this precious package, me. But after awhile I grew fond of them, even as they passed me around like a plate of canapes at a cocktail party. Anybody would have, especially a young person like myself who thought he was "different." I watch the E Channel and see all these parents of boys, parents who are suing Michael Jackson, and I want to tell them, your boys are saying two things, one out of each side of their mouth, or maybe three things, one of them being, "Let me go back to Neverland Ranch where at least I was *appreciated*."

Unlike Michael Jackson, the religious staff of St. A— wore ropes around their waists to remind themselves, and us, of the constant poverty of St. Francis of Assisi. One of them quoted St.

Therese to me, to illustrate his humility: "I am the zero which, by itself, is of no value but put after a unit becomes useful." I pulled the rope from around his waist, teasing him. I took one home as a souvenir. These fat long ropes, wheaten color, thick as my penis and almost as sinuous. I believed in those ropes. I said to myself, why don't *you* become a monk, think of all the side benefits? I walked down to the grove of trees by the river's edge one April afternoon, thinking these grand thoughts of joining the seminary. Beneath my feet small pink flowers, a carpet of wood sorrel or wild hepatica, leading down to a marshy space tall with field horsetail, up to my waist. "God," I called out, "give me a sign I'm doing the right thing." I felt guilty that I had sinned in a car, guilty and stained, like a slide in a crime lab. I waited for His sign, but zilch. Above me a pair of laughing gulls, orange beaks, black heads, disappeared into the sun. *Is that my sign?* thought I, crestfallen. *How oblique.* But right around that time I began to realize that there was something stronger than a Franciscan brother.

Marijuana leads to heroin, they used to say. I don't know about that, but after awhile friars just don't cut it, you want something stronger, something that'll really *take you there.* You want a priest. Ever see *The Thorn Birds,* the way Rachel Ward longs for Richard Chamberlain? Or Preminger's *The Cardinal,* with Romy Schneider yearning for some other gay guy, it's a thrill to think, y'know, with a little luck, this man licking my cock could turn out to be the Prince of the Whole Church, the Supreme Pontiff, in ten or fifteen years and right now, you can almost see his soul shining right through his thinning blond hair, already he's godly—Again the dreaming self rises above the squalid air of the black back room, the hush of the confessional, breaking free into a world of pleasure and Eros and hope, all I continue to pray for and more. Out in the snowy East of Long Island I bent over Frank O'Hara's grave and traced his words with my tongue, the words carved into his stone there: "Grace to be born and to live as variously as possible." Another lapsed Catholic trying to align the divine with the human.

And because I was so willful, I made spoiling priests a kind of game, like Sadie Thompson does in *Rain*. Under those robes of black, I would think, are the white limbs of strong men. I trailed one priest, Fr. Carney, from assignment to assignment. I was his youth liaison—encouraged to inform on my peers' drug habits, I had first to increase my own. You have to be a little hard, a little speedy, to become what we then called a "narc." He also got me to bring along other youths to retreats staged on isolated Long Island mother houses. When I graduated from St. A— I continued to traipse after Fr. Carney, like Marlene Dietrich slinging her heels over her shoulder to brave the desert at the end of *Morocco*, all for Gary Cooper's ass. "You don't have to call me Father Carney," he would say to me. "Call me Paul." I felt like king of the hill, top of the heap. Oh, Paul, I would say, why am I being treated so well? "Because you are who you are," he told me. "You are someone special. You are Kevin Killian."

I grew more and more spoiled, and he must have enjoyed my ripeness, up to a point; and then he left me, in this valley of tears. I remember standing in his room watching the cold green spectacle of Long Island Sound, leaves of yellow acacia tapping into the window, with this pair of black gym shorts pulled down just under my buttocks, and thinking to myself, I'll bring him back to me with my hot skin and my healthy boy type sweat. And him, Paul, slouched on his king-size bed, turned away from me, bored, extinguished, his breviary pulled next to him like a teddy bear. "There's a list on my desk," he said. "Some of them may be calling you." So when I pulled up my pants I'd have this list to turn to, the names of other priests, *next!*—Like one of those chain letters, filled with the names of strangers, to whom you have to send five dollars each or Mother will go blind. "You're trading me too," I said, before the door hit me on the ass. Thump.

So the next guy called me, Father some Polish name, and he turned out to be—really into the Rosary . . . Around this time I got to thinking that despite what they told me, I was not someone special after all.

These men were connoisseurs all right. They pulled out my cork and took turns sniffing it. Meanwhile the *sommelier* stood by, a smile in his eyes, attentive, alert. Disillusioned, dejected, I began to read the whims of these men not as isolated quirks, but as signs of a larger system, one in which pleasure, desire endlessly fulfilled, *jouissance*, are given more value. Within the Church's apparently ascetic structure, the pursuit of pleasure has been more or less internalized. By and large, the pursuit (of violence, danger, beauty) is the structure. I had to hand it to them! Under their black robes those long legs were born to *can-can*. Pleasure, in a suburbia that understood only growth and money. Aretha Franklin said it best, singing on the radio while I moped from man to man. *"Chain-chain-chain,"* she chanted. *"Chain of fools."*

I met Dorothy Day in a private home in Brooklyn, when Father Paul took me to meet her. She was seventy then, and had been a legend for forty years, both in and out of the Church, for her activism, her sanctity, her saltiness. I had read all about her in *Time* magazine. She sat on a huge sofa almost dwarfed by these big Mario Buatta-style throw pillows, gold and pink and red.

Her hands were folded neatly in her lap, as though she were groggy. The way to get closer to Christ, she asserted, is through work. Father Paul argued mildly, what about the Golden Rule? Isn't love the answer? No, she responded sharply,—work, not love. Last night on TV I watched *The Trouble with Angels*, in which mischievous Hayley Mills raises holy hell at a Long Island girls' school, till she meets her match in imperious, suave Mother Superior Rosalind Russell. At the denouement she tells her plain girlfriend that she won't be going to Bryn Mawr or even back to England. She's decided to "stay on," become a nun, clip her own wings. I remember again wavering on the brink, of becoming a priest, saying to myself, why don't you do the— *Hayley Mills thing?* Saying it to myself from the back row of this cobwebbed movie house in a poky town on the North Shore of Long Island, fingering the beer between my legs, all alone in the dark.

Now I'm all grown, Dorothy Day is dead, and when I open *Time* magazine I read about altar boys and seminarians suing priests. One quarter of all pedophile priests, they say, live in New Mexico. I have no interest in pursuing my "case" in a tribunal, but I'd like to view such a trial—maybe on Court TV? Or sit in the public gallery, next to John Waters, while my teachers take the stand and confess under pressure or Prozac. I'd get out a little sketchpad and charcoal and draw their faces, older now, confused and guilty and perhaps a little crazy. Then their accusers would come to the stand, confused, guilty, crazy, and I could draw in my own eyes into their various faces, into the faces of my pals and brothers.

Oh how I envied them their privilege, their unflappable ease, the queers of the church. If they were as lonely as they claimed, weren't there enough of them? If their love lives were dangerous, surely they would always be protected by the hierarchy that enfolded them. I remember one monk who had been sent away years before to a special retreat in Taos and he said, *I didn't want to have to come back and see any boys. But then I wanted to come back, it must have been to meet you, Kevin.* And I pictured this empty desert sky with nothing in it but one of Georgia O'Keeffe's cow skulls staring at me through time. My face broke into a smile and I said, "That is so sweet."

I broke with the Church over its policies on abortion, women's rights, gay rights, just like you did. Perhaps its hypocrisy angered you, but that's just human nature, no? What scared me was its monolithic structure. It's too big either to fight or hide within, like the disconcerting house of the Addams Family. I tried to talk to It, but It just sat there, a big unresponsive sack of white sugar. So good-bye. And yet I suppose I'm a far better Catholic now than then. I dream of this god who took on the clothes of man and then stepped forward to strip them off at the moment of humiliation. This renunciation for a greater good remains with me an ideal of society and heaven. I try to get closer to Christ through work. I tried love for a long time but it only lengthened the distance between Him and me.

So I try to call the number of St. A— to see where the 20th high school reunion will be. So that's when I find out the school's now defunct, for the usual reasons: indifference, inflation, acedia. I continue to see the Church as the house of Eros, a place of pleasure and fun, and I continue to regard men in religious costume as possible sex partners, yearning to break free. Such was my training, my ritual life. I can't shake it off, I'm not a snake who can shed its skin. Every time I pass a crucifix I wonder, what if it had been me up there instead, could I have said, *Father, forgive them, for they know not what they do?* I don't think I'm so special, not any more. At the church here in San Francisco, I bow down and make the sign of the cross, the logo of the Church, an imprint deep within forces me to replicate this logo. Up, down, left, right, the hand that seeks, then pulls away frustrated. The hand tightens, becomes a fist, the fist is raised to the sky, on the desert's edge, angry and queer. Inside the Church burns incense, tricky and deep-penetrating, strong, perdurable, like the smells of sand cherry, silverweed, trillium.

Hobbits and Hobgoblins

Randall Kenan

The world whispers to those who listen. Secrets collide in the air with visions of truth and particles of fancy. *Listen.* Hear the murmurs of owls speaking of buried treasures, the sparrows conversing over great battles of yore, the squirrels telling tales in hushed voices of the time an angel lighted on the shoulders of a young girl and allowed her to see the ghosts of her future. The voices canter about unceasing, sibilant and silken and silvery in the ether, containing all the wisdom of the great world; all the knowledge ever needed floats about in the air simply to be heeded, contained in faint hummings slightly louder than the chiming of the spheres. Any boy can hear. If he only listens.

Malcolm sits in his grandmother's chair, a great chair it is. In truth, a throne once owned by an Egyptian empress. Malcolm knows. She sat here, as he does, nibbling peacock's brain and honey-covered hippopotamus eyes, fanned from behind by a Nubian, naked but for a blindingly white turban and gold bracelets. He fans Malcolm now, an idle coloring book in Malcolm's lap while the gossamer plumes create an imperial breeze. Malcolm sighs.

"Brandon, I'm really tired of discussing it."

"Don't call me Brandon again, Denise. It's Fetasha. Fetasha Yakob."

"Jesus, Brandon—"

"Denise!"

Malcolm's father cannot see it, but a cobra slithers about his feet. Malcolm can see it. He does not worry. Malcolm knows it will not harm his father. The snake has a bright red hood and is striped like a barber's pole in orange and black. It has no venom; but it can breathe fire when it is angry.

"You have no respect for me or my beliefs."

"Brandon, *you* have no respect for you or your beliefs. You've changed your damn mind so much you don't even know what you believe."

"Don't use language like that in front of the kid."

"Jesus, Brandon. He's six."

"Exactly. Set an example."

"Mother, can you believe this?"

"Hm."

Malcolm grins when he sees that his grandmother, who sits ignoring his quarreling parents, trying to read a magazine, has a hobbit on her lap. The hobbit's name is Fidor. He winks at Malcolm. Fidor's orange hair is pulled back in a long ponytail and he wiggles his big toes in contentment, enjoying the grown-ups' argument.

"*You* are the one who hasn't held a job in ten fucking years."

"Denise. The boy."

"Don't come into my house and lecture me on how I should raise my son, Brandon. My god, you haven't seen him in three months and suddenly you've decided you can't live without him."

"He's my son, Denise."

"You noticed. Finally. Took you six years."

"Don't be mean, Denise. There's no reason."

Malcolm is pleased to see that the blue cockatoo—a very rare creature, with the ability to fly through walls—is perched atop his mother's head. The blue cockatoo sings in a Tibetan dialect taught to it by the great pirate Yeheman, a friend of Malcolm's who invited him onto his flying pirate ship, the galleon *Celestial*, once. Yeheman wanted to take Malcolm on an expedition to the other side of the sun. But Malcolm had to go to school. Yeheman left the blue cockatoo with Malcolm as a bond of friendship. The cockatoo is named Qwnpft.

"The answer is no, Brandon. No."

"The name is Fetasha, Denise. It means 'search' in Amharic, the Ethiopian tongue."

"I don't care. No. You can't take him."

"Only for a month, Denise."

"Not for a day."

"I have rights, you know."

"Sue me."

"Denise. I am his father."

"Brandon, I was there. For both events. The conception and the delivery. I know who the father is."

"You're trying to be funny, Denise. This is not productive."

"You're being flaky, Brandon. This is not sane."

The curtains are covered with speckled lizards, they chirp like birds and create melodies in eight-part harmony; gifts from the Maharajah of Zamzeer. He keeps sending gifts to Malcolm to gain his hand in marriage for his royal daughter, the ugly Princess Zamaha. Malcolm plans to hold out.

"Mother, do you hear what your *former* son-in-law proposes to do?"

"Hm."

Fidor giggles and slaps his knees; Qwnpft trills in Tibetan. Yamor, the black winged horse, another gift from the Maharajah, wanders into the room, up to Malcolm, and nuzzles him softly behind the ear. Yamor is lonely and wants to go for a fly. But Malcolm can't right now. His parents are arguing.

"Denise, I know how to take care of him. He'll be well looked after."

"Brandon—"

"*Fetasha!*"

"*What*ever. You can't even look after yourself. How on earth do you expect me to allow you to take my son to Jamaica for a month? Has this Rastafarian bullshit really messed your mind up that much?"

"Denise. Your language."

"I cussed like a sailor when you met me, remember? That's what you liked about me, or so you said."

A green orangutan hangs from the ceiling lamp; giant fire-red

Amazonian toads play leapfrog in the thick carpet; a yerple sea turtle swims the length of the room, turning somersaults as he completes laps over everyone's head. Underneath the coffee table perch three demons, Ksiel, Lahatiel, and Shaftiel, whom Malcolm caught a week ago trying to punish a knight. He has made them his slaves. They smoke long pipes of blue tobacco, which puffs up in pungent clouds of pink.

Today is Malcolm's sixth birthday. Jerome, Sheniqua, Perry, William, Davenport, Clarise, Sheryl, Tameka, Yuko, Bharati, John, Björn, Ali, Federica, Francesca, and Kwame came to his party. School will be over in three weeks, his grandmother says, and he will be taken from his Kingdom in the Land of New Jersey to his summer residence in the Land of the Carolinas, to rule with his Imperial cousins at the Imperial Palace at Tims-on-the-Creek. But now his father, who used to be a sorcerer named Mahammet al-Saddin and has now become this Prince Fetasha Yakob, plans to steal him away to the island principality of Jamaica, where rules, Malcolm has heard tell, the sinister Lord Jam-Ka. His father must need him to do serious battle. But Prince Fetasha must convince the Empress, his mother. Malcolm is worried.

"Just stop asking, Brandon. You are not going to let my son smoke ganja and commune with Ja and fiddle with some crystal around his neck. And what on earth are you wearing anyhow, Brandon? You look like . . . Jesus, what does he look like, Mama?"

"Hm."

"What's that around your neck?"

"Cowrie shells. And the name is Bran—I mean Fetasha."

"Your name is Brandon Church Harrington, okay? And that's what I'm going to call you."

"You continue to disrespect me, just as you always did. That's what ruined our marriage."

"O Lord, here we go. How dare you—"

Prince Fetasha came to Malcolm's party as a surprise. He tiptoed around back, in through the wood, and made a grand entrance in the backyard, coming through the hedges. He scared Malcolm's friends. Malcolm was surprised and happy. Malcolm's mother was angry. They fail to "communicate," his mother once told him. They're just from different worlds, child, his grandmother said. His grandmother likes Prince Fetasha. He likes Prince Fetasha too.

"How can a man, a black man, with your background, with a degree from Morehouse with Honors, no less, with a J.D. from fucking Yale, *fucking Yale*, go around with his head twigged up like a reggae singer, wearing—what the hell is it you have on, Brandon? I liked last year's getup much better—Do you know how much you'd be pulling down if . . . ? I have to take a Valium every time I think about it—"

"It's always money with you."

"*You* were the one born with a trust fund, okay? Don't talk to me about money. I worked my way through med school, fool. *You* don't even pay alimony, which I could still contest."

"I don't *caaarre* about money, Denise. Can't you get that through—"

"You don't c*aaarre* about anything. Except your hair."

Malcolm's mother, the Empress of the Kingdom of Orange, in the Land of New Jersey, is a baby doctor, a pediatrician. Her office has walls of tangerine and licorice and lime and lemon and blueberry. Grandmother, the Queen Mother, takes him there sometimes. All their subjects, waiting for an audience, sit in the candy-flavored room playing with blocks and trucks and rainbow-assorted animals—toys Malcolm now finds boring. The Empress doesn't have any video games there.

"Okay, for the last time—now I'm going to say this slowly, Mr. Rasta, so you can possibly, perhaps, maybe, understand me: Under. No. Circumstance. Will. I. Allow. You. To. Take. My. Son—the one who's sitting over there in that chair. With. You. Any. Where. Not Jamaica. Not Ethiopia. Not Newark. Not New York. Not to the convenience store down the road. After your last escapade, Mr. 'I'll-have-him-back-Sunday-night,' Malcolm is OFF LIMITS. If you want to see him, you do it *here*. There he is. Now look."

"Denise. You're being unreasonable again."

"Unreasonable? Again? Need *I* remind you that you kid-napped—"

"Kidnapped is unfa—"

"You were gone for a week—"

"Should we really be arguing in fron—"

"—instead of a weekend."

"—of him?"

Malcolm likes to go to the Savage Land with Prince Fetasha. He likes the caverns and the canyons, the mountains of steel and glass. They speak in loud booming voices. Sometimes they scream. The roads are wide and black with strange hieroglyph-ics painted about them, and the inhabitants rush about, surely chased by some monster like Godzilla or Smaug or Bigfoot. Prince Fetasha, when he was Mahammet al-Saddin, married Malcolm on his shoulders when they were in the Savage Land. He could smell the scent on his father called M-cents. Malcolm liked the smell. Prince Fetasha's hair is in long black snakes like Medusa's. He says they are called deadlocks. Malcolm likes to play with his father's deadlocks. They feel spongy and soft, and they smell of M-cents. Once Fetasha, who was then Mahammet al-Saddin, gave Malcolm a necklace of shells like the one he's wearing now. The shells told Malcolm where a magic amulet, long lost, lay in Africa. But when he got home his mother, the Empress, tore the shells from his neck and said he might get funjus from them and threw them into the trash compactor. The amulet will never be found.

"Denise."

"No."

Yamor, the black winged horse, is getting antsy, and the floating yerple turtle seems to be slowing down. A mask on the wall winks at Malcolm, and the hobbit is climbing down off his grandmother's lap. Malcolm stands up, and his wing'd sandals take him across the room to his mother and father.

"Mom, can I get some deadlocks like Daddy's?"

His mother, the Empress, raises her hands in the air and rolls her eyes—the look she has when his grandmother says his mother is "disgusted with the world again." His father, Prince Fetasha, pats him on the head. But before either of them say anything, his grandmother pops her magazine shut.

"Okay, Boo"—his grandmother always calls him Boo—"time for your bath and bed, birthday boy. It's been a big day."

Malcolm's grandmother, the Queen Mother of the Empress, sells castles and palaces when she's not being Queen Mother. They call her a Real Tor and she wears a man's jacket with a house decal on the breast that looks just like his F-16 decal. Each day she meets people looking for a new castle. Sometimes she takes him with her. People make very strange noises when they look about and ask the Queen Mother weird questions. Malcolm likes to explore the castles, looking for ghosts and lost elves, always on the lookout for hobgoblins, his sworn enemies.

Sometimes his grandmother, the Queen Mother, takes him to the movies and gives him candy and makes him swear he won't tell his mother, the Empress, since she'd be "disgusted with the world." Malcolm isn't allowed to have candy. But he sneaks plenty.

In the bathroom his grandmother helps him undress. He lifts his arms to get his shirt off. The water sloshes into the tub with a river's rush. The Queen Mother sprinkles the secret magic special potion into the water and it begins to bubble like a witch's cauldron.

"Okay, soldier. In you go."

"Gramma?"

"Hmmm?"

"Am I going to go to Jamaica with Daddy?"

"I doubt it very seriously."

"Will I get to go to New York with him?"

"I don't think so baby. Not for a while."

"Can I get deadlocks like his?"

"Hell no."

"Why?"

"Into the water."

The silly octopus with the glasses caresses Malcolm's ankle as he steps into the water; the bubbles tickle his hind parts as he eases down. When each one pops it says a magic word. The water is warm and heavy and fun.

"Now don't forget to wash behind your ears."

The Queen Mother leaves, and Malcolm closes his eyes and says the magic words and—Qwiza!—he is a merman with a fish-tail wide as the dining-room table, its scales diamond-shaped and sparkling and the color of oil on water, and it flops grace-fully in the air like a sail in the wind. When Malcolm is in the water he is transformed into the Lord of the Sea (a part-time job), and he must save his Dominion from the evil sea-wizard Nptananan who takes on many forms, his favorite thing that of a merwolf with fangs like a viper.

Malcolm knows when it is about time for his grandmother to come to fetch him out of the water, "so your skin won't wrinkle," she says, so in a flash he turns back into a boy. He lathers himself with the secret magic special potion soap that will make him invincible to arrows and bullets and swords and hexes. He remembers to wash behind his ears.

Grandmother, the Queen Mother, dries him off in the huge towel that could eat him whole—yet another gift from the Maharajah. In times of trouble, with the right magic words, it becomes a flying towel.

After saying good night to the Empress and the former Prince-Consort Fetasha, who once was the Crown Prince Mahammet al-Saddin, Malcolm is tucked into bed, the Nubian still fanning him. The yerple turtle sleeps bobbing in the air current; the lizards are aligned on the curtain in the pattern of the family coat-of-arms; the flying horse, Yamor, is ZZZZZZ-ing on the floor, his wings fluttering ever so gently with each breath; Fidor, the hobbit, is curled underneath the covers with Malcolm; Qwnpft, the blue cockatoo, nestles in Malcolm's hair; and the barber-pole-striped cobra coils into a perfect O at Malcolm's feet. The demons, Ksiel, Lahtiel, and Shaftiel, are secure in the closet and Malcolm can smell the pink smoke as it wafts up from underneath the door.

"Sweet dreams, Boo. Happy birthday."

"'Night."

The Archangel Rafael, right on schedule, appears in the corner when the lights go out, his blazing sword at the ready.

Voices drift up through the ventilation shaft.

"Denise, you know it would really be a good experience for him at his age."

"I've already paid for his trip down South with Mama."

"Money, money, money."

"I know, I know. I was the Marxist once, remember? I still . . . well, you know . . ."

"Oh yeah, the occasional freebie at the clinic, the volunteer work at the soup kitchen, the checks to Amnesty and the NAACP and Klanwatch and Greenpeace. You mean the payoffs for the guilt ghosts?"

"Now who's being mean? I'm not going to be a hypocrite, Bran—Fe—I can't. Mr. Dreadlocks. I've worked hard for this life. If you don't like it, fuck you and the horse you rode in on. It's my life, okay? I'm the one going to Capitalist Hell."

"But do you have to take Malcolm with you? I don't want my son to grow up to be a vain, pampered, spoiled, over-educated, suburbanite airhead with no sense of history and no sense of self."

"Like you, you mean?"

"Hey, I'm trying, okay? At least I'm—"

"Well, so am I."

". . ."

". . ."

"Look. I don't want to take the bus to the PATH to the subway to home."

"Brandon? I don't know why you won't just buy a car."

"Can I . . . ? Well . . . you know . . ."

"Oh, you're such a baby, Brandon; a cute baby, but a thirty-six-year-old baby just the same."

"Please, Dr. Harrington, ma'am, *please*. I'll wash your

turbo-engined-diesel-guzzling-air-polluting-whatever-the-hell-it-is in the morning. Please . . ."

"Stop that. You know . . . I'm . . . ooooh . . . Now quit that. Brandon. *Brandon*. You . . ."

" . . ."

" . . ."

"Remember the time we got ourselves holed up for a whole weekend and listened to nothing but Carmen MacRae and ate nothing but fruit and did it till we were sore?"

"Hmmmmmm . . . Where do you plan to sleep?"

"Right here."

"But Mama'll . . ."

"She *is* a grown woman, you know."

" . . ."

" . . ."

"I do like the way those feel."

Through the open window Malcolm can see four red eyes aflame. He knows they belong to the hobgoblins, Gog and Magog, on the lookout for him, lurking in the whispering New Jersey night. But the Archangel will protect him and there is no cause for worry. The castle is secure. The drawbridge is drawn. The Imperial Family is one. And he is six years old.

Once in a great while, now and again, deep with dreams of dreams of dreams, we may chance to hear our true selves speak, and in those words are kept the keys to ourselves; but we must listen softly, listen soundly, listen silently, or we may never hear our voices telling tales of who we are.

A Good Man

Rebecca Brown

Jim calls me in the afternoon to ask if I can give him a ride to the doctor's tomorrow because this flu thing he has is hanging on and he's decided to get something for it. I tell him I'm supposed to be going down to Olympia to help Ange and Jean remodel their spare room and kitchen. He says it's no big deal, he can take the bus. But then a couple hours later he calls me back and says could I take him now because he really isn't feeling well. So I get in my car and go over and pick him up.

Jim stands inside the front door to the building. When he

opens the door I start. His face is splotched. Sweat glistens in his week-old beard. He leans in the door frame breathing hard. He holds a brown paper grocery bag. The sides of the bag are crumpled down to make a handle. He looks so small, like a school boy being sent away from home.

"I'm not going to spend the night there," he mumbles, "but I'm bringing some socks and stuff in case."

He hobbles off the porch, his free hand grabbing the railing. I reach to take the paper bag, but he clutches it tight.

We drive to Swedish hospital and park near the Emergency Room. I lean over to hug him before we get out of the car. He's wearing four layers—T-shirt, long underwear, sweatshirt, his jacket. But when I touch his back I feel the sweat through all his clothes.

"I put these on just before you came." He sounds embarrassed.

I put an arm around him to help him inside. When he's standing at the check-in desk, I see the mark the sweat makes on his jacket.

Jim hands me the paper bag. I take his arm as we walk to the examination room to wait for a doctor. We walk slowly. Jim shuffles and I almost expect him to make his standard crack about the two of us growing old together in the ancient homos home for the prematurely senile, pinching all the candy stripers' butts, but he doesn't.

He sits down on the bed in the exam room. After he catches his breath he says, "Nice drapes."

There aren't any drapes. The room is sterile and white. Jim leans back in the chair and breathes out hard. The only other sound is the fluorescent light. He coughs.

"Say something, Tonto. Tell me story."

"–I . . . uh . . ."

I pick up a packet of tongue depressers. "Hey, look at all these. How many you think they go through in a week?"

He doesn't answer.

I take an instrument off a tray. "How 'bout this?" I turn to show him but his eyes are closed. I put it back down. When I close my mouth, the room is so quiet.

I can't tell stories the way Jim does.

A doctor comes in. She introduces herself as Dr. Allen and asks Jim the same questions he's just answered at the front desk—his fevers, his sweats, his appetite, his breath. She speaks softly, touching his arm as she listens to his answers. Then she pats his arm and says she'll be back in a minute.

In a few seconds a nurse comes in and starts poking Jim's arm to hook him up to an IV. Jim is so dehydrated she can't find the vein. She pokes him three times before one finally takes. Jim's arm is white and red. He lies there with his eyes closed, flinching.

Then Dr. Allen comes back with another doctor who asks Jim the same questions again. The doctors ask me to wait in the private waiting room because they want to do some tests on Jim. I kiss his forehead before I leave. "I'm down the hall, Jim."

Jim waves, but doesn't say anything. They close the door.

Half an hour later, Dr. Allen comes to the waiting room.

She's holding a box of Kleenex.

"Are you his sister?"

I start to answer, but she puts her hand on my arm to stop me.

"I want you to know that hospital administration does not look favorably upon our giving detailed medical information about patients out to non-family members. And they tend to look the other way if family members want to stay past regular visiting hours."

"So," I say, "I'm his sister."

"Good. Right. OK, we need to do some more tests on Jim and give him another IV, so he needs to stay the night." She pauses. "He doesn't want to. I think he needs to talk to you."

She hands me the box of Kleenex.

Jim is lying on his back, his free elbow resting over his eyes. I walk up to him and put my hand on his leg.

"Hi."

He looks up at me, then up at the IV.

"I have to have another one of these tonight so I need to stay."

I nod.

"It's not the flu. It's pneumonia."

I nod again, and keep nodding as if he were still talking. I hear the whirr of the electric clock, the squeak of nurses' shoes in the hall.

"I haven't asked what kind."

"No."

He looks at me. I take his sweaty hand in mine.

"I don't mind going," he says, "Or being gone. But I don't want to suffer long. I don't want to take a long time going."

I try to say something to him, but I can't. I want to tell him a story, but I can't say anything.

Because I've got this picture in my head of Jim's buddy Scotty, who he grew up with in Fort Worth. And I'm seeing the three of us watching "Dynasty," celebrating the new color box Jim bought for Scotty to watch at home, and I'm seeing us getting loaded on cheap champagne, and the way Scotty laughed and coughed from under the covers and had to ask me or Jim to refill his glass or light his Benson & Hedges because he was too weak to do it himself. Then I'm seeing Jim and me having a drink the day after Scotty went, and how Jim's hands shook when he opened the first pack of cigarettes we ever shared, and how a week later Jim clammed up, just clammed right up in the middle of telling me about cleaning out Scotty's room. And I think, from the way Jim isn't talking, from the way his hand is shaking in mine, that he is seeing Scotty too.

Scotty took a long time going.

Jim stays the night at Swedish. The next night. The next. He asks me to let some people know—his office, a few friends. Not his parents. He doesn't want to worry them. He asks me to bring him stuff from his apartment—clothes, books. I ask him if he wants his watercolors. He says no.

I go to see him every day. I bring him the *Times*, the *Blade*, *Newsweek*. It's easy for me to take off work. I only work as a temporary and I hate my jobs anyway, so I just don't call in. Jim likes having people visit, and lots of people come. Chubby Bob with his pink, bald head. Dale in his banker's suit. Mike the bouncer in his bomber jacket. Cindy and Bill on their way back out to Vashon. A bunch of guys from the baseball team. Denise and her man Chaz. Ange and Jeannie call him from Olympia.

We play a lot of cards. Gin rummy. Hearts when there are enough of us. Spades. Poker. We use cut-up tongue depressors for chips. I offer to bring real ones, but Jim gets a kick out of coloring them red and blue and telling us he is a very, very, very wealthy Sugar Daddy. He also gets a big kick out of cheating.

We watch a lot of tube. I sit on the big green plastic chair by the bed. Or Dale sits on the big green chair, me on his lap, and Bob on the extra folding metal chair: We watch reruns, sitcoms, *Close Encounters*. Ancient, awful Abbot and Costellos. Miniseries set between the wars. But Jim's new favorites are hospital soaps.

He becomes an instant expert on everything—all the characters' affairs, the tawdry turns of plots, the long-lost illegitimate kids. He sits up on his pillows and rants about how stupid the dialogue is, how unrealistic the gore:

"Oh come on. I could do a better gun-shot wound with a paint-by-numbers set!

"Is that supposed to be a bruise?! Yo mama, pass me the hammer now. Now!

"If that's the procedure for a suture, I am Betty Grable's legs."

He narrates softly in his stage aside: "Enter tough-as-nails head nurse. Exit sensitive young intern. Enter political appointment in admin, a shady fellow not inspired by a noble urge to help his fellow human. Enter surgeon with a secret. Exit secretly addicted pharmacist."

Then during commercials he tells us gossip about the staff here at Swedish which is far juicier than anything on TV. We howl at his trashy tales until he shushes us when the show comes back on. We never ask if what he says is true. And even if we did, Jim wouldn't tell us.

But most of the time, because I'm allowed to stay after hours as his sister, it's Jim and me alone. We stare up at the big color box, and it stares down at us like the eye of God. Sometimes Jim's commentary drifts, and sometimes he is silent. Sometimes when I look over and his eyes are closed, I get up to switch off the set, but he blinks and says, "I'm not asleep. Don't turn it off. Don't go." Because he doesn't want to be alone.

Then, more and more, he sleeps and I look up alone at the plots that end in nothing, at the almost true-to-life colored shapes, at the hazy ghosts that trail behind the bodies when they move.

Jim and I met through the temporary agency. I'd lost my teaching job and he'd decided to quit bartending because he and Scotty were becoming fanatics about their baseball team and consequently living really clean. This was good for me because I was trying, well, I was thinking I really ought to try, to clean it up a bit myself. Anyway, Jim and I had lots of awful jobs together—filing, answering phones, xeroxing, taking coffee around to arrogant fat-cat lawyers, stuffing envelopes, sticking number labels on pages and pages of incredibly stupid documents, then destroying those same documents by feeding them through the shredder. The latter was the only of these jobs I liked; I liked the idea of it. I like being paid five bucks an hour to turn everything that someone else had done into pulp.

After a while, Jim got a real, permanent job, with benefits, at one of these places. But I couldn't quite stomach the thought of making that kind of commitment.

We stayed in touch though. Sometimes I'd work late xeroxing and Jim would come entertain me and play on the new color copier. He came up with some wild things—erasing bits, then painting over them, changing the color combos, double copying. All this from a machine that was my sworn enemy for eight hours a day. We'd have coffee or go out to a show or back to their place so Scotty could try one of his experiments in international cuisine on us before he took it to the restaurant. Also, Jim helped me move out of my old apartment.

But Jim and I really started hanging out together a lot after Scotty. Jim had a bunch of friends, but I think he wanted not to be around where he and Scotty had been together so much: the dinner parties and dance bars, the clubs, the baseball team. So he chose to run around with me. To go out drinking.

We met for a drink the day after Scotty. Then a week later,

we did again. Over the third round Jim started to tell me about cleaning out Scotty's room. But all the sudden he clammed up, he just clammed right up and left. He wouldn't let me walk home with him. I tried calling him but he wouldn't answer.

Then a couple weeks later he called me and said, "Wanna go for a drink?" like nothing had happened.

We met at Lucky's. I didn't say anything about what he had started to talk about the last time we'd met, and he sure didn't mention it. Well, actually, maybe he did. We always split our tab, and this round was going to be mine. But when I reached for my wallet, he stopped me.

"This one's on me, Tonto."

"Tonto?"

"The Lone Ranger." He pointed to himself. "Rides again."

He clinked his glass to mine. "So saddle up, Tonto. We're going for a ride."

We had a standing date for Friday, six o'clock, the Lucky. With the understanding that if either of us got a better offer, we just wouldn't show up and the other would know to stop waiting about 6:30 or so. However, neither of us ever got a better offer. But we had a great time talking predator. We'd park ourselves in a corner behind our drinks and eye the merchandise. Me scouting guys for him; him looking at women for me.

"He's cute. Why don't we ask him to join us."

"Not my type . . . but mmm-mmm-mmm I think somebody likes you."

"Who?"

"That one."

"Jim, I've never see her before in my life."

"I think she likes you."

"I think she looks like a donkey. But hey, he looks really sweet. Go on, go buy him a drink."

A few times I showed up at six and saw Jim already ensconced in our corner charming some innocent, unsuspecting woman he was planning to spring on me. I usually did an abrupt about-face out of Lucky's. But one time he actually dragged me to the table to meet whoever she was. Fortunately that evening was such a disaster he didn't try that tactic again.

After a while our standing joke began to wear a little thin. I cooled it on eyeballing guys for him, but he kept teasing me, making up these incredible stories about my wild times with every woman west of the Mississippi. It bugged me for a while, but I didn't say anything. For starters, Jim wasn't the kind of guy you said shut-up to. And then, after a longer while, I realized he wasn't talking just to entertain us. His talk, his ploys to find someone for me, were his attempts to make the story of a good romance come true. Jim had come to the conclusion that neither he, nor many of his brotherhood, could any longer hope to live the good romance. He told me late one bleary, double-whiskey night, "Us boys are looking at the ugly end of the Great Experiment, Tonto. I sure hope you girls don't get in a mess like us. Ya'll will be OK, won't you? Won't ya'll girls be OK?"

Because Jim still desired, despite what he'd been through with Scott, despite how his dear brotherhood was crumbling, that some of his sibling outlaws would find good love and live in that love openly, and for a good long time, a longer time than he and Scott had had. He wanted this for everyone who marched 3rd Avenue each June, for everyone that he considered family.

He's sitting up against his pillows. I toss him the new *Texas Monthly* and kiss him hello on the forehead. He slaps his hands down on the magazine and in his sing-song voice says, "I think someone likes you!"

I roll my eyes.

He gives me his bad-cat grin. "Don't you want to know who?"

"I bet you'll tell me anyway."

"Dr. Allen."

"Oh come on, Jim, she's straight."

"And how do you know, Miss Lock-Up-Your-Daughters? Just because she doesn't wear overalls and a workshirt."

"Jim, you're worse than a Republican."

"I am, I am a wicked, wicked, boy. I must not disparage the Sisterhood." He flings his skinny hand up in a fist. "Right On Sister!"

I try not to laugh.

"Still, what if Dr. Allen is a breeder? I'm sure she'd be very interested in having you impart to her The Love Secrets of the Ancient Amazons."

"Jim, I'm not interested . . ."

"Honey, I been watching you. I seen you scratching. I know you been itchin' fer some bitchin'."

He makes it hard not to laugh.

"Jim, if you don't zip it up, I'll have to shove a bedpan down your throat."

"In that case I'm even gladder it's about time for Dr. Allen's rounds. She'll be able to extract it from me with her maaaar-velous hands."

And in sails Dr. Allen, a couple of interns in tow. I get up to leave.

"Oh, you don't have to leave." She smiles at me. "This is just a little check-in with Jim."

Jim winks at me behind her back.

I sit down in the folding metal chair by the window and look at downtown, at Elliott Bay, the slate gray water, the thick white sky. But I also keep looking back as Dr. Allen feels Jim's pulse, his forehead, listens to his chest. She asks him to open his mouth. She asks him how it's going today.

"Terrific. My lovely sister always cheers me up. She's such a terrific woman, you know."

I stare out the window as hard as I can.

Dr. Allen says how nice it is that Jim has such nice visitors, then tells him she'll see him later.

"See you," she says to me as she leaves.

"Yeah, see you."

The second she's out the door, Jim says, more loudly than he usually talks, "That cute Dr. Allen is such a terrific woman!"

"Jim!!" I shush him.

"And so good with her hands," he grins. "Don't you think she's cute? I think she's cute. Almost as cute as you are when you blush."

I turn away and stare out the window again. Sure I'm blushing. And sure, I'm thinking about Dr. Allen. But what I'm thinking is why, when she was looking at him, she didn't say, "You're looking good today, Jim." Or, "You're coming right along, Jim." Or "We're gonna have to let you out of here soon, Jim, you're getting too healthy for us."

Why won't she tell him something like that?

There's a wheelchair in his room. Shiny stainless steel frame, padded leather seat. Its arms look like an electric chair.

He's so excited he won't let me kiss him hello. "That's Silver. Your dear friend Dr. Allen says I can go out for some fresh air today."

"Really?" I'm skeptical. He's hooked to an IV again.

"Gotta take advantage of the sun. Saddle up, Tonto."

He presses the buzzer. In a couple of minutes an aide comes in to transfer the IV from his bed to the pole sticking up from the back of the chair. The drip bag hangs like a toy. I help Jim into his jacket and cap, put a cover across his lap and slide his hospital slippers up over his woolly socks.

"Are you sure you feel up to this?"

"Sure I'm sure. And if I don't get a cup of non-hospital coffee, I am going to lynch someone."

"OK, OK, I'll be back in a minute. I gotta go to the bath-room."

I go to the nurses' station.

"Can Jim really go out today?"

The guy at the desk looks up.

"Dr. A says it's fine. You guys can go across the street to Rex's or something. A lot of patients do. They uh . . . don't have the same rules as the hospital." He puckers his lips and puts two fingers up to mime smoking.

"Uh-huh. Got it."

Back in the room I take the black plastic handles of the chair and start to push.

Jim flings his hand in the air, "Hi-Yo Silver!"

I wheel him into the hall, past doctors and aides in clean white coats, past metal trays full of plastic buckets and rubber gloves and neat white stacks of linens. Past skinny guys shuffling along in housecoats and slippers.

The elevator is huge, wide enough to carry a couple of stretchers. Jim and I are the only ones in it. I feel like we're the only people in a submarine, sinking down to some dense, cold other world where we won't be able to breathe. Jim watches the elevator numbers. I watch the orange reflection of the lights against his eyes.

When the elevator opens to the bustling main entrance foyer, his eyes widen. It isn't as white and quiet as he's gotten used to. In his attempt to tell himself he isn't so bad off, he's made himself forget what health looks like. I see him stare, wide-eyed and silent, as a man runs across the foyer to hug a friend, as a woman bends down to pick up a kid. I push him slowly across the foyer in case he wants to change his mind.

When the electric entry doors slide open he gasps.

"Let's blow this popcorn stand, baby." He nods across the street to Rex's. "Carry me back to the ol' saloon."

I push him out to the sidewalk. It's rougher than the slick floor of the building. Jim grips the arms of the wheelchair. We wait at the crosswalk for the light to change, Jim hunching in his wheelchair in the middle of a crowd of people standing. People glance at him then glance away. I look down at the top of his cap, the back of his neck, his shoulders.

When the light changes everyone surges across Madison. I ease the chair down where the sidewalk dips then push him into the pedestrian crossing. We're the only ones left in the street when the light turns green.

"Get a move on, Silver."

The wheels tremble, the metal rattles, the IV on the pole above him shakes. The liquid shifts. Jim's hands tighten like an armchair football fan's. His veins stand up. He sticks his head forward as if he could help us move. I push us to the other side.

We clatter into Rex's. There's the cafeteria line and a bunch of chairs and tables. I steer him to an empty table, pull a chair away and slide him in.

"Jesus," he mumbles, "I feel like a kid in a high chair."

"Coffee?"

"Yeah. And a packet of Benson & Hedges."

"Jim."

"Don't argue. If God hadn't wanted us to smoke, he wouldn't have created the tobacco lobby."

"Jim."

"For god's sake Tonto, what the hell difference will a cigarette make?"

While I stand in line, I glance at him. He's looking out the long wall of windows to Madison, watching people walk by on their own two feet, all the things they carry in their hands—briefcases, backpacks, shopping bags, umbrellas. The people in Rex's look away from him. I'm glad we're only across the street from the hospital.

I put the tray on the table in front of him. He puts his hand out for his coffee, but can't quite reach it. I hand him his cup and take mine.

"Did you get matches?"

"Light up."

"It's good to be out . . . So tell me, Tonto, how's the wild west been in my absence?"

"Oh, you know, same as ever . . ."

"Don't take it lightly, pardner. Same as ever is a fucking miracle."

I don't know whether to apologize or not.

When we finish our cigarettes, he points. "Another."

I light him one.

"You shouldn't smoke so much," he says as I light another for myself.

"What?! You're the one who made me haul you across the street for a butt."

"And you drink too much."

"Jim, get off my case."

He pauses. "You've got something to lose, Tonto."

I look away from him.

He sighs. "We didn't use to be so bad, did we Tonto? When did we get so bad?"

I don't say, After Scotty.

He shakes his head as if he could shake away what he is thinking. "So clean it up, girl. As a favor to the Ranger? As a favor to the ladies? Take care of that luscious body-thang of yours. Yes? Yes?"

I roll my eyes.

"Promise?"

"Jim . . ." I never make promises; nobody ever keeps them.

"Promise me."

I shrug a shrug he could read as a no or yes. He knows it's all he'll get from me. He exhales through his nose like a very disappointed maiden aunt. Then slowly, regretfully, pushes the cigarettes towards me.

"These are not for you to smoke. They're for you to keep for me because La Dottoressa and her dancing Kildairettes won't let anyone keep them in the hospital. So I am entrusting them to you to bring for me when we have our little outings. And I've counted them; I'll know if you steal any."

"OK."

"Girl Scouts' honor?"

"OK, OK."

The cellophane crackles when I slip them into my jacket.

"Now. Back to the homestead, Tonto."

The Riding Days:

One hung-over morning when Jim and I were swaying quea-sily on the very crowded number 10 bus to downtown, I bumped into, literally, Amy. She was wearing some incredible perfume.

"Hi," I tried to sound normal. I gripped the leather ceiling strap tighter. "What are you doing out at this hour? On the bus?"

"Well, the Nordie's sale is starting today and I want to be there early. But Brian's car is in the shop so he couldn't drop me off."

"Jeez. Too bad."

"Oh, it's not that bad. He'll be getting a company car today to tide us over."

"How nice."

She smiled her pretty smile at Jim but I didn't introduce them. She got off at the Nordstrom stop.

After she got off, Jim said, "She's cute, why don't you—"

"She's straight," I snapped. "She's a breeder. Now. She used to be the woman I used to live with. In the old apartment."

"The one you've never told me about," he said.

I stared into the back of the coat of the man squished in front of me. "Jim, shut up."

"I'm sorry, babe . . ." He tried to put his arm around me.

I wriggled away from him.

"Hey, she's not that cute," he said when I jumped off the bus at the next stop. It was several blocks from work, but I wanted to walk.

That afternoon, Jim sent me a box of chocolates. The chocolates were delivered to me in the xerox room. They were delivered with a card. "Forget the ugly bitch. Eat us instead, you luscious thang." I shared the chocolates with the office. They made the talk, the envy of the office for a week. I kept the contents of the card a secret.

Jim sweet-talked my apartment manager into letting him into my tiny little studio apartment so he could leave me six—*six*—vases of flowers around my room when I turned twenty-seven. He taught me how to iron shirts. He wore a top hat when we went to see the Fred and Ginger festival at the U. He knew that the solution for everything, for almost everything, was a peanut butter and guacamole sandwich. He placed an ad in the *Gay News* for Valentine's Day which said, "Neurotic lesbian still on rebound seeks females for short, intense, physical encounters. No breeders." And my phone number. Then let me stay at his place and laughed at me because I was afraid the phone might ring. He brought me horrible instant cinnamon and fake apple flavored oatmeal the mornings I slept on his couch, the mornings after we'd both had more than either of us could handle and didn't want to be in our apartments alone, and said, "This'll zap your brain into gear, Mrs. Frankenstein," and threw me a clean, fresh, ironed shirt to wear to work. He fed Trudy his whole-food hippie cookies to keep her quiet so he and I could sneak out to Jean and Ange's porch for a cigarette and a couple of draws on the flask.

He wore his ridiculous bright green bermuda shorts and wagged his ass like crazy, embarrassing the hell out of me, at the Gay Pride March. He raised his fist and yelled, "Ride On, Sister, Ride On!" to the Dykes on Bikes. He slapped high-heeled, mini-skirted queens on the back and said in a husky he-man voice, "Keep the faith, brother." I got afraid some guy might slap him or hit him with his purse, or some woman might slug him. When I started to say something, Jim stopped. The march kept streaming down 3rd Avenue beside us. The June sun hit me on the head and Jim glared at me. He crossed his arms across his chest like he was trying to keep from yelling.

"Tonto, what the hell are you afraid of anyway? You may like to think of us all as a bunch of unbalanced, volatile perverts, but every single screaming fairy prancing down this boulevard and every last one of you pissed-off old Amazons is my family. My kith and my kin and my kind. My siblings. Your siblings. And if you're so worried about their behavior you should just turn your chickenshit ass around and crawl back into the nearest closet because you are on the wrong fucking ride."

I didn't say anything. He stared at me several seconds. Then a couple of punky women dancing to their boom box dragged Jim along with them. I watched their asses wag off in front of me. I started to walk. But I was ashamed to march with him again. Then, when he saw the Educational Service District workers contingent in front of us, their heads covered in paper sacks because you can still be fired from your state school teaching job for being queer, Jim turned around and hollered, "At least you don't have to keep your sweet gorgeous sexy face covered like that anymore, Tonto." I stared at my pathetic, scared, courageous former colleagues. Jim pranced back to me and yanked me into a chorus line where everyone, all these brave, tough pansies, these heroic, tender dykes, had their arms around each others' backs. Jim pulled me along. I felt the firmness of his chest against my shoulder.

"This is the way it's gonna be, Tonto. Someday it's all gonna be this great."

He laughed at his own stories and he clapped at his own jokes. And he never, never, despite how many times I asked, told me which stories he'd made up, which ones were true.

And sometimes, when he's holding court from his hospital bed, and he's in the middle of telling us some outrageous story, making all of us laugh, and we're all laughing, I forget. When he's telling it like there's no tomorrow—no—like there *is*—I just forget how he is in his body.

He gets over something, then gets something else. Then he gets better then he gets worse. Then he begins to look OK and says he's ready to go home. Then he gets worse. Then he gets something else.

On the days they think he's up to it, they let me take him out. A couple times both of us walk, but other times he rides. They call it his constitutional. We call it his faggot break.

I bring him a cup of Rex's coffee and throw the cigarettes across the table to him. He counts them, purses his lips and says, "You *are* a good Girl Scout." Then he leans toward me, gestures like a little old lady for me to put my ear up close to him.

"She's just trying to make you jealous," he whispers.

"What?"

"Doc-tor A-llen," he mouths silently.

He nods across Rex's to a table in the no-smoking section. Dr. Allen is having a cup of coffee with a woman.

"She knows we come here, she hopes you'll see her with another woman and be forced to take action."

"Jim . . ."

I'm sure Dr. Allen has seen us, Jim and me and the ciga-rettes, but I'm hoping she's taking a break from being doctor long enough to not feel obliged to come over and give Jim some healthy advice.

"She likes you *very much*, you know."

"Jim, I've probably had five minutes of conversation with the woman," I whisper, "all about you."

"Doesn't matter. It's chemistry. Animal maaag-netism."

He wants me to laugh.

"Come on, Jim. Give it a rest . . ."

He turns around to look at Dr. Allen. Then he looks back at me. He takes a long drag on his cigarette. He tries to sound buoyant. "Hey, I'm just trying to get you a buddy, Tonto. Who you gonna ride with when the Ranger's gone?"

One time Jim told me, this is what he said, he said, "A lie is what you tell when you're a chicken shit. But a story is what you tell for good."

"Even if it isn't true?"

"It's true. If you tell a story for good, it's true."

I had had them twice and they were always great. They truly, truly may have been the best sour cream enchiladas on the planet. But that time, after two bites, Jim threw down his fork.

"These suck."

"Jim, they're fine."

"They suck."

He pushed the plate away. "I can't eat this shit."

I handed him the hot sauce and the guacamole. "Add a little of these"

"I said I cannot eat this crap." He lifted his hands like he was trying to push something away. I started to clear the table.

"Leave it. *Leave it.*"

I put the plate down. I looked away from him. Then at him. "Let's go out for Chinese."

He didn't say anything, just nodded.

I ordered everything: egg rolls, hot and sour soup, moo goo gai pan, garlic pork, veg, rice, a few beers. He asked me to tell him a story and I did. A lewd, insulting, degrading tale about a guy at the temp agency, a swishy little closet case we both despised. I told about him being caught, bare-assed, his pecker in his paw, in the 35th floor supply room by one of the directors. Jim adored the story. He laughed really loud. He laughed until he cried. He didn't ask if it was true.

We ate everything. All the plum sauce. All the little crackers. Every speck of rice. But we didn't open our fortune cookies.

On the way home, Jim put his arm around me and said, "You're learning, Tonto."

The enchiladas were a recipe of Scotty's.

The door is half closed. I take one step in. There's a sweeping sound in the room, a smell. The curtain has been drawn around the bed. I see a silhouette moving.

"Jim?"

"Go away." His voice is little. "I made a mess."

An aide in a white coat peeks around the curtain. He's holding a mop. He's wearing plastic gloves, a white mask over his mouth and nose. I leave.

I go up to the Rose. Rosie sees me coming through the door. She's poured a schooner for me by the time I reach the bar.

"Jesus, woman." She leans over the bar to look at me as I'm climbing onto the barstool.

"Shrunken body, shrunken head . . . gonna be nothing left of you soon, girl."

I reach for the beer. She stops my hand.

"We don't serve alcohol alone. You have to order something to eat with it."

"Gimme a break, Rosie. I have one dollar and—" I fish into my jeans, "55 . . . 56 . . . 57 cents."

"Sorry pal. It's policy."

"Since when."

"Since now. It's a special policy for you."

"Rosie, please."

"Don't mess with the bartender."

I drop my face into my hands. "Please Rosie."

She lifts my chin and looks at me. "If you promise to clean your plate, we'll put it on your tab."

"You don't run tabs."

She points to her chest. "I'm the boss."

As I'm finishing my beer she slaps a plate in front of me—a huge bacon-cheeseburger with all the trimmings. A mound of fries. A pint glass of milk.

She writes out the bill and pockets it. "We'll talk."

"Thanks."

I take a bite. She puts her elbows on the bar.

"How's Jim?"

"The same." My mouth is full.

She cocks her head.

I swallow. "Worse."

"Jeez . . ." She touches my arm. "Eat, honey. Eat something."

I eat. Sesame seed bun. Bacon. Mustard. Lettuce. Pickles. Tomatoes. Cheese. Meat. Grease on my fingers. I chew and swallow. It is so easy.

Jim on the drip-feed. Jim not keeping anything down. Or shitting it out in no time. His throat and asshole sore from everything that comes up, that runs through him. His oozy mouth. His bloody gums.

A hand on my back. "Hi."

I turn and almost choke. "You're Jim's—"

I nod. "Yeah, right." I swallow. "You're Doctor Allen. Hi."

I wipe my mouth and hands on the napkin.

She's saying to the woman she's with, "This is Jim's sister," as if her friend's already heard of Jim. Or of, me. Dr. Allen extends her hand to me. "Please, my name's Patricia."

I shake her hand.

"And this is my sister Amanda. It's her first time here—I mean—here in Seattle." She does this nervous little laugh. "She's visiting from Buffalo."

It's the woman she was having coffee with at Rex's.

"Oh Buffalo," I say, "How nice."

"I've come to see if poor Pat's life is really as boring as she tells me it is. Doesn't have to be does it?" the sister says with a grin.

I don't know what to answer. I do this little laugh.

They both look around the bar. Not wide, serious check-out sweeps of their heads, but shy quick glances. They certainly aren't old hands at this. And I think I see two different varieties of nerves here. I try to read which is the tolerant, supportive sister, and which is the one who wanted to come to this particular bar in the first place.

"Mind if we join you?"

"Uh, no. Sure. Great."

I gesture to the empty barstool next to me, then I stand up and gesture to my own. "But I was just going, actually . . . here, have my stool." I down half the glass of milk. "Gotta be at work early in the morning," I lie.

They look at each other and at me. I feel like one of them's about to laugh, but I don't know which. Dr. Allen sits on my stool. Jim's right. She is pretty cute.

I gulp down the rest of the milk, slap my hands on the bar and shout into the kitchen, "I owe you Rosie!"

I say to the sister, "Nice to meet you. Have a nice time in Seattle." And to the Doctor, "Nice to bump into you. See you 'round."

Then I'm standing outside on the sidewalk, shaking.

Because maybe, if I had stayed there in the bar with them, and had them buy me a beer or two, or coaxed a couple more out of Rosie, maybe I would have asked, "So which of you is the supportive sister, and which of you is the dyke?" Or maybe I would have asked, "So how 'bout it ladies. Into which of your lovely beds might I more easily insinuate myself?"

Or maybe I would have asked—no—no—but maybe I would have asked, "So, Dr. Allen, you are pretty cute, how 'bout it. How long 'til Jim goes?"

I bring him magazines and newspapers. The *Times*, the *Blade*, the *Body Politic*. They all run articles. Apparent answers, possible solutions, almost cures. Experiments and wonder drugs. A new technique. But more and more the stories are of failures. False starts. The end of hope.

Bob's been coughing the last few times he's been here. He's still at it today.

Bob coughs. I look at Dale. He looks away.

One evening in the middle of "Marcus Welby," Jim announces, "I'm bored outta my tits, girls. I wanna have a party."

Mike, who's been drooping in front of the TV set, sits up.

"I say I am ready for a paaaaar-tay!"

Mike says, "Jimmy boy, you're on."

We OK it with Dr. Allen. Mike raids the stationery store on Broadway for paper hats and confetti and party favors and cards. We call everyone and it's on for the evening after next. They limit the number of people allowed in a room at a time so Mike and I take turns hanging out by the elevator to do crowd control. Jim shrieks, he calls me "Tonto the Bouncer" and flexes his arm in a skinny little she-man biceps. It's great to see everybody, and everyone brings Jim these silly presents: an inflatable plastic duck, a shake-up scene of the Space Needle, a couple of incredibly ugly fuzzy animals, a bouquet of balloons. Somebody brings him a child's watercolor set; it's the only gift he doesn't gush about.

When I start to clean the wrapping paper, he says, "Oh leave it a while." He likes the shiny colors and the rustling sound the paper makes when he shifts in bed.

When anybody leaves, he blows a kiss and says, "Bye-bye cowpoke," "Happy Trails."

He knows what he's doing.

I see it when I'm coming down the hall, a laminated sign on the door of his room. I tiptoe the last few yards because I don't want him to hear me stop to read it, acting as if I believe what it says. It's a warning, like something you'd see on a pack of cigarettes or a bottle of pesticide. It warns about the contents. It tells you not to touch. I push myself into his room before I can give myself a chance to reconsider.

I push myself towards his bed, towards his forehead to give him his regular kiss hello.

"Don't touch me."

When he pushes me away, I'm relieved.

"Do you realize they're wearing plastic gloves around me all the time now? Face masks? They've put my wallet and clothes into plastic bags. As if me and my stuff is gonna jump on 'em and bleed all over 'em, as if my sweat—"

"Jim, that's bullshit. This isn't the Middle Ages, it's 1984. And they're medical people, they should know they don't need to do that. Haven't they read—"

"Why don't you go tell 'em, Tonto? Why don't you just march right over to 'em with all your little newspaper articles and you just tell 'em the truth."

"I will, Jim, I'll—"

"Oh for fuck's sake, Tonto, they are medical people. They know what they're doing." He covers his eyes with a hand and says wearily, "And I know what my body is doing."

He holds his skinny white hand over his eyes. I can see the bones of his forearm, the bruises on his pale, filmy skin. He looks like an old man. The sheet rises and falls unevenly with his breath.

I ought to hold him but I don't want to.

"Jim?" I say, "Jim?" I don't know if he's listening.

Inside the belt-line of my jeans, down the middle of my back and on my stomach, I feel myself begin to sweat. I start to babble. A rambling, unconnected pseudo-summary of articles I haven't brought him, a doctor-ed precis of inoperative statements, edited news-speak, jargon, evasions, unmeant promises, lies.

But I'm only half thinking of what I say, and I'm not thinking of Jim at all.

I'm thinking of me. And of how my stomach clutched when he said that about the sweat. I'm thinking that I want to get out of his room immediately and wash my hands and face and take a shower and boil my clothes and get so far away from him that I won't have to breathe the air he's breathed. Then further, to where he can't see how I, like everyone I like to think I'm so different from, can desert him at the drop of a hat, before the drop of a hat, because my good-girl Right-On-Sister sympathies extend only as far as my assurance of my immunity from what is killing him. But once the thought occurs to me that I might be in danger I'll be the first bitch on the block to saddle up and leave him in the dust.

I don't know what I say to him; I know I don't touch him.

After a while he offers me a seat to watch TV, but I don't sit. I tell him I've got to go. I tell him I have a date. He knows I'm lying.

I look around for Dr. Allen. She tells me she thinks this recent hospital policy is ludicrous. "It just increases everybody's hysteria. There's no evidence of contagion through casual contact. If these people . . ." But I don't listen to the rest of what she says. My mind is still repeating *no evidence of contagion through casual contact.* I'm so relieved I'm taken out of danger. I realize I'm happier than if she'd told me Jim was going to live.

I don't listen until I hear her asking me something. I don't hear the words, just the tone in her voice.

"Huh?"

She looks at me hard. Then shakes her head and turns away. She knows what I was thinking, where the line of my loyalty runs out.

The next day before I visit him, I ask Dr. Allen, "Are you sure, if I only touch him . . ."

It's the only time she doesn't look cute. She practically spits. "You won't risk anything by hugging your brother."

Her eyes make a hole in my back as I walk to his room.

I hug him very carefully, how I believe I can stay safe. He holds me longer than he usually does. He doesn't say anything, when I pull away, about the fact that I don't kiss his forehead, which shines with sweat.

"Come here," he says in his lecher voice, "Daddy's got some candy for you."

He hands me a hundred dollar bill.

"What's this?"

"What I still owe you for the TV."

"What?"

"The hundred bucks I borrowed for the color TV."

Jim wanted to buy it for Scotty when all Scotty could do was watch TV. Jim wasn't going to get paid until the end of the month so I lent it to him. He wanted to pay me back immediately but he kept having all these bills.

"Dale withdrew it from the bank for me."

"I don't want it."

He glares at me. "The Ranger is a man of honor, Tonto."

"OK, OK, but I don't want it now."

He keeps glaring. "So you want it later? You gonna ride into Wells Fargo bank and tell them part of my estate is yours?"

"Dale can—" I close my eyes.

"I owe you, Tonto. Take Dr. Allen out for the time of her life."

"Jim . . ."

"Goddammit, it's all I can do."

He grabs me by the belt loop of my jeans and tries to pull me toward him but he's too weak. I step toward the bed. He stuffs the bill into my pocket.

"Now go away please. I'm tired."

Was this a conversation? Was it a story?

I wish Scotty knew how I felt about him.

He knew.

I never told him. I wish I'd said the words.

He knew.

How do you know?

He told me.

Did he? What did he say?

Scotty told me, he said, Jim loves me.

Did he really?

Yes.

Did he say anything else?

Yes. He said, I love Jim.

He said he loved me?

More than anything.

Is that true?

Yes, Jim, it's true.

This is how I learn to tell a story.

We stay away for longer than we ought. I tell him it's time to go back, but he whines like a boy who doesn't want recess to end. He chatters. For the first time since I've known him, he starts retelling stories he has told to me before, stories that lose a lot in the retelling. But finally he runs out of things to say and lets me wheel him out of Rex's.

There's a traffic jam. Cars are backed up to Broadway and everybody's honking. A couple blocks away a moving van is trying to turn onto a narrow street. People at the crosswalk are getting impatient. They look around for cops and when they don't see any, start crossing Madison between the cars.

"I'm cold," says Jim.

He puts his free hand under his blanket. I lean down to tuck the cover more closely around his legs. His face is white.

"I'm cold," he grumbles again, "I wanna go back in."

"In a minute, Jim. We can't go yet."

"But I'm freezing." He looks up. "Where's the fucking sun anyway?"

I take my jacket off and wrap it around his shoulders. The cellophane of the cigarette package crinkles. I take care not to hit the drip feed tube.

People start laying on their horns. The poor stupid van ahead is moving forward then back, inch by inch, trying to squeeze around the corner.

"It's moving, Jim. The truck's going."

"About time," he says loudly, "Doesn't the driver realize what he's holding up here?"

Then the truck stalls. There's the gag of the engine, silence, the rev of the motor, the sputter when the engine floods.

"Someone go tell that goddamn driver what he's holding up here."

People in their cars look out at Jim.

"I've got to get back in," he screams, "Go! Go!" He starts shooing the cars with his hands. The drip feed swings.

I grab his arm. "Jim, the IV."

"Fuck the IV!" he yells, "Fuck the traffic. I'm going back in. I have to get back in."

"We're going, Jim, the traffic's moving now," I lie. "We're going in. Settle down, OK?"

He pushes himself up a couple of inches to see the truck. "The truck isn't moving, Tonto."

He kicks his blanket awry and tries to find the ground with his feet. "I'm walking."

"Jim, you can't."

"So what am I supposed to do. Fly?"

"You're supposed to wait. When the traffic clears—"

"I'm sick of waiting. You said it was clearing. You lied to me. I'm sick of everyone lying. I'm sick of waiting. I'm sick—" His voice cracks.

I put my hand on his arm. "When the traffic clears I'm going to push you and Silver across the street."

"It's not a horse," he screams, "it's a goddamn wheelchair!"

He starts to tremble. He grips the arms of the chair. "It's a wheelchair full of goddamn croaking faggot!" He slaps his hands over his face and whispers, "Tonto, I don't wanna. Don't let me—I don't wanna—I don't wanna—"

I put my arms around him and pull him to me. His head is against my collarbone. His cap falls off his sweaty head. I try to hold him. He lets me a couple of seconds then he tries to pull away. He isn't strong enough. But I know what he means so I pull back. He grabs my shirt, one of his.

"I don't wanna—" he cries, "I don't wanna—"

I put my hands on his back of his head and pull him to my chest.

"I don't wanna—I don't wanna—" he sobs.

His hands and face are wet. I hold his head.

He grabs me like a child wanting something good.

When we get back to his room he's still crying. I ring for Dr. Allen. Jim asks me to leave.

I pace around in the hall. When Dr. Allen comes out of his room, she says, "He's resting. He isn't good but he's not as bad as you think. He won't want to see you for a while. Now we can't pretend he's not afraid. You can call the nurses' station tonight if you're concerned, but don't come see him till tomorrow. And call first."

I want to tell her to tell him a story, to make him not afraid. But I don't. I say, "I'm going to call his parents."

She looks at me.

"*Our* parents," I mumble.

"He hasn't wanted his family to know?"

"Right."

"Call them."

I call his parents that night. They say they'll fly out in the morning and be able to be with him by noon. I tell them I'll book them a hotel a five minute walk from the hospital. They want to take the airport bus in themselves.

I call him in the morning.

"Hey, buddy."

"Yo Tonto."

"Listen, you want anything special today? I'm doing my Christmas shopping on the way down to see you."

"No you're not."

"Who says?"

"Santa says. I called Jean and Ange this morning and you're going down there for the week. That remodeling you were supposed to help them with way back is getting moldy. So it's the bright lights of Olympia for you, Sex-cat."

"Jim . . ."

"You have to go. They're going to pay you."

"What?!"

"They said they'd have to pay somebody, and they're afraid to have a common laborer around the priceless silver. So they want you. And it's not like you've been earning it hand over fist since you've been playing candy-striper with me."

"Jim, they don't have any money."

"They do now. Jeannie managed to lawyer-talk her way into some loot for her latest auto disaster and Ange is determined to spend the cash before Jeannie throws it away on another seedy lemon. So, Tonto, you got to go. It's your sororal duty."

It was impossible to talk Jim out of anything.

"Give my best to the girls and tell Trudy the Sentinal Bitch I said a bark is a bark is a bark."

"Doesn't Alice get a hello?"

"Alice is stupid. I will not waste my sparkling wit on her."

"OK . . ."

Were we going to get through this entire conversation without a mention of yesterday?

"So Tonto, the Ranger is much improved today . . . My folks called a while ago from DFW airport. They're on their way to see me. Thanks for calling them."

"Sure."

"We'll see you next week then."

"Right."

He hangs up the phone before I can tell him goodbye.

I drive to Olympia. Ange is outside chopping wood. When I pull into the yard she slings the axe into the center of the block. She gives me a huge hug, her great soft arms around my back, her breasts and belly big and solid against me. She holds me a long time, kisses my hair.

"Hi baby."

"Ange."

She puts her arm around my back and brings me inside. The

house smells sweet. They're baking. Jeannie blows me a kiss
from the kitchen.

"Hello gorgeous!"

"Jeannie my darling."

I warm my hands by the wood stove. Ange yells at Gertrude,
their big ugly German shepherd, to shut up. She's a very talk-
ative dog. Jeannie brings in a plate of whole wheat cookies. I
pick up Alice the cat from the couch and drop her on the floor.
She is a stupid cat. She never protests anything. I sit on the
place she's made warm on the couch. Jean hands me the plate.
The cookies are still warm. I hesitate. It always amazes me they
can, along with Jeannie's law school scholarship, support themselves by selling this horrible homemade hippie food to health
food joints.

I take a cookie. "Thanks."

"How's Jim?"

"OK . . ."

"Bad?"

"Yeah."

"He sounded incredibly buoyant on the phone, so we figured . . . we told him we'd come up to see him next week when
we've finished some of this." She nods at the cans and boards
and drywall stacked up outside the spare room.

"Let's get to work."

"Yeah. Let's do it."

Ange puts an old Janis Joplin on the stereo. We knock the
hell out of the walls.

They cook a very healthy dinner. As she's about to sit down,
Jeannie says, "Hey, we got some beer in case you wanted one.
Want one?" Ange and Jean haven't kept booze in their house
for years.

"No thanks." There's a jar of some hippie fruit juice on the table. "This is fine."

They look at each other. We eat.

I sleep on the couch in the living room. Gertrude sleeps in front of the wood stove. I listen to her snort. She turns around in circles before she settles down to sleep, her head out on her paws.

Jim and I used to flip for who got the couch and who got the tatami mat on the floor next to the dog. I lean up on my elbow to look at Trudy the Sentinal Bitch. Only Jim could have re-named her that. In the bedroom Ange and Jean talk quietly.

All the junk has been moved from the spare room into the living room. Some of it is stacked at the end of the couch. I toss the blanket off me and sift through the pile. Rolled-up posters, curling photographs. There's a framed watercolor of Jim's, a scene of Ange and Jeannie by the pond, with Gertrude, fishing. They look so calm together. They didn't know Jim was painting them. They didn't know how he saw them.

I find one of all of us, three summers ago when we climbed Mount Si. Jim is tall and bearded, his arms around the three of us, me and Jeannie squished together under his left, Ange hugged under his right. All of us are smiling at the cameraman, Scotty.

Two nights later the phone rings late. I'm awake, light on, blanket off, before they've answered it. When Ange comes out of the bedroom I'm already dressed.

"That was Dr. Allen. His parents are with him. You should go."

They won't let me drive. We all pile into the truck; Jeannie driving, Ange in the middle, me against the door. Jeannie doesn't stop at the signs or the red lights. She keeps an even 80 on the highway. For once, Ange doesn't razz her about her driving.

I-5 is quiet. The only things on the road are some longhaul trucks, a few cars. We see the weak beige lights of the insides of these other cars, the foggy orange lights across the valley. We drive along past sleepy Tacoma, Federal Way, the airport.

"Look, would you guys mind if I had a cigarette?"

"Go ahead baby."

Ange reaches over me and rolls down the window. I root around in my jacket for Jim's cigarettes. I'm glad I didn't make that promise to him.

We pull into the hospital parking lot. My hand is on the door before we stop.

"You go up. We'll get Bob and Dale and meet you on the floor in ten minutes."

In the elevator is a couple a little older than me. Redeyed and sniffling like kids. We look at each other a second then look at the orange lights going up.

When the elevator opens I run. But when I see the guys in white taking things from the room in plastic bags, I stop. The man at the nurses' station looks up.

"Your parents are in the waiting room."

"My what?"

"Your parents."

Then I remember how that first night, a million years ago, when Dr. Allen had told me she couldn't tell me about Jim unless I was in his family, I had told the story of being his sister.

"Oh Christ."

"They told me to send you in when you came."

"Oh Jesus."

They've left the waiting room door open a crack. I look in. His father is wearing an overcoat. His hands lay loose around the rim of the hat in his lap. His mother is touching her husband's arm. Neither of them is talking.

I knock on the door very lightly. They look up.

"You must be Jim's friend. Come in."

I push the door open. They both stand up and put out their hands. I shake their hands.

"Mary Carlson."

"Jim Carlson."

I introduce myself.

"The young man at the desk told us that, before she went into surgery, Dr. Allen called our daughter and that she was on her way. But we don't have a daughter."

"I'm sorry, But I—the first night Jim was here I told Dr. Allen—"

Mr. Carlson is still shaking my hand. He squeezes it hard.

"You have nothing to apologize for. Jim told us what a good friend you'd been to him. Both after Scotty, and more recently."

"Jim was a good friend too. I'm sorry I didn't call you sooner."

"We know he asked you not to. We had a few good days with him. I think he wanted to get better before he saw us," says Mrs. Carlson. "He didn't want us to have to see him and have to wait the way he had to wait with Scotty."

"Yes."

"Did you know Scotty?"

"Yes."

"He was a lovely young man."

"He was good to Jim," says Mr. Carlson. "There were things about Jim it took us a long time to understand, but he was a good son." He says this slowly. "He was a good man."

"Yes."

"We loved him." Mr. Carlson's mouth is open like he's going to say more, but then there's this sound in his throat and he drops his face into his hands. "Dear God," he says, "Oh dear God."

Mrs. Carlson pulls her husband's head to her breast. His hat falls to the floor.

I pick the hat up off the floor and put it on the table. I leave the room. When I close the door, I hear his father crying.

Ange and Jean and Bob and Dale are standing at the nurses' station. The boys are in pj's and overcoats and houseslippers. They look at me. I look at them. We all look at each other. Nobody says anything.

Dale walks over to the wall and puts his forehead against the wall. His shoulders shake. Bob goes over and puts his hand on Dale's back. Nobody says anything.

We get in the truck to go back to Bob and Dale's. We all insist Bob sits up front with Jean and Ange. Dale and I sit in the open back. We haul the dog-smelling woolly blanket over our knees and huddle up next to each other. I can feel the cool ribbed metal of the bottom of the truck through my jeans. Jeannie pulls us away from the bright lights of the hospital onto Madison.

It's dark but there're enough breaks in the clouds that we can see a star or two. The lights are off at Rex's, the streets are empty. Jean drives so slow and cautiously, full stops at the signs and lights, and pauses at the intersections. There's not another car on the road, but I think she hopes if she does everything very carefully, things might not break apart.

Jean stops at the light on Broadway. Dale and I look into the back window of the pickup and see their three heads—Jeannie's punky hairdo sticking up, Ange's halo of wild fuzz, Bob's shiny smooth round scalp. The collar of Bob's pj's is crooked above his housecoat. He's usually so neatly groomed, but now he looks like a rumpled, sleepy child.

Dale begins to tremble. I put my hand on his knee.

"Jim was a great guy, the greatest, but now it's like he was never here. What did he ever do that's gonna last? It's like his life was nothing."

"Jim was a good man," I say.

Dale nods.

"And he loved a good man. He loved Scotty well."

"And that's enough?"

"It's good," I say, "It's true."

Dale takes my hand. He holds it hard. It's the first time I notice he wears a ring.

He takes a breath. "Bob . . . you know Bob . . . I'm afraid maybe . . . I think Bob . . ."

He can't say it. I see his eyelashes trembling, the muscles in his jaw as he tries to keep from crying. He swallows and closes his eyes.

"Bob is a good man," says Dale.

"Yeah Dale, I know. Bob is a good man, too."

So we all go back to Bob and Dale's. I call the Carlson's hotel to leave Bob and Dale's phone number. We drink tea and sit around in the living room until someone says we ought to get some sleep.

"Well, there's plenty of pj's," says Bob. "We can have a pajama paaaaaaar-tay."

He says it before he realizes it's a Jim word. Ange and Jeannie and I try to laugh. Dale closes his eyes.

Bob and Dale get pj's for us. They wash the teacups as Ange and Jean and I change. We all look really silly in the guys' flannel pj's. When the boys come out of the kitchen and see us, they laugh. It's a real laugh. It sounds good.

Ange and Jean are going to stay in the guest room. Ange says to me, "You wanna stay with us, babe?"

Dale says, "Or you can sleep on the couch in our room."

"Thanks guys." I plop down on the living room couch. "This is fine with me."

Dale goes to the linen closet to get some sheets and blankets.

If I lie next to someone I will break apart.

I wake up first. I put the water on to boil. When Jean and Ange come out of the guest room, I say "The Katzenjammer twins."

They look at my pj's. "Triplets," Jeannie says.

"Quads," says Ange when Dale comes into the kitchen.

He gives us each a scratchy, unshaven kiss on the cheek.

"Good morning lovelies."

Jeannie nods towards the guys' room. "Our fifth?"

"Bob's asleep now. He was sweaty last night. I don't think we'll go to Jim's."

He goes to phone the bank and Janet, Bob's business partner. Jean and Ange and I look at each other.

"You want me to stay with you?" asks Jean when Dale gets off the phone.

"Naaaah," he smiles like nothing's wrong. "Bob'll be alright. You guys go help the Carlsons."

We take turns in the shower while we listen for the phone. We hear Bob coughing in the bedroom.

The Carlsons call. They want to meet at Jim's about ten to clean out the apartment. We say OK, and plan to get there a half an hour early in case there's anything we need to "straighten up." Not that we expect to find anything shocking, but if we were to run across something, even a magazine or a poster, it might be nicer if the Carlsons didn't see it.

We leave Dale sitting at the kitchen table, his hands around his coffee mug. He looks lost. He looks the way he's going to look after Bob is gone.

We take the truck and stop by the grocery store to get a bunch of cartons. I've got the keys to Jim's place. When we walk up the steps I think of Jim standing there when I came by to drive him to the hospital. We climb the gray-mustard colored carpet of the stairs. The hallways smell like food. Living people still live here.

When I open the door to the apartment everything looks different. We set the empty boxes on the living room floor and begin to look in closets and drawers, intruding in a way we never would if Jim was around. There's nothing in Jim's drawers but socks and T-shirts and underwear, nothing beneath the bed but dust, stray pennies, a couple of crusty paintbrushes.

The Carlsons get there before we can go through all the rooms.

The Carlsons don't think there'll be anything they'll want from the living room, so I start packing the books and records, wrapping the TV in towels before I put it in a box.

Jeannie and Mrs. Carlson start in the kitchen. I hear Mrs. Carlson telling Jeannie about the first time Jim made scrambled eggs, about her trying to teach "my Jims," as she calls her husband and son, to cook. She laughs as she remembers the story of the eggs. It's good to hear her laugh. In Jim's room Mr. Carlson and Ange are packing shirts into cardboard cartons. I glance in. Mr. Carlson looks so small, like a schoolboy being sent away from home. He's very slow and careful as he fastens buttons and smooths collars and folds sleeves. He creases the shirts into neat, tidy rectangles. Ange says a couple of things but Mr. Carlson doesn't answer much. So after a while she leaves him to sort through his son's ties and loafers, his jackets and suits, his baseball things, alone.

"This must have been Scotty's room," says Mrs. Carlson.

I'd been in there when Scotty was around. But after Scotty, the door was never open.

The handle of the door is colored silver. Mrs. Carlson puts her hand on it. It clicks. She pushes it open. The curtain is drawn, the room is dark. But we can see around Mrs. Carlson, in front of us, that the bed and dresser and the night-table are gone. The only piece of furniture is the long desk by the window. The desk is crowded with clutter. There are pale gray-white rectangles on the walls. Ange flips on the light.

And all around is Scotty. Scotty in his red-checked lumber jacket. Scotty smiling with a three-days' growth of beard. Scotty sitting cross-legged on a mat. Scotty with long hair, a tie-dyed shirt, and sandals. Scotty in his ridiculous bright orange bermuda shorts. His firm brown stomach, his compact upper arms, him holding up a Stonewall fist and grinning. His fine hands holding something blue. His profile when he was a boy. Him resting his chin in his palms and looking sleepy. His baseball hat on backwards. His pretty shoulders, his tender sex, his hands.

In every one, his skin is tan, his body is whole, his eyes are blue and bright. We recognize some poses from old photographs, and some from Scotty as we remember him. But some are of a Scotty that we never saw; Jim's Scotty. Painted alive again by Jim.

"Dear Scotty," Mrs. Carlson says, "my Jim's beloved."

We take some stuff to a center that is starting up. We leave most of it in both their names. The TV in Scotty's. The hundred dollar bill in Jim's.

A few days later everything is over. The Carlsons are flying back to Texas. They don't want a ride to the airport but they invite us all down for coffee at their hotel. They tell us if we ever get to Texas to come see them. We all thank each other for everything and say if there's ever anything we can do. The Carlsons take some paintings to share with Scotty's family. When the airporter arrives we put their suitcases in the storage place beneath the bus. Mr. Carlson carries the paintings rolled up into tubes. When the bus pulls out Mrs. Carlson waves to us for both of them. Mr. Carlson won't let go of the tubes.

We go back to Bob and Dale's and drink more coffee. We all get pretty buzzy. Then Jean says they shouldn't put it off anymore, they need to get back to Olympia. I mumble something about starting up temping again.

Jean says, uncharacteristically, "Oh, fuck temping."

Bob laughs. "Listen to that potty mouth."

Ange reminds me that I have to go back to Olympia to get my car, and I ought to help them finish the remodeling. Both of which are true, but it's also true they know what I can't say: how much I need to be with them.

So we say "See you 'round" to Bob and Dale and get in the truck to drive back down to Oly. Ange makes me sit in the middle, between the two of them.

"Wha-chew-wont, baby I got it!!" Ange howls as she shoves Aretha into the tape deck. Aretha takes a second to catch up with Ange, but then it's the two of them singing. Ange cranks the tunes up as Jean pulls the truck out onto 15th. We turn at

Pine. Jean slows the truck as we pass the Rose in case anyone cute is casually lounging around outside; no one ever is. There's a moment of stillness at the red light on Broadway, a moment of stillness between the tracks, then "Chain of Fools." Ange cranks it up even more as we turn left onto Broadway, then turn right again onto Madison and right into a traffic jam.

Ange rolls down the window as if she needs the extra room to sing. She loves the chain-chain-chaaaaain, chain-chain-chaaaaaain parts and always does this ridiculously unsexy jerk of her shoulders and hips when she sings it. She gets especially crazy at the cha-ya-ya-ya-ya-in part near the end. She squints and tries to look very mean, meaner with each ya-ya-ya. Jeannie is good at the hoo-hoo's, which she accompanies with some extremely precise nods of her chin, and some extremely cool finger points. I sit between them and laugh.

But as the song is nearing the end and we haven't moved more than ten yards, I growl, "What is this traffic shit?"

Ange pops the cassette out of the tape deck.

"What?"

"I said, what is this traffic shit."

"Quarter of four," says Jean, "I thought we'd miss it."

"The old 'burg ain't what it used to be baby. New folks movin' in all the time. And they all have six cars and they all love traffic jams. Reminds them of good ol' LA."

"Where they can all go back to in a goddamn handtruck, thank you very much."

We inch along a few minutes then come to a complete stop in front of Rex's. Pedestrians on the sidewalk look around for cops then start walking in between the cars. Someone squeezing by in front of the truck does a knock-knock on the hood and grins in at us.

"Smug asshole bastard," I snarl.

Cars start honking.

"Jesus this traffic sucks," I say louder.

Ange looks at me.

The car behind us is laying on the horn.

"Fuck the traffic," I shout.

"Hey, babe, take it easy," says Ange, "We'll get outta here soon."

I ignore her. "Fuck the traffic," I cry. I put my hands over my ears. "Fuck the traffic."

Then I hear Jim screaming, "Fuck the traffic! Don't they realize they're holding up a wheelchair full of dying faggot!" Then I hear him yelling, "So what am I supposed to do, fly?" Then he looks at me, "Tonto, I don't wanna, I don't wanna die."

Then my head is against the back of the seat. I'm rigid.

Ange's hand is on my arm.

"Baby?"

Jean grinds the truck into reverse, backs up a couple inches, whacks it back into first and climbs over the sidewalk into the Seattle First National Bank parking lot. She cuts the engine.

"Baby." Ange says it hard.

She yanks me away from the back of the seat and throws her arms, her whole huge body around me. Jeannie grabs me from behind. I'm stiff I'm like a statue. My body can't bend and I can't see. They sandwich me in between them. Spit and snot are on my face.

"Let it go, baby, let it go."

I can't say anything. My jaws are tight. "Let it go, babe."

Ange pulls away from me enough to kiss my forehead. I break. She squeezes herself around me tight. Then they're both around me, holding me.

And then, dear Jim, held close between the bodies of our friends, I see you.

I roll you and your wheelchair out to the sidewalk. I'm worried because in the few minutes it's taken us to get from your room to here, the sky has turned gray. I tell you we ought to get back inside, but you wave that idea away. I stand above you at the pedestrian crossing and look down at the top of your cap, the back of your neck, your shoulders.

There's a traffic jam. The cars are pressed so close not even pedestrians can squeeze through. A wind is picking up. People are opening umbrellas. Cars are honking, drivers are laying on their horns. I start to say again, that we really ought to go back in, but you find my hand on the wheelchair grip and cover it with your own. You sigh like a tolerant, tired parent. You shake your head. You pat my hand then squeeze it.

"The traffic'll break in a minute, Jim."

But you aren't listening to me. You slip your hand from mine, and before I can stop you, you've unhooked the tooth of the dripfeed from your arm.

"Jim, the IV."

"Ssssh." You put your finger to your lips like you are finally going to tell the truth about a story you've been telling for so long.

You slip the blanket off your knees. You stand up alone, not needing to lean on anyone. You're tall as you used to be. You stretch your arms out to your sides and take a deep breath. I see your chest expand. You stretch your neck up and look at the sky. You throw your arm around my shoulder and pull me to you. I feel the firmness of your body and smell the good clean smell of your healthy skin the way it was the summer we climbed Mt. Si. You pull my face in front of you. You hold my face between your hands and look at me. You look inside where I can't see, where I can't look away from you. Beneath the fear the covered love, you see me, Jim. Then, like a blessing that forgives me, and a healing benediction that will seal a promise true, you kiss my forehead.

You tell me, "Tonto, girl, I'm going for a ride."

You fling your Right-On Sister Stonewall fist up in the air then open your hand in a Hi-Yo Silver wave. I watch your hand as it stretches above you high, impossibly high. Your feet lift off the sidewalk and you rise. Above the crowded street, the hospital, above us all, you fly.

The rain begins. Cold drops hit my face when I look up at you. But you fly high above it, Jim. Your firm taut body catches glints of light from a sun that no one here below can see.

I raise a Right-On fist to answer you, but then my fist is opened, just like yours, and I am waving, Jim.

Good friend, true brother Jim, goodbye.

Dorothy Allison is the author of *Bastard Out of Carolina*, *Cavedweller*, *Trash*, and *Skin: Talking About Sex, Class, and Literature*, among other books. A recipient of numerous Lambda Literary Awards and a National Book Award finalist, Allison is also one of the founders of the Lesbian Sex Mafia, and serves on the advisory board of the National Coalition Against Censorship.

Christopher Bram is the author of nine novels, including *In Memory of Angel Clare*, *Almost History*, and *Father of Frankenstein*, which was adapted into the film *Gods and Monsters*. A Guggenheim Fellow, he received the Bill Whitehead Award for Lifetime Achievement from the Publishing Triangle in 2003, and the Randy Shilts Award for *Eminent Outlaws: The Gay Writers Who Changed America* in 2013.

Dodie Bellamy is the author of *Feminine Hijinx*, *Real: The Letters of Mina Harker and Sam D'Allesandro*, and *Cunt Norton*, among several other collections of fiction and nonfiction. Her 2015 collection of essays, *When the Sick Rule the World*, was named one of the fifty best independent books of the year by Flavorwire.

Bruce Benderson is the author of several works of fiction and nonfiction, including *User*, *Pretending to Say No*, and *The Romanian: A Story of Obsession*, which won the Prix de Flore in France. *Toward the New Degeneracy* is an homage and epitaph and eulogy to the old Times Square, while *Sex and Solitude* examines the loss of urban spaces and rise of the Internet.

Rebecca Brown is the author of more than a dozen novels and short story collections, including *The Haunted House*, *The Terrible Girls*, *Annie Oakley's Girl*, and *The Gifts of the Body*, which won numerous literary awards. *American Romances* is an examination into nature of the American creativity, with essays on pop culture, sexuality, religion, and art.

Raymond Carver (1938–1988) was one of the most well-known writers from the 1980s. His collections *Will You Please*

Be Quiet, Please?, *What We Talk About When We Talk About Love*, *Cathedral*, and *Where I'm Calling From* are iconic works of the period, and helped revitalize the short story form. Carver was also an accomplished poet, and author of numerous collections.

Dennis Cooper is the author of the George Miles Cycle of novels (*Closer*, *Frisk*, *Try*, *Guide*, and *Period*) as well as several other works of prose and poetry, including *My Loose Thread*, *The Sluts*, *God Jr.*, *The Weaklings*, *The Marbled Swarm*, and *Smothered in Hugs: Essays, Interviews, Feedback, and Obituaries*.

Gil Cuadros (1962–1996), among the first Chicano voices to document the AIDS pandemic in Los Angeles, was an early recipient of a PEN Center USA/West grant for writers with HIV. His 1994 book *City of God*, published by City Lights Books, is now taught in many Chicano and Queer Studies programs.

Sam D'Allesandro (1956–1988) is the author of prose that has been collected in several posthumous collections, including *The Zombie Pit*, *Real: the Letters of Mina Harker and Sam D'Allessandro* (with Dodie Bellamy), and *The Wild Creatures*.

Bret Easton Ellis is the author of *Less Than Zero*, *The Rules of Attraction*, *American Psycho*, *The Informers*, *Glamorama*, *Lunar Park*, and *Imperial Bedrooms*, as well as the screenplays *This Is Not an Exit*, *The Informers*, and *The Canyons*. Since 2013, he has been the host of a popular weekly podcast.

Mary Gaitskill is the author of *Bad Behavior*; *Two Girls, Fat and Thin*; *Because They Wanted To*; *Veronica*; *Don't Cry*; and *The Mare*. *Veronica* was a finalist for the National Book and National Book

Critics Circle awards, and her stories have appeared frequently in *The Best American Short Stories* and *The O. Henry Prize Stories* anthologies.

Suzanne Gardinier's poetry has been published in *Usahn, The New World, Today: 101 Ghazals*, and *Dialogue with the Archipelago, Iridium*, as well as the essay collection *A World that Will Hold All the People*. She is the recipient of an Associated Writing Program Award, Kenyon Review Award for Excellence in the Essay, and the Pitt Poetry Prize, as well as fellowships from the New York Foundation for the Arts and the Lannan Foundation.

Robert Glück is the author of *Elements of a Coffee Service, Jack the Modernist, Reader, Margery Kempe, Compound Fracture*, and *Denny Smith*. One of the co-founders of the New Narrative movement, Glück has been director of San Francisco State's Poetry Center, codirector of the Small Press Traffic Literary Center, and editor for Lapis Press and the literary journal *Narrativity*.

Brad Gooch is the author of fiction and poetry including *The Daily News, Jailbait, Scary Kisses*, and *The Golden Age of Promiscuity*. He is also an acclaimed biographer, including *Flannery: A Life of Flannery O'Connor*, which was a National Book Critics Award finalist, and *City Poet: The Life and Times of Frank O'Hara*. His other books include *Godtalk: Travels in Spiritual America*, and *Smash Cut: A Memoir of Howard & Art & the '70s & '80s*.

Jessica Hagedorn is the author of, among other books, *Chiquita Banana, Pet Food and Tropical Apparitions, Dangerous Music,*

Mango Tango, Dogeaters (a recipient of an American Book Award and National Book Award finalist), *Danger and Beauty*, and *Gangster of Love*, as well as the editor of *Charlie Chan Is Dead: An Anthology of Contemporary Asian-American Fiction*.

Amy Hempel's fiction has been collected in *Reasons to Live, At the Gates of the Animal Kingdom, Tumble Home*, and *Collected Stories*. She is the recipient of numerous awards and grants, including the Hobson Award, a Guggenheim Fellowship, a USA Fellowship grant, the Ambassador Book Award, the Rea Award for the Short Story, and the PEN/Malamud Award.

Essex Hemphill (1957–1995) was a poet and activist whose writing appeared in *High Performance, Gay Community News, RFD Magazine, The Advocate, Pyramid Periodical*, and *Essence*, among other publications, as well as the collections *Conditions* and *Ceremonies*.

A.M. Homes is the author of the novels *This Book Will Save Your Life, Music for Torching, The End of Alice, In a Country of Mothers*, and *Jack*; the short-story collections *Things You Should Know* and *The Safety of Objects*; and the memoirs *The Mistress's Daughter* and *Los Angeles: People, Places and The Castle on the Hill*. She collaborates frequently with artists, has written for television and the movies, and has received numerous fellowships from the John Simon Guggenheim Foundation, the National Endowment for the Arts, NYFA, and The Cullman Center for Scholars and Writers at The New York Public Library, among others.

Gary Indiana is the author of well over a dozen books, including the story collections *Scar Tissue* and *White Trash Boulevard*;

the novels *Horse Crazy*, *Gone Tomorrow*, *Rent Boy*, *Resentment: A Comedy*, *Depraved Indifference*, *Do Everything in the Dark*, and *The Shanghai Gesture*; the essay collections *Let It Bleed* and *Utopia's Debris*; and the nonficton works *The Schwarzenegger Syndrome* and *Andy Warhol and the Can that Sold the World*. He is also the author of several plays, as well as an actor, filmmaker, and visual artist.

Denis Johnson's fiction includes *Angels*, *Fiskadoro*, *The Stars at Noon*, *Resuscitation of a Hanged Man*, *Jesus' Son*, *Already Dead*, *The Name of the World*, *Tree of Smoke*, *Nobody Move*, and *The Laughing Monsters*. His poetry collections include *The Man Among the Seals*, *Inner Weather*, *The Incognito Lounge*, *The Veil*, and *The Throne of the Third Heaven of the Nations Millennium General Assembly*. *Tree of Smoke* won the National Book Award and was a finalist for the Pulitzer Prize. He is also the author of several plays and screenplays, and the essay collection *Seek: Report from the Edges of America*.

John Keene is the author of a novel, *Annotations*, a collection of short stories and novellas, *Counternarratives*, and a book of poems, *Seismosis*. He was longtime member of the Dark Room Collective and Cave Canem. He translated Hilda Hilst's *Letters from a Seducer* from the Portuguese, and has translated several other works from French and Spanish as well, and is the recipient of an AGNI John Cheever Short Fiction Prize and a Whiting Award.

Randall Kenan is the author of the novel *A Visitation of Spirits*, the story collection *Let the Dead Bury Their Dead*, the monograph *A Time Not Here* (with photographer Norman Mauskopf), the biography *James Baldwin: American Writer*, and the nonfiction books *Walking on Water: Black American Lives at the Turn of the 21st Century* and *The Fire This Time*. He is also the editor of *The Cross of Redemption: The Uncollected Writings* of James Baldwin. He is the recipient of a Guggenheim Fellowship, a Whiting Award, the John Dos Passos Prize, and the Rome Prize from the American Academy of Arts and Letters, among others.

Kevin Killian's several books of fiction, nonfiction, and poetry include *Bedrooms Have Windows*, *Shy*, *Little Men*, *Arctic Summer*, *Argento Series*, *I Cry Like a Baby*, *Action Kylie*, *Impossible Princess*, *Tweaky Village*, and *Spreadeagle*. With Peter Gizzi, he edited *My Vocabulary Did This to Me: The Collected Poetry of Jack Spicer*, which won the American Book Award. He has edited several other books, written numerous plays, and is the co-founder of Poets Theater and the publishing house Small Press Traffic, as well as the editor of the poetry zine *Mirage*.

Jamaica Kincaid is the author of the novels *Annie John*, *Lucy*, *The Autobiography of My Mother*, *Mr. Potter*, and *See Now Then*. Her nonfiction books include *A Small Place*, *My Brother*, *Talk Stories*, *My Garden Book*, and *Among Flowers: A Walk in the Himalayas*. Her short fiction has been collected in *At the Bottom of the River*. Among the many prizes and fellowships she has received are the Morton Dauwen Zabel Award, a Guggenheim Fellowship, a Lannan Literary Award, and the Prix Femina Étranger, as well as induction into the American Academy of Arts and Letters and the American Academy of Arts and Sciences.

Jim Lewis is the author of the novels *Sister*, *Why the Tree Loves the Axe*, and *The King Is Dead*. In addition to his fiction, he is a noted art critic and journalist. He has written monographs for more than thirty artists, including Richard Prince, Christopher Wool, and Larry Clark, with whom he also collaborated on the story for Clark's film *Kids*. His journalism has appeared in *GQ, Granta, The New York Times, Rolling Stone,* and *Vanity Fair,* among dozens of other publications.

Jaime Manrique has written more than a dozen books, including *Los adoradores de la luna; El cadáver de papá; Colombian Gold; Scarecrow; Latin Moon in Manhattan; My Night with Federico Garcia Lorca; Sor Juana's Love Poems; Twilight at the Equator; Eminent Maricones: Arenas, Lorca, Puig, and Me; The Autobiography of Bill Sullivan; Our Lives Are the Rivers;* and *Cervantes Street.* He was awarded Colombia's National Poetry Award for his first book of poems, as well as an International Latino Book Award, a Guggenheim Fellowship, and a Foundation for Contemporary Arts Grants to Artists Award.

Patrick McGrath is the author of the novels *The Grotesque, Spider, Dr. Haggard's Disease, Asylum, Martha Peake: A Novel of the Revolution, Port Mungo, Trauma,* and *Constance,* as well as the short story collections *Blood and Water* and *Ghost Town: Tales of Manhattan Then and Now.* He also wrote the screenplay adaptations for *The Grotesque* and *Spider.*

Susan Minot is the author of the novels *Monkeys, Folly, Evening, Rapture,* and *Thirty Girls,* as well as the short story collection *Lust.* She has also written a book of poetry, *Poems 4 A.M.,* and the screenplays *Stealing Beauty* and *Evening* (with Michael Cunningham). Among her prizes are the Prix Femina Étranger, an O. Henry Prize, and a Pushcart Prize.

Eileen Myles's poems, stories, and essays have been collected in *Not Me*; *Chelsea Girls*; *On My Way*; *School of Fish*; *Cool for You*; *Skies*; *Sorry, Tree*; *Tow*; *The Importance of Being Iceland*; *Different Streets*; *Snowflake*; and *I Must Be Living Twice*. She is also the author of the novel *Inferno*. With Liz Kotz, she edited the anthology *The New Fuck You: Adventures in Lesbian Publishing*. She is the recipient of a Guggenheim Fellowship in nonfiction, an Andy Warhol/Creative Capital Art Writers grant, a Lambda Book Award, and the Shelley Prize from the Poetry Society of America.

Sarah Schulman's novels are *The Sophie Horowitz Story*; *Girls, Visions and Everything*; *After Delores*; *People in Trouble*; *Empathy*; *Rat Bohemia*; *Shimmer*; *The Child*; *The Mere Future*; and *The Cosmopolitans*. Her nonfiction books are *My American History*, *Stagestruck*, *Ties That Bind*, *The Gentrification of the Mind*, and *Israel/Palestine and the Queer Imagination*. Her plays include *Mercy*, *Carson McCullers*, *Manic Flight Reaction*, and *Enemies, a Love Story*, adapted from the story by Isaac Bashevis Singer. Among her many prizes are a Guggenheim Fellowship, a Fulbright, two New York Foundation for the Arts Fellowships, a Revson Fellowship, and two American Library Association Stonewall Book Awards.

Lynne Tillman is the author of the novels *Haunted Houses*, *Motion Sickness*, *Cast in Doubt*, *No Lease on Life*, and *American Genius: A Comedy*, as well as the nonfiction books *Bookstore: The Life and Times of Jeannette Watson and Books & Co.*, and *The Velvet Years: Warhol's Factory 1965–1967*. Her short story collections include *Absence Makes the Heart*, *The Madame Realism Complex*, *This Is Not It*, and *Someday This Will Be Funny*, while her nonfiction has been collected in *The Broad Picture* and *What Would Lynne Tillman Do?* She is the recipient of a Guggenheim Fellowship and was a finalist for the National Book Critics Circle Award for Criticism.

Laurie Weeks is a writer and performer whose 2011 novel *Zipper Mouth* received the Lambda Literary Award Best for Best Debut Novel and was shortlisted for the Edmund White Award. Since the mid-80s her work has appeared in such publications as *LA Weekly, The Baffler, Vice, The Best American Nonrequired Reading, Pussy Riot: A Punk Prayer For Freedom, Whitney Biennial 2012, Nest, Apology*, and Semiotext(s)'s *The New Fuck You*. A contributing screenwriter to *Boys Don't Cry*, her latest chapbook is *I Watch the Human* (New Herring Press). Weeks directed the original incarnation of Eileen Myles's opera *Hell*; toured with Sister Spit; and co-founded—with artists Charles Atlas and Nicole Eisenman, among others—NYC's underground cult series *The Summer of Bad Plays*. Weeks has performed widely, including downtown NYC venues including the Pyramid Club, The Kitchen, P.S. 122, LaMama, and Jackie 60. Currently she runs The Dr. Weeks Institute for Ecstatic Juvenile Delinquency and its workshop division The School for Vulnerable Little Tinies.

David Wojnarowicz (1954–1992) was an artist, writer, and activist whose books include *Sounds in the Distance, Tongues of Flame, Close to the Knives: A Memoir of Disintegration, Memories That Smell Like Gasoline, Seven Miles a Second* (with James Romberger and Marguerite Van Cook), *Waterfront Journals, Rimbaud in New York 1978–1979* (edited by Andrew Roth), *In the Shadow of the American Dream: The Diaries of David Wojnarowicz* (edited